The Profiteer: War with Iran

Author: Mark Williams

*To Greg and Starla,
What a great family you have!
I appreciate the years of support
you provided, up to today even,
to make ASG great.
Mark W.*

Book Review

"An exciting novel...Through it all, what stands out is Steve's unbending determination, he is always going to do the right thing." Douglas Horn, Colonel, United States Army (retired)

First Chapter Preview

"The story lines are engaging...and the leadership lessons are important."

"very intriguing"

"Ok, I am hooked! So when can I buy the entire book? The first chapter is great "

"Wow! That's a lot of action...! Great story! It pulls you in."

Copyright © 2015 Kratos Enterprises, LLC

All rights reserved.

ISBN-10: 069242220X
ISBN-13: 978-0692422205

This book is dedicated to my family, especially my wife, Sherry, and children, Meriah Park and Marcus Williams. I want to thank the many people who provided input and review comments that helped shape this story. In particular I thank my wife and my brother, Patrick Williams. I offer my sincere gratitude to my development editor, Dorrie O'Brien, for her patient guidance.

1

Jake Turner brought his eighteen-wheeled armored Mercedes truck to a shuddering stop. First, he'd felt the explosion. It shook him so hard that his teeth rattled, and the ringing in his ears rendered him near deaf for several minutes it was so loud. The fully-loaded tractor-trailer rig bucked like a bronco at the rodeo and slid upright for fifty feet with Jake standing on the remaining brakes. Then the day went dark as the sky filled with gray and black smoke.

Jake could see the rounds ricochet off his truck hood and crack his windshield before he could hear them. He couldn't see the shooters and he didn't waste time sitting in the front seat of the truck cab trying to find them. He grabbed his radio and hopped in the back of the cab, hoping the armor plating would protect him until help arrived.

"I'm hit, I'm hit!" Jake's shrill voice, raised two octaves with excitement, hit the short-range FM convoy radio net like a bolt of lightning.

Training taught Jake to keep driving after an attack, if possible. But Jake's truck was disabled, and it gave the attackers a target to focus on and a location to draw in other vehicles and soldiers. His only viable choice was to take cover and wait for help.

"Cargo 7, this is Alpha One-Zero. What is your status, over?"

Lieutenant Bruce Williams, Platoon Leader with the Alpha One-Zero call sign, wasn't receiving satellite video or external convoy communications.

Jake keyed his mike. "Alpha One-Zero, Cargo 7 was hit by a mortar shell or a roadside bomb. My truck slid off the road near this two-story apartment. I'm alone and will remain in the rear cab of the vehicle for protection. I can't go forward without getting shot. I'm not injured now, but I'm taking small arms fire on my left. There appear to be at least a half dozen shooters firing at me. I can't get to my weapon to return fire. I need help!"

As Jake moved around in his truck to get better cover, he accidently keyed his radio and everyone in the convoy could hear his pleas. "Lord Jesus Christ, help us. I don't want to die, Lord. Please, please, save me. My son, my wife, what will they do without me? God help me. Our Father which art in heaven, hallowed be thy name. Thy kingdom come, thy will be done on earth as it is in heaven." Jake moved again and the transmission stopped.

Williams, though moved by his pleas as much as anyone, needed his team to keep their heads and maintain radio discipline. "Jake, watch your mike. Everyone, keep the radio clear except for emergencies."

The withering gunfire was coming from both a building on the convoy's left and the brick security wall surrounding it. This kind of heavy, coordinated attack indicated a higher level of pre-planning than was normal for the usual roadside vehicle assault by Iranian mujahideen fighters.

"Alpha One-Zero, this is Alpha One-Two. I see Cargo 7 and will provide cover." Sergeant Marie Olivera moved her Mind Resistant

Ambush Protected armored vehicle to the left of Truck 7. She blocked incoming fire and her team returned the full firepower at hand: a .50 caliber gun, an M-240 machine gun, grenade launchers, and M-16 rifles from a team of three Marines. She was the squad leader for the second MRAP gun truck in the convoy. The nervousness of her first combat encounter had long-since passed. She was an experienced Marine and reacted that way. Olivera, though her adrenaline was pumping, was outwardly calm as she surveyed the site. She could see Truck 7 and knew Jake was secure in the rear cab, for now. Other trucks were rolling by quickly, but Truck 7 held the attackers' attention. She saw heads popping up on the building occasionally and could tell the fire was coming from many locations.

Olivera rapidly located the direction of incoming fire with the multiple sensors in their MRAP Boomerang system to measure muzzle blast and bullet shockwave, and focused return fire on the shooters. She directed her team's fire zones for optimum effectiveness, however limited: blasting snipers out of well-protected positions is difficult. She was confident she could defend the area as long as her ammunition lasted.

Jake's adrenaline was surging through his body, bringing heightened awareness to his senses. His hands trembled with the acute feeling of the weapon he held, his nostrils burned from the smoke and gunpowder, his pupils dilated with a clearer, brighter vision of the shooters, both friend and foe. His emotions were raw and uncontrollable, and his mouth was outrunning his mind. "Thank God, the cavalry has arrived! Shoot those maggots, ma'am! I can shoot now, too. Damn you, Iran!"

***

There were sixty-five freight trucks in this convoy, carrying fuel, food, water, vehicles, and supplies hundreds of miles every day. They delivered to dozens of Forward Operating Bases (FOBs) near Neka,

Iran and throughout the region from the central distribution center at Joint Base Mashad. The armored tractor-trailers and heavy equipment transport vehicles provided protection against improvised explosive devices, mortars, and small arms. The truck drivers were active duty soldiers who in peacetime worked for Kratos Energy and Logistics Company, a U.S. Department of Defense contractor.

Gun Trucks operated by members of the Marine's 3rd Battalion, 23rd Marine Regiment escorted the convoy. The Gun Trucks were spaced about ten cargo trucks apart from each other to provide uniform protection for the convoy.

The supplies were critical to the success of the mission, and these convoys were the most efficient way to supply the hundreds of FOBs throughout Iran. There were over a thousand trucks on the roads on any given day, delivering supplies to the 250,000 service members throughout the country.

The team had driven into the town of Neka in northern Iran, and then lost all contact with their headquarters at Mashad. The convoy team could talk on their radios, but no one outside the immediate area was answering them. Small arms fire and mortars continued to hit them as the other trucks rolled through the fire.

"Everyone else, keep moving and get the hell out of that kill zone! Maintain your spacing." Williams didn't want to make a bad situation worse. It took discipline, training, and leadership not to send more reinforcements to the downed vehicles and injured truckers—halting the convoy would only provide easy targets and potentially prevent the convoy from reaching the FOBs—a victory for the mujahideen. Pushing through the ambush was the first priority; rendering aid to comrades had to be the second priority.

Disabled vehicles were increasing; casualties began to rise.

"Alpha One-Zero, this is Cargo 14. Cargos 12 and 13 are down." They were down well beyond the disabled Truck 7 by now. Truck

14's driver continued to roll-on as he reported the disabled vehicles.

It was a typical type of attack employed by the mujahideen on these convoys. Gallons of fuel were poured into a hole in the road and set on fire. The smoke would billow black and gray while the red, orange, and yellow flames shot up as combustion varied unevenly across the pool, causing confusion and sometimes over-reaction by the drivers. The enemy often used children to throw a sticky-bomb — a sock covered with adhesive or containing a magnet, and filled with TNT — against the side of a truck just in front of the fuel fire. The soldiers hesitated to shoot a child. Exactly what the mujahideen counted on.

"Alpha One-Three, keep going. I repeat, don't stop for Cargos 12 and 13. Copy?" Williams needed armed escorts for the vehicles still rolling ahead of the wreck. The next Gun Truck's crew's first instinct would be to stop, return fire, and render assistance to the drivers.

"Roger. Alpha One-Three still rolling."

"Cargo 12 or Cargo 13, do you read me?" Williams called. He tried to raise them several times, but got no response. That didn't mean they were dead. Perhaps their radios weren't functioning or they were out of reach. Williams wouldn't assume they were dead, and he wouldn't abandon them, either.

"I see Cargo 12 in a watery ditch off the side of the road. Cargo 13 is stopped in the fuel fire," Gun Truck 3 reported as he rolled through.

The sticky bomb that had been stuck near the front wheel of Truck 12 had blown the tire out, causing the truck driver to lose control; it rolled on its side and slid up just short of the fuel fire. Truck 13 struck Truck 12 from behind when it rolled over, causing Truck 12 to slide through the fire and into the ditch.

Williams responded, "Alpha One-Four, do you read me?"

"Alpha One-Four reads you."

"Stop and cover the two wrecked vehicles ahead of you."

"Roger One-Zero." They would provide cover and look for survivors. The Gun Truck team would render first aid as soon as they could reach the drivers. Their suppressing fire would protect other trucks as they rolled by as well.

Williams evaluated the situation. Ambushed when intelligence said the threat was low, they'd had no external communications' links working to call for assistance or to get a better look at the enemy positions and strength in the surrounding area. Some trucks were getting through, but many of the convoy trucks had been disabled and were taking increasingly heavy fire. Continuing with this drive-through game of dodge-the-bullets and run-like-hell wasn't working. Lieutenant Williams could see it would result in many more casualties and possibly loss of the mission. He needed a different approach.

"Alpha One-One, this is Alpha One-Zero. Do you read me?" Williams was in the lead, moving vehicles out of harm's way, and the first Gun Truck was moving a few vehicles behind his command vehicle. "Alpha One-One, this is Alpha One-Zero. Do you read me?"

"Alpha One-One. Over."

"Alpha One-One, stop your truck at my position."

Within one minute, Alpha One-One arrived. Gun Truck 1 leader stepped out of his vehicle without salute in combat. Williams was standing outside his vehicle in full-dress combat gear. The command vehicle was facing the opposite direction, its motor running. Williams was going back into the fight. If there was going to be a massacre, he was going to save as many good guys and kill as many bad guys as possible.

"Sergeant, I want you to take the convoy lead and get those trucks out of this fire zone safely and don't stop until you reach the FOB, no matter what you see or hear on the radio," Williams said. "And when you get to that FOB, you tell them to send a few Black Hawks in here to wipe out this nest of vipers. If you do that and I make it out alive, I will personally pin a medal on your chest. Now get going!"

"Yes, sir!"

As Gun Truck 1's leader prepared to pull away, he turned to the Marine in the seat next to him and said, "Take a long look at him as we go by, Private. If you die in this God-forsaken place with half the balls Williams has, they'll sing songs about you in the Marine Corps for a hundred years."

Hearing those words, the gunner stood up in his hatch. Bucking protocol and overcome by pride, the gunner snapped a salute and yelled, "Give 'em hell, Lieutenant."

"I'll give 'em more than hell. I'll put a 5.56 millimeter round in the ass of every murdering bastard that dared to pick up a weapon and shoot at my people today." Bruce's nose was running, his eyes were watering, his face and even his ears were red, his speech was a little slurred, and he could hardly stand still for the Gun Truck to pass. When he got this mad, his whole body reacted.

Williams got back into his command vehicle, stomped the gas pedal to the floor and sped back down the road he came from, weaving in and out of his convoy vehicles as he reentered the shooting area. The first scene he came to was Trucks 12 and 13.

"Alpha One-Four, this is Alpha One-Zero. I'm stopping in front of Cargo 12. Lay down covering fire. Do you copy?" Bruce could smell the heavy, oily scent of diesel fuel pouring from the trucks and burning in the road. The air was thick and difficult to breathe.

"Roger One-Zero."

All guns from Gun Truck 4 opened fire, suppressing most of the enemy's fire while Williams ran to Truck 12. The Iranians used both the AK-47 and AK-74 guns and rounds were kicking up dust and pinging off the nearby vehicles as he slid behind the truck.

When Bruce got to the vehicle lying on its side, he grabbed the step of the passenger's side door, which was now above him, to propel himself up. There were two passengers inside: the driver and a ride-along trainee. Crouching on the door, he looked through the window and saw the passenger returning fire through the blown-out windshield. The driver was sitting face down in the water still buckled into his seat and apparently dead.

"Private, is your driver dead?" Bruce could see the fear in the private's face. Bruce had seen that look many times when soldiers first encountered combat. Some succumbed to it and ran away while most others overcame the fear. In this situation, the private couldn't run away even if he wanted to. He either fought or died. The fact that he was returning fire at all showed he was conquering his fear.

"Yes, sir. He took a bullet in his head before we went into the water."

"Give me your hand, Private, and let's get out of here." When the private grabbed Bruce's arm and unbuckled his seat belt, Bruce snatched him out through the vehicle window and threw him to the ground all in one motion.

AK-47 rounds continued to ping around Bruce and the truck. Bruce jumped down with the private, using the vehicle to shield them from incoming fire.

"Grab your weapon and run to the command vehicle. I'll cover you."

After the private had made it safely back to the command vehicle, Bruce motioned to Gun Truck 4 leader to cover him as he ran from Truck 12 to 13.

Bruce had amazing acceleration, taking only two steps to reach his peak speed. He ran through the short opening between the two disabled trucks, and dived head-first behind Truck 13 and well behind the burning fuel fire. He skidded his body across the dirt and rock road, arms extended up, holding his M-16 in one hand, planted the knuckles of the gun hand and palm of the free hand and brought himself back to a standing position in fluid action, like a runner sliding head-first into second base.

Bruce couldn't get into the burning cab of Truck 13, but he could see into it from behind the cab. Bruce saw the burned corpse and smelled the unmistakable scent of burning human flesh. He sat back momentarily and thought, *Two out of three of my soldiers dead. It shouldn't be this way.*

"Alpha One-Four, Cargo 13's driver is dead. I want your team to load up and catch up with the convoy. Do you understand?"

"I understand. Alpha One-Four respectfully asks the lieutenant's permission to cover you back to command vehicle, then we will move out."

"Negative, One-Four. Move out and draw fire. I'll get back to my vehicle and work my way back to the other downed vehicles."

"Roger. Moving out."

***

The next report came in just as Williams reached his Command Vehicle.

"Cargo 63 is hit. I can't see anything except his hood, smoke, and fire," Truck 64 reported and drove on.

"Alpha One-Zero, this is Alpha One-Seven bringing up the rear. We're deploying with Cargo 63."

Sergeant Major George Bird and Steve Holmes weren't leaving their soldier-employees on Truck 63 behind. As the smoke thinned and the dust began to settle, they could see the significant destruction from a large explosive detonation. The explosion had caved-in the truck cab and peeled the trailer open like a can of sardines. The driver for Truck 63 wasn't visible. They had to find him, provide protection, and render whatever medical aid they could.

More trucks were hit. Gun Trucks responded. Fatalities were mounting quickly. Steve now understood how the soldiers, immortalized in *Black Hawk Down*, must have felt making their last stand at Mogadishu.

George Bird pitched Steve Holmes a spare M-16 and ammo bandolier from under his seat. Civilians weren't supposed to have weapons in combat, but this was a desperate situation. George, using his armored door for cover, rolled low out of the vehicle and continued rolling to the short wall surrounding the buildings where the mujahideen were hiding. The wall had two entranceways spaced about twelve feet apart in front of him. With the heavy fire they were receiving, he couldn't stand up or stay in one position to continue returning fire, so he scattered his attack from a prone position. He'd fire several semi-automatic, three-shot bursts at specific enemy firing positions, then roll hard to the other entranceway and fire several bursts from this position. George's constant changing angle of fire forced the mujahideen to shift position to avoid getting shot, but not all of them were lucky enough to avoid George's aim.

Steve and George blocked the incoming fire with their vehicle and returned a barrage of small arms and grenade fire. The smell of gunpowder mixed with dust filled their nostrils. Vision was poor, so their return fire was inaccurate but heavy. Their response was sufficient to cause the snipers to keep their heads down. After a few minutes of this, Steve crawled out on the passenger's side of the vehicle to look for Truck 63 survivors. He stayed low as he lifted the handle to open the Gun Truck door. Then he slid down the side of the vehicle to lay flat on the ground. He did a low-crawl to the wreckage of Truck 63 while George continued to fire.

Additional fire started up on their right. The situation seemed to be deteriorating; trucks damaged, soldiers killed or wounded, freight destroyed, and now new fire from the opposite direction. Steve wondered if the situation could get any worse.

"We have incoming fire from the right side of the road," Sergeant Major Bird reported. "Repeat. Alpha One-Seven has fire coming from the right."

Steve took cover under the wreckage of Truck 63, which protected him from fire coming from both directions. He began to see vehicles and personnel moving in from the right, but he couldn't make out any distinctive markings from his distance. He could tell they weren't firing at him. As he listened, he heard the distinct difference between the shots on his right and those on his left; a difference he'd learned years ago during FBI training at Quantico. It told him the fire on the right was likely American. The smaller caliber and lighter M-16 shells fired by the Americans sounded distinctly different from the AK-47 some of the Iranians used. As the vehicles drew nearer on his right, he saw combat vehicles in the distance that looked American.

Steve transmitted, "We've run into a pitched battle between the Iranian and American forces." *How did that happen?* he wondered. *Where was the intel? Why weren't they receiving communications from anyone outside the convoy?* Questions raced through his head while he maintained cover and searched for survivors in Truck 63.

George transmitted, "Alpha One-Zero, can you raise the friendlies on our right? Tell them we're the good guys. We'd like to avoid fratricide." They must recognize the convoy vehicles and the ambush scene. If he could reach them, he could help coordinate assistance.

"Negative One-Seven. They aren't responding on our radio frequency and we've lost all comms with HQ."

As the force on the right moved closer, Steve Holmes confirmed they were U.S. troops. Their assault was causing the Iranian mujahideen fire to slow down enough to get a closer look at the damaged Truck 63.

The friendly force was U.S. Army Rangers aided by the U.S. Army

10th Mountain Division and local Azerbaijani-speaking, western Turkic Iranians. They were leading a planned assault to clear out several hundred mujahideen fighters in the Elburz Mountains/Neka area. The fighters were the remnants of the Iranian Republic Guard regulars supported by Hizballah and local recruits. The Rangers were sweeping down the valley to drive them into their blocking divisions that occupied high ground. The convoy had driven directly into the middle of the battle.

After surveying the scene and checking both vehicle occupants, Steve transmitted, "No survivors, repeat, no survivors from Truck 63." Steve clicked off the radio. "God have mercy on their souls."

Steve sat next to the destroyed hulk of Truck 63 and thought about their families. He would be the one who had to tell them their loved ones weren't coming home. He'd done it before, but it was never easy. He and Kratos' Human Resources representatives would accompany the grief team the military sent in uniform to the front door of the family's home.

The company name symbolized the job they did in support of the military. Kratos was the winged enforcer for the Olympian God Zeus. It was an appropriate symbol to honor their service and sacrifice.

As Steve slumped with one hand against the destroyed hulk of Truck 63, his stomach churned and heaved, vomit rose in his throat and stopped there, leaving a burning, sickening taste in his mouth. The ghastly sight of those two dead soldiers, with gaping, bloody wounds lying in the position where they'd felt their last sputtering heartbeat in Truck 63, etched a mental mural of Steve's first combat deaths from his first combat experience. Other dead and wounded mujahideen in their last spastic motions of death or writhing pain flooded his ears and eyes in and around the building where they fought. The smell of burning flesh and the shrieks of pain and pleas for help in Farsi, Arabic, English, or other tongues were the most gut-wrenching, vomit-inducing scenes and sounds.

Before Steve could get up from his position, a Humvee with a Tactically-Operated, Wire-guided missile launcher rolled up and slid to a stop beside him in a cloud of dust. He could see the Army fire-control Ranger gripping the weapon, staring through his sight, concentrating on the sniper target. With the optical sight zeroed-in on the image of the building housing the mujahideen fighters firing mortars, the Ranger called out, "Fire in the hole!"

Kaboom! The TOW missile exploded out of the launch-tube with brilliant fire from its solid rocket propellant engine, momentarily blinding Steve. The Ranger held fast to the weapon, keeping the optical sight fixed on the sniper nest to steer the missile. Signals from the Humvee guidance computer to the missile traversed along two wires, which spooled from the back of the missile to the onboard computer control system. The guidance commands moved the missile fins through actuators to steer it in for a kill. The missile came whistling in and exploded in the building, creating a ball of fire and eliminating most of the mujahideen fighters at the scene. The remaining fighters rushed back away from the explosion.

Lieutenant Williams rounded up functioning trucks and any people who were still operational, formed a new convoy and security line-up, and pushed the team and supplies on toward the FOB.

George took charge of the Neka scene. He and Steve rendered immediate life-saving and first-aid assistance for the wounded until the Army UH-72A and H-60 helicopter Medevac teams arrived. They also had to examine and repair the vehicles, sort through and salvage the cargo with help from the drivers to determine its disposition and return what they could to Joint Base Mashad.

2

Joint Base Mashad, Iran

Steve Holmes arrived back at Joint Base Mashad late that evening, drained of energy and needing sleep, but with his mind doing somersaults and replaying the Neka battle over and over, he needed to wind down first. Steve and George traipsed into the almost-empty Joint Base Mashad bar near closing time. Shell-shocked, they had hardly spoken to each other on the ride back.

"Bring us two cold ones of whatever you've got on tap, Mack," George called out as the two dragged their weary bodies to the nearest table and slumped down hard. An attractive waitress, who was probably a Kratos employee from the States on contract in Iran for two years, carried the two mugs on a tray above her shoulder, sloshing some out as she came to the table and set them down. "Here ya go, boys. Drink 'em up. We close in thirty minutes."

Steve gulped his beer noisily and slammed the empty mug down on their table near the bar. "Haaaa!" The guttural yell broke their shock-filled silence. "This is screwed up!"

"What? Your head or this mission?"

"Maybe both. Our people died for no good reason today."

"That's the damn shame of it. We don't know what the reason was."

"I sure don't, but I'm mad as hell." Steve shoved back hard from the table, his chair sliding several feet. "No way in hell we should have wound up in that shootout today. We checked the routes. Checked the intel. How did it happen?" Steve couldn't sit still. He jumped up to work off the anger, pacing back and forth. "Something or someone caused that FUBAR mess."

"That's right! That's right! But what? Who?" George exclaimed.

Steve kicked the chair across the floor. It crashed into the bar and bounced against an empty table.

The bartender yelled, "Alright, men, you don't want me to call the MPs. Keep it down."

"Come on, Steve, sit back down. I know you, and you'll figure this out."

Steve picked up the chair and slid it back under the table. They ordered two more beers and sipped them quietly for a few moments.

"I'll make you a promise on this spot, George. Those thirty-five soldiers and Marines at Neka will not die in vain. I'll find out who or what caused this mess if it's the last thing I do. People died on my watch and I'm going to find out why."

***

Steve's phone in his CHU rang early the next morning, waking him from a dead sleep.

"Get up, Steve," George said. "I've got the meeting you asked for last night, set for oh nine-hundred hours with the Army's Commander Huggins."

Steve groaned and rolled over to look at the clock that he didn't have on the table. "How much time do we have?"

"Just enough time for you to shave and shower before I come get you. I'll be there in twenty minutes."

George briefed Steve on Lieutenant Colonel Patrick Huggins, U.S. Army 3rd Ranger Battalion, 75th Ranger Regiment, on their way to the meeting. Huggins had first served with the 75th Ranger Regiment as a platoon captain in Afghanistan and received the Silver Star for valor in Operation Ringo. During the operation, he'd led over two hundred Rangers to capture a critical airstrip and kill the Taliban holding it. Wounded and almost overrun by the Taliban, he called in a C-130 airstrike close to his own position. His courage and the precision of the Air Force C-130 team enabled them to defeat the Taliban and set up a base near Kandahar in Helmand Province to conduct NATO military combat operations, psychological operations, and CIA missions in Afghanistan and Pakistan.

Huggins would be anxious for Steve's rundown on the Neka fight and he would know if his Rangers had had the same communications and intelligence problems.

They went by armored SUV through Joint Base Mashad, a camp protected by imposing twelve-foot-high, steel-reinforced, concrete T-Walls on the inner perimeter and two treacherous barbed-wire outer layers of fencing. It was all guarded by heavily armed soldiers constantly patrolling on foot and vehicle while electronically and visually monitoring for threatening movement. The sand bags stacked two-or-three-columns deep around bomb shelters and buildings and the anti-mortar netting on the top of those buildings contributed to the distinctly military feel of the camp. A Counter-Rocket Artillery and Mortar 20-millimeter Phalanx system mounted at several locations throughout the base provided lethal defense.

With thick dust swirling outside their closed windows, Steve heard the gravel and dirt grinding under the SUVs big tires as they rolled through the camp. The normalcy of the camp struck Steve as deceptive. It made him feel insulated from the war. He saw the civilized comforts everywhere. They drove past the waste treatment plant, reverse-osmosis water purification and bottling plant, fire department, post office, Army Air Force Food and Exchange Service building, chow hall, hospital, laundry, and gym. Before he visited these camps, he'd never envisioned that the AAFES facility would be available for soldiers to shop for toiletries, snacks, and small, civilian personal appliance needs in a combat zone. It never occurred to him he'd find a Pizza Hut, Starbucks, and McDonalds and even a professional masseuse in the camp.

"How's the food in our chow hall, George?"

"As good as home, except they don't serve lobster and steak every Friday night at home."

The chow hall was a big morale booster that got a lot of the base commander's personal attention.

"I want to visit our people working in the chow hall, laundry, and other facilities before I leave."

"I'll set that up, Steve. You know they found another grenade in the laundry yesterday?"

"No, I hadn't heard that, but it doesn't surprise me." Kratos employees did the laundry. Soldiers just threw it in a bag and dropped it off at the base laundry, then the cleaned, folded, and hung clothes arrived back at their CHU later. It was amazing what his employees found in that laundry in addition to an occasional grenade: money, unspent rounds, and drugs were not unusual.

The commander's clerical assistant escorted Steve into the 3rd Ranger Battalion waiting room. She then stepped into the lieutenant colonel's office. Steve admired the roominess and comfort of this reinforced tent structure. The semi-circular shape, like the old metal Quonset huts used in previous wars, gave it that no-nonsense Army feel. The smell of gun oil and pipe tobacco wafted through the air like a gently waving flag; the gun oil was familiar, the tobacco was unique. The cool air blew loud from the air conditioner as an old-time clock ticked off the seconds in the still room.

The assistant stepped back in the room and told them the commander would see them now. Steve walked in with George and, at the commander's invitation, took their seats around the rectangular meeting table. The assistant provided thirty-two-ounce bottles of water for all attendees—keeping hydrated was a priority year-round.

"Good morning, Colonel Huggins. I brought Sergeant-Major Bird with me so we could give you our full account of the convoy attack."

Lieutenant Colonel Huggins thanked Steve, introduced his executive officer and the Judge Advocate General's representative. There weren't any meetings between contractors and commanders that didn't have the military lawyer present. Huggins had individual and group debriefings scheduled all day, but this was his only meeting with a contractor.

"Mr. Holmes, I want to thank you for lending a hand in helping us defeat the mujahideen attack and save the lives of our soldiers. Lieutenant Williams briefed me this morning by phone from the FOB and his comments about you and George were commendatory."

Officially, Steve wasn't supposed to participate in the fight. His weapon wasn't officially issued and the one George provided could be a difficult issue if the commander chose to press the matter. Steve knew the rules: They shot spies. Spies and mercenaries carry weapons in a war zone without a uniform. Either way, the Status of Forces Agreement and Geneva Conventions wouldn't apply to him.

"Thank you, sir. I had the incredible fortune of being protected by Sergeant-Major Bird."

Colonel Huggins winked at Steve, then smiled at George. "Yes, I am aware of Sergeant-Major Bird's contribution. Lieutenant Williams extolled both his gallantry and spontaneous actions to save lives and repel the enemy. Although there have been some reports of a spare weapon appearing out of thin air and winding up in your hands, I want you to know that I don't believe those accounts. I chalk the story up to the fog of war. I know you picked up your M-16 lying on the ground near the convoy, and I am glad you knew how to use it. If anyone has a problem with that explanation, they should speak now." This was a commander who knew how to dispense with the chaff and focus on what was important.

George stood up abruptly, came to attention, and started to speak, "Sir, I want to explain—"

"Sit down, Sergeant-Major."

George had been ready to admit to providing the weapon—and that he would do it again under similar circumstances. Nonetheless, he was glad to remain silent.

"Okay, Mr. Holmes, give me a rundown on this convoy from the pre-departure briefing until my Rangers arrived on the scene."

"This was a regularly scheduled supply run from Joint Base Mashad to the FOB. We had sixty-five cargo trucks, one hundred-ten convoy drivers and passengers, seven gun trucks and twenty-five Marines in the security team, and one civilian, me. The morning of departure, we received a route reconnaissance briefing that indicated no major delays or detours were expected. The security briefing indicated a low-risk trip: While the convoy might receive harassment in the form of occasional small arms fire, IED, or some non-lethal threats, the route was green. There was a brief reference to planned action in the Elburz Mountains well away from the convoy route. I now realize that action was your Rangers, except the fight occurred in the city, not in the mountains as the pre-brief indicated. Lieutenant Williams briefed us on the safety and security procedures and protection. At approximately fifteen-hundred, while driving through Neka on the Army-designated major supply route 'Chicago,' we started receiving heavy fire from attackers in and around the buildings. Our communications external from the convoy back to Joint Base Mashad were not working. Lieutenant Williams directed defense of the convoy while ushering the remaining convoy out of the fire zone and on to the FOB as quickly as possible. After approximately thirty minutes of this, we saw your Rangers firing from the east."

Lieutenant Colonel Huggins maintained eye contact, listening intently as Steve described the events. "So, your convoy was experiencing the same communications blackout as our Rangers?" Huggins reached into his pocket for a pipe. He started filling it with tobacco as Steve replied.

"Yes, sir. If you don't mind, can I ask when the Rangers lost airborne communications?"

"The comms were fine when the Rangers parachuted into the Elburz Mountain Valley the night before to execute a planned assault on a group of Iranian fighters. They were made up of elements of the Iranian Republic Guard Army, the Mahdi Special Forces, and supported by Basij local militia. They had good communications when they set out for Neka the next morning. It wasn't until they got about five miles out of Neka that they lost comms. The platoon commander made the battlefield decision to continue the mission despite the loss of AWACS communications."

Colonel Huggins' calm demeanor changed almost imperceptibly as he pushed back his shoulders and straightened his head slightly. He wanted his officers on the battlefield to make command decisions. The commander had fought too many battles with Monday-morning quarterbacks in their safe and secure staff jobs who were all too anxious to criticize initiative. "Their battle plan and intelligence updates to that point were sufficient to continue the assault. I fully endorse that decision." Huggins then relaxed a little and sat back in his chair. After packing his pipe full of tobacco, he struck a match off the wooden desk and lit it.

"Did your Rangers see the convoy before they lost AWACS communication?"

"No, they didn't see your convoy until the Iranians started firing on you. It took them a few minutes after that to get in range to fire. My Rangers move slower than your convoy. You weren't even in the picture when they lost comms."

"Where were your Rangers expecting to engage the Iranians?"

"The night before the assault, we expected to find them about five kilometers southeast of Neka. However, before the platoon broke camp, my Rangers received an intelligence update that said they'd moved back into Neka. The platoon adjusted their plans and carried on."

Which meant the Rangers didn't know the mujahideen were in Neka until after the convoy departed Mashad, Steve thought.

The cherry-scented tobacco smoke was making Steve's eyes water. He took a long drink of water, which gave him a moment to blink hard and clear his vision. "Our convoy never received an intelligence update after departure that morning."

"So your convoy didn't get the update on the threat. From what you told me, you would have been near Neka when we received the intel update."

There was no intelligence failure. It was just that no one in the Neka area could receive an intel update, which eliminated one problem. Now, Steve could focus on the communication snafu. "I covered this with Lieutenant Williams. He had no further information on the enemy that would have caused him to change his route or scrap the mission," Huggins said.

"Sir, do you have any idea what caused the enemy to move to Neka?"

"Not yet. They like to run small convoy attacks and harass our patrols in the cities. They use the close proximity and cover of buildings to hide in as they attack the passing convoys. If they know there's going to be a fight with regular forces, they prefer to do it in the mountains, Al-Qaeda-style."

After a few more questions, Lieutenant Colonel Huggins stood up, with everyone in the room following his lead, thanked Steve, and said goodbye.

3

Joint Base Mashad, Iran

At the end of the workday, Steve gathered up his papers, closed down his computer, then sat back in his chair and recalled his arrival into Iran the day before the Neka ambush. He kept thinking back to those few days in hopes of coming up with more answers to all the questions troubling him...

***

The turbulent C-17 flight from Turkmenistan for the last leg of Steve's flight into Joint Base Mashad was made all the worse by the tactical maneuvers flying at treetop level once they crossed the Iranian border. Bumping up and down like riding the pothole-filled dirt roads of his childhood farm back home in Bonifay, the aircraft would pitch up to climb a little, and then pitch down to drop, all with sudden motion. Even a little drop down was worse as small negative gravity forces made him grip the seat arm harder. The constant up and down in total darkness inside the plane made some air sick, but it just tensed him up.

Steve turned up the collar and buttoned up his blue sports coat as he deplaned, to fend off the chill from the forty-degree weather and stiff wind that greeted him on the flight line on this brisk March day in Iran. It seemed too late in the year for the gloves, scarf, and knitted hat he slipped on to keep him warm.

George Bird, Steve's Convoy Program Manager, peacetime employee, and friend picked him up in an armored SUV to escort him to his CHU. Stepping into the vehicle, "Fortunate Son" by Creedence Clearwater Revival played on the radio.

Steve thought, *now there's a problem that still exists today. The senators' sons and daughters of wealthy, well-connected parents were still getting their children draft deferments, just as they did sixty years ago.* The Vietnam-era protest songs got lots of play in Iran on the Armed Forces Radio station. They struck a sympathetic cord, especially among the poor who didn't have connections or wealthy parents to get them deferments.

George had retired from the Marine Corps as head of the Presidential helicopter security team positioned at Quantico. He flew with Presidents Bush and Obama wherever they went during his eight years in this role, which included a lot of trips to Camp David in Maryland. George was a security professional, expert military combat Marine, and physical fitness nut.

"How're your family and my godson doing, George?" George and Cathy's third son, Danny, had been born with severe brain defects; the doctors hadn't been sure Danny would survive childhood.

"They're all doing really well. Cathy quit teaching math a while back so she could spend more time at home with the boys. All three are glad to have mom around more. Danny amazes us every day. Now that she's there all the time, we let the physical therapist go. I take over when I'm home on leave."

"What you two have done and the sacrifices you've made for Danny are incredible. The time and money you've spent on doctors and physical therapy. The way you've made Danny's life as normal as possible. The education and special equipment you've provided. The sports you participate in with him. You two are incredible! I'd love to see the family and have dinner with everyone when you're back in the States."

"That'll be great, Steve." George switched off the radio. "We should discuss your itinerary. Tonight at nineteen-hundred you'll have dinner with six Defense of Freedom Medal winners. Then, our convoy pulls out at oh-six hundred tomorrow morning."

Adding it up, Steve would only get five or six hours of sleep that night. Even if there was plenty of time to sleep, he wouldn't be able to for several days while his body adjusted to the time zone difference. "Who are the honorees for our dinner tonight?"

"The six are all truck drivers and will be in the convoy tomorrow."

"Every one of them has been wounded, and yet here they are, back again, driving a truck? What pushes them to do that?" Steve shook his head, awed.

"I hope you ask each of them that question tonight. Their answers will vary, but they all care about the mission and the soldiers they are supporting. They are all brave and dedicated."

"It will be a privilege for me to meet them."

"So, a little background on each. Marc Blum is thirty-six and has a nine-year-old daughter in Florida. His wound from an IED occurred in Afghanistan in twenty-thirteen. Jake Turner is fifty-two, has a wife and two children in Houston, Texas. He was injured by an IED explosion in Iraq in twenty-ten and again in Afghanistan in twenty-twelve."

Steve removed a 5x7 card from his shirt pocket and started making notes. He jotted down names and just a note or two about each honoree he would reference. "Wounded twice and he still comes back. Wow."

"He will be the only driver at the dinner tonight who was wounded twice."

"Please seat Jake across the table from me for dinner. I'm interested to hear his story."

"Will do. Moving on, Meriah Parkson is forty-one. She has a husband and three sons back in Beavercreek, Ohio. She was wounded in Afghanistan in twenty-twelve."

"Doug Harris, Dennis Michaels, and Teresa Faircloth are all single and were wounded in Iraq."

"Think about it, George: If these drivers got wounded now as active duty military, they'd get a Purple Heart. The DOFM went a long way to giving contractors who were injured or killed while supporting the troops the recognition they deserve, but still, it isn't the same as the Purple Heart. But we have made progress; the Secretary of Defense didn't even include contractors in their casualty reports in previous wars."

"Yeah, contractors have come a long way since Afghanistan."

George reached under his seat, pulled out some papers and handed them to Steve. "Here are the plans for tomorrow; you need to know what to expect, what route we're taking, who's going with us and all that. Despite some general intelligence warnings about attacks on the first anniversary of the start of the war, we don't expect any trouble on our route. We're prepared just in case, of course. We've used this route hundreds of times in the past few months and the mujahideen have been cleared, except for one pocket north of Neka, and we won't go near there."

"Tell me about the convoy, Sergeant Major Bird."

"We have sixty-five diesel-powered tractor trailers and Heavy Equipment Transports carrying fuel, water, ice, MRAPs, supplies, and mail to our FOB outside Tehran. There will be a Marine security detail escorting us. As usual, we'll have one Gun Truck for every ten vehicles armed with a fifty-caliber gun, M-240 machine guns, and soldiers carrying small arms. We'll have a platoon of twenty-five Marines, commanded by Lieutenant Bruce Williams, and I will be his second-in-command."

George turned off the main road and stopped at the housing security gate. After showing their IDs, they drove down narrow dirt roads in between rows of trailers in the housing compound. Their heavy, armored SUV pulled to a stop. George handed Steve his keys, dropped him off at his Contaierized Housing Unit, and said, "You have about twenty minutes to get ready if we're going to make it to the chow tent on time for the ceremony and dinner."

The trailer was small and designed mainly for sleeping; it had bare plywood walls, a single bed, a wooden nightstand, and not much else. It had a light metal exterior and was about the size of a single-commode public restroom. The CHUs sat six feet apart in row upon row in the housing section of the camp. They had electricity and Wi-Fi, with a communal bath and toilet facility located nearby.

Steve and George stepped ahead of the line awaiting service at the chow tent. They presented their identification and went to the room for their dinner honoring the Defense of Freedom Medal winners. It was a private dining room with a rectangular folding table and chairs for about a dozen people and space for a podium and projector. Steve reviewed his note cards before the honorees arrived.

George stood beside Steve at the entrance to the private dining room to greet the truckers. Referring briefly to his note cards, Steve stepped forward to each honoree as they entered the room, shot out his right hand for a firm shake, and placed his left hand on their shoulder. He looked them in the eyes, addressed each by name, and welcomed them.

The first honoree arrived five minutes early. "Hello, Dennis. I'm Steve Holmes, the Kratos Energy and Logistics Corporation Executive

Vice President for Government Services."

"Howdy, Steve. Call me Whiskey. Prit-near half the truck drivers don't know me by any name but Whiskey."

"Okay, Whiskey, it is."

"We use call signs for truckers when we ain't in uniform. Only when we drive as whatchucall 'civilian contractors' can we use 'em on the radio. Commander don't think they fit that military protercol, and he's the boss."

Steve got the call sign from each of them. Marc was Baller. Meriah was Ohio Girl. Jake was Hatchet. Doug was Colonel. Teresa was Filly.

George pulled out a bottle of Jack Daniels whiskey from his backpack that Steve had smuggled into this Muslim land and offered each honoree a shot in their soda or straight up. The oak flavor from the barrels that stored the sour mash combined with the distinct Tennessee whiskey taste, gave the guests a treat in this foreign post away from home. The straight shot burned with the first sip but tasted better with each additional sip.

Steve got to know the drivers a little better, and he thanked each of them for their sacrifice and dedication. They in turn each thanked him and Kratos for the support they received while contractors, and especially when they were injured. That care contributed greatly to their loyalty to Kratos.

They had to go through the chow line to get dinner. No catering staff in a war zone; not unless you are a high-ranking military officer. The food was plentiful. Chicken grilled or fried, steak done to your desire, fish, hamburger, hot dogs, pizza, breads, vegetables, and big salad and dessert bars. You could refill your plate as often as you liked. Steve's favorite was all the ice cream he could eat. A lot of soldiers gained weight while they were in the combat zone.

During dinner, Steve asked each honoree around the table why they would continue to drive after they'd been wounded.

Whiskey was first. He said he needed the money. "Only God knows when our time here on earth is up. Not a damn thing we can do to change that."

Baller wasn't eligible to serve in the regular military when he'd first joined Kratos, because he had severe scoliosis requiring him to wear a back brace. The Army grandfathered him into active duty when they started the Sponsored Reserves. "They still won't let me in the infantry with my back problems, so I'm glad to do my duty driving trucks."

Filly wanted to see the world and didn't really know how dangerous the work was until she got over to Iraq the first time. Once she was there, the drivers and soldiers all became like family to her and she became like a mother to them.

Colonel and Ohio Girl came back after their injuries because they loved supporting the young soldiers. "It's dangerous for us, but it's dangerous for everyone," Ohio Girl said.

Hatchet was the last trucker to answer. Wounded twice and with twenty years working for Kratos, his story was the most compelling. While they all expressed the desire to serve their country as a motive as well, it was Hatchet who said he came back after two injuries to fight the Iranians.

"I came for the money and stayed for the mission. What we do here is important to everyone, especially the young combat soldier. With the average age of a trucker nearly twice that of a young combat soldier, they look to us for guidance and reassurance."

Steve said, "I've talked to many soldiers, enlisted and officer, junior and senior ranks. They all say they love the support our men and women in Kratos give them." Jake fidgeted with his fork and looked around the room at others as Steve spoke. It was clear there was more Jake wanted to say. "So what else is on your mind, Jake?"

"I am proud of what we do, and Kratos is the leader for taking care of its employees in a combat theater, but it wasn't always so good, you know. Company actions to rush into the war without good preparation were misguided. For example, using trucks without sufficient armor on contractor vehicles was stupid."

"Yes. The generals planned for the initial war, but not the occupation and rebuilding of Iraq after Baghdad fell. Corporations rushed in to help, without being prepared to handle the huge volume of business and extreme circumstances. Some of that neglect was criminal."

Jake grimaced, his face blushed. "It damn sure was criminal. I lost close friends driving trucks that had no armor and no security protection. When the military was too busy, security for the truck convoys disappeared. Truckers knew the fuel and supplies were critical for the mission, and we often went ahead with the trips even without armed protection. We were getting shot at every day with or without security. It was hell."

Whiskey exhaled loudly, cleared his throat, and said, "I got what you might call a less-than-honorable wound."

The few snickers broke the icy mood in the room.

"What kind of wound was that?" Steve asked.

"Sub*cooo*taneous gl*ueteee*us acute lead poisoning."

"What's that?"

"I got shot in the ass! But, it twern't no retreat to the rear. Ain't no pun, neither. No sir, there twern't no armor and an IED frag rikerchetted through the door up my seat and up, well, you know."

"Those unarmored vehicles. I'll be damned if I know how you all had the courage to drive them on the Iraqi highways like that every day."

"Twern't no courage I was feelin' back then. I just didn't wanna die. Didn't know we was gonna be the main course in a hadji turkey shoot."

Steve grabbed Whiskey by the shoulder. "You shouldn't have been put in that situation."

Dinner ended with a prayer for all those dead and living who received the DOFM and for the safety of their convoy the next day. Then Filly handed Steve a sheet of paper with what looked like verses on it.

"We'd like you to join us in singing the truckers song. It's a tradition when three or more of us meet socially. We call it the 'The Persian Truckers Battle Hymn.'"

"What's the tune?"

"You sing it to the tune of the 'Battle Hymn of the Republic.'" Then, they broke out in mostly off-key voices.

I heard the mighty thunder of the rolling eighteen wheels,
We are trucking down Persian highways where the wrath of hell reveals,
No bullet, rocket, or mortar will deter the sword He wields,
By God, we're rolling on.
Glory, glory hallelujah
Glory, glory hallelujah
Glory, glory hallelujah
By God, we're rolling on.

Through the shrapnel and the bullets we shall never sound retreat,
We'll get the cargo through it and will never accept defeat,
As He died to make men holy, let us live to make men free,
By God, we're rolling on.
Glory, glory hallelujah
Glory, glory hallelujah
Glory, glory hallelujah
By God, we're rolling on.

The group ended the song with smiles all around, said their goodbyes and headed back to their CHU for a few hours sleep before they had to get up to join the convoy.

Steve arrived at the rallypoint for the convoy the next morning just in time to hear Lieutenant Williams give the security update. It hadn't changed from the night before. Though there was one aspect of the security briefing that Steve had forgotten about until now: The Intelligence Officer mentioned that this was a regularly scheduled trip, but they'd moved the trip ahead by one day this week to avoid other major military operations on their normal travel day. The schedule had changed less than one week before departure. That meant only people directly involved in the operation or those who regularly received convoy movement schedules knew the information on where and when this convoy would travel. If the communications failure was deliberate, the schedule change would at least narrow down the list to those who knew when and where the convoy would travel.

4

Springfield, Illinois

The scene was electric. Thousands of supporters packed the auditorium to hear the senator declare victory. Streamers shot, then floated through the air. Kazoos blared, the crowd cheered, laughed, and screamed, and the "William Tell Overture" blasted from speakers, creating a deafening cacophony. "Jobs Now, Jobs Tomorrow, Jobs Forever!" and "All the Way!" banners dotted the audience, signs pumped up and down in the hands of excited supporters, and slogan-painted balloons floated throughout the room.

The senator and his wife waded through the enthusiastic crowd on stage, shaking hands, smiling, hugging the cheering and crying staff, until they finally reached their family and closest supporters at the podium. Reporters from news agencies around the world covered every step of the victory celebration for the primary winner and assumed-to-be Democratic presidential nominee.

"Thank you. Thank you!" The senator tried to speak, but the cheering, yelling, and general din continued. He turned, hugged, and kissed his wife and each of his children one more time. Holding up one hand, he managed to get some of them to quiet down.

"Thank you, Illinois!" The crowd erupted in thunderous applause at even higher decibels. The senator hugged and slapped the backs of his closest supporters standing on stage while the cheering continued. Raising both hands, he asked for quiet as he waited to speak, and then finally, "They said our campaign was in the toilet. They said our ideas weren't relevant. They said we couldn't win." The crowd booed in a long, deep growl. "I say, it's jobs, jobs, jobs, and we are going to take that message all the way from the outhouse to the White House!"

As the crowd exploded in applause and voices rose to their loudest, Senator Alex Shankle reached over and turned off the television that he and his small group of supporters were watching.

In the small conference room on the opposite side of Springfield, with no media, few signs, and little noise or music, Shankle turned and looked into the faces of his supporters gathered around. Their somber mood and quiet chatter contrasted with the scenes on TV. The light tap, tap, tapping of rain on the windows was the loudest sound in the room.

With one arm around his wife, Audrey, Shankle said, "It all seemed so easy after we won the straw poll in Iowa." He paused for a moment to choose his words. "We cannot continue this campaign as we have been. Senator Rockefeller is running away with it. The voters have spoken again and again since Iowa and they're saying they aren't interested in the war. They care about jobs." The senator's adult children, Adam and Amy, stepped in closer to hug their dad.

It started with one comment blurted spontaneously by a supporter, "Don't stop now, Senator." Others agreed and the small group began to chant, "Don't stop now, don't stop now."

The senator and his family all hugged a little tighter as they stared out at his most loyal supporters. "I want to continue, but without a win in Illinois we don't have the funds to go on as we have been. We don't have the support of the Party and our message is not catching on." The chanting stopped. He looked around the quiet room, briefly making eye contact with each of them. Their disappointment felt coarse and hard like stale bread too hard to chew or swallow. "But I'm not quitting. I didn't quit in my first political race for county commissioner. I didn't quit in the race for state senator, governor, or United States senator, and I'm not quitting now."

Slowly the sadness shifted to hopeful optimism in the small room with supporters holding hands, smiling, and voicing their approval and love for their leader. Many of those in the room had been with Alex Shankle since the beginning. They believed in him because they saw his humanity, felt his care and concern for the common man. When a tornado struck his community during his first term as county commissioner, he'd climbed on board a Caterpillar bulldozer and helped clear city streets so emergency crews could get through. He'd spent his Christmas holidays serving meals to the poor and delivering blankets and encouragement to the homeless. He always had time for his constituents, and he never tired of helping his community.

A supporter at the back of the room called out, "Tell us what to do, Senator."

"Well, ah," Shankle stumbled over his words with no script or campaign slogan to provide a pat answer off the cuff. "Well, ah, we should . . ." He hadn't thought this through. A small sheen of nervous sweat shone on his upper lip.

Audrey Shankle squeezed his hand hard. "Go on."

His eyes brightened and his face relaxed. "We have to go on!" He paused as the ideas came slowly at first, then faster. "We can continue to get the message out. We won a few delegates in the primaries and when people get behind our antiwar message, we can gear up the campaign again. We'll keep the website open and continue to take contributions. We can seek out support from other like-minded organizations. The Catholic Church is against the war. Let's get their support. Let's text our voters directly with our message and solicit their support. I will continue to make speeches and remind voters from the Capitol just how dangerous this war is for Americans. The very future of our country is at stake. I believe the American people will in time understand that importance and rally to our campaign."

On the edge of the small crowd, Jodie Arenas, Shankle's top aide and campaign manager, stood with arms folded, face red, seething with anger.

Shankle's largest financial benefactor, Frank Zorbos, asked her, "You think this is the end? Can we ever really get back in the race?"

"Hell no, it's not over! I won't let it be over."

"What can you do?"

"I can do plenty. We've come too far and worked too hard to have it all end here. The people might not be interested in the antiwar message today, but it only takes one catastrophe with lots of dead soldiers coming home in body bags to get their attention."

"He can't go on without support. I've given him all the money I can, but it's not enough."

"I'll get us money. I can start by mortgaging my home or, if that's not enough, sell my soul to the Devil. I'll do whatever it takes."

Jodie's eyes opened wide as if a thought had just occurred to her. She pulled out her smartphone and thumbed over to her contact list. The list of donors labeled "Last Chance" popped up on her screen. The first number started ringing as she walked outside into the light rain.

5

Washington, DC

Steve Holmes' first appointment, after getting back to DC, was with Bernie Tyler, Kratos' CEO and Chairman of the Board of Directors. No one had free access to Tyler. His direct subordinates couldn't just walk in and speak to him.

Steve arrived early, as usual, for the meeting with his boss. He parked in the company garage and used the covered crosswalk to enter Kratos' headquarters. He came in through the glass double-doors of the third-floor reception area, waved to security, showed his badge, walked through the security scanner, and entered the elevator with a half-dozen other employees. With multiple stops, it took a few minutes to get to the 40th floor at the top of the building. He got out at another secure area where the company's executive leadership team worked.

Steve took a seat on the leather couch outside Tyler's door while Tyler finished a phone call with one of the Board's Directors. From the pieces of the conversation he could hear, Steve could tell that Tyler was questioning Linda Hines about some of the Board members' loyalty.

"Janice, get me the Board file," Tyler yelled. Janice went to the file cabinets just outside Tyler's office and returned with a file. Just as she sat down again, he yelled, "This won't do, I need the reports from last month's Board meeting. It's the blue file." Janice went back to the file cabinets and delivered the blue file to Tyler. "Janice, I need the file with the résumés of each Board member as well." Looking exasperated, Janice got up again and retrieved the file. "Oh, hell, none of this is what I need. Just forget it."

Steve had had a very candid discussion with Linda Hines at a recent reception preceding the Annual Stockholders Meeting that had highlighted some of Tyler's problem behavior. Steve recalled the discussion vividly.

With drink in hand and other Board members and executive employees milling around, Linda had quietly asked Steve, "How would you characterize Bernie's leadership style?"

"I can salute and follow orders with the best of them," Steve replied. If Linda wanted Steve to be candid, she had to ask for it. Perhaps Bernie Tyler had told her this was a cohesive team that worked closely together, all pulling in the same direction.

"That's not a very encouraging leadership description or your relationship with Bernie, or is it?"

Steve swirled his near-empty glass of pinot noir, recalling the scents of vanilla, black cherry, wood, and apple. "Perhaps not, but do you mind telling me why you're asking?"

"It's my job to know how he's doing. We have these social interactions with the company's top executives to get to know you and get a feel for how the operation is running."

Steve looked around at the place where they were meeting. Plush leather bar stools stood around high tables convenient for standing or seated conversation for two or three guests. A waiter in black tie, white shirt, and black suit carrying a tray of empty glasses, asked for drink orders. "Very good," he'd say. "I'll have those out immediately. Dinner will be served in the private executive room next door."

The exclusive restaurant had private rooms like this for their upscale private parties. On any given night you'd see players from the local baseball team ordering the mammoth forty-eight-ounce T-bone steaks or city and state executives enjoying the five-star meals with their spouses or friends.

"First, you'll have to tell me which Tyler you're talking about: Tyler, the Chairman of the Board, or Tyler, the CEO?"

"Does your relationship vary that much with him?"

"Yes, it does. Tyler dictates the relationship with his subordinate based on which role is most advantageous for him. His behavior is the biggest argument against combining both the CEO and chairman's role that I know of. See, it's the CEO's job to run the company. The chairman's job is to monitor performance of the company and to protect the interests of shareholders. When it's convenient, Tyler looks at the business and heaps blame on subordinates in his CEO role. Yet, in reality, he is a micromanager who doesn't trust anyone else to make decisions. When it's time for the CEO to be accountable, Tyler behaves as the chairman and questions how the executives are running their part of the business, always claims he wasn't informed or didn't know what was happening, and talks about shareholder interests as if that's his only concern. When it really counts, he never takes responsibility for problems or failures in his operational leadership role as CEO. Not when it counts."

"When does it count?"

"When there is something on the line for Tyler to lose, like part of his bonus or his job. Surely you've noticed this. For example, I've never seen him take responsibility in front of the Board for anything that has gone wrong in company operations."

"I'm not sure I have noticed. Can you give me an example?"

Steve knew that Linda had to be very careful in her Board role to avoid meddling in the operation of the company. She could oversee and she could receive complaints, but anything that gave even the appearance that she was interfering with the day-to-day operation would be in violation of her duties.

Steve set his wine glass down carefully on a folded cloth napkin on the barroom table. When he got going in a conversation, his hands often moved as fast as his mouth. "Sure, I'll give you an example you'll remember. Last fall, when we were nine months into the integration of that IT company we bought, Burns and Coswell, the Board asked for a report on how the acquisition was going." Steve gestured for acknowledgment with a turn of his head and his hands open, palms up.

"Yes, I remember it; you gave a summary of the activities. You all were having some major problems with both the acquisition and the integration phase. As I recall, you accepted responsibility for the integration failures."

"Yes, I took responsibility. It happened in my organization. I made decisions and appointed key people to run that integration within Kratos. I owned it. More importantly, I owned the responsibility to fix it." Steve made a chopping motion with his right hand to emphasize the point.

"So, what was the problem with Tyler in that meeting?"

"Tyler did not say a word during the discussion. He cowed in the corner, never taking responsibility for his or his team's actions. At the very minimum, he should have taken responsibility for the fouled-up acquisition decision to purchase Burns and Coswell. He absolutely made that final decision himself."

"He told us in private session that you and the VP of Mergers and Acquisitions fouled that up. He said you all kept him in the dark until it was too late."

"That's absurd, Linda. He's a micromanager. He makes the decision on these deals. He ran the M&A meetings. He drove the financial analysis to achieve the kinds of outcomes he expected, which did not reflect the estimates provided by his due diligence team. He drove the Burns and Coswell acquisition valuation and decision himself." Steve's hands were moving quickly now. "No one, and I mean no one, could tell Tyler that the value of that company was anything less than what Tyler wanted."

"Did you challenge the acquisition decision?"

Steve shrugged his shoulders. "I wasn't invited to most of the Mergers & Acquisition meetings to be involved enough to challenge it. That was pretty amazing to me: We were doing an acquisition of a company that I would be responsible for running, and I wasn't involved in many of the discussions. Tyler treated the M&A meetings like his own stage and it was a one-man act. In fact, he made it clear he didn't think anyone else understood this kind of financial estimation as well as him. I gave my opinion when asked, and I had an operational team supporting the acquisition."

"What did you expect Tyler to say during your briefing to the Board?"

Steve shook his head in disbelief as he thought about Tyler's behavior. "As leader of the company, and the one who made the ultimate decision, he should have said, 'I am responsible. I own this problem.' After that, he should go back into the operation and fix the problems that led to the failure. He might even need to fire people but, if he never owns the problem, never holds himself accountable, the problems never get fixed. As a demonstration of that very lack of accountability for acquisitions, this isn't the first one that has gone bad." Steve raised his index finger and shook his head. "The last flop was a manufacturing engineering company in Huntsville, Alabama two years ago. Tyler never told me there had been previous acquisition problems. If he had, we might have avoided some of them this time around. Tyler doesn't own it, so he doesn't fix it."

Linda swirled her drink, looked around the room, let out an audible sigh, and said, "The Board members have certainly seen Tyler's temper and discomfort when we criticize anything he does. He doesn't take it well."

Steve couldn't suppress a small smile, knowing the Board recognized Tyler's behavior problems more than they acknowledged.

At the maitre d's invitation other guests moved toward their seats at the dinner table, eyeing the names set at each position, looking for the spot that Tyler had personally selected for them, and wondering about the significance of each seat.

Steve retrieved his glass from the table as Linda spoke about Tyler's behavior while they strolled into the dining room. The large cherry wood table and heavy leather upholstered chairs gave the room an exclusive feel.

He took a sip, wondering what else the Board members knew about Tyler's behavior. "Therein rests the problem with Tyler's behavior and our relationship, as far as I'm concerned. As the CEO leader of the company, he does not take responsibility when things go wrong, when it really matters. More than just blaming his subordinates, his management style is to position them so he has a fall guy or gal when things go wrong. All the while, he wants to make every decision. Tyler will come to you privately, on small issues and take responsibility one-on-one, but not when it matters. I've come to see that as a 'nuclear nuance' of leadership."

Linda and Steve found their seats and waited a moment for everyone to arrive before sitting down. "The Board does recognize this shortcoming with Tyler and we've brought it to his attention. We even sent him through a leadership program that addressed ownership and another area he needed to improve in: people management."

Steve cracked another small, knowing smile. "If Tyler went to charm school, it didn't work. No one in the business would conclude that your discussion with him or the training did any good. You can't be the critic and the actor, too; few people are objective enough to fault their own performance regularly, and Tyler certainly would never fault his performance in front of the Board."

Fifteen minutes after their scheduled meeting was to start, Tyler's secretary called Steve's name and shook him out of his flashback.

"Mr. Tyler said you can come in now."

He stepped through the office door behind the secretary and walked toward Tyler. It was a clear, dry spring day. The warmth of the sun shining through windows on two sides of Tyler's room reminded Steve of the early spring and cherry blossoms beginning to bloom in DC.

Tyler reached over his desk to make the greeting. He made no attempt to get up or to make eye contact as he shook hands with Steve. "Sit down over there."

Tyler was in his seventies and wasn't prone to small talk, so Steve had gotten to know his background through friends and associates.

Tyler had had a difficult relationship with his father, and there were rumors of physical abuse in Bernie's childhood. His father had started a small dry cleaning business, worked hard, built it into a substantial business, and wanted his son to run the business after college. But Bernie rebelled and went out on his own.

Tyler avoided the Vietnam War with a deferment to go to college and now was never comfortable with the military side of his business. He didn't understand the patriotism and commitment to supporting the troops that his contractors and Sponsored Reserve employees displayed. He thought their terms of respect, like "Yes, sir" and "No, sir" were more kowtowing for show than true respect.

"I'm proud of the Kratos mission to support our troops and the dedicated people who deliver that support every day under dangerous conditions," Steve Holmes had often said to Tyler. To which Tyler would often stare back blank-faced, or comment, "They do it for the money." On one occasion Steve got the opportunity to explain further. Reaching for the company Annual Report, he pointed to the men and women pictured in it supporting the military in a combat zone. He turned to the first page. "This is Joe Gonzalez. He's prior active duty military and worked as a Deputy Sheriff in Holmes County, Florida before he joined Kratos as a Sponsored Reserve employee."

Joe's creased uniform and muscular upper body filled the shirt, giving it a triangular look as he reached for an Army post visitor's ID badge.

"There were many, safer jobs he could have here at home, but he wanted to support our troops. His experience in combat and life do a lot to encourage the junior regular active duty soldiers in their teens and early twenties who are often away from home and experiencing combat for the first time. Like many of our employees, he cares for them as he would his own family."

It was beyond Bernie Tyler's comprehension.

Steve now stepped back a bit awkwardly and sat down across the desk from Tyler. Steve knew the barrier made Tyler feel more comfortable. Tyler never started the conversation with pleasantries, although Steve often tried casual conversation at the beginning. Steve doubted that Tyler knew if he was married, had a dog, or had hobbies; he was sure the man didn't care to know.

Tyler swiveled around in his chair to face the window, ninety degrees from his line of sight to Steve. He crossed his legs and leaned back. "Tell me about the Neka convoy."

Surprised that Tyler showed concern, Steve gave him a rundown of the attack and its aftermath. Steve said, "It's a shame that so many brave men and women were injured or killed, many of them former Kratos employees."

Tyler said, "We lost materiel, too. What do you think this will cost Kratos?"

"It will cost us very little. DOD paid for the equipment and supplies on the convoy that we bought through our contract. All our former employees injured or killed were on active duty. We'll have a little cost, like the one hundred thousand dollars bereavement bonus we pay to the family for their needs when a Sponsored Reserve employee dies on active duty; maybe five million dollars in total."

Then Tyler asked Steve to give him a rundown of Kratos's Iranian contracts. Steve discussed the people, contracts, and risks. Tyler was particularly interested in the work going to a Turkish company. Kratos had hundreds of subcontractors, so his interest in this one was unusual.

"How has Sadik Dost performed on the work we've awarded them?" Tyler asked.

"Their performance has been spotty. They generally provide construction management and food service workers. If they get the right people assigned, they do a pretty good job. However, they're not open to our audits and they're not cheap. Still, we invite them to bid and compete for new work." Steve wasn't exactly sure what Tyler was driving at, but Steve's judgment of their behavior should have been enough to cause Tyler concern.

"What I hear you saying is that they get their work done. Is that right?"

How Tyler extracted that out of the conversation was unknowable. However, Steve knew Tyler was looking to make a point. Steve would approach this as he always did: be brutally honest and state the facts, so that he knew Tyler clearly understood what he meant.

"The tasks get completed because of a lot of assistance from Kratos. As the prime contractor, we're ultimately responsible so we can't let them fail. I'm concerned about their lack of openness, too. We've had past problems with subcontractors mistreating employees and human trafficking. Some of these subs took passports away from the workers and wouldn't let them leave the country. When those passports are withheld, that often leads to other employee mistreatment."

Tyler's face remained expressionless. He alternately turned his head to look at Steve and scratched what appeared to be doodles on a pad of paper. Slow, circular movement or faster movement with the pen tilted as he filled in the geometric shapes he had drawn.

Steve waited for some reaction to his concern, but receiving none, he continued, "That's slavery, Bernie! Some of the women have been forced into prostitution. Human trafficking is a serious problem and Kratos will be held liable by the Defense Department if we haven't done everything we can to prevent these crimes."

"I know you'll make sure that doesn't happen, Steve."

Tyler leaned his chair forward, stood up, and began to pace in front of the windows. It was uncomfortably quiet in the room for a few minutes as Tyler appeared to ponder Steve's comments. He stopped in front of Steve, looked down, and for the first time that day made eye contact with a clear focus that suggested interest and purpose.

"You say they are competing for new work. Are they winning work?"

Steve could tell that Tyler already knew the answer to his question. "They haven't won any recent work for the reasons I told you." Steve couldn't make it any clearer. "They're too expensive, they don't provide good people, their performance is poor, and their lack of openness is a big risk for Kratos."

"Let me give you my optics on the situation." That was Tyler's way of saying: *I don't buy what you just told me, I've looked into this matter, and you're full of shit.* "The president of Sadik Dost tells me you won't let them bid. You tell me they are bidding, but just aren't successful. They've successfully worked for us in the past. What am I to think?"

Steve glared at Tyler for a few moments. His anger registered with a slight straightening of Tyler's head as Steve remained silent. Steve stood up, faced Tyler, and spoke in a slightly raised voice. "You should pay attention to *me*, and you should think they're working you to get an advantage in their bidding. More than anything, you should believe what *I* tell you. If not, you should get someone in this job you trust."

Steve paused, expecting some reaction from Tyler, but once again he got nothing. Frustration growing, he walked a couple steps to the side to break the tension-filled locked stare, then walked back when he added in a lower tone, "While their performance is spotty, I worry more about their behavior. They appear to be more concerned about which of their family members they do business with and what members of the United Arab Emirates royal families they are close to than they are about getting the job done *right*. In addition, they treat foreign workers poorly. I've increased the training and assigned additional auditors to oversee their work, but their behavior still worries me."

Without commenting on Steve's concerns or clarifying his implication that Steve had lied, Tyler walked back to his desk, sat down and picked up a single piece of paper with numbers aligned in columns. "We make good profit on their work and I'm using them to build relationships for more work throughout the Middle East." Tyler laid down the paper and looked at Steve again. "We can make billions in the Middle East if we have the right partners. We can use Sadik Dost's well-connected relationships there to leverage our way into new business, but that all hinges on your ability to get them work on our contracts. Quid pro quo, ya know? You need to do whatever it takes to get them more work in Iran, immediately."

Steve was stunned. Tyler's last statement showed a total lack of understanding or care for what you must do when contracting with the U.S. government, specifically the Department of Defense. "Our government contracts require that we compete and award task orders on an objective basis of cost, technical, management, and past performance factors. To get an award, Sadik will have to improve their scoring in these areas. To deviate from that approach guarantees us a challenge by the Defense Contract Audit Association, and the potential for unallowed costs, which become write-offs to profit," Steve said emphatically.

Tyler was back on his feet in a hurry, talking fast and loud and gesturing wildly with his hands, first pointing at Steve, then pointing out the window at the world. "Do I need to remind you that I'm the CEO and you are a pissant around here? I make fifteen million dollars a year to think big and make big decisions. No one tells me how to run this business. I tell them. Now, I believe I've made myself clear, Mr. Holmes. You do what you have to do to get Sadik Dost more work or I will get someone who will!"

Steve sat, staring at him as Tyler turned and walked to the door, opened it, and in a calm voice, said, "Thank you, Mr. Holmes. I'll be looking forward to hearing from you soon."

Steve stood up again and walked out, glaring at the man as he did.

6

Steve walked to the elevator, preoccupied with Tyler's insult and demand to get Sadik Dost more work. "Whatever it takes." He passed Janice outside Tyler's office, Mark Darrow walking in the hall, and the receptionist, without greeting. Stepping onto the elevator just ahead of Steve was the CFO, John Carpenter.

"Steve. You look like you're off in dreamland."

"I'm sorry, John, good morning. I just left Tyler's office with plenty to chew on."

"Ah, yeah, our Bernie can be difficult to deal with. You want to talk about it over a cup of coffee in the cafeteria?"

"Sure, if I'm not interrupting your schedule today."

"I've always got time to listen to the problems of operations executives."

Descending to the bottom floor where several commercial vendors prepared, scooped, tossed, and served fast food mainly for the building's office employees, Steve and John got coffee and found a remote table away from the ears of other employees.

"So, what was Tyler's burning issue for today?"

"He sees our work with the DOD in Iran as a way to leverage relationships to expand our commercial business in the Middle East."

"That makes sense."

"Yes. We already have several subcontractors doing work for us in Iran who we team with for other work in Saudi Arabia, Iraq, and Kuwait."

"I'm aware that some of our largest commercial construction contractors in those countries are under our contract with the military in Iran. They are the slowest paying customers we have. The leverage of our work in Iran helps to pressure them to pay faster on the commercial contracts."

"It's not cash flow I'm worried about right now. It's Tyler's desire to send this one company more work despite the performance and behavior problems they've demonstrated."

"Can you shore up their performance to get the projects done?"

"You mean can we do their job for them? Yeah, we can do that, though it seems pretty stupid to me to create more work for ourselves rather than to give the work to a more competent company."

"I don't see the problem. Just help them do a better job."

"*The problem* is they aren't cheap and they have poor past performance. With the criteria we must use to select subcontractors, they won't beat other competitors. Tyler expects us to 'do whatever it takes' to get them work."

"I see. What will you do?"

"This one is easy. We'll run the source selections according to the rules and we'll make our awards to the best-qualified bidders. I suspect Sadik Dost won't be winning a lot of work, but I can see the brown feces in violent collision with the turbine blades on this one, John."

John chuckled. "I haven't heard it put quite that way before."

"Their performance isn't my biggest concern. Their behavior

toward their third-country national employees is where I'm really worried. They don't always treat these employees humanely, and that can be a bigger problem for us with the Department of Justice and FCPA. But, Tyler isn't at all concerned."

"That certainly gets my attention. Has this company violated any FCPA rules?"

"If I knew of any, they would have been prosecuted already."

"Can you keep the company straight?"

"I don't know, we'll try, but I'll bust them the first time I find them misbehaving."

"I'm sure you'll do the right thing, Steve. How are you handling Bernie's impersonal style?"

"I wish I could punch him every now and then, but I can handle it."

"This may be talking a little out of school about Tyler, but I heard a story about him from his mother that might help explain why he is like he is. As a child, he was the local bully's favorite target. One night, he stopped to play at a friend's house and the friend's older brother pushed Bernie around, then punched him in the eye. Bernie went running home. His father caught him as he came in the door, saw the blood on the cut cheek, and demanded Bernie go back and stand up to the kid. When Bernie was too afraid and refused, his father beat him with a belt—one of many times his father thought a beating would toughen his kid up. I think he takes some kind of medication today to control his moods, but I don't know what the ailment is."

"So, you think Bernie's callous treatment of workers and his questionable ethics are due to the physical abuse he experienced as a child?"

"What I'm saying is that he's taking medication that helps him to be a more normal human being. I don't think that excuses his behavior, but it makes him a little easier to understand."

***

Steve seethed about the conversation with Tyler all day at work. That evening, with a tall glass of iced tea in his hand, and sitting out back on his apartment patio on a cool April evening, he gave his friend, Sergeant-Major George Bird, a call in Iran.

"Good morning, George. I knew you'd be in your CHU at oh-five-hundred hours."

"No kidding. It must be important, or you wouldn't wake me up, I hope."

"Yes and no. It's important to me because you're the only person I can talk to about this, but it's probably not going to seem so important to you in a combat zone."

"So hit me with it."

"Tyler wants me to get work for his pet contractor, Sadik Dost, despite the fact their performance stinks, their cost is too high, and I'm concerned they're going to treat their employees like slaves the first chance they get. Even worse, that son of a bitch called me a liar!"

"Just like that, he called you a liar?"

Steve stood up and began to pace on the patio. "Oh, hell, no. He's too slick for that. He questioned the veracity of the story I told him about Sadik Dost."

"So, what are you going to do about it?"

"As for Sadik Dost, I'll personally look into their subcontracts with Kratos more closely, and ensure we're treating them fairly, which I'm confident is the case. Then I'll meet with their president. I'll invite him to bid on all future work. I'll even give him a list of upcoming procurements. I'll assure him that they have an opportunity to win all work based on Sadik's ability to score higher than other bidders. I'll tell them I spoke with their friend Bernie Tyler, and I understand the importance of the relationship. I won't tell them that I expect my personal attention to this matter will result in them getting zero work in the future. Then, I'll tell them if they so much as misplace a passport of one of their employees, I will personally kick them off every subcontract they have with Kratos."

George rolled in his bed laughing. "You're a real ass-kisser. What about him calling you a liar?"

"Now, that's serious. I can't work for someone who doesn't trust me and I won't stand for someone calling me a liar. But, I also won't let my animosity toward Tyler get in the way of my duty to our employees, either. I'll stick it out as long as I can to ensure things are done right, but this is the beginning of the end of my working for Bernie Tyler."

"If it helps any, I find that liars think everyone else lies, too."

"Thanks for the words of wisdom, George. Now try to get some sleep and I'll do the same."

***

Steve's first sight of the early dawn light that was just now painting his room introduced the new day with a brand new vision. He rubbed his eyes, extended his legs and arms out, fists clenched for that stretch that moved him from slumber to stir. He rolled over and glimpsed the fluorescent digits that confirmed daylight was burning. *You gotta get up, you gotta get up, you gotta get up in the mornin'* . . . was the tune playing in his head that wouldn't go away on this morning.

I gotta get up and sort out this FUBAR Neka mess, he thought was exactly his theme for the day. He had meetings setup and conversations planned. He needed answers.

He stumbled into the kitchen and flipped the switch on the single-cup coffeemaker to let it brew, as he got ready for work. The aroma of the rich Dutch coffee was enough to get a jumpstart on his first shot of caffeine. He filled his thermal cup, took the elevator to the basement, and slowly maneuvered his old Cadillac CTS out of the garage, accelerating once outside to get him started toward Langley. He maneuvered in and out of the morning traffic quickly to get through the growing number of cars he encountered on his way to his first appointment with Lieutenant General Amanda Miller, Air Force Deputy Air Combat Command commander and acting Command and Control commander.

How old was Mandy now? Forty-six, forty-seven? He tried to remember. Amanda had been his brother's girlfriend at the Air Force Academy. She was way more ambitious than Wayne, and when she moved on, she'd advanced rapidly. Steve had bumped into her over the years but not much more than that.

Steve was relieved she took his call personally a few days earlier when her receptionist said he wanted to schedule a visit.

"Hey, Steve. Business must be slow if you're coming to see me." She spoke with the same soft-toned southern accent; her voice hadn't aged at all.

"Slow would be a good thing, chaotic is not. I appreciate you taking my call, and I want to apologize again for those pranks I played on you when you and Wayne came home on holidays."

"You mean like the time you let that mouse loose in the house?" Steve recalled her long brunette hair highlighted with blond strands that always seemed to flow in slow motion when she walked. Her soft complexion and easy laugh fed the crush of a teenage boy. "You were funny when you jumped and ran, but Wayne was funnier. Remember how he actually screeched and jerked his legs up? He was more afraid than you were. Of course, he said he heard you and thought it was a snake before he saw the mouse. After he caught me and spanked me like a baby, I did regret it."

"How's that hard-working mom of yours? I always had a lot of respect for her raising eight children and working two jobs with an alcoholic husband."

"She finally retired after we all got out of the house. She lives in Florida, works with the church, and dotes on her grandchildren."

"She deserves a peaceful old age. Now, what can I do for the big Kratos executive?"

"I wanted to talk to you about the AWACS' performance with that new Army Airborne Command and Control System, A2C2S. Tomorrow, if possible."

"We can do that. I'd like to know what you think happened to the Neka convoy. How about oh-nine hundred?"

Langley, Virginia

After driving the three hours to Langley and getting through security, Steve and Amanda met in her office. Although the room was austere, it had a comfortable feel to it. The metal desk, plain wooden bookshelf, and roundtable were functional office pieces without plush. She had the usual ego wall with diplomas and certificates. The picture with her hair pulled back in a bun, the loose-fitting green flight suit, cool-looking dark sunglasses, and well-worn desert combat boots showed a proud pilot standing below the wing of the light-gray E-3 AWACS. She loved to fly. She also had her personal wall with pictures of her husband, son, and two daughters. There were pictures of her piloting the AWACS, finger-paintings, electronic gadgets, and hand-written cards. You could tell a lot about what was important to her, just by looking around.

Steve could hear the roar of aircraft engines and envision the powerful planes as they landed and took-off from the Langley runway as he stood in her office. The whine of the big C-5 Galaxy engines and that sight that seemed to defy gravity as the giant plane took off at what looked like too slow a speed to remain airborne. He could hear the distinctive whirl of propellers on the C-130 and V-22. The power buildup, then release of brakes and blast of afterburners as the F-35 and F-22 fighter jets slowly rolled forward, increasing speed and accelerating rapidly down a long runway until first the front wheel then the rear wheels lifted off the ground, catapulting the powerful and agile planes, nosing up ever more to quickly climb to their cruising altitude. It was a vivid reminder of the awesome power and complexity of the planes Amanda saw every day.

Amanda walked out from behind her desk, hugged Steve, sat down at the small round table in her office, and motioned for him to do the same. Steve stepped her through the Neka pre-convoy planning, route reconnaissance, and intelligence briefings. He explained the ambush, their response, and the Rangers' presence. Finally, he told her what he'd learned about the communications problems.

Lieutenant General Miller asked questions and took notes. When Steve finished, Amanda gave him the background on the recent AWACS system upgrade which integrated the Army A2C2S and advanced electronic countermeasures, ECM. The rapid-prototyping program had been initiated by President Rubina to get the armed services more integrated in the battlefield and reduce costs. All command and control functions checked out satisfactorily in the ground and flight tests. The Army and Air Force tested networking, software, sensor, ECM, and communications systems at Hanscom AFB and it had all performed appropriately since deployment in 2019.

After a half hour, Steve hadn't learned anything that would explain the Neka communication failure. He asked, "Did your AWACS receive satellite communications during the conflict?"

"I can't discuss the details of the system operation, other than to say that as far as we can tell right now, the system was working as designed everywhere that day except around Neka."

"Do you think taking the Army system off helicopters and

integrating it into the Air Force's AWACS could have contributed to the problems?" If it wasn't working well, the Army had every reason to make that well known.

"We haven't identified any problems caused by the integration. We're working with the Army Aviation and Missile Command in Huntsville, Alabama to assess the A2C2S system."

Steve thought about his friend, Alf French, who worked in Huntsville. He'd risen from a working engineer to group vice president of the defense company Intuit3D. They'd been close friends and colleagues. This would be a good excuse to see him again.

"Having the Air Force work together seamlessly with the other branches of the armed services improves combat effectiveness. It doesn't make common sense that one branch of service should develop systems that duplicate the same capability in another branch. Gone are the days when the Army and Air Force had teams working side-by-side who couldn't communicate electronically with each other's systems." Amanda said.

Well, not completely, Steve thought. He couldn't communicate with the Rangers on the Neka convoy. "Have you had this problem before, on other missions?"

"We have no reports of the problem occurring on any other mission."

Still, it was just too coincidental that the mujahideen moved down from the mountains at the last moment and lined up along the route the convoy would take that day. Steve could envision the jihadis packed tightly and moving quickly in trucks, vans, buses, and cars, some wearing shirts and pants, others wearing robes, trying to blend into traffic and avoid satellite and drone eyes. Kalashnikovs clenched in hand, RPGs stacked on floorboards, and carrying just enough spare boxes of ammunitions to get them from one pre-positioned stockpile to another. Steve didn't believe in coincidences.

"When do you expect to complete your investigation?"

"We should be finished in a week, but we're also supporting the Congressional inquiry of the Senate Armed Services Committee and I don't know how long that will take, or where it's going."

"Who is your liaison with SASC?" He knew Alex Shankle would be involved in this inquiry in some way. He was famous for attacking the contractors and he'd want to score political points against the President for poor management of the war.

Amanda stood up before answering the question and began to pace, a frown on her face. "Do you know Jodie Arenas very well?" Amanda's voice carried concern; she was clearly bothered by something.

"I've met her, but I can't say I know her well."

"I've had a lot of interaction with her. We've gotten these Congressional inquiries ever since I first joined the military. I recognize it as a legitimate role Congress must play. But the frequency of these inquiries has really grown in the past year. It's difficult to get your job done and respond to continual Congressional inquiries within the budgets we have. And, off the record, this Arenas has been particularly obnoxious. She asks for a lot of information, then asks for more. But it's obvious they're not reading what they get. I found it unusual in our one-on-one conversations that she asked a lot about Kratos' involvement. Watch out for her, Steve; she is ruthless."

"I'm sure she will come after me once she's determined how to blame Kratos for the problem. I'll visit her after I go to Quantico."

"Why focus on Kratos?"

"'Cause we're the biggest. Many think the enactment of Sponsored Reserves was done as a political favor to protect defense companies from prosecution and to prevent employees from their right to sue these companies."

"We borrowed the Sponsored Reserves concept from the British. I see the difference those additional troops have made, Steve. Fewer combat tours, fewer cases of PTSD, and fewer suicides."

"The critics ignore the improvements and focus on the contractor to uniformed military ratio. That figure approached one to one in Iraq. There are four contractors for every uniformed soldier in Iran today, including the Sponsored Reserves. Allegations of corruption, fraud, inefficiency, and profiteering are already flying around the halls of Congress. Since Kratos is the largest contractor in Iran with prior employees and contractual involvement in the convoy, we'll be an easy target for Congress to attack."

Steve thanked Amanda, then set out on his return trip to Washington. He placed a call to Shankle's office on the way and setup a meeting with Jodie Arenas for the following day.

***

Steve had plenty of time to think about his meeting on the drive back to DC. Senator Alex Shankle had been very busy looking for mismanagement of the war, particularly in the use of DOD contractors. Steve or members of his team had appeared before numerous Congressional hearings, committees, subcommittees, and task forces to explain Kratos' roles and actions. One particular exchange between Shankle and Mark Darrow stood out:

"Mr. Darrow, could you explain to this Senate panel why Kratos would allow innocent civilians and military personnel to breathe cancer-causing particles in a hazardous work environment while your company sat on information that could have warned them of the extreme danger they were in?"

Darrow had lifted the letter notifying the Army contracting command at Rock Island, Illinois of the asbestos hazard in the buildings at Joint Base Mashad. It was the same letter the senator's staff had requested and received weeks before the hearing. He glanced up, incredulous, and looked at Shankle for what felt like several minutes, but was in fact only a couple seconds. "Sir, I have in my hands—"

"I didn't ask you to read something to me, Mr. Darrow. I asked you why you didn't report that information."

"The document shows—"

"There you go again, Mr. Darrow. Let me ask you a simpler question, and I just want a one-word answer. I read here that you have a Doctor of Jurisprudence degree from Stanford University. Is that correct?"

"Yes."

"Now we're making progress, Mr. Darrow. You can succinctly and honestly answer a question put to you. So, I'm going to give you one more opportunity to come clean to the American people, who may not have the advantage of your expensive education, about the careless and callous manner in which your company disregarded the toxic particles in those buildings that threatened the safety of others."

Mark Darrow put the paper he was holding down, and simply said, "We did not hide the information. We informed Rock Island of the asbestos hazard immediately after we did our inspection of the building as we are required to by our contract."

"Now, that is a damned lie, sir. Your task order with Rock Island was dated October first, twenty-nineteen and your letter notifying them was dated November fifteen, twenty-nineteen. You withheld that information for six weeks, exposing hundreds of innocent people to deadly airborne fibers."

The senator didn't tell the audience that Kratos was assigned to inspect hundreds of buildings or that the military had ownership of those buildings for months before assigning the project to Kratos. It was only because Kratos insisted on a thorough inspection of each building that problems like asbestos, faulty wiring, contaminated water, and other hazardous conditions were uncovered in the first place.

Quantico, Virginia

The discussion with Shankle's staff would have to wait for now. First, Steve wanted to stop at Quantico to visit the Marine Corps Information Operations commander and his friend, General Ronald Lee. He was a technology expert who just happened to be a Marine. He had been a key expert for the most advanced information technology developments for the Defense Advanced Research Projects Agency, the Navy, and Marines, in the past twenty years. He frequently advised the President and worked with NSA from time-to-time on national security issues involving advanced technology systems.

As Steve entered the main gate at Quantico, he saw Marines with rippling muscles protruding through their perfectly pressed and fitted uniforms, standing guard at the main gate. Marines in full combat gear and backpacks ran effortlessly along Fuller Road past the golf course and into the main base, unconcerned about their load, the distance, or the heat. Pristine grounds and austere buildings named after fallen heroes lined the streets: Mann Hall, John Henry Balch Health Clinic, and Lejeune Hall. He pulled into Walt Hall, named for General Lewis Walt, who'd served the Marine Corps for forty-one years, spanning WWII, Korea, and Vietnam. General Walt received the Silver Star, Bronze Star, and two Purple Hearts.

"Good morning, General Lee," Steve said as he reached out his hand to the General and felt the cold, round, metal object as they shook hands. Steve closed his fist to keep the object from falling out, and then opened his palm to reveal a bright, shiny, decorated emblem. "You have a new coin!"

"Yeah, it's new since we last met. It's got the Information

Operations command logo on the front with my name on the back."

"Well, I'll be sure to keep it with me at all times. You know so many people who might 'coin' me at any time. Thank you; I'd be buying a lot of drinks if I didn't have this with me, especially around a Marine Corps base."

"How's your Marine friend, George Bird, doing?"

"I just spoke with him last night. He's in Iran leading convoys and doing well."

"I remember the story he told me about you at Bethlehem high school when he had a drug problem. He respected the fact that you stuck by him, even though teachers and other parents falsely accused you of being involved in drugs, too."

"Yeah, I was unusually thin because I didn't eat right and exercised like a demon as a varsity athlete. I guess I looked like a druggie. George is a great Marine, and like most of us, had problems in his life. I'm proud to call him a friend."

After getting a rundown on the Neka incident and Steve's findings, General Lee reminded him that he couldn't discuss the classified details of the investigation. Then he sat back and looked out the window. "Advanced combat computer systems are extremely difficult to sabotage from the outside. The system is designed to block the introduction of any uncontrolled external data or signals. And our countermeasures systems are designed to detect, counter, and overcome any external jamming by the enemy. We detected no jamming during the time the Neka convoy was attacked."

"Could it be an equipment malfunction?"

"We're investigating that, but it's unlikely for such a narrow area and limited time frame like this. That leaves only the deliberate actions by someone who had legitimate access."

"So, you think an AWACs operator could be the culprit?"

"Improper access could happen during the design, development, deployment, maintenance, or operation of the system. I don't have one shred of evidence to prove any of this, but I believe it's possible."

Steve privately worried about foreign perpetrators as well. He knew the world had been probing, testing, and learning the limitations and weaknesses of U.S. systems since the earliest days of information warfare. Chinese, Russians, jihadists, and even U.S. allies had all tried to play catch-up since the U.S. and Israeli employment of the Stuxnet virus in 2010. U.S. sabotage of Iranian nuclear facilities was a clear demonstration of that leadership. The virus had successfully shutdown the Iranian centrifuges at the Natanz nuclear facility, among others.

Steve said goodbye, and he replayed what General Lee said all the way back to DC. An insider could have done this, but why would he do it? Personal gain, revenge, or fanaticism could be motives. General Lee didn't go so far as to suggest a motive. If he was right about the insider, the Army investigators would find out why.

Washington, DC
Jodie Arenas had agreed to meet Steve at Alex Shankle's Washington DC office at 1:00 PM the following day. He entered the Dirksen Senate Office building and made his way to Shankle's office. He stepped inside and noticed one other visitor seated on the couch, waiting, though not necessarily for Jodie Arenas. He took a seat in an armchair and picked up a magazine with a picture of Shankle shaking hands with his largest benefactor, Frank Zorbos, on the front.

Turning to the article with the headline ONE WORLD ORDER TO END ALL WARS, Steve read that Zorbos was giving millions to the campaign through SuperPACs, his companies, and private contributions. Zorbos was embracing Shankle's antiwar theme to achieve his larger aim: a union of all nations.

When Steve entered Jodie's office, she was hard at work with a phone in one hand and typing on the desktop computer with the other. Steve sat on the couch that faced her desk while she continued to work. He crossed his legs and noticed a small hole was beginning to wear on the bottom of his Florsheim loafers. It was time to get his favorite Vietnamese cobbler to sew on another sole.

Steve had learned a lot about Jodie from friends that dealt with her, like Ambassador Richard Allenby, a Kratos director, and Lieutenant General Amanda Miller, as well as Internet blogs and media insiders. Jodie Arenas wasn't confused about what she wanted, and she would do anything it took to get it. The higher she raised Shankle's star, the more power she could wield, and the greater opportunity she'd have for a top government job. She was always the first one at work and the last to leave. She had come up with innovative approaches using satellite systems and social media to get more voters, made the plans, put together the material, and saw it through. Her intelligence and drive enabled her to become his right-hand staff assistant. After his election to the U.S. Senate, she quickly got the position of chief of staff by pushing others out of the way any way she could.

Amanda pointed out that Jodie controlled the senator's agenda. That meant that anyone who wanted to speak with him had to go through her. She made herself indispensable by always being the first to deliver what the senator needed. If it was votes for infrastructure funding for his district, Jodie knew which senators needed favors she could sway. If that didn't work, she also knew the secrets they didn't want to be exposed. An affair here, a drug problem there, a gambling debt with another, she learned all the secrets and used them to her advantage. Jodie kept records on each senator and actively worked the local staffers and contacts to add to her information.

If the senator was having difficulty getting a bill passed and Jodie knew another senator was a little dirty, she'd help make them extra dirty. For instance, there was an education bill to improve literacy that would help the senator's image, and there was one female senator opposing the bill because it competed with her own. What Jodie knew was that that senator was a closet bi-sexual and lonely during her long stays in Washington DC away from her husband. Jodie arranged meetings with local prostitutes for the woman. Eventually, she found the senator a local partner to share her bed every night in DC. All the while, she was collecting compromising photos that could come in useful—as she did to get the education bill passed.

After a few minutes, she finished her other conversations and turned toward Steve. Heaving her IPAD out of her desk, she slid the screen into her transportable keyboard, sat the computer on her lap, and started typing before she started talking. Jodie wasted no time with pleasant conversation. "Did you direct your employees to take a short-cut through Neka to save money for Kratos?"

Steve knew that in lieu of a clear motive to justify accusing Kratos, Jodie was trying out a line of questioning the senator might pursue in the hearings.

"Ms. Arenas, you forget that my employees became full-time, regular soldiers the minute this conflict began." Steve knew that a denial in a public hearing sounds like an admission of guilt, no matter whether or not you are guilty. Saying, *"No, I didn't direct Kratos employees to do it,"* and *"No, we didn't do it for the money,"* are truthful answers that would only serve to plant suspicion in the public's mind.

Jodie's typing was going clickety-click as Steve spoke. "You can sell that crap to your corporate friends, but not to me. You make money on the supplies shipped, the vehicles leased, and fuel used. And those 'soldiers' don't forget where their bread is buttered in peacetime. They aim to please you." She had the false accusations all lined up with just a little accurate, but unrelated data thrown in to make them sound even more plausible.

"You dishonor their service to our country, Ms. Arenas. You and your kind heap criticism and false allegations on them. It's a wonder anyone who ever held a job in the defense industry would go fight for their country when they know that people like you will be there to smear their reputation." Steve saw no reason to pull punches at this point. It was clear that Arenas had her mind made up, and she was working to form a convincing argument.

Jodie slammed the keyboard down and bounced up out of her chair. Walking out from behind the desk, pointing down at Steve with a menacing stare, she said, "Senator Shankle is a patriotic American who serves his country in the U.S. Senate. He has supported programs that ensure equality, promote diversity, and provide health care for service members and their families. You, Holmes, only care about the bottom line dollar for your business."

She didn't, of course, mention that the senator never served in the military and his children, Adam and Amy, had deferments so they didn't have to serve, either.

"Take it easy. I'm not the only one who questions the senator's motives. Others believe he's looking to use defense contractors to score political points in his bid to become president."

"I don't have the time or desire to explain what a great man he is. You wouldn't understand. I ferret out the scum in our system and expose them. You corporate executives sit in your plush offices and sneer at honest public servants while you sport around in your Land Rovers and BMWs paid for by government contracts that you time and time again fail to perform on."

She was sounding out another theme for the senator: *Companies that pay their leaders enough to afford expensive automobiles must be corrupt.* She would never question the money that a professional baseball or football player made, but if you made it by running a corporation, you were dirty, to some factions of government. Top sports athletes make tens of millions of dollars per year to play a game and bring money in for the owners of the team. Top executives deliver hundreds of millions or billions of dollars for their owners. In addition, corporate executives are the ones that generate jobs in America that produce wealth.

"You're right. I wouldn't understand, Ms. Arenas. I do, though, recognize that waste, fraud, and abuse by government employees and contractors alike have occurred in the past. It is regrettable and at Kratos we do everything we can to ensure it doesn't happen." With no response coming from Arenas, Steve said, "Moving on, I'd like to know what your Commission is finding out about the communication failures at Neka."

Jodie sat back down at her desk and began thumbing through some papers. "Our findings are not complete. There will be hearings before we can get to the bottom of this. You can bet you'll be front and center to answer their questions, Holmes." Jodie seemed a little nervous about those hearings. Maybe she didn't feel her case against Kratos was strong enough yet.

"Are you at least investigating potential causes other than contractor error and greed?"

She looked down and started reading another document.

Steve continued, "For example, why did the equipment fail at just that time and for just that limited region? Who had access and motive to sabotage the systems? I think the American public will want to know. Is this failure linked to other similar events that have resulted in hundreds of lives lost, billions of dollars of equipment destroyed or stolen, and disruption that has bogged this war down? Or, is your investigation mainly political, trying to accuse the President of favoring contractors and mismanaging the war?"

Jodie did not respond initially and continued to appear to be reading a document. It was obvious that she did not like answering questions, especially from Steve Holmes. She finally looked up. "Of course we are investigating. We stand behind our Commander-in-Chief and do all we can to win this war. Now get out of my office, I have other meetings to attend, Holmes."

Steve left the Capitol Building feeling depressed. He'd grown up loving his government and he'd spent his life defending and supporting it. Now, to have your Congress and a powerful senator's aide attacking him and the company he worked for was unnerving. The upcoming Congressional hearings were worrying. He strolled through the National Mall to soothe his emotions as he searched for his proper course. Argue Kratos' case and destroy his reputation and career? There didn't seem to be a lot of upside in that approach. Delegate it to subordinates so he could keep his name clear? That's certainly what his boss would do. Bernie Tyler always positioned a fall guy. Quit and run—get out while the gettin' was good? That was the easiest option. There were risks no matter what he did.

As Steve strolled by the Washington Monument, World War II, Martin-Luther King, and Lincoln memorials, he read the inscriptions carefully and rubbed his hand over the words, trying to find the right approach to a difficult dilemma: to understand what these great men honored here had done in much more dire circumstances. What had sustained them in the moments when they questioned what action to take? Steve wasn't saving the nation, freeing a race of people, or anything nearly that important, but these men must have searched their souls more than once for the right course. Whatever their rationale, they didn't choose the easy path. They didn't delegate the responsibility, and they didn't quit.

Steve decided there on the Washington Mall to confront those who would dishonor the service of his employees.

7

Washington, DC

Senator Alex Shankle was busy on any day, but even more so this day when the senate was in session. Riding down George Washington Memorial Parkway in his black chauffeur-driven limousine before breakfast, he was on the phone with a mayor from his district.

"We need federal funding for this new bridge to bring more tourism into our area," the mayor said.

"I've got that earmarked in the Transportation Bill. I believe it will pass before the budget."

"Thanks, Senator. Don't forget you have a lot of supporters in my city."

He met with four of his hawkish colleagues for breakfast in the Senate Dining Room, to discuss the vote on the North Korean treaty. While enjoying his pancakes with real maple syrup and smoked sausage, Shankle said, "Seventy years after the Korean War ended, we need to give this new North Korean government a chance to expand the economic and political reforms they committed to."

The junior senator from Alabama, Randy Coltrane, said in his slow Southern drawl, "I don't think we can trust those Ko-reeuns. General Kim Woo-ha has done knocked over 'ol Supreme Leader Kim Jong-un, but he ain't demonstrated whether he'll be any less crazy. That said, the kooop has done brought the greatest chance for peace. I'm a-gonna vote for the treaty."

Senator Harper McCastle from Illinois said, "I'm with you on this, Alex, as always. Let's give peace a chance."

When the senate was in session, Shankle was up and about, meeting in the Senate Chamber with other senators, aides, and staffers in the aisles during the proceedings. He told one senator's staffer how he was leaning on an upcoming bill. He signed a letter from his own staffer to recommend the appointment to the Air Force Academy for a bright young student from his district, who was also the son of a wealthy supporter.

As Shankle was standing, talking with two aides, he felt a firm slap on his back. Turning around, the Senate Majority Leader, Cary Breed, said, "Alex, I'm counting on your vote for Marsha Bennett for the DC Federal District Court judge today."

Shankle reached up and patted the Leader's shoulder. "I'm expecting the same from you for the vote on the Ambassador to Turkey."

There were continuing resolution bills to fund the war to consider, committee and subcommittee meetings, including the Senate Armed Services Committee that Alex Shankle chaired. On top of all that, he met with well-heeled, prominent, and the most influential constituents visiting Washington, DC every working day.

***

Meanwhile, at the White House, President Rubina was talking with Vice President Luke Walker and Senate Minority Leader Lisa Bronkowski. "What's holding up Marsha Bennett's approval?"

Walker said, "She's just one of a long list of appointees the

Democrats are sitting on."

Bronkowski said, "Your judicial nominees are doing better as a whole than others. We have one hundred twenty-three federal nominees awaiting approval; twenty-six of those are judges."

Rubina replied, "I want a conservative in there before I leave office. The DC judge rules on a lot of federal actions; let's have eggs and pancakes with the senators who need a push, Browny."

"There's a vote later today. It'll have to be club sandwiches, but I'll give you the three swing votes you should call."

***

Back in Shankle's office, his staffers did the in-depth review, planning, and wrote the position papers and questions for each of the senator's meetings. Jodie Arenas was ramrod-in-chief of staff in the old-school style. She used the carrot-and-stick method, except there was no carrot. She drove the team mercilessly to get the senator's duties completed.

In this case, Jodie had scheduled a meeting with Alex immediately following her meeting with Steve Holmes to update the senator on the convoy investigations.

"Come in and have a seat, Jodie." Shankle walked around his desk to give Jodie a long hug. The senator watched every move her body made under the short skirt and tight blouse she wore as she moved to the leather-backed chair, sat, and crossed her legs. He said, "I've just come from a SASC hearing on waste, fraud, and abuse by contractors in the Iran war. We are throwing away billions of dollars of taxpayer's money on useless projects or systems that don't work. The Under Secretary of Defense for Acquisition, Technology, and Logistics testified to some incredible failures.

"The 'bridge-to-nowhere' that Bechtam is building would be a laughable example of that waste if it wasn't so damned big. We are spending a billion dollars to build a bridge from Iran to the Basra oil fields in Iraq. Why? So the president can help his wealthy oil and gas companies do business in both countries. He also gets to reward his donors, like Bechtam, with a fat contract. It should be a crime."

Arenas said, "That information will serve as a great introduction for your hearings on the contractor's role in the Neka convoy disaster."

"The senate subcommittee hearings have been scheduled for June fifteenth. How long will it take you to wrap up your data-gathering on the Neka investigation?"

"We should have the preliminary findings in the next two weeks. The Army is leading the fifteen dash six investigation. They are working with the other agencies to cover the communications and intelligence systems, people, and processes. I want to talk to the operational and technical teams a little more. Your letter of congressional inquiry is keeping them on their toes."

"The president is entirely too close to these contractors. The Neka incident is a prime example of how the president is mismanaging this war with his extreme reliance on contractors. What kind of evidence do you have against Kratos?"

"First, there is no indication of any malfunction of the equipment transmitting to the convoy. That should eliminate the AWACS as a source of the failure and put more focus on Kratos. Second, the Kratos employees have the contract to maintain the FM radios and equipment on the convoy vehicles used for communications. They had access and opportunity to cause the malfunction of the receiver and transmitter equipment on these trucks. I'm not sure if we can build a case to show it was deliberate, but we can certainly show their incompetence. I'll attack their level of training and show a profit motive for their actions—bad equipment means more contracts for them. The publicity will be good for you politically."

"How do you explain that Kratos employees would lose their

lives in such a scenario? They had an executive riding in the convoy in addition to former employees now on active duty."

"It will be easy to show that those who had access to sabotage the equipment were not going on the convoys. They work back in the camps. And Steve Holmes riding along on the Neka convoy was a screw-up and just shows their further incompetence." Jodie moved in her seat to cross her legs in the other direction.

Shankle caught every move and his eyes lingered. After a pause, he said, "We need more solid evidence against Kratos. The charges have to be more than our conjecture."

"I might have an informant who will testify to Kratos' complicity in all this." There were always disgruntled employees in a company of this size. Arenas was a master at finding the right disgruntled employee, feeding their ego with attention, and supplying them with information to construct accusations.

"Does your informant know enough to be convincing?" Shankle said with a little excitement. He needed more supporters like Jodie. People who could make things happen.

"He has firsthand information on some minor incriminating actions. I'm coaching him on his testimony. I'll have him ready for your June subcommittee meeting."

There was one more related matter Jodie needed to discuss with him. "Alex, the senate is voting tomorrow on the president's nominee to the Federal District Court in DC, aren't you?"

"Yes, there's a lot of support for the nominee. They'll call for unanimous consent to fast-track her, and I think she'll be approved, no problem."

"What if you dissented to the call for unanimous consent?"

"Well, I promised Majority Leader Breed I'd support his man, ah, woman in this case. I'm trading my vote here for another nominee I want to get approved later in the session. Why should I dissent?"

"Who has the power in a vote requiring one hundred percent consensus, Alex?"

"I suppose we all do, collectively. The nominee needs everyone's vote."

"No. The power and control are in the hands of the dissenter in a consensus vote. You should say no 'til hell freezes over."

"They'll just move to a vote anyway with a cloture motion."

"That's where you can use your influence to prevent the votes needed for cloture. You can horse-trade your votes on other nominees to get enough senators to vote against cloture. Let the clock run out on this nominee. Don't let her get approved."

"Why are you so hell bent against this one district court nominee?"

"This judge has clearly indicated she'll be hard on drug dealers and I have a friend whose case is coming before that court. He's part of an antiwar group. You need the support of these groups to foment distrust in President Rubina's leadership of the war."

"Okay. She *is* one of Rubina's appointees. I'll do some arm-twisting to make sure this nominee doesn't get approved."

"Thanks, Alex. I'll see you after work at our usual location."

8

Arlington, Virginia

The day was rainy, windy, and cold in DC as those gathered at Arlington National Cemetery took their solemn position for this somber occasion. Umbrellas and raincoats cloaked the audience as they made their way to the burial shelter. Many of the two hundred or so family, employees, reporters, guests, and government officials, wept as the citizen-soldiers descended to their final resting places. They heard the honor guard call cadence and saw them snap to attention, then to arms, as if they were seeing it for the first time. Startled at first, they swelled with pride as three volleys rang out. This would be the peaceful, honorific resting place for brothers and sisters, mothers and fathers, and heroes who once again stood in the breach between enemy and friend, terrorist and country. They would no longer breathe, laugh, or wonder. Couldn't play with their children or tell their mother they loved her. They had no more aspirations to achieve, work to complete, or duty to fulfill. They had given the most precious gifts they could offer: their lives and futures, for their country.

Steve Holmes stepped to the podium to honor the brave citizen-soldiers who'd died in the Neka firefight. He tried to still his emotions with a deep breath and exhale. He withdrew the typed notes he'd made and practiced and lay them on the podium. He wouldn't need them.

He looked out over the assembled crowd, and began. "No one cheers the defense contractor! Yet, these brave men and women were courageous to the very end. They strove to prepare themselves, their equipment, and services to perform proudly in war. They endeavored to persevere the risks, hardships, separation, and loneliness of combat assignments. They aspired to achieve the freedoms we hold dear by defending our country until their last breath. It was their last act of courage; let it be known that they did so freely, in service to their country.

"It was certainly not their first act of courage. One early act came when they pledged to protect and defend the U.S. from all enemies, as both civilian contractor and active duty soldier, when called to service.

"But it was not truly their last act of courage, either. The legacy of what they did, how they served, will survive and inspire others. Their courage and sacrifice echo for the millennia of contractors at war, from biblical times to contractors in the War on Terror, to Kratos today. These selfless individuals we honor today are the very personification of strength and power for our military. Though our cause may be questioned, their service never will. The critics will not be deterred. The politics will not be deferred. The lawsuits will not be dismissed. But, the citizen-soldier will march bravely on earth and in heaven, with honor, pride, humility, and the everlasting gratitude of a free nation."

Steve stepped back, choking back tears. He had more to say, but not the composure to say it. He folded his notes, reinserted them into his coat pocket, and walked off stage. President Mark Rubina met him on stage, grabbed his hand and firmly squeezed his shoulder. "Thank you, Mr. Holmes, for speaking so eloquently for these brave men and women."

Steve managed a nod. Silence filled the area, broken only by the sobs of the family members as Steve took his seat.

President Rubina stepped up to the podium to deliver his address in this election year. "Abraham Lincoln said over one hundred-fifty years ago in another battlefield bathed in American blood that few would remember the three-minute speech he gave that day. He felt inadequate to the task of properly honoring those fallen heroes. I feel the same. Without these brave men and women, our country would not be free. The sacrifices made by those Sponsored Reserves and regular military soldiers and Marines in the Neka convoy allow us to be free from the constant threat of nuclear attack. They cannot give more.

"But *we* must give more. This war is not over and only through persistent, dogged determination through men and women like these will we prevail. Lincoln worried no one would remember his words. Yet, we do remember his words that speak as plainly today for the Neka warriors as it did for those at Gettysburg. We honor those who sacrificed all."

A solitary bell rang, and a moment of silence followed for each fallen hero after President Rubina recited his or her full name. At the conclusion, the wind grew calm and Taps rang out amid the peace and quiet, joined only by the sounds of light rain clapping the umbrellas and funeral coverings as if it were applause from the Almighty.

As the ceremony ended, George and Cathy Bird walked with Steve, silently at first, through the cemetery. Cathy could see how tormented Steve was by these deaths. She sensed his guilt and anger. Cathy reached for and held Steve's cold, wet hand.

Searching for words of comfort, Cathy said, "You can't blame yourself for this, Steve. These men and women knew what they were getting into. They knew the sacrifice they might have to make."

There was a long pause as Steve got his emotions sufficiently under control to talk. He sighed a deep breath. "I'm not so sure they really knew, Cathy. Yeah, they knew it was war and they were told they could die. But, do you think deep down they really thought they would die in Iran?"

George said, "It's impossible to know how they thought about death, but you know like all of us they had to rationalize it somehow. Some certainly accepted that death was a possibility. Whether because of their faith, commitment to the cause, or just pragmatism, they accepted it. No doubt others dealt with the fear by telling themselves it wouldn't happen to them or by just blocking it out altogether. But none of them would blame you. You, above anyone else they knew, worked to make sure they were as safe as they could be."

Steve murmured, "Safe, yeah. I really did a bang-up job of that."

George replied, "More would die if you didn't care enough to get them armor for their vehicles and guards for their convoys. You didn't make the decision to go to war, Steve, the President and Congress did. You can't carry all the weight of other people's decisions."

Steve thought back to the incremental decisions that led to war. War seemed to evolve so rapidly; it seemed like only yesterday they were just talking economic sanctions on Iran and monitors for their nuclear program. The more Steve thought about it, the madder he got. "Other people's decisions. That's right. Assholes in Washington make decisions and people die! They must have run their cold-hearted statistical models over and over to calculate how many Americans would have to die to conduct this war. Then, they'd change the input parameters until they reached a politically acceptable number of deaths. Cold-hearted as hell. They said it would all be over in six months. Six months! They had to know that was wrong. No modern war in the middle east lasts six months!"

"Perhaps the U.S. models were wrong, but Congress was getting plenty of support from our British and Israeli allies," Cathy replied. "You know that when the U.S. escalated the pre-war tensions with that Iranian embargo and no-fly zone, the Iranian mullahs took it as an act of war. They felt threatened; boxed in a corner. Their people were beginning to revolt, and their economy started failing and there were bigger and deadlier street protests every day. The mullahs were scared and when they blamed all their problems on the U.S. and threatened a nuclear attack on Israel, what were our politicians supposed to do but attack first?"

Steve was seething mad at this point. His eyes were watery, not in sadness but anger. "If more of the politician's sons and daughters had to serve and die in these wars, I bet they wouldn't be so quick to attack. Now look at what a mess we have. The Iranian military simply dissolved into the population and launched a guerilla war. They can't win in a direct battle with our military, so they're attacking all the soft targets where more of my people are: convoys, logistics depots, and our lightly guarded forward operations bases."

George put a firm right hand on Steve's left shoulder as Cathy hugged him from the other side. They walked silently out of Arlington National Cemetery and back to Steve's car.

9

Washington, DC

Bernie Tyler's stated objective for this quarterly financial review was to do whatever it took to maximize profit in the next few months. The anticipation in the room was unlike any other QFR Steve Holmes had attended. Every business unit president and his or her financial controllers were in the room or on the phone dialing-in from around the world. The fit and athletic-looking president of manufacturing sat next to his controller whispering quietly with serious, worried looks on their faces. They sat as far away from and as much out of the line-of-sight from Tyler's chair as they could get. The president of construction arrived early and took the seat on the corner of the table, close to Tyler. Steve sat in the center of the long side of the table with his controller so he could easily talk to anyone in the room.

Tyler's instructions to his secretary, Janice, were to wait until everyone arrived and checked-in on the phone before calling him into the room. Entering the room with an enthusiastic "Good morning, everyone," his massive frame made a swoosh sound as he sat down in the oversized recliner at the head of the table. John Carpenter, Chief Financial Officer, sat on his right. Janice sat in a small chair directly behind Tyler to run any errands.

"I'll make a short opening statement, and then we can start with your reports. Our revenue and profits soared during the pre-war build-up. Since the war started, we've transferred billions of dollars of our work revenue to the government as our Sponsored Reserve employees went on active duty. Our stock has taken a beating. As I said in my memo to you this week, to counter that stock trend, we will maximize our profit in the next quarter. I have set new, challenging financial goals for each business unit for the remainder of the year. It will drive our stock price up when Wall Street sees how well we are growing the bottom line. It will also put money in the pocket of every executive in the room with substantial Kratos stock holdings. As each of you presents your financial projections for the upcoming quarter this morning, I'd like you to identify the top action you're taking to boost profit. Let's start with manufacturing."

The manufacturing president discussed his revenue, sales, overhead, and profit improvement plans. He would be exceeding his projected goals for the quarter by twenty-five percent. "Our key initiative to improve profit is to halt all capital equipment purchases and save the depreciation costs and cash. We're delaying upgrades and fixing whatever breaks. The new equipment in our business plan for the year was to improve our piping production. With pipe prices at an all-time high, the delay will hurt our manufacturing capacity and sales volume in three months when the new equipment was scheduled to come on line, but it does result in higher than projected profits in the next quarter."

Tyler reviewed the operating profit from manufacturing with Carpenter. The executives sat in hushed silence as the two carried on their discussion. Tyler punched some numbers into his calculator, showed them to Carpenter, then turned to the manufacturing president. "That's not enough. I want you to lay off seventy-five percent of your overhead management and administrative staff today. That will get us another twenty-five percent profit."

The manufacturing president was shocked, but nodded his acceptance, glad to escape without any further cuts.

"I'd like to hear from our executive vice president of government services next."

Steve was prepared to explain the rise and fall of the government services business. He showed the significant growth of his organization leading up to the war, then the decline in the last year. In the last year his organization had held its own as most of the Sponsored Reserve employees transferred to active duty. Transforming their sales workforce, they were able to win sufficient new work to keep their revenue at the pre-war build-up levels. "I will cancel bid and proposal activities for the next three months and layoff twenty-five percent of the sales force to maximize profit in the next quarter. We project a thirty percent improvement in profit for the quarter with these changes."

Once again, Tyler and Carpenter huddled and reviewed financial sheets. Tyler laid out several financial sheets to compare other business units to Steve's. They calculated more numbers. Finally, Tyler turned to Steve and said, "Put up the histogram on the screen that shows the breakdown of your overhead costs, Steve." After looking at the chart, he said, "Sales is about forty percent of your total costs, is that correct, Steve?"

"That's the cost of our sales and marketing staff, proposals, consultants, and services. Yes, it's about forty percent."

"How many people do you have in sales and marketing?" Tyler asked.

"Fifty-five," Steve replied.

"Lay them all off today, Steve. That should double your profit for the quarter."

"Yes, but you'll be eating your own seed corn."

"How's that?"

"Stopping all the sales and marketing activities and laying off all the people will ensure we won't grow new business for the remainder of the year. It would take us at least six months to re-staff and grow a new sales and marketing workforce."

"I know you, Steve. You'll overcome any obstacle. Your people call you 'Man in the Arena,' after that speech Roosevelt gave. You try and try again, despite the difficulties. You tried and failed on five bids over four years until you succeeded in getting us into the Air Force logistics engineering business, when everyone said you couldn't crack that business. You established new customers for us with the Marine Corps and Department of Homeland Security. You opened up new lines of business for information technology and acquisition engineering services. Determination is your forte."

"While I appreciate the confidence, I need to point out the fall-off in profit we will see after this big gain next quarter if we eliminate our sales and marketing staff and budget. Our profit will start to plummet as projects end and we have nothing to replace them with for the rest of this year and at least through mid-year next year. It would take us that long to recover."

"We'll cross that bridge when we come to it."

"I don't see how this makes any sense, Bernie. Yes, our profits will rise in the next quarter and our stock would likely go up, but the stock price will crash when the Street finds out about the artificial, short-term cuts we made to manufacture that short-term profit increase."

"You'll find a way, Steve. I'm setting the challenge goals. It's up to the business unit leaders to make it work. I've never cut too deep. I've always looked back at cost reductions and realized I could have done more. And every time I led the organization to make cuts, we always came out better in the long-run."

The president of construction had bad news to deliver in his presentation. "I regret to report that we won't even make our target profit next quarter. The coal mine we are constructing in the Amazon jungle is losing ten million dollars a month. Our workers are on strike, our vendors can't produce the steel they committed to deliver, and our buildings are sinking in what seems almost like bottomless quicksand."

After lambasting his incompetence for getting into this mess, Tyler put up a series of slides on the display screen for everyone to see. "I assigned a team of engineering and construction experts, led by Tom Price, my personal financial controller, to re-evaluate the project and develop a plan to get us out of this. They reassessed the project schedule and cost estimate-to-complete for the project, and have a completely different view. Their schedule shows you completing this project six months earlier. That shifts your profit from negative to positive for the upcoming quarter."

Steve knew Tom Price as Tyler's 'fixer 'who was used to making problems go away.

The construction president said to Tyler, "Your team assumed the problems I mentioned didn't exist. There is no plan to achieve their unrealistic schedule and cost projection. If we forecast the profit they're showing for next quarter, and we don't deliver, we'll be restating earnings and may get serious criminal questions from the Security and Exchange Commission."

Tyler replied, "Well, then, I guess you better make sure that doesn't happen."

When the meeting ended, Steve's financial controller asked, "How *are* we going to recover from these draconian sales and marketing cuts?"

"We'll all be doing double duty. I'll be back in the proposal and business development role and so will you. We'll set up consulting arrangements with some of the people leaving, so we can use them later on. And we'll have to hire other sales consultants to augment our sales force once the next quarter is over as we start building our staff back up. It will be difficult and I don't expect we'll win any new work for the rest of this year. But, we will recover and rebuild our sales and marketing team in time to bid and win new work late next year."

"Tyler was right—you don't give up, do ya, Steve?"

"We don't have a choice. I don't know what Tyler is doing or why he's doing it, beyond the statements he made here. My job is to carry out his instructions to the best of my ability, while continuing to build a thriving business that services our people, customers, and stockholders."

10

The eight-year-old girl stepped onto the stool so she could see over the podium and speak to the thousands of people gathered. Holding her handwritten notes with both hands to keep the wind from blowing them away, she had to let go again and again to brush the hair from her face to see the words. The barrette with a yellow butterfly helped, but her hair was just too long to pin it all back with just one clip.

She wasn't nervous at all. Her Nana said she was a smart girl who shined brightest when she was in front of a crowd for a gymnastics competition, spelling bee, or acting in her school plays. Stretching to reach the microphone that was pointed down as low as it could go, she said, "Don't let my daddy die." She brushed the hair from her eyes and gripped the paper with both hands once again. "My mommy went to heaven and I cried. I still cry. My mommy was in the Army. Nana said a Iramium shot her. I don't know any Iramiums. I hide under the covers with my Miffy at night. She's not afraid. That's all."

The three thousand antiwar protesters gathered at the Washington Monument in Washington, DC were completely silent, except for a few sniffles, as she stepped down from the stool.

The protesters had gathered after Internet postings on social media, and Senator Alex Shankle's personal invitation on his website, called for a day of solidarity among those who were against the war in Iran. They crowded around the monument in hats and t-shirts adorned with antiwar slogans, listening to the speeches, sitting on the lawn, milling about talking, and some carried signs and chanted slogans. The celebrities, politicians, and antiwar groups in the subdued crowd came from across the country. They came from churches, synagogues, and mosques. Cardinal O'Daniel who represented the Catholic Workers Movement, moved through the crowd, laying a hand on each person he met, making a sign of the cross, and blessing them for protecting God's children everywhere. Colt Wayne, Hollywood's newest and most famous leading man, carried a sign and walked among the crowd in an antiwar cap and dark sunglasses promoting the Communists Against the War group. Senator Randy Coltrane spoke on the podium and passed out pamphlets to the crowd, advocating the Libertarian Party's isolationist philosophy and his objections to the war.

Frank Zorbos, the billionaire supporter of Shankle's presidential campaign and leader of the non-profit movement, One World Order, stood near the podium talking to Shankle. "I'm not giving you my money out of the goodness of my heart, Alex, I expect something in return."

"I've voted for and against judicial nominees on your behalf and I've sponsored legislation that tightens environmental emissions that you favored. What else do you want, Frank?"

"That's minor crap. A single world government would end all wars. It won't happen if you're not elected."

"I'm trying."

"I don't want you to try. I want you to make it happen. When you're willing to risk everything, then you'll find a way to get elected."

Seventy-five Capitol Police officers patrolled the perimeter, stood at highway crossings, rode on horseback nearby, or waited near patrol cars and police motorcycles to ensure public safety. They stood prepared for any contingency, wearing high-visibility yellow smocks over their blue-and-white uniforms and bulletproof vests, their batons and pistols ready on their belt. Police observers watched for troublemakers at the checkpoints as other officers scanned people and bags. Traffic moved a little slower around the monuments with some streets closed, tour buses rerouted, and pedestrians steered away from the main protest gathering area, but there was no reason to expect trouble.

Adam and Amy Shankle stepped onto the small, crowded stage and stood together at the podium. Adam, the oldest, spoke first. "My sister and I are here to introduce the greatest man we know. You know him as Senator Alex Shankle. His grandparents lived through the Dust Bowl and depression of the early twentieth century. They boarded a train for Ohio with barely enough for train fare during the war to bring the family to the heartland—to Dayton, Ohio. It was here that his parents met and he was born on the poor side of town in the shadow of the Church of the Holy Angels. A church that formed the center of their community and daily life.

"Alex Shankle was baptized, confirmed, and married in the same church that held the funeral for both his parents, who were tragically killed in a house fire when he was sixteen. Alex went on to the University of Dayton where he went from team manager to starting forward on the Flyers basketball team. He met and married our mom, Audrey, while at the school. Armed with a degree in law, he opened his own firm in nineteen ninety-seven while also working at Legal Aid of Ohio, providing free services to the poor.

"Our mother provided assistance for abused and neglected children for others to help pay the debt they both incurred for education in these lean years. They were great parents!

"He was first elected to serve his community as county commissioner. Alex Shankle was a tireless defender of the poor, labor, and farmers. Four years later as state senator, he helped usher in better health care for senior citizens. He tasted bitter defeat when, as Ohio's democratic leader for Al Gore's presidential campaign, they lost a bitter fight with Bush. Since being elected senator, my father and mother have fought tirelessly for the poor and downtrodden who couldn't fight for themselves. Now, we want them to go to the White House to fight for all Americans."

Taking the microphone, Amy said, "We are so very proud to introduce to you the greatest father, American, and the next President of the United States, Alex Shankle."

Their father hugged Adam and Amy as he stepped to the podium to applause. "I am a rich man to have the love of a family like this." Turning, he looked back at his family. "But this is a serious day. A time for all men and women of conscience to have their voices heard. Today, we are engaged in a terrible foreign war, unprovoked, and unjust; fifty-three of our soldiers were killed needlessly in the past month alone."

As the senator continued to speak, Jodie Arenas made her rounds to stir the crowd and speak to some of the more radical attendees. Here, she pumped a sign up and down before handing it to a passive protester. There, she pulled three people sitting on the ground to their feet as they joined her, yelling, "No more war, No more war!" Everywhere, she pumped her fist, urging one protester after another to get on their feet and let their voices be heard.

Stopping to speak to Colt Wayne, she said, "The time will come for action. Today, we rally together so our voices will be heard by the media, Congress, and the president."

"I have to tell you, Jodie, the Communists Against the War are prepared to do much more than protest."

"The day will come when too many casualties and too much war threatens the peace and stability of the United States. On that day, hundreds of thousands will take to the streets to demand an end to the war. And, on that day, perhaps we'll have to do more than talk."

Fifteen minutes into the speech and Shankle was just now getting to his criticism of the president. "I'm a proud American. I love our country. The American people don't want war. The contractors want war. They don't love our country, they love money. President Rubina wants to give them their war. He wants to reward his friends and campaign contributors. He cloaks that purpose in rhetoric about protecting Americans and ensuring freedom. He plays on people's fear of terrorist attacks in their homes. All the while, he's feeding his private contractors billions of dollars of contracts to reward the rich executives who put him in office. He's graduated from the days of a six-hundred-dollar toilet seat from Lockheed Martin and a seventeen-thousand-dollar oil pan from Sikorsky, to giving billions to companies like Kratos and Bechtam, for worthless projects like the hundreds of millions of dollars wasted on the bridge to no where. We have to send a clear message to the President: Stop the war! Stop the war! Stop the war!"

On cue, his staff picked up the chant: "Stop the war! Stop the war!"

Jodie seized this moment to escalate the protest. She marched up to the podium, walking arm-in-arm with Colt Wayne, Senator McCastle, and Frank Zorbos, pumping her fist, and chanting, "Stop the war! Stop the war!" Alex, Audrey, Adam, and Amy Shankle joined the marchers and followed by other celebrities, elected officials, and protestors, marched across the National Mall toward

Pennsylvania Avenue and the White House. The hundreds of protesters enthusiastically followed the leaders, chanting and marching like walking rows of linked chains one after the other.

The Capitol Police moved their forces along the path the marchers were taking. Two dozen police in riot gear, batons at the ready, stood in front of the fence protecting the White House. Meanwhile, Secret Service agents and the police inside the White House property moved onto the South Lawn to discourage anyone who might attempt to scale the fence. Sharpshooters and spotters on the roof of the White House scanned the crowd and the sky looking for any trouble.

The crowd remained peaceful as they moved across the Ellipse between 15th and 17th streets. When they got to E Street, the crowd stopped, blocking traffic. The Capitol Police captain approached the senator and the other leaders of the march. He first asked them quietly, then with a bullhorn, to clear the street and stop the unlawful blocking of traffic.

The senator said, "You'll have to arrest us, Captain. We're not moving."

A team of backup police officers arrived in several vans. Vehicles screeched to a halt, doors flew open, and police officers spilled out with plastic flexcuffs dangling from their belts. They came prepared, working in pairs to cuff and search each of the protesters on the road. After a dozen of the protest leaders were arrested and hauled away in the paddy wagon, the crowd began to disperse.

The news media recorded the arrests and interviewed protesters. Each of the arrested protestors were taken to the police station, officially booked into jail with the misdemeanor of obstructing traffic, charged a small fine, then released. The stories and pictures didn't make the splash in the national news they expected, but Shankle and Arenas were satisfied they had consolidated the antiwar voices. They would work to make these voices louder as the election approached.

11

New York, New York

Each pre-invited guest was carefully patted down and scanned by Secret Service agents as they entered the Metropolitan Museum of Art Terrace Room that overlooked New York's Central Park. The three dozen political supporters, politicians, and aids chatted and sipped champagne and cocktails as they waited for President Mark Rubina to arrive.

Steve Holmes arrived with Kratos board member, and former Ambassador to Saudi Arabia, Richard Allenby. Looking around at the other guests, Steve said, "There are some heavy hitters at this fundraiser, Richard."

"A swanky affair for the biggest contributors."

"I guess that explains why Kratos is here."

"You should feel honored. These are the corporate leaders for the largest defense companies in America, and they're big financial supporters for President Rubina's run for a second term."

Recognizing a familiar face, Steve said, "Come on. I'll introduce you to Jerry Hunter."

Steve walked across the room and made eye contact with Jerry, who smiled and stepped forward to shake his hand, "Hello, Steve. Did you bring your checkbook?" he asked with a smile.

"Good afternoon, Jerry. I brought the checkbook for my PAC. I couldn't get into the parking lot of this place with what my personal check could do. I wanted to introduce you to one of our Kratos directors, Ambassador Richard Allenby. Richard, this is Jerry Hunter, CEO of Lockheed Martin."

"Yes, I know of the ambassador. Nice to meet you, sir."

"Good evening. I have always been impressed by the outstanding systems Lockheed Martin produces for our military. The Joint Strike Fighter is a superb machine."

"Thank you. I could arrange a courtesy flight sometime if you'd like."

"That would be thrilling."

Steve said, "Don't let this guy deceive you, Richard. They do more than hardware. They compete with us in the services and construction business as well."

"And you seem to regularly kick our asses," Hunter said.

President Rubina entered the room a few minutes later, accompanied by his wife and an aide. They moved quickly to shake hands and greet each guest. His aide whispered in his ear as they approached Steve.

"Now this is an unlikely group! A diplomat and a couple of sharks." After greeting each of them by name, the President said, "Judy and I need your support. The general election is gonna be a brawl."

Steve said, "Are the Democrats better off with a primary fight?"

"They'll just give us good material to attack them with. I'll save our money and ammunition to fire at them in September and October."

Richard said, "With Judy as your lead strategist again, they won't stand a chance."

Judy Rubina replied, "Thank you, Richard, but we won't take the Democrats for granted. We're preparing for a hard fight."

President Rubina said, "Mr. Holmes, I want to thank you again for the outstanding service and sacrifice of your employees serving on active duty. The speech you made at Arlington to honor those heroes was moving."

At that moment the Speaker of the House, Lionel Johnson, stepped into the group. "I hope he's asking each of you for your financial support. He's a bit shy about it, so I just make sure we let everyone know we have to raise over a billion dollars."

When dinner was served, the President, First Lady, and the Speaker ate their meal making small talk with those around them. Then the President asked for questions.

In an abrupt manner and without waiting to be recognized, a donor said, "I'm Harry Strap, CEO for World Food, the largest food supplier to the Army. When are you going to get us some tax relief? We have the highest corporate taxes in the world."

"Thank you for posing the question, Mr. Strap. It's clear you're anxious for an answer, and it's important for American business, so I'll take your question first. As you know, Speaker Johnson has put forth a bill to decrease corporate taxes based on an index of the taxes offered by the developed nations who compete with us. The index would be different for agriculture versus manufacturing machinery, for example, because the countries we compete with would be different. The formula has more complexity to allow for Third World countries and allies who we don't want to disadvantage, but that tax rate, if used today for manufacturing machinery, would amount to a fifteen percent corporate tax. That's less than half the tax rate corporations pay today."

"So you say. I haven't seen any change in the law."

"That's right. We're trying to work out a compromise with the Senate where there is a Democratic majority. We'll find common ground, but it is taking some time to get this legislation passed."

"Try? I don't give you my money to have you try."

President Rubina chuckled, then looked at his wife. She could see his face was a little red. Not so red that anyone else would notice, except her. He took a small breath after the pause, then locked eye contact with Strap and said in a calm, steady voice, "I'm sorry it is not moving faster. I'll ask the Speaker to go into more detail with you after we're through with dinner. I would also politely correct your thinking that you 'give' me any money at all. You make a campaign contribution to a party and candidate who you believe represents your values. You elect that individual to make decisions, enact laws, and support causes that are consistent with their principles. You, as a constituent, get an opportunity to voice your opinion. My staff relentlessly reaches out to the voters on-line, in town hall meetings, at public appearances and through indirect polling to solicit your feedback. If you dislike the job your elected official is doing, you have the right to voice that dissatisfaction in many ways, including voting against the candidate next time there is an election.

"Now, I'll tell you what you may not fully grasp. Your suggestion that there is some kind of quid pro quo because you 'give' me money, if it were true, would be illegal. It is, of course, not true. It is only your ignorance and rude behavior that leads you to even suggest I would engage in something illegal.

"Now, with your permission, Mr. Strap, I'll answer a question from one of our other guests who have waited patiently."

As Rubina fielded the next question, Steve leaned over to Richard, and whispered, "I bet Strap wishes he'd worn his brown pants today to hide his embarrassment."

Richard almost laughed out loud.

After dinner, Rubina's aid caught Allenby and asked him to make an appointment to see the President about a matter of importance in the next week. Richard would sit on the President's volunteer council of advisors for military affairs.

12

Washington DC

The weather in DC was rainy and windy on this early April morning as Steve Holmes pulled on his running clothes, laced-up his shoes, fit his earphones in, slipped his radio armband above his bicep and started to stretch. He'd run in worse weather. He grabbed the kitchen countertop, extended his right and then his left leg behind him, keeping his back straight with his heels flat on the ground to stretch the calf muscles and loosen the Achilles tendons to prevent another tear. He repeated the position with first his right and then his left leg behind him, but now with the ball of the front foot on the ground, heel up, pressing the center of his body toward the ground to loosen his thigh muscles. Finally, he bent over at the waist, feet together, reaching for the floor with both hands to stretch his back.

Huh, he thought and chuckled in a sarcastic way. *When I was twenty-five, I just put on my jogging clothes and ran out the door. Before long, my stretching routine will exceed the length of my run.*

***

Just after arriving at his office at 8:00 AM, the secretary buzzed him. "Steve, there's someone from the FBI on the phone for you."

When Steve answered, he heard a soft voice with a Boston accent and perfect diction, say, "Mr. Holmes, this is Special Agent Sherry

Adkison with the Federal Bureau of Investigation. I'd like to ask you a few questions about the Neka convoy."

"I wasn't aware this had become a case for the FBI."

"We're assisting the Army's Criminal Investigation Division with their investigation. I can explain all that when we meet."

"Okay. Where would you like to meet?"

"Could you come to our headquarters on Pennsylvania Avenue this afternoon?"

"Yes. Is one o'clock okay?"

"I'll see you then, Mr. Holmes. Once you clear security, the receptionist will be expecting you."

Steve finished a little paperwork, then walked out of his office and down to the metro station in time to grab a quick lunch in Pentagon City and still make his afternoon meeting. Steve sat alone on the sparsely populated late-morning metro train, trying not to think about his meeting with the FBI. He tried to read his newspaper on the short ride from King Street in Alexandria to Pentagon City as the ta-tump, ta-tump of the steel rails, station announcements, and the banging of the electronic doors opening and closing at each stop distracted him. After a Thai wrap and hummus, he road several stops on the Blue Line to Federal Triangle and Pennsylvania Avenue. The walls of the tunnel passed by slowly at first in this dim subterranean world as the train moved out, then faster and faster until it was hard to read the signs for the stations they passed. After clearing security at FBI headquarters, Steve was escorted to an interview room to await the FBI agent.

Special Agent Sherry Adkison entered the room a few minutes later. Her beauty caught Steve's eye immediately. Her shoulder-length brown hair and green eyes seemed to beam as he shook her small, warm hand. She removed her badge from her briefcase and showed it to Steve as they sat down across from each other at the table.

"I hope you found the office easily, Mr. Holmes."

"Um . . . I, ah, I had to google the location. It's one of the few DC government buildings I haven't visited."

"I'm the lead FBI agent for this investigation. As I told you, we're supporting the Army's CID investigation of the Neka convoy disaster."

"Why does the Army need the FBI's help?"

"When their investigation involves potential crimes by civilians, they usually ask the proper civilian police agency to assist them."

"The Army can't investigate civilians?"

"They can investigate to some extent, but they can't enforce civilian laws. There may have been civilian laws broken in this case, so they called the FBI."

"Ah, the Posse Comitatus Act that protects civilians from military rule?"

"Exactly."

"What civilian laws are you investigating?"

"One is the potential that someone with knowledge and access to the communications systems was involved in the failure. That might involve civilian sabotage and espionage laws. Since your former and current Kratos employees supported the convoy, I thought I'd start the investigation with you."

"Is this where you tell me you're here to help, and then I tell you I'm glad you're here?" Both Steve's nervousness and his sudden infatuation coaxed a lame attempt at humor.

Sherry smiled. "I've heard that one before, Mr. Holmes. Could you start by telling me about yourself and why you were riding in the convoy the day it was attacked?"

How dumb! But she didn't throw me in handcuffs for that joke. Steve thought.

Her broad smile, white teeth, and full lips caught his attention for a moment. "I'm the Executive Vice President of Government Services for Kratos. That includes all the work we do in support of the war. We provided many of the supplies on the convoy. We purchase food, clothing, and medical supplies. We manage the fuel supplies, maintain vehicles, and bottle the water in the camps. Before they went on active duty, many of the soldiers and Marines in the convoy worked for Kratos as part of the Sponsored Reserves, as you said. And the vehicles they drove were purchased by Kratos. I was riding along on the convoy as an observer when the attack occurred."

"You also worked at the FBI."

"I was a Special Agent for a few years; Quantico class, summer of 'ninety-five. I left the FBI and joined Kratos for the mission and the opportunity to grow."

"What went wrong with the convoy?"

"Soldiers and Marines got killed when the route was expected to be green that day and we couldn't call for help."

"Green?"

"Intelligence and pre-route reconnaissance assessments said it would be a low-threat, green trip that day. Yet, we were attacked and found ourselves in a pitched battle between Rangers and Iranian mujahideen fighters."

"Yes. I understand the Rangers got a threat update that said the mujahideen had moved into the city, but your convoy did not receive that information."

"That's correct, from what I saw and heard from Lieutenant Williams."

"Tell me what you know about the communications failure."

"I heard Lieutenant Williams say they'd lost all radio and data communications with Mashad headquarters. I found out later the satellite phone wasn't working, either. The only communications that appeared to be working were the short-range tactical convoy radios and a small airborne drone deployed by Lieutenant Williams."

"Who has the contract to service the convoy communications systems?"

"Kratos has the maintenance contract for all military vehicles, including the communications systems, at Joint Base Mashad."

"So, your technicians serviced the equipment before the convoy departed?"

"They have maintenance logs for each vehicle. I don't know which communications systems were serviced and which were not before the convoy went out, but yes, in general, we service the equipment."

Sherry reached in a box beneath the table, picked up a stack of papers, and spread them on the table in front of Steve. "Are these the maintenance logs your employees filled out?"

Steve immediately recognized that she was good and she was prepared as an investigator. Anyone lying to her wouldn't get far. Steve examined the papers. The maintenance logs listed the type of repair, what was done, and who did the work. "I recognize the forms and the signature of the maintenance supervisor, so yes, they appear to be our forms."

"The forms show that your employees conducted repair and maintenance on several of the MRAP vehicle Falcon long-range radios. Were you aware of these repairs?"

"Not specifically, no. I knew we maintained the systems, but I wasn't involved in day-to-day repairs. Our program manager at Mashad could verify the work, although I have no reason to suspect the records are inaccurate."

"I'll need to get a list of the names and contact information for your program manager and maintenance supervisor after we finish. Is there any reason to suspect that any of these maintenance employees might want to sabotage the system?"

"I wouldn't suspect any employees would do that. We do a background check and psychological testing for all our employees to identify potential threats. And the Army conducts a background check of their own for any foreign nationals we employ on-site. Some of the U.S. citizens have security clearances as well, so they've had additional screening."

"Have you had any discipline problems with your maintenance crew?"

"I know of two incidents within the past year. We fired one employee who was falsifying the hours she reported on her time card and maintenance log. And we disciplined one employee for showing up to work legally intoxicated."

"Where did the employee get the liquor from? I didn't think they could sell it in a Muslim country."

"He had returned from a regularly scheduled leave in Bahrain late the evening before his shift started. His blood alcohol content at oh-six-thirty the next morning was still above point oh-eight."

"I'll need those names and contact information as well, along with your human resources manager and financial controller. What do you think caused the communications failure on the Neka convoy, Mr. Holmes?"

"I really don't know what caused the failure. I do think it was deliberate and I think it could have only been done by someone who had legitimate access to the system."

"Like your radio technicians?"

"They can't be ruled out, but I don't see a scenario where they could cause a total blackout of all radio communications back to Mashad when they work on only a few trucks at a time. Let's just say, hypothetically that someone from Kratos' maintenance shop did it. How could they cause all the individual radios in all the MRAP vehicles to fail at once? It's not logical."

"Do you think profit could be a motive?"

"I don't see how. We work under the MANPower Civilian Augmentation Program, MANCAP, a cost-plus-fixed-fee contract. We don't get more profit if we do more work; the fee pool was fixed when the contract started. The cost we might expend for supplies and equipment that we purchase for the military is reimbursed to us at cost, with no more fee mark-up."

"So, you don't get more profit for selling more supplies or equipment."

"No, we don't. It's smart contracting by the military. I'm sure they wanted to avoid just the kind of scenario you were thinking about where contractors are incentivized with more profit to sell more and more expensive equipment."

"Thank you, Mr. Holmes. That's all I have for now, but I'd like to see you again in a few days after we question these other Kratos employees."

"I'd like to see you again as well, ah, I mean, ah, I'm glad to be of any assistance I can."

Sherry blushed just enough to let Steve know his Freudian slip of the tongue flattered her.

13

Steve Holmes stood outside his apartment in the pre-dawn darkness waiting for Ray to arrive to take him to Dulles Airport. Fog hung in the air like a wet blanket as Ray's headlights cast two smoky cones of illumination on the lonely street.

Talking with Ray was always enjoyable and on this morning it provided a welcome break from worries about the upcoming senate hearings and FBI investigation. Ray kept up with all major sports and could recall the stats from almost any era. Whether they discussed basketball or professional baseball, Ray knew the players, history, and averages.

"I sure am ready for the NBA playoffs to start. You think Durant will get another title?" Steve asked as Ray pulled away from the apartment.

"He deserves it. Oklahoma City's stacked with talent."

"Yeah, and they got him in one of the weakest NBA drafts in history."

"Right. Durant, Al Horford, and Joakim Noah are the only two thousand-seven draftees who've pulled out decent careers from it."

"Not like the 'seventy-nine draft when Magic Johnson and Larry

Bird came out of college. That was the best draft ever."

"Nah. Bird was drafted by Boston as an underclassman the year before. The greatest draft ever was nineteen eighty-four when Michael Jordan and Hakeem Olajuwon were drafted."

"You win again, Ray. I don't know how you remember all that stuff."

Hoping the fog would burn off in two hours before his flight departed for Huntsville, Alabama, Steve cleared the security checkpoint and got to the frequent flyers' lounge to read the newspapers and grab a cup of coffee. He was going to visit his old friend, Alford French, and meet with the Army at Redstone Arsenal, home to the development agency responsible for the Army Airborne Command and Control System, continuing his personal investigation into the Neka convoy attack.

The gate agent scanned his electronic boarding pass from his smartphone at 7:30 AM. Steve walked down the short jetway, took the first aisle seat in coach he found and sat down in the economy section with ever-diminishing leg room. The plane boarded on time, and Steve had fallen asleep before the wheels left the ground. That always happened.

Huntsville, Alabama

He awoke ten minutes later, finished reading his newspapers, then started reviewing his paperwork for the meeting with the Army Aviation and Missile Command. Alford French met Steve at the airport with a firm handshake and man hug. A friend and former employee, Alf worked in the engineering design and development field as a defense contractor. He filled Steve in on the people he would meet as they drove along Interstate 565 from the airport to downtown Huntsville for a late morning breakfast.

Alf pulled his truck into the busy High Cotton diner parking lot off Sparkman Drive. The popular restaurant was still crowded with the Army, NASA, and contractor workers noisily talking and eating their breakfast. Steve recognized several people as he squeezed through the tightly packed tables.

"Steve Holmes, you old dog. What brings you to Huntsville?" an old business associate asked as he stood to shake Steve's hand.

"I'm in town for a meeting at Redstone. How are Sandy and your two girls? They must be grown by now?"

"They're doing great, thanks for asking."

Once they sat down, Steve ordered pancakes, grits, and bacon, his favorite meal, whether for breakfast or dinner. After they discussed their families a little, Steve was interested to hear about Alf's new job.

"How do you like being Intuit3D's Group VP?"

"It's fun. I've got a lot more responsibility if things go wrong, but I also got to pick the team I wanted, and can make decisions to 'go' on projects that I think will work without somebody breathing down my neck."

"So why Intuit3D and not somewhere else?"

Alf smiled and started to speak, but was interrupted as the waiter arrived with the food. Alf spread his red paper napkin in his lap and leaned back to give the piping hot serving of hash browns, poached eggs, and ham room as they passed in front of him on their way to the table. After a prayer of thanks for the food they were about to eat, Alf continued.

"Arnie Banks, the company owner, convinced me to take this job. They needed an experienced executive to lead them as they graduated from their world of small, disadvantaged set-aside business to full and open competition. But it wasn't just the challenge or even the money that convinced me to take it. Arnie clinched it when he invited my entire family to stay with him and his family at their home over the weekend."

"You stayed in his house?"

"Yes. Arnie flew all of us first class to Pasadena, California. First class! We came in on a Friday and left on a Sunday afternoon. They had two spare rooms at their place on Orange Grove Avenue for us."

"The cost of the trip alone had to mean you were high on his radar. That had to be flattering."

"It impressed the hell out of me! And my wife was thrilled."

"Did you talk business?"

"None. It was all social. My wife met his wife. My kids played with his grandkids. Arnie and I jogged around the Rose Bowl on Saturday morning while the ladies took the kids and went shopping. On Saturday night, we strolled along the beautiful palm-lined streets in that year-round mild weather and stopped in Old Town Pasadena on Colorado Boulevard for a great meal. We talked about family, hobbies, news, whatever came up, but never about business. On Sunday, we went to his church early, then toured Los Angeles before going back to the airport.

"I found out later that it wasn't something he typically did. I thought a lot about why he invited us, and I think he wanted to get to know me and my family in a different way than most leaders know those who work for them, even after years of employment. Arnie wanted to know he could trust me to think the way he did."

"That was a great new recruiting tool for both of you. I can see how it would make you want to take the job."

"What about you, Steve? How's it working with Bernie?"

"A hundred-eighty degrees different from the deal you have with Arnie. I have unfortunately had a string of lousy corporate bosses and Bernie is the worst of the bunch. I stay because of my people and the mission to support the military. They're both that important to me."

"That's gotta be difficult. Let me know if there's anything I can do to help."

"I'll keep you informed, Alf."

Alf promised to keep tabs on the Army's investigation and let Steve know if there were any new developments. After breakfast, they walked through the U.S. Space and Rocket Museum before going to the arsenal for Steve's meeting.

At 11:00 AM, Steve sat down with the civilian director of the Aviation and Missile Command, Dr. Reed Elliot, at Redstone Arsenal. Dr. Elliot brought his chief engineer and judge advocate general's representative to the meeting with him.

"Thank you for seeing me, Doctor Elliot. I know you're all busy with the forensic analysis of the Neka A2C2S system in addition to the work you do here every day."

"Please, Mr. Holmes, you're not intruding on us. I'm aware of the great job you and your company are doing in support of our troops. And any friend of Alf's is welcome here. I'm glad to do anything I can to help."

"How is your analysis of the A2C2S equipment coming along?"

"We took it out of the box and checked it out to make sure everything was there and functioning properly. We tested the equipment and reviewed digital records of operation."

"Any surprises or malfunctions found?"

"We haven't found any problems so far. But it's a complex bit of equipment. The state-of-the-art airborne command post gives our ground commanders battle space information awareness for command and control on the move. That's critical for the conduct of modern, fast-moving ground forces whether in full battalions or small convoys."

"Do you know exactly what information was blocked during the Neka convoy attack?"

"Effectively, Lieutenant Williams was looking out of one eye with myopic vision. He couldn't see all the hostiles and friendlies in the area, and he didn't have the intel he needed. And he couldn't communicate with Joint Base Mashad. The system provides an integrated picture of all the digital surveillance and intelligence sources needed to make command decisions. Exactly the type of information Lt. Williams could have used on the Neka convoy."

"Have you ever seen this kind of outage on other missions?"

"No. The A2C2S is a pretty new addition to AWACS. The system has performed well on Blackhawk helicopters in the past and on the few AWACS missions where it has been used as well, until the Neka convoy."

"Do you have a working theory about what happened?"

Dr. Elliot replied, "I'm an engineer by training and DNA make-up. I deal with facts. I don't have any facts at this point to explain the outage. I leave the guessing to the lawyers and politicians."

Their analysis wouldn't be complete for another week. While they couldn't discuss their detailed results with Steve, the commander assured him the equipment had checked out satisfactorily so far.

Steve continued with his questions. "Have you examined the training records for the ground and airborne operators?"

"In general, we keep all training certificates up to date with the latest equipment for both the ground and airborne personnel. That wouldn't be any different for the Neka convoy. We designed the training program with the initial equipment development at Redstone. It's a built-in feature of the equipment itself. And we updated the training when it went into AWACS."

Steve thanked Dr. Elliot and his staff, stood up feeling a little down, and walked out the door. As he departed the building and walked through the sea of parked cars to reach Alf's truck, he thought about why all the investigations were coming to a dead end. No evidence of a clear cause for the loss of communications had arisen, but he realized this was one more possible point of failure eliminated, pending final tests by Redstone.

After reviewing what they'd heard in the meeting while they were driving back to the airport, Steve turned to Alf. "Are you up for another call to Mr. Magic tonight?"

"Are you still pulling that stunt?"

"Yeah, I'm literally a one-trick pony. Besides, it's fun."

"Sure, I'll do it."

"I'll call you later tonight."

As they turned back onto Interstate 565 heading for the airport, his cell phone rang.

"Hello, Mr. Holmes. This is Special Agent Adkison. I have some follow-up questions. Could we meet somewhere today to discuss them?"

"I'm in Huntsville and won't be back into Dulles until this evening. Can it wait until tomorrow?"

"It could, but I'm leaving town for a week. What time does your flight arrive?"

"Around eight PM"

"I'll meet you at the little bar and grill they have just outside of security."

***

Washington, DC

When Steve arrived, Sherry was sitting at a table in the corner of the small restaurant with drink in hand. "What would you like to drink, Mr. Holmes?"

"Won't it be suspicious if you're buying a suspect drinks, Agent Adkison?"

"You're not a suspect, Mr. Holmes, unless you had some type of suicidal wish when you rode in that convoy."

"I'll take a Guinness. What are you having?"

"Oh, I don't drink, Mr. Holmes. This is iced tea."

"Please call me Steve so I won't feel like a perp anymore."

"Okay, Steve. You can call me Sherry. I guess your days in the FBI weren't fulfilling enough to make a career out of it?"

"I saw an opportunity to support an important mission and perhaps run a company someday. I enjoyed my days as an FBI agent."

"I won't keep you long, Steve. We're still doing background investigations and interviews on some of your people in the field. In fact, I'm leaving for Iran in the morning to interview a few of your employees."

"So, you think some type of sabotage by a Kratos employee is likely?"

"We're focusing on the sabotage theory more, and not just for Kratos employees. None of the equipment tests identified failure. We don't see a plausible way simple human error could have caused it. Sabotage is looking more likely."

"How can I help?"

"You've been on both sides of the street. You worked for the FBI and now you're in civilian contracting. Where would you look to find the saboteur?"

"I'm flattered you'd ask me. I know the FBI is not out of leads."

"Yes, we have plenty of theories, but narrowing the list of suspects down could help tremendously."

"I think you're looking at two distinct events, not one. The so-called saboteur, if there is one, could be responsible for one or both events. The first event is the failed communications equipment, and you're all over that. The second event is the convoy schedule."

Sherry squinted at Steve, then looked down to her folder and began to paw through it. She shuffled one bound set of papers after another, looked only at the first or second page, then threw each rejected document aside on the table. She got a little faster, a little more aggressive with the papers, and a little more agitated as she discarded set after set, until she finally reached one, and said, "Here it is." Sherry scanned the document, flipping through the first few pages quickly, then finally she stopped. Everything was calm and quiet now as Sherry read. It was just a few moments, before she said, "You said in your deposition that a week before the convoy was to depart, the schedule was moved up one day. Who authorized that change?"

"I don't know. Perhaps the Army Transportation Command commander. I do know that only a small number of people had that kind of short-term access to the schedule. That convoy ran every week on the same day, except that week. When you get the list of people who knew about the change in the schedule, you'll find the person who informed the jihadis, deliberately or not."

"You believe there are foreign agents involved in this sabotage?"

"It's the only logical conclusion I can see."

"Once an FBI agent, always an FBI agent. I'm glad we got together tonight."

"Why don't we meet again when you get back from Iran? I'll buy you another glass of tea. Perhaps I can answer any remaining questions you have about Kratos or our people you interview."

"Are you asking me out on a date, Steve?"

"I was hoping to be subtle about it, but yes, I am."

"I'll tell you what. We'll go Dutch for dinner at McCormick and Schmick's. I'll give you a call to set it up."

"Okay, it's an, ah, ah, appointment date. Got it." He smiled.

***

It was late when Steve called Ray to pick him up at Dulles. Ray was parked in the cell phone waiting area, so it only took a few minutes before he pulled to the passenger arrival curb. Steve stepped into the car and said, "Sorry about the late hour, Ray. I had an interview at the airport that delayed me."

"No problem. I was listening to NBA radio."

"That reminds me. I'd like to get some good seats if the Oklahoma City Thunder plays the Washington Wizards again this year in the finals; I know you have good contacts."

"I can try, but I can't promise you anything."

"Let's see about that. I have a deck of cards here, Ray. Would you like to see some magic?"

"I don't believe in magic."

"Pick a card, Ray, and show it to me."

Ray drew the four of clubs and held it up as Steve dialed his cell phone.

"Hello, Mr. Magic. I'm sitting in the car with my friend Ray and he doesn't believe you can read his mind. I just— Yes, Mr. Magic, yes. I just wanted to show Ray how real magic works. He doesn't— Yes, Mr. Magic, yes, he's sitting right here and you can talk with him. Yes, yes, Mr. Magic, I'll put him on." Steve handed the phone to Ray.

When Ray said, "Hello" the voice said, "Your card is the four of clubs," and hung up. Ray laughed. "How'd you do that?"

"It was magic, Ray."

"You've gotta tell me, so I can show my wife."

"If you promise to get me floor-level seats for the opening game of the Wizards versus Thunder playoffs, I'll show you. I'll even pay for the tickets."

"I'll have to call in a favor, and it won't be cheap. But, yeah, tell me how it was done."

"I called my friend, Alf French, in Huntsville. We play this card trick game together. When I said 'Hello, Mr. Magic,' that signaled to him that the game was on. He first ran down the suits – spades, hearts, diamonds, clubs. When he said 'clubs,' I said, 'Yes, Mr. Magic, yes.' He then ran down the value of the card, Ace, two, three, four.

When he said 'four,' I said 'Yes, Mr. Magic, yes.' Mr. Magic then asked me, 'Is the card the four of clubs?' and I said, 'Yes, yes, Mr. Magic,' and I handed the phone to you."

They both laughed about it and talked about other gags as they rode back to Washington.

14

Baltimore-Washington International Airport

Driving fast in her BMW with the top down and cool wind blowing her raven black hair in the early Saturday morning hours in southern Maryland, beat the boredom of Jodie Arenas' daily commutes into DC on the Metro. Speeding up and down the small hills, decelerating only slightly to hug the tight turns, then accelerating quickly on the straightaway, Jodie was exhilarated as she made her way to meet, of all people, a defense contractor near Baltimore-Washington International airport. It was a departure from her typical weekend, catching up on the Congressional investigation reports, researching background material, or planning her work for the following week. Nonetheless, ensuring Jack Uttman was prepared for the Subcommittee on Intelligence and Communications Failures in Iran hearings that would occur next month was her top priority.

***

Jack fumbled with his wallet as he pulled out his credit card and swiped it through the taximeter to pay his $22 fare from BWI. He looked nervous and unsure of himself as he scanned the coffeehouse, looking for the face that matched the picture he had. The truth was, he'd filed his whistle-blower claim to get revenge against Kratos for his employment termination and to collect the fee for any judgment that came as a result of his testimony. He never in his wildest dreams thought he'd be telling his story to a panel of senators. That would terrify anyone in his position.

Jodie had chosen the coffeehouse and time for the meeting to be sufficiently away from Washington DC to avoid recognition or eavesdropping. DC is really a small world and people who know people who know you are often sitting within earshot of any conversation you have in the city. A company, agency, or person's name overheard in a conversation caused ears to perk up and people to take notice.

Jack bumped the chair, then caught it as he sat down half on the seat and half off.

"Thank you for coming, Jack. I hope you had a pleasant flight?"

"Yes."

"I was going to have an espresso. What can I order for you?"

"Coff— ah, coffee."

Jodie ordered a European double espresso for herself and a Grande Latte Americano for Jack and started some small talk to get him relaxed.

Jack wore thick, black-rimmed glasses. His wrinkled Dockers and polo shirt didn't match. He looked like he had slept in them. He spoke quietly, without confidence, and he made little eye contact with her. It would be a challenge to make him convincing in front of the senate panel.

Jodie started out by reviewing his claims. "What documentation did you expect to have on hand at the hearing to substantiate any fraudulent purchases?"

"There had to be a signed purchase order. We would have a list that was either generated by one of our operations leaders or a request that came directly from the military. But I don't have any of those documents with me. They were all kept by Kratos." That was an easy question for Jack, and he didn't have to lie, yet.

"Can you remember a time when you didn't have that documentation for a purchase?"

Jack's eyes cut away to the floor. He blinked several times and touched his face with his hand. He lied, "Not that I can recall. I was meticulous. I always had something approved in writing before I made a purchase."

"So, you wouldn't know what the basis was for that purchase or even if someone above you fabricated those lists. Your job was simply to make sure the items requested on the list were properly purchased. Is that correct, Jack?"

Jack looked up, smiled, and made direct eye contact for the first time. "That's right." Sounding a little embarrassed, Jack added, "But it seemed that we were buying too much stuff. In my twenty-plus years in procurement, the volume was unprecedented."

Jack had no proof for these excessive invoices. He couldn't substantiate the purchases of items like how many radios and how much food.

"Did anyone at Kratos ever direct you to sign invoices that you hadn't confirmed?"

Jack thought about the question for a long moment. "I can't remember a specific instance, but you can bet they were buying equipment that wasn't needed."

"Are you aware of the DCAA Form One findings for questionable costs that have been made against Kratos in the past few months?"

"Not since I left the company earlier this year. We always had the DCAA doing audits, but they seldom dug deep enough to find the real dirt. There were a few Form Ones issued, but they didn't amount to much."

Jodie lifted her backpack from underneath the table, reached in, and pulled out a stack of papers. "I've copied the most recent DCAA Form One reports for you to review. They're alleging over a billion dollars of fraud occurred in the past year. Everything from timesheet errors to disappearing fuel supplies, to unsubstantiated vendor purchases." It wasn't hard for Jodie to get these reports. Once Shankle placed a call to the DCAA director and threatened to make him testify to defend his department's poor record of recovering money from contractors, he was glad to help.

Jack took the documents and began to look through them. Jodie ordered another espresso and watched Jack as he read. His eyelids opened wider, and he nodded and smiled with some excitement. "Yeah, that's exactly what I meant about buying unnecessary supplies."

"I want you to read those reports in detail. When you speak at the hearing, you should cite some specific examples in here to substantiate your claims."

"These are just allegations that are often refuted when Kratos has an opportunity to respond. Won't the senators want me to provide more concrete proof?"

"Don't worry about that. These findings are sufficient to substantiate your allegations. It makes them look guilty as hell in the hearings. Let me ask you another question." Jodie paused and maintained penetrating eye contact with him. "I've heard some allegations that you destroyed equipment and didn't report it. Is that true?"

The shock on Jack's face was obvious. "I never destroyed equipment! Who said I did?"

Putting Jack on the defensive helped to get his mind in the position Jodie wanted it. "Well, Kratos may be spreading the rumor to smear your testimony. It's going to look bad in the hearing when they accuse you. How are we going to counter that?" Make a false accusation, and then give him an opportunity to fix it. She was experienced at this game.

Jack was speechless, and his mind was racing to find a way out of this. He knew that he was lazy, and his recordkeeping wasn't good. There were sure to be pieces of equipment that had been destroyed or disposed of without proper documentation.

"Well, I haven't brought this up yet, but I saw Kratos employees destroying equipment. I could tell the committee that."

Bingo! Jodie smiled, leaned back and relaxed. Mission accomplished. She thought, *I should write a book on how to influence people and win without really trying.* "That is an outstanding plan. The best defense is a good offense. You throw those claims at them and leave it to them to disprove."

Jack sat back and crossed his legs in a relaxed and comfortable position. Jodie could see his confidence building. He made better eye contact, smiled freely, and spoke more confidently.

"I think you're just about ready for this, Jack. I have a couple of assistants I will send over to help you polish your testimony for the hearings. They will work with you on your appearance and presentation. They'll give you the questions we prepared for the senate committee to ask you. You can dry-run your presentation and answers with them. They are experts at this Capitol Hill game."

Jodie left the coffeehouse knowing that the subcommittee hearings would be a slam-dunk and implicating Kratos in the Neka communications failures was a *fait accompli*.

15

Dubai, United Arab Emirates

As Bernie Tyler stepped out of the Dubai International Airport terminal and into the bright, ninety-five degree midday weather, the humidity and light wind hit him like a hot towel. Small beads of sweat formed on his forehead and stained his shirt as he walked the few minutes to his waiting car. Stepping into his limousine without speaking to his company chauffeur, Khalid Abu Ahmet—which literally meant "Khalid Father of Ahmet" to establish his first-born son as heir to his tribe and fortune—he immediately picked up the folder and began to read papers forwarded to him from his office in Washington.

They drove on the wide, palm-lined, and manicured Sheikh Zayed Road heading for the Burj Al Arab hotel, past the massive Emirates Towers, towering Burj Khalifa, expansive Safa Park, opulent Mall of the Emirates, and the busy Gold Souk. The lavish hotel, shaped like a large sail and located on land reclaimed from the sea with help from Dutch and Belgian engineers, was visible for miles before they arrived. Located on some of the most expensive real estate in the world, it was just the kind of place where Bernie Tyler liked to do business: ostentatious, exotic, and located in an emerging world business center.

After checking in and taking a dip in the pool, they were going to a traditional Arab feast as a guest of Sheikh Mohammad Khaleed, a distant relative of the ruling Al Maktoum family. Sheikh Khaleed was a key business partner and minority owner for Sadik Dost, Kratos' subcontractor in Iran and other Middle East countries. To do business successfully in this area, you needed partners who had connections to the decision-makers in the government, partners whose principals were related to the ruling family. Businesses had to be extra careful about violating western corruption laws if they were scrupulous. If not, they hoped they didn't get caught.

Bernie listened to the message on his cell phone as he dried off on the pool deck. Dialing the international number, his investment adviser answered, saying, "Kratos' stock is soaring!"

"As I expected it would after we cut costs and announced our revised earnings estimates for the year."

"You're a lucky investor, Bernie. That monthly programmed sale you filed with the SEC back in November is paying off now. With a strike price of half the current trading price, you'll make millions."

"Luck has nothing to do with it. I beat the high cost out of our system and now all our stockholders will reap the rewards. I expect to make ten million by the time we announce our financial results in early June."

"I'll pretend I didn't hear that Bernie. Be careful."

***

They arrived at Sheikh Khaleed's palace in matching, armored black SUVs; Bernie thought the place looked like a military complex from the outside with all the razor-wire fencing on top of the high-security Adobe walls, except for the minarets peeking up on the roofs. Once inside the gate, the estate was a marvel of neatly trimmed lawns, high palm and date trees, swimming pools, fountains, and a number of luxury cars parked in neat rows: a two-tone, dark metallic-colored Rolls Royce for the sheikh, black Bentleys for the children, and Mercedes, BMWs, and Range Rovers for anyone who wanted them. Expensive cars were an obsession with the sheikh's family. There were several smaller palaces for the families of the sheikh's married children. Bernie saw an outdoor tent-like structure that reminded him of the nomads with their camels stopping for an evening in the desert.

The sheikh's eldest son came out wearing the traditional long, white jalabiya to greet their guests. The women were never seen in the palace, although many were there. A male accompanied them whenever they were in public, and were always wearing the long, black abayas.

The son greeted Bernie with a kiss on each cheek and a limp handshake.

They walked into the palace, which was gargantuan and divided into dining rooms, washrooms, meeting rooms, and living quarters for the sheikh's family. They turned into a rectangular room that was vacant except for the decorative, cushioned armchairs positioned with their backs to the wall all around. It felt like a room made for a king, with walls trimmed in twenty-four-carat gold crown molding, and a spectacular crystal chandelier that Bernie guessed was twenty-five feet wide and forty feet high, hanging from the center of the ceiling. After some small talk, everyone stood as the sheikh entered the room, personally greeted each guest, starting with Bernie, and sat in the corner, facing Mecca. Bernie sat at the guest of honor's position to the sheikh's right and to his left was the Sadik Dost president, Ahmet Gul, the son of Bernie's driver.

"*As-salaam alaikum,* and welcome my friends," the sheikh said.

"Thank you, Sheikh Khaleed. We are pleased to be here in your beautiful home," Bernie replied.

Ahmet replied with the traditional "*As-salaam alaikum.*"

After some small talk and inquiries about the well-being of Bernie's family, the sheikh continued. "I hear good reports about our business in Iran with the U.S. Department of Defense through your contract, Bernie. As a minority owner of Sadik Dost, we consult with our friend Ahmet and his team frequently."

Bernie replied, "We value your guidance for our business together. Your involvement is important to ensure that all our family and friends in the Middle East are taken care of."

"Yes, and everyone is very happy to be making lots of money, thanks to Kratos's generosity."

They all chuckled.

Bernie's only real concern about the sheikh's family and friends was how that relationship would translate into wealth for Bernie. He saw the opportunity for new construction contracts in Dubai and Abu Dhabi worth billions. After Dubai had been selected for the 2026 FIFA World Soccer Cup, it had announced a plan to spend a hundred billion dollars in new facilities and infrastructure. New highways, high-speed railways, stadiums, and even complete cities were to be constructed. Kratos garnered a piece of the new business, but there were still major facilities to construct and operations contracts to award. They were building a new city to house the 50,000 foreign workers just to support that World Cup construction. There were massive stadiums under construction which were both open-air and air-conditioned temporary facilities that could be disassembled and sold to poorer countries after the games. That would take some technology and know-how to pull off in the desert that would mean huge profits to a company like Kratos.

Sheikh Khaleed said, "As a token of our appreciation, I offer this small gift." The small gift was two million U.S. dollars in cash. Exactly the kind of appreciation Bernie expected. This was uncirculated money with the smell of ink still noticeable. The sheikh's bank ordered its American dollars directly from the U.S. Treasury. They didn't like money that touched unclean hands before it touched their hands. Spreading work around in Iran to get work in Dubai and the payoffs from all those vendors would make Bernie as wealthy as a sheikh.

"You are very generous, Sheikh Khaleed. I have spoken to my operational leaders, and I will put my own financial controller in place on our U.S. federal contracts to ensure Sadik Dost will do even more work in the future." Bernie was almost giddy as he opened the satchel and gazed at the crisp new stacks of hundred dollar bills.

"Thank you, my friend. Now, we will feast on young halal goat meat and then celebrate with our friends in the beautiful city of Dubai."

The meal commenced with the washing of hands in an outer room lined with imported marble sinks and gold-trimmed mirrors. An attendant was there to hand each guest a fresh towel monogrammed with the sheikh's coat of arms. The sheikh guided Bernie to his seat of honor. The sheikh's son positioned the other guests. The dining hall had the kid, head, eyes and all, centered on the long, rectangular table with other Arab breads and yogurt dishes spread around. The aroma was that of an open, wood-burning fire slowly roasting seasoned meat on a cool desert night.

The sheikh offered the *Bismillah* blessing, then dipped his bare hands into the main dish and served the guests of honor a handful of goat and rice, saving the eyeballs for Bernie. Bernie wasn't prepared for the barehanded scooping by the sheikh. He looked at Ahmet, who assured Bernie he should accept the great courtesy the sheikh displayed and eat what was given.

After the meal, they all loaded into their separate vehicles. The caravan headed for the Stratosphere Restaurant and Lounge on the

122nd floor of what had once been the tallest building in the world: the Burj Khalifa, the "Caliph's Tower." By now, the streets were crowded and the city was lit up. You could easily imagine you were in any western city.

At the restaurant, there was more food and plenty of liquor served for the westerners. The guests could also have the company of Russian prostitutes of the highest quality. The young, beautiful, well-educated Russians came to Dubai to bed rich Arabs and make a lot of money fast before returning home to their university studies or regular jobs.

Bernie feasted on all the delights with drunken abandon. Drunk or sober, he lusted openly after women wherever he went. His eyes bulged and his tongue nearly rolled out of his head in the presence of attractive women. This behavior had resulted in several sexual harassment allegations in the U.S., followed by hefty financial settlements.

On this night, Bernie was in rare form. He danced in his boxer shorts with his pants on his head. "Who wants to fuck Bernie?" was his hedonistic mantra all night.

A brunette in knee-high black boots, tight shorts, and a sheer blouse wandered over to Bernie. "*Habibi ana behibak!*"

"You'll have to speak English for me, honey. What's your name?"

"I said, 'Honey, I love you.' You can call me Sonja, baby. See anything you like?"

"Hell, yeah, I like what I see. And I'd like to see what I can't see. How much, doll?" Bernie ran his hands down her backside.

"You're no Arab. Do you think you can afford me, baby?"

Incensed, Bernie removed his hand and stood back. "Can you afford to pass me up? That's the question you should be asking yourself. I may let one of these other girls have me."

The Russian prostitute couldn't tell if he had money, but she could sure see how homely he was. Homely, old, and arrogant. He must have money, she thought. "Yeah, baby. That's why I came over here to you. You're too hot to let someone else have. I'll give you a special rate, a thousand dollars."

"I'm insulted, doll; I'll pay twice that. Now let's find a quiet place to complete our business."

16

Washington, DC

Steve had a light schedule at work this morning. He had meetings in the afternoon to prepare him for the upcoming senate hearings on Intelligence and Communications Failures in Iran; that left plenty of time to get in a good midday workout.

Shortly after 11:00 AM, he changed from his work clothes into his gym shorts and shirt, grabbed his worn-out tennis shoes, jumped into his old Cadillac CTS and sped off to the gym. The midday sun bathed his car with warmth as he drove down Army Navy Drive. The traffic was heavy and it took him twenty minutes to get to the Pentagon gymnasium where he often played pick-up basketball with his friend, General Ronald Lee, when they were both in DC. It was a very exclusive gym in a protected area frequented by high brass and politicians. The games regularly included military and civilian DOD, members of Congress, and other executive civil service employees.

As he approached the building, he peered through the window and could see Ron and several other players, including Alex Shankle, warming up. Shankle comically wore the short-shorts, the high-top canvas Converse All-Star sneakers, and the tube socks that were in vogue back in the '70s.

Steve sat on the bench and laced up his shoes. He chatted with Ron as they stretched and loosened up, followed by dribbling, lay-ups, and then short- and long-range jump shots to warm up. Steve and Ron sized up the competition like a couple young bulls sizing-up an opponent before locking horns. The players stretched or shot around, hoping for enough players to arrive to make at least a four-on-four, full-court game.

When enough players had arrived, they divided up teams. Everyone shot free-throws to determine the teams. Shankle was on one team, and Steve was on the other. With both teams decided, Steve shot and made the make-it-take-it three-pointer to give his team the first possession of the ball.

Steve's team included Ron and a big 6' 7" Defense Department civilian named Bud, who could shoot and rebound well. He didn't recognize the other two players. Ron was a strong, big body that clogged up the middle.

Shankle, their main opponent, was big, burly, and not particularly athletic. At 6'6" and 250 pounds, he ate up a lot of space under the goal. They also had junior Florida Congressman Rodney "Buggs" Boggs; a short, 5'5" ball handler with a sweet jump shot.

Steve pushed the ball up the court on their first possession and hit Bud with a two-handed chest pass for a short baseline jumper score. Buggs brought up the ball for their first possession and passed it to Shankle, who was posted low near the basket. Shankle muscled up a jump hook shot through an onslaught of hacking and holding that passed for defense. He missed.

Ron got the rebound and dribbled the ball back to the opposite end of the court. Steve took the pass, drove the ball down the lane to the basket, around the senator, and made the lay-up. Steve tried the same move on the next play on offense, but Shankle blocked the shot, and said, "Get that shit out of here." Buggs pushed the ball up and hit a short jump shot. On the next play, Steve pump-faked once to take the senator out of the play, drove to the basket, and shot a floater. Shankle grumbled that Steve elbowed him, but play continued.

Bud stole their inbound pass and scored on the next play. That made the score 8-2 for Steve's team. On the next play, Steve was defending Shankle as Buggs missed a jump shot. Shankle got the rebound despite the box-out and a little pushing from Steve. They scored a few more baskets as Steve continued to battle Shankle for the rebounds. The trash-talking from Shankle was getting louder.

Trailing by a bucket with only one shot needed for the win, Steve threw the ball to Ron in the corner and cut through the middle off Bud's screen to the opposite side of the floor, getting an elbow from Shankle on the way. Ron reversed the ball around the top of the key back to Steve. Dribbling toward the free-throw line, Steve peripherally saw the defense shift when Bud moved to an open position near the goal. Steve made a one-hand, no-look bullet pass to Bud that hit Shankle square in the face when he stepped in the path of the ball. He was sliding with his man on defense and did not see the ball coming. Play stopped and Shankle sat down on the bench as Steve approached him.

"Are you all right, Senator Shankle?"

Red-faced with anger, Shankle ignored the question.

"I'm sorry you got hit. It was an accident."

Shankle turned away without comment. He sat out the rest of the game and another player took his place.

After the game, Steve sat on the bench near Shankle and apologized again. Ignoring Steve, Shankle turned to Buggs, and said, "Nothing's broken, but I didn't appreciate the deliberate pass thrown at my face by a profiteer and would-be soldier."

Steve was astounded. He slid closer to Shankle, "You can't honestly think I would deliberately hit you in the face?"

Shankle responded with a cold stare.

It did not help Steve's situation to know that two weeks later he would be testifying in front of the senator at the hearing on Intelligence and Communications Failures in Iran.

17

Senator Harper McCastle entered the room walking quickly, both arms wrapped around her documents, followed by four staffers carrying their computers and more documents for the hearing. Distinguished-looking with a full set of gray hair, she smiled and nodded at the faces she recognized in the Senate chamber gallery. She took the center seat on the semi-oval-shaped, raised table for the senators on the Senate Armed Services Committee's Subcommittee on Intelligence and Communications Failures in Iran. The other nine senators, four Democrats and five Republicans, were intermingled on either side of her, making last minute preparations for the hearing. Senator Alex Shankle sat at the table huddled with his aides, two seats to McCastle's left. After spreading her documents on the table in front of her, she greeted each of the senators while her staff plugged-in and set-up behind her.

The audience of about a hundred spectators, mostly contractors, civil servants, and news media, were already in their seats awaiting the start of the hearing. Those new to these meetings sat quietly, in awe of the powerful panel in front of them. The half-dozen media representatives prepared their electronic recording devices and greeted old friends, while other frequent attendees talked quietly, pointing at one senator or the other.

The hearing convened at 8:00 AM on June 15, 2020, chaired by McCastle, in the Dirksen Senate Office Building in Washington. McCastle sat with both arms on the table, leaning over her papers, with her reading glasses pushed far down her nose as she opened the hearing. "I want to thank all of you for attending this hearing. Our focus today is very narrow. We want to investigate to what extent the communications and intelligence failures in Iran may be due to the actions of contractors like Kratos, and its employees, many of whom become active duty military when called up for service. We'll hear from two witnesses, Mr. Jack Uttman, a former Kratos employee, and Mr. Steve Holmes, Kratos' Executive Vice President of Government Services.

"I particularly want to thank Mr. Uttman for being here today. You sir, courageously sacrificed your job and career to ensure that the American taxpayer and our troops knew the truth. I and this subcommittee greatly respect your courage and your patriotism."

Looking down both sides of the table, she said, "We'll start with opening remarks from our panel, beginning with Senator Shankle."

Jack Uttman sat alone at the small rectangular table isolated at the center of the room between the senate panel and the audience. "Thank you, Madam Chairman. I also want to thank Mr. Uttman for being here today. I've got to say—you showed true honesty and fortitude. For that, you lost your job, and Kratos has vilified you in the press! For protecting the taxpayers, you lose your job. That's just wrong in my book. We're going to get to the bottom of this, and I hope you get every penny you deserve when you sue Kratos."

Sitting in the gallery, listening to Shankle's remarks, Steve Holmes was feeling more and more uncomfortable. Shankle had already moved from biased interrogator to chief accuser.

After the other senators had made their brief opening remarks,

Harper McCastle pushed her reading classes up over the bridge of her nose to read her prepared notes. "On May twenty-six, twenty-twenty, the Commission on Contractor Failures in Iran, led by Senator Alex Shankle, presented its final report to Congress. All of you should have received and read that report. Just to remind everyone, the report found minor system and procedural problems by the Army and Air Force, but nothing that would cause the major failures we've seen. Its primary conclusion was that Kratos' employees deliberately sabotaged equipment and covered up faulty intelligence reports. The mujahideen attacks on the Neka and similar convoys have resulted in the loss of hundreds of lives and billions of taxpayer dollars over the past year. Kratos provides mechanics, equipment, supplies, and many logistical functions, but their primary role here was maintaining the vehicles, including the communications systems, and providing much of the materials on the convoy. Many of the truck drivers were working at Kratos as Sponsored Reserve employees before becoming active duty soldiers. Numerous other contractors and subcontractors play a role in these convoys, from supplying equipment to supporting the convoy planning and preparations.

"Will the witness please stand and raise his right hand to be sworn in," McCastle said as she stood to state the oath.

Jack Uttman stumbled as he pushed his chair back and swore his oath.

"Mr. Uttman, you may proceed with your testimony."

Jack placed a hand on the back of his seat to steady himself as he slowly sat back down. There was a pause as he shuffled his papers and cast his eyes down, avoiding the stare of the powerful panel. He poured himself a glass of water, spilling as much as he managed to get in the glass. His hand shook and he sloshed the water as he took a sip.

"Chairman McCastle and members of the Committee, thank you

for this opportunity to come here today and share my experience working for Kratos in Iran. During my time as Chief of Contracts, I personally saw Kratos submit over one billion dollars' worth of unsupported costs on these contracts with the Army's Rock Island Contracting Command. The Defense Contract Auditing Agency, the DCAA, found one point eight billion dollars in questionable costs during that period. I personally uncovered fraudulent financial payments, inadequately trained craft and support services workers, and equipment sabotage by Kratos' employees."

Sitting in the audience awaiting their turn to testify, Steve Holmes turned to his chief counsel, Mark Darrow and whispered, "How can they allow a witness to make unsubstantiated claims like that?"

Darrow replied, "This is not a criminal trial. The witness can say anything he wants so long as he doesn't perjure himself."

"How do they know he's not?"

"A member of the panel would challenge the veracity of Jack Uttman's statements. Probably a Senator sympathetic to us."

"In that case, there won't be any challenges."

Uttman continued, "When I reported that fraud to my superiors at Kratos, I expected a full investigation to identify the problems and prosecute the guilty parties. Instead, I was branded a liar, told to be quiet, and fired from my job." Jack paused and noticed many senators nodding acceptance. Others were looking attentively at Jack or glaring accusingly at Steve Holmes. Jack's hands steadied and his speech was a little clearer. "Today, I finally get an opportunity to be heard."

McCastle leaned forward and pulled her microphone close. "Mr. Uttman, I'd like to start the questioning by asking about the military managers who oversaw the Kratos contract: Rock Island's contracting officer and the technical manager. How vigilant were they in watching out for the taxpayers' money?"

"They were very lax. Early on in the war there were problems with Kratos' systems and serious deficiencies in the financial reporting to the Army. Instead of tightening the Army's oversight and financial controls on Kratos, the contracting officer for what they call MANCAP—you know, the MANPower Civilian Augmentation Program—outsourced the oversight by hiring a third-party contractor to oversee Kratos. That's the fox watching the hen house! And, Rock Island waived its standard fifteen percent withholding of payment that is standard before final pricing is approved. The whole process was highly unusual. Kratos' financial and business interests, not the interests of the Army, soldiers, or taxpayers seemed to be paramount."

Shankle threw his papers on the table, rocked forward, slapped his arms on the table, and said, "Was this treatment of Kratos unusual? Were other contractors treated the same?"

"There was very lax management of contractors from what I saw, but I wasn't closely involved with other contracts."

"But you witnessed this favored treatment for Kratos, is that right?"

"Yes. In all my years of contracting with the military, I have never seen anything like the way Kratos' unsupported charges were handled by the Army contracting officers. Not until DCAA investigated did any real accountability begin to occur."

McCastle said, "Do you know why the government oversight of these contracts was so poor?"

"I was told it was due to a lack of manpower. Rock Island awarded numerous task orders to Kratos on a cost-reimbursable basis, which required more oversight than fixed-price work. With the commencement of the war, the number and size of the task orders increased exponentially. Awards under Kratos' MANCAP contracts alone tallied over ten billion dollars. Oversight support by the

Defense Contract Management Agency, DCMA, and the DCAA, was understaffed."

McCastle said, "Can you be more specific? What problems resulted from this lack of proper oversight?"

Jack sat up a little straighter and looked confidently into McCastle's eyes. "I'll give you two examples. First, we had hundreds of procurement specialists buying supplies and equipment from local and regional suppliers, as much as possible. This was the so-called Iranian First program. The objective of this program was to help the Iranian economy and provide jobs for Iranians, some of whom might otherwise join the Basij local militias fighting with the mujahideen."

Shankle turned to the senator beside him, whispering, "Those jobs should go to Americans."

Uttman continued, "Through the efforts of my contract team and with great difficulty, we identified several cases where Kratos' procurement specialists were taking kickbacks from these companies for the right to cheat our soldiers. In one example, a Kratos procurement manager and a government contract manager were arrested for approving bogus vendor purchases for food services that were paid to the bank account of a fictitious company. The two men then withdrew these funds and used them to buy boats, cars, houses, and luxury vacations.

"The second example of the lack of oversight involves the one point eight billion dollars' worth of improper charges documented by DCAA. DCAA declared that Kratos' projected costs were unacceptable, that they overstated costs and used incorrect algorithms to estimate future costs." Jack started to smile as he saw the senators nodding approval and taking notes.

McCastle turned to her aide and asked for the summary of DCAA's report. Shuffling through a large folder, the aide produced the single-page summary alleging wrongdoing. McCastle pulled the mike to her. "Did you observe any events that substantiate those DCAA charges, Mr. Uttman?"

"Well, uh, I, uh, I don't know." Jack loosened his tie and reached for a glass of water.

"We want to hear your observations on what happened, Mr. Uttman. Those DCAA reports were issued after you left Kratos. Please stick to what you know."

Well, thank you for a little objectivity, Senator, Steve thought.

Shankle interjected, "Madam Chairman, if I may ask the witness a question. Mr. Uttman what was the quality of training for Kratos employees?"

"I saw firsthand how inadequately trained the Kratos staff was. New employees were rushed into the battle theater with one week of training and put to work. Many of them complained about not knowing what their job was or how to do it. It was chaos."

Steve shook his head in disbelief, then turned to Mark Darrow, and scribbled a note. *He's lying. Jack was responsible for ensuring that our training met contract requirements.*

"And what about sabotaging equipment, Mr. Uttman?"

"I witnessed employees falsifying reports to cover up for stolen or damaged equipment." Jack removed his handkerchief to wipe the sweat building on his upper lip. "For example, they would smash radios and then turn them in for replacements. This allowed Kratos to buy more equipment and gain more profit on the government contracts."

Questions followed for two hours that served to reinforce the conclusion that Kratos was capable of sabotaging the communication systems.

Shankle asked the final questions. "Mr. Uttman, do you believe Steve Holmes is a loyal American?"

The people in the gallery from Kratos murmured. Jack's eyes

opened wide with surprise, and he sat back a little in his seat.

"I-I don't really know Mr. Holmes that well."

"Okay, fair enough. Do you consider Kratos to be a patriotic company?"

"Absolutely not! They're motivated by the dollar, not any sense of national pride."

At the end of the questioning, the panel of senators all looked either mad or at best, passive. It would be difficult for Steve to turn those opinions around.

Chairman McCastle said, "Thank you, Mr. Uttman. Your testimony here is truly eye-opening. The level of corruption you attest to is almost unbelievable. We will take a short break and reconvene at ten-thirty when we hear from Mr. Steve Holmes of Kratos."

Jodie Arenas met Uttman at his table with a smile and pat on the back. They spoke quietly as they walked out of the room.

Steve and Mark Darrow met with George Bird out in the hall.

George said, "Jack's testimony was pretty damning, and sure as hell misleading. He mixed in a little truth with a lot of fabrication."

Steve replied in a depressed tone, "I know, but in the court of public opinion and politics, will anyone care about the facts or the truth? I'm afraid Shankle has made up his mind about who's guilty and he's just using this hearing for publicity. Hell, he thinks I'm a traitor! If you noticed, Jack didn't offer any documented proof that he reported any of the incidents he talked about. He's just taking the DCAA's documentation of allegations and acting like he reported the same thing."

"Yeah, I noticed, Steve. What do you think will come of the DCAA allegations?"

"Over ninety percent of the time those allegations are proven false when we provide the detailed records in response to their Form One findings. If we find we made an error, we will admit it and pay up. If there is wrongdoing, and it occasionally does happen, we always support prosecution of the criminals. In the one example Jack cited for the bogus food service invoices, it was a Kratos internal investigation that found that fraud. We self-reported the crime to the Departments of Defense and Justice and worked with them to prosecute the criminals involved. Jack conveniently left that detail out."

"Well, anyway, I don't envy you having to testify in front of that hostile audience. They were patting each other on the back and high-fiving just before the break. You're in for a difficult time when we reconvene."

"Thanks for the vote of confidence, George. I'm going to rely on the truth and documented facts. That's what has to win out in the end."

18

When the subcommittee reconvened, McCastle swore Steve in and asked him for opening remarks.

"Thank you, Madam Chairman and senators. I welcome the opportunity to answer your questions about communications and intelligence problems and, most importantly, help resolve what caused the Neka convoy disaster. I'll start by saying simply that there is no evidence to support any claims that any Kratos employees were responsible in any way for the Neka debacle, through sabotage, incompetence, or any other means."

"Before I go further, though, I'd like to address Mr. Uttman's testimony. I did not come here today to have allegations made by a former employee stand without being able to respond." Steve didn't pause here. He hoped to avoid the objection of any senator to his rebuttal. "The patriotic, ambitious, hardworking Kratos men and women would demand that Mr. Uttman's accusations be challenged. Have there been individual criminal acts and misbehavior? Yes, just like with any population of a mostly blue-collar workforce anywhere in the world. And, just like the mayor of any large city regrets those criminal acts in his or her city, so Kratos regrets them as well. It doesn't make the mayor a criminal. Kratos has fully supported the prosecution of employees who commit crimes."

McCastle interrupted Steve. "Let's just pick up the questioning from here, Mr. Holmes. Mr. Uttman and members of this committee are alleging sabotage by Kratos. Take the destroyed radios, for example. Can you prove they are wrong?"

"I can. The Army conducted its own investigation of these allegations, and it could find no evidence to support Mr. Uttman's accusations."

Shankle said, "That doesn't mean it didn't happen, Mr. Holmes. This is not a court of prosecution. We're gathering facts. I personally would take the word of an honorable citizen like Jack Uttman over that of a Kratos executive."

Steve replied, "Let's, for argument's sake, say that some of that activity Mr. Uttman testified to is accurate. If it were, then he'd be incriminating himself. For example, we researched the allegation that employees were destroying radios and there is simply no evidence that he either presented, or that we could find to document, that he ever reported fraud or sabotage while employed at Kratos. We interviewed all the members of his team, and none of them can verify his claim that they participated in an investigation that found fraud and sabotage."

McCastle responded, "What possible reason could Mr. Uttman have to lie?"

"I don't know. Maybe revenge for losing his job. Maybe the millions of dollars he would receive if the whistleblower allegations result in criminal penalties. Maybe for immunity for himself." Steve paused and again looked each senator in the eyes. It was important that they heard the other side of this story. Some senators were paying attention. Some were checking their smartphones or talking to aides without much interest in what Steve said. "I'd like to turn now to other specific allegations Mr. Uttman has made."

Senator Shankle broke in. "No. Stop right there, Mr. Holmes. Your inquisition has gone far enough. When we want your input on something, we'll ask the questions."

Steve interrupted the senator. "I was told that I had ten minutes to make any comments I wanted, Senator."

Shankle shouted, "I don't need you or your high-paid lawyer to cross-examine Mr. Uttman's testimony! He earned his right to speak without being shut up by the likes of you!"

Steve was prepared for the bullying tactics and responded calmly. "It is precisely because we cannot cross-examine Mr. Uttman that I want to address the unsubstantiated allegations he made."

"I don't want to hear it, Mr. Holmes. You don't make the rules here, I do!" The senator flipped his microphone away from him, pushed back from the table, crossed his legs, and rocked back in his chair, glaring at Steve.

Steve watched Harper McCastle, who was looking at Alex Shankle during his rant. He could tell McCastle agreed with Shankle's sentiments until he said he made the rules. Then there was just a small change in her expression, a tightening of the lips, and furrowing of the brow. McCastle looked at Holmes, then back at Shankle. It was an uncomfortable moment in the room as she stared at Shankle, then turned back to Steve. "Given the latitude we gave Mr. Uttman in his opening statement, I will give Mr. Holmes the same courtesy."

Steve thought, *Hell, yeah! Thatagirl! Finally, some fairness is creeping into these hearings.*

"What kind of three-ring circus are you running here, madam? I'm the Chairman of the Senate Armed Services Committee; I don't take shit from anyone," Shankle said in frustration.

McCastle responded with excellent poise. "It is a McCastle circus and not a Shankle circus, sir. I make the rules on this subcommittee, not you. Mr. Holmes, you may continue." McCastle was often quoted as saying she was privileged to have Shankle's guidance in her political career, but her glare at Shankle seemed to say she was just his junior senator, not his bitch.

The side conversations by the senators stopped and one senator began examining the systems and training documentation Steve had provided.

"Thank you, Madam Chairman. First, I'll address the allegation of fraud. We work to prevent any fraud through corporate policies and procedures emphasizing ethical behavior, new employee and recurring ethics training, employee honesty and integrity certifications, checks and balances through regular audits, and emphasis from all Kratos leadership in meetings and communiqués. Nonetheless, some employees will still try to break the law. When that occurs we fully support the data gathering and prosecution of the criminals involved."

Picking up a separate stack of papers, Steve continued, "Second, as to the allegations of inadequate systems and improperly trained staff, the evidence is strongly to the contrary. All critical Kratos financial systems, including time-keeping, procurement, and accounting, have been certified by the government's DCMA. We have an overall training manager and she provided you with the technical and business certifications and training dates for all our people. In every case, that training meets or exceeds both the contractual requirement and the U.S. industrial code.

"Finally, as to the failure of equipment, I'd like to walk through a systematic examination of each possible cause for the equipment failure, focusing specifically on the Neka convoy." Steve produced a chart summarizing the potential causes and the evidence for/against each. "Could it be simply normal failure of the equipment? The Army and Air Force tested all systems employed in the Neka area. Other than the lack of long-range communication with Mashad and those between the ground forces and AWACS for a relatively brief period, all other equipment in the area operated appropriately.

"Could the problem be a lack of proper operation of the equipment? In addition to the certified Kratos staff, all operators had proper training, government and contractor alike, and no instances of improper operation during this attack were identified. This finding was based on a review by the Air Force.

"Could the problem be sabotage by Kratos' employees? There is no evidence, beyond Mr. Uttman's general allegation, which is unsubstantiated, about this sabotage. It would be impossible for anyone operating the equipment in each of the separate trucks on the ground to simultaneously turn it all off at once without an electronic jammer, which AWACS didn't detect. Again, the Army investigated and found no evidence of sabotage by ground personnel."

McCastle said, "If it wasn't the equipment, human error, or sabotage, what do you think caused the failure?"

"I didn't say it couldn't be sabotage. I do think sabotage is a likely cause of the equipment failures during the Neka attack." Steve now had the full and undivided attention of every senator, except Senator Shankle, who appeared uninterested as he thumbed his iPhone.

"Having eliminated all the probable causes, we're left with the improbable likelihood that someone inside the military communications design, development, operations, or maintenance regime intentionally sabotaged communications."

McCastle said, "No one has suggested sabotage by someone inside the military establishment. What makes you think that happened?"

"This disruption occurred at the precise time and location of the Neka convoy attack. Think about how complex that would be to coordinate. This communications disruption could only be caused by someone who knew where the convoy would be, where the Iranian mujahideen fighters would be, and when they would all be at the same location."

The senators were listening now, taking notes, and focusing on the discussion. Some of their aides were updating their blogs with developments. Members of the gallery were getting out short text messages through social media.

"How would an insider pull this off?"

"He would've needed an inside technology expert with access to AWACS systems to cause the equipment failure. And an intelligence contact to make sure the Iranians and convoy were at the same place at the same time. In today's compartmented military organization, those would not be the same person. Since the Neka convoy wasn't planned until one week before the attack, it is highly likely that one saboteur had access to the convoy schedules while another was knowledgeable about AWACS operation. And since that sabotage benefited the mujahideen, it leads to the inevitable conclusion that foreign saboteurs were involved in the communications failure."

Steve sat back in his chair, scanned the panel members, and sighed with relief. Senators and their staff were busy typing notes or discussing his testimony. For the first time, they appeared to consider an insider as a likely suspect in the sabotage and foreigners as the potential saboteurs. Everyone except Shankle. The sweat beading up on Shankle's brow betrayed his concern.

Shankle said, "Mr. Holmes, that was some fantastical storytelling. You should write fairy tales for a living. With your high-priced legal team and deep corporate pockets you clearly fabricated a story aimed to sway this panel. But I'm not swayed one bit. Let's explore your testimony, just a little." Shankle looked around the room and smiled. "Please answer my questions with a simple yes or no, Mr. Holmes. You said there was no evidence of fraud or sabotage against Kratos, is that correct?"

"Yes."

"Now, Mr. Holmes, DCAA has identified one point eight billion dollars of fraud in your contracts with the military, but you say most of it is unfounded. You are willing to accept that some of your employees might have committed crimes. You clearly don't mind letting your poor, defenseless employees take the blame for crimes your company commits. Now, I'd like a simple yes or no answer to my question, Mr. Holmes. Did Kratos pay five hundred fifty thousand dollars for fraudulent accounting practices in twenty-nineteen?"

Steve knew where that figure originated. Shankle was adding all the payments Kratos made in 2019 to settle claims by DCAA for work totaling over $600 million dollars. That $550,000 represented less than one-tenth of one percent of the claims. Agreeing to some small payment without admitting guilt allowed the DCAA investigator to save face and companies could move on. Otherwise, DCAA had absolutely no incentive to ever closeout an investigation and corporate leaders would remain bogged down with investigations rather than running their businesses.

"That settlement is one-tenth of one percent—"

Shankle cut him off. "A simple yes or no, Mr. Holmes!"

"Those settlements are—"

"Yes or no!"

"Can you provide detail on the claims?" Maybe Steve could expand the discussion to show the rationale for settlements.

"I'll do the questioning, Mr. Holmes, not you. If you refuse to answer the question, I can have the documented evidence presented here to show that Kratos did, in fact, pay the five hundred fifty thousand dollars in twenty-nineteen for fraudulent charges on their MANCAP contract. I know admitting the truth feels like a basketball slammed in your face, Mr. Holmes." Shankle stared at Steve with a look of satisfaction.

"You can't show fraud, Senator, because it didn't happen!"

"The panel will take your attempt to sidetrack the discussion rather than answer the question as a yes. Let's move on to a question about your motives to commit fraud and sabotage, Mr. Holmes. I see from the most recent Security and Exchange Commission's required Proxy Statement for Kratos that you take home over four million dollars a year. Do you think that compensation is fair when your average employee in Iran takes home less than one hundred thousand dollars a year?"

"You're comparing apples and oranges, Senator. Over half of that total compensation figure you show for me is an estimate based on how Kratos' stock will perform in future years, which right now isn't looking good. The one hundred thousand dollars you mention is the employee's annual salary, a hundred percent of which is paid out in the calendar year."

"Of course you're embarrassed to be challenged on your pay, Mr. Holmes. I understand that. But, don't dodge the question. Is it fair?"

"It is neither fair nor unfair. It is what the market demands."

"Don't avoid the question, Mr. Holmes! Fair or unfair?"

"Okay, it's fair in a free-market economy, but unfair in a socialist society." The only part of that answer that would make the news is that Steve Holmes, Kratos executive, said his multi-million dollar salary was a fair wage despite the fact that the people who worked for him in a war zone made orders of magnitude less.

"As I look at the financial reports for Kratos, Mr. Holmes, I am shocked at the hundreds of millions of dollars pocketed every year to pay exorbitant salaries for fat cats like you. My final question is, and I'd like a simple yes or no: Is your company motivated by profit?"

Beaten down by the senator, Steve lost the will to try to explain the many reasons for a company to exist, including being the engine for prosperity. "Profit is of course one reason public companies exist."

"Madam Chairman and fellow committee members, I want to note that after direct questioning, Mr. Holmes has admitted that Kratos has committed fraud. They have a clear profit motive for their behavior. I am proud to have led the charge to protect our citizens from the greed of the military-industrial companies. Our president has recklessly wasted taxpayer's money and the lives of soldiers in order to garner votes and financial contributions for his party. We are nothing short of a country at war with private sector profiteers who would sell out our freedom at any price. I will continue to champion the fight against these profiteers."

After another hour of questioning from other senators, the hearing adjourned. Alex Shankle was mobbed by reporters who were yelling questions and sticking microphones in his face as he exited the hearing.

"Senator, have you seen the headlines for the afternoon papers?"

The AP reporter held up the paper with the headline in large font, "KRATOS ALLEGES FOREIGN SABOTEURS WHILE SENATOR SHANKLE ACCUSES PRESIDENT OF MISMANAGEMENT."

"There are no foreign saboteurs. That is a ridiculous attempt by Kratos to shift blame. The real story is the president's handling of the war. The American people need to get outraged to get us out of this war."

19

Baghdad, Iraq

The Predator drone was loitering silently above the block and mortar building like so many others in this dusty, dirty part of Baghdad. The infrared signatures of the two Americans from Oklahoma City had been easy enough for Predator to follow in the tortuously slow streets from the Baghdad airport to Sadr City as their vehicle stopped at the many checkpoints throughout the route. What these two Americans from Oklahoma City were doing here was a more difficult matter to determine.

The FBI had started monitoring the mosque in Oklahoma City after several of its members had joined ISIS fighting in Syria. They'd tracked several of the Muslims who regularly traveled back and forth to Iraq. The CIA was called in for assistance when foreign agents entered the picture.

There was an informant in the room when Muqtada Al Sadr greeted the two Americans. Muqtada said in Farsi, "*Salâm aleykom*, and welcome back, my brothers."

"Allah is great and has protected us as we traveled from the home of the infidels, Sayyid," said the older American who did the talking for both of them.

"I want you to meet Amir Ahmadi, my brother from Iran. We can help the mujahideen defeat the infidels through Amir."

The guests were served small cups of traditional sweet tea with cardamom by Al Sadr's servants. After some social discussion, the Americans returned to their purpose for the trip.

The American said, "We have a believer, Sayyid, who can help us ambush the American beast?"

Amir asked, "Is this where we have gotten the information to attack the American trucks?"

"It is. But those attacks were minor compared to what else he can do."

Al Sadr said, "You have done well. Allah will reward you. Let us eat, then you and Amir can talk of targets."

Quantico, Virginia

Army Criminal Investigation Division, CID, Captain Catherine Murphy, placed the noise suppression ear protection in place, and affixed her goggles so they fit snuggly on her face as she prepared to maneuver through the firing range at Quantico.

She removed the Sig Sauer P228 pistol from her shoulder holster and, pointing it into the weapons clearing barrel, slid the empty clip out of the pistol handle, loaded the thirteen 9mm blank shells, reinserted the clip, and then slid and released the slide to chamber the first round. She was ready for the simulated shooters in the blank-fire search-and-clear practice facility. The team systematically searched the practice facility from the ground floor up, sequentially moving, covering, and clearing each room.

As Murphy finished her training and removed her goggles and hearing protection, she saw the contractor for her ten hundred appointment walking into the CID Major Procurement Fraud Unit weapons training building. After unloading her weapon and walking into the visitor's area, she extended her hand, and said, "Thank you for coming, Mr. Holmes. I appreciate you driving down from DC to meet me."

Steve Holmes replied, "It's not every day that I meet at a shooting range."

"I have to keep my weapons training current. Going back into DC for a meeting would have cost me an entire day. Please have a seat. We have an ongoing investigation into a fraud case involving a munitions supplier in Iran, and we need some help immediately. The blanket ordering contract we have with Kratos allows the CID's Fraud Unit to get specialized contractor support at a fixed hourly cost to the Army."

"Yes, we can provide support. You tell me the requirement and I'll get the people to support you."

"I'll give you some information now, with a more detailed brief to follow once we have the task order in place with Kratos. I don't want the names and activities of these alleged criminals to leak out because too many people are involved."

"I understand that, Captain Murphy. I just need enough information to help me find the right people to support you."

It was a busy morning at the weapons training center. There was a steady flow of CID agents coming and going as Steve talked with Catherine in the waiting area lounge.

"We are investigating Army munitions suppliers and Army contracting officials that may be providing ammunition illegally from embargoed countries in exchange for bribes and kickbacks. The prime Iranian contractor, First Persia, is not delivering the quantity of 5.56 mm ammunition it contracted for. As the lowest bidder on the Rock Island munitions contract, First Persia committed to supply nearly ten percent of the Army's small ammunitions requirement. We suspect their Hungarian manufacturer, Loszer Vallalat, is buying Chinese manufactured ammunition to fill their ammunition shortage—an ally of Iran and a country on the U.S. Embargo List. Loszer Vallalat is running the blockade. The ammunition is manufactured in China, secretly shipped to Hungary, and then trucked into Iran. And, we suspect there are some bribes by subcontractors going to the Army's Rock Island contracting officer to cover up the shortages."

"Why would China, an ally of Iran, sell us ammunition?"

"Not only does China supply poor quality ammunition, but they ensure there are shortages, which may enable them to influence the outcome of the war."

"What kind of help are you looking for?"

"You'll be tracing the money coming from China. That means banks, wire transfers, surveillance, and criminal investigation support. We'll work the Army procurement side of the investigation. I'll lead the investigation with an experienced financial fraud investigator to support the overall effort. We'll need you to supply the rest."

"Just off the top of my head, I think you're talking about expertise in international finance, money-laundering, some technical experts, and some clerks, accountants, and finance specialists. I have an experienced money-laundering investigator just coming off another project. His name is Neal Blum. He worked for the FBI on financial fraud and money-laundering cases after graduating from college with a degree in International Finance. After leaving the FBI, he worked in the banking industry. He worked with all the major world banking centers. He would be the right person to lead Kratos' side of the investigation."

"Neal sounds like a good choice. I want your involvement as well, Steve. Not only are you qualified with your FBI experience, but having you will ensure I'm getting the best people from Kratos when the work demands someone immediately."

"I can support the project, Captain Murphy, but I won't have time to run it. Neal will do that."

"You may change your mind about how much time to spend on this project when I tell you one other aspect of the company we're investigating. It's been reported that First Persia was the only supplier to withdraw their cargo from the Neka convoy after the scheduled trip was moved up by one day."

"You think they knew the convoy would be attacked?"

"They could have been tipped off, maybe they played a role in the attack, or maybe it was just coincidence. If we follow the money trail, it may lead to the Neka convoy attack as well."

"Is the FBI aware of this investigation?"

"We informed FBI Director Elliott Stephens this week."

"Count me in!"

***

The following week Neal was on the job working with the Army. Red-haired, overweight and speaking with a Texas drawl, Neal much preferred to live on his vast Texas ranch tending his longhorn cattle. He did spend his weekends on the ranch, horseback-riding across the two hundred acres, herding the cows from one field to another or shooting coyotes that his donkeys didn't scare off. If the donkeys were nearby, they'd bray, paw the ground, chase after and kick the coyotes with such ferocity they protected the cattle. Neal expected to retire to his ranch someday, but for now he still had to earn a living.

A routine check of the reports from the Financial Crimes Enforcement Center, FinCen, didn't reveal any payments from the Hungarian company to Norinco, the suspected Chinese ammunitions manufacturer, in violation of U.S. law. Neither did other standard international reports. When the FBI provided assistance in tracing the financial transactions by interviewing witnesses and tracking emails and text messages, the investigation revealed that Loszer Vallalat sent the illegal payments from Hungary directly to Norinco at the People's First Bank of China. Proving that the Chinese were paying Loszer Vallalat kickbacks to buy their ammunition for the U.S. Army would be more difficult.

After several weeks of tracing the money supply, Neal and Steve went to Beijing to determine how the money moved from Norinco to Hungary for the suspected payoffs and kickbacks they were making.

Beijing, China

Neal and Steve arrived in Beijing after a fourteen-hour flight from New York. They entered China with visas stating they were supporting the U.S. embassy. They made their way to the Holiday Inn in Beijing's financial district. After freshening up, they met Catherine in the hotel lobby and ordered drinks.

Catherine summarized their task. "We proved the Hungarian munitions manufacturer violated U.S. law by doing business with a company on the Treasury's embargo list. We can bar the company from doing business with the U.S., but if we want to put the criminals in jail for a long time, we have to show there were kickbacks."

Steve asked, "Do we have anything to guide our surveillance of Norinco?"

"I think we can catch them paying kickbacks. We have a list of several known Chinese nationals here in Beijing who've made payoffs on other contracts in the Middle East. We narrowed the list down to one who's made frequent trips to Hungary recently. If we put a surveillance team on him, perhaps we can prove he's involved or makes contact with others who are involved. One way or the other, we should be able to determine how the money is getting back to Hungary."

They setup their surveillance across the street from the home of the suspected Chinese money man in a first-floor apartment inside the Second Ring Road near Beijing's Financial Street. They watched the agent coming and going frequently, sometimes carrying a backpack when he left the building, but not when he returned. He'd leave empty-handed on other trips, but return with a backpack. They decided to follow him to see where he went.

Although Steve and Neal would normally stick out among the much shorter citizens if there were only Chinese around, Beijing has become one of the most active financial centers and cosmopolitan cities in the world. The joke is: "What's the second most spoken language in Beijing?" The answer is: "Chinese." Westerners don't stand out in Beijing, especially around the Beijing Financial Street.

The Chinese agent didn't appear to be concerned about being followed. He never took evasive action as he traveled from his home to his stops in Beijing. He walked slowly, used the same trains, taxis, buses, or cars, and at similar times, and seemed to be unconcerned that anyone might follow him.

Steve and Neal followed the agent to several locations in the first week. He frequently drove his Cadillac Seville, but occasionally took a taxi to his meetings. He most often went to a lawyer's office, Ming Han. Occasionally the agent went to the Peoples First Bank of China in the financial district. It seemed likely that the agent was bringing cash to Ming Han and the bank, but they didn't know where he got the money.

Things changed abruptly the following week. On Monday morning, the agent walked quickly out his front door. Steve saw the agent and jumped out of his car to follow. A city bus was pulling to the stop in front of the agent's apartment at the same moment the agent arrived. Quickening his pace without running, Steve tried to catch the bus, but it was too late. The driver pulled off immediately after he picked up his lone passenger. Surprised by the quick getaway, Steve stood looking inconspicuously away while cursing himself for losing the agent. The agent moved around for the remainder of the week once again without visible concern for who might be following.

On the next Monday, the agent again changed his tactic. *Bam!* The backdoor slammed just after dawn as the agent raced out of his apartment and hit the sidewalk on the fly.

Steve and Neal were ready this time. Neal followed the agent to the taxi on foot as Steve drove their rental car around the block.

The agent took a shortcut through the parking lot across the road to the next street, stepped into a waiting taxi, and sped off.

When Steve saw the taxi speeding off, he picked up Neal, and they followed several car-lengths behind. As the taxi slowed to stop at a subway station, the agent stepped out of the moving vehicle and bolted down the stairs.

Neal jumped out of his vehicle and boarded the train in the car behind the agent. Neal could see the agent watching for anyone who boarded the train after him. He alerted Steve to pick up the tail when the agent got off the train at the next stop. Steve left his car and picked up the agent's trail as he departed the train station. Neal got off at the second station, stole an untended bicycle, and returned to pick up his car to rejoin Steve in the chase.

Steve was strolling well behind the agent as he walked unhurried up the street for about ten minutes. The agent stopped at a newsstand and picked up a paper. Steve had ducked into a restaurant doorway before the agent noticed him. After several minutes, the agent put the newspaper down and walked back down the street the way he had come. Steve radioed Neal to pick up the trail. Neal put on sunglasses and removed his coat to continue trailing the agent. The agent stopped frequently to look behind him, sometimes with a look over his shoulder and at other times looking at the reflection in a store window.

The agent spent two hours walking, doubling back, and hopping buses, taxis, or trains to lose anyone who might be following him. Once he was confident he wasn't being followed, he took a taxi to the Chinese military central headquarters for the People's Liberation Army, PLA, in Beijing. All its top Army commanders worked in the building. Steve and Neal watched him enter the base from across the road.

Steve stopped the car opposite the military headquarters, got out, retrieved the tire iron from the trunk, and removed the rear tire of his car, so they could watch the entrance as they worked inconspicuously. They removed the spare tire and jack from the trunk, and began to replace the tire. They took as much time as they could. When the agent departed the building an hour later, he was carrying a backpack. Quickly tightening the final lug nuts on the tire, they lowered the jack and followed the agent back to the Ming Han law office, where he departed ten minutes later without the backpack.

Steve and Neal felt sure the backpack was full of cash. The money trail went from the Chinese military to the Ming Han law office. Next, they needed to prove where the money was going from there. They took two immediate actions to get their proof. First, Catherine agreed to setup surveillance on the Ming Han law office. And, second, she would get the FBI to search FinCen again for related financial records from Ming Han.

While they conducted their surveillance the next morning, Catherine turned to Steve and Neal, and said, "The involvement of the PLA changes our approach to security. This isn't just corporate espionage. These are the big boys, and they play rough. We need a plan."

Steve agreed. "Right now, we don't know how much they're involved and what broader dealings with the Chinese military there may be. But we know they don't always play nice. Before we discuss security, Catherine, do you have yourself covered politically?"

"I notified my commander at CID and he has in turn notified the Army Chief of Staff, and also the Department of Justice. Right now, all I've been asked for are weekly reports on our activities and an immediate report if the Chinese involvement escalates in any way. I have an appointment tomorrow to inform the Deputy Chief of Station at the U.S. Embassy about our activities as well."

"It could damn sure escalate! It could blow up into an international incident if we're not careful. I'm worried about our own level of security now, too. We're dealing with people who carry guns, not ammunition manufacturers."

"We can't carry weapons over here, so you'll have to carry whatever you can find and rely on your training to protect yourself. If you get in trouble, head for the U.S. embassy. We will not engage in any offensive action."

Neal said, "Hey, I was an analyst. I can protect myself if we're attacked by a stack of intelligence reports or by a coyote back at my ranch with a gun in my hands, otherwise I'm better off giving up to any trained Chinese agent who might come after us."

Steve replied, "I'll stick close to Neal. I think we can handle ourselves."

Steve and Neal continued to watch Ming Han in Beijing. They cataloged everyone who came and went. With the help of local intelligence sources at the embassy, they were able to verify most of the visitors. The clients were commercial or government customers who didn't seem suspicious.

The next day several people left the office with packages and went directly to the Peoples First Bank. The surveillance team couldn't be sure what they were doing in the bank without examining their briefcases and bags. They couldn't verify what was happening with the suspected cash from the Chinese agent without breaking into the office and planting bugs and cameras. That evening, after the Ming Han law office closed, they all met in the hotel lobby bar for a drink where they assumed all conversations were being recorded.

Steve started the cryptic discussion. "We haven't seen any of our friends today. This trip may not prove beneficial after all."

Neal responded, "Perhaps we'll have better luck tomorrow. I'd like to get a look at the merchandise our competitors are carrying around. I just know it will be a gold mine of information if we could get our hands on it."

"We know the merchandise is carried by our friend from the government to the lawyer. We think the lawyer takes the merchandise into the bank. If we don't see our friend tomorrow, we'll have to figure a way to look at that merchandise. Perhaps there is someone in town who would sell it to us?"

Catherine responded, "I've spoken with our business associates today. They're confident they can buy our competitor's merchandise. So, one way or another, we'll get to examine it in the next few days."

The waiter came to take their order for another round of drinks. The team was suspicious of everyone, including the waiter. They watched him carefully as he moved through the bar.

After a dinner of Peking Duck in hoisin sauce, the team went to bed to get rested for another long day of surveillance.

Their break in the case came when they met with the U.S. Embassy Chief of Station, who also led CIA activities in Beijing. The CIA—Catherine's "business associates"—had an informant who was a bank official at Peoples First Bank and felt they could get the data for which accounts were being used.

Neal gave them the names and addresses of people coming and going from the Ming Han office and provided the account numbers for the Hungarian company, Loszer Vallalat. Two days later, the informant provided detailed information on the accounts.

The people coming from the law office were depositing cash in multiple bank accounts. No electronic transfers and, presumably, no paper trails to trace back to the law office or the Chinese military. There were lots of small deposits that presumably came from one large amount delivered from PLA by the Chinese agent in the backpack. Catherine called this smurfing. The accounts all belonged to shell companies setup by the lawyer. The informant also provided records of the transfer of these accounts to the Barbuda Caribbean Bank. All the accounts were numbered, so there were no names to associate with them.

The team decided it was time to close up shop in Beijing. Perhaps they would be back, but for now, they needed to follow the money to Barbuda.

20

Washington, DC

Wearing a faded and frayed baseball cap and dark sunglasses, Alex Shankle walked slowly as he approached the Washington Monument from the direction of the Capitol Building. As he strolled through the mall, he turned and looked at the museums, back toward the Capitol or just at tourists passing by, watching carefully for anyone who might be observing him.

Jodie Arenas approached from the opposite direction on Constitution Avenue, wearing a floppy hat and carrying a White House tourist shopping bag. They sat on a bench at the base of the monument, far away from other visitors so their conversation would not be overheard.

Mid-morning was a quiet time on the Washington Mall; too early for most tourists and too late for people driving to work.

Shankle spoke without looking at Jodie. "We have to do something to fire up public condemnation of the war, or I'll never get back in the presidential race."

Arenas said, "I think we're strong when we exploit the setbacks in the war and get public support to blame Rubina. The hearings last month helped us focus more attention on the contribution contractors are making to the problems. But, it doesn't feel like a ground swell right now."

Shankle looked around to see if anyone had recognized him or was watching. Satisfied they were not being observed, he continued, "We've got the typical antiwar protesters, the isolationist Libertarian activists, and left-wing liberal supporters. That's hardly mainstream America. We need something to get the general mass of voters behind our campaign."

Jodie reached into her briefcase and pulled out a copy of the *London Chronicle* from the day before. "Take a look at this article and tell me what you think, Alex."

Shankle sat down, put on his reading glasses and read the first part of the article. "It says Sir Angus Pringle, the Liberal Democratic Leader, is against the war. I was aware of that."

Jodie rolled her eyes at Shankle's tendency to not read much beyond the title of a story before he jumped to conclusions. "Keep reading, there's more to the story."

Shankle took a few extra minutes to read the entire article. "Sir Angus is very critical of President Rubina. I like that. It doesn't say how much support he has for his views with the British public, though."

"The polls in London show the British citizens are against an expansion of their role in the war. They don't want their government to commit ground combat troops. The Liberal-Democrats are campaigning against the Anglo-American aggression and what they are calling a new era of colonialism. The Archbishop of Canterbury has been speaking out against the war from the very beginning. He's starting to get more public support. The antiwar protesters are becoming more vocal and visible as President Rubina pressures

Europe to take a more active role. If we can channel that dissatisfaction toward Rubina and fuel even greater U.S. dissatisfaction, we'll pick up more supporters."

Shankle tore the article out of the *Chronicle* and wrote a note on it before looking up at Jodie again. "Get our staff working on this. I want to know how deep this sentiment goes with Britain's political leaders."

"I'll start with my friends in the media. They need to re-run the *Chronicle* story and get their editors talking about the growing dissatisfaction with the war. And we can use social media to drum up support."

"What about our other allies? Israel's Prime Minister, Menachem Peres, has talked about conducting negotiations. How wide-spread is the dissatisfaction for the war in Israel?"

"Peres's father got the Nobel Prize for peace in nineteen ninety-four for the Oslo Accord. Peres junior is seen as a dove in his country, just like his dad. The minority Labor party feels the allies have already accomplished their goals by wiping out Iran's nuclear capability in the first months of the war. They are clamoring for peace negotiations. And there is a growing peace movement among the Israeli people. Polls show the majority of its citizens think the war should end."

Shankle continued to make notes on his newspaper. "I think we can use the dissatisfied factions in England and Israel to increase the U.S. focus on Rubina's mishandling of the war. Many of our conservative politicians are particularly attuned to Israeli concerns. That can help our cause."

Jodie pulled out her smart phone and started thumbing the screen. "There is a meeting in London next month among the coalition heads of state. Perhaps you should attend in your role as Chairman of the SASC?"

"I agree, but we should keep my attendance low key. Let's try to get meetings with Sir Angus and President Peres's staff while we're in London." Shankle pulled Jodie close to him. She responded by molding her body firmly into his. "The time alone will do us both some good."

After a long moment, they remembered where they were and separated.

Shankle had one more topic he wanted to cover while he was away from anyone who might overhear. "What about our Chinese friend? Is he in any danger of exposure?"

Surprised at Shankle's mention of the Chinese, Jodie said, "We have been very careful. You and I are the only ones who know about them. As long as we don't slip up, no one else should know. One issue they are very concerned about is this investigation into the Neka convoy. They fear that Kratos is getting too close to the truth. It's in Kratos' interest to find someone else to blame for that disaster. With the FBI involved, others are starting to look harder for a foreign saboteur as well."

"See what our friends can do about shutting Steve Holmes up."

"I'll talk with them today."

Shankle nodded. "It was inevitable that the agencies investigating this disaster would start to consider potential foreign saboteurs. But if we build a strong enough case against Kratos, and they don't have any hard evidence to the contrary, we should be able to divert their attention away from any potential Chinese connection."

"Just relax, Al. I've got that under control. We'll show that Kratos is the saboteur. And I've been extremely careful with any communication with the Chinese. No one will ever suspect them."

"Okay. Get those meetings scheduled for me in London. Get the staff to make our travel reservations as well."

"I'll work on it this afternoon and then I'll stop by your office to show you what I've got."

"Somehow, I don't think we're talking about work anymore. I can't wait."

21

Barbuda, Antigua and Barbuda

The Barbuda Codrington Airport was small and looked deserted from the air as Steve Holmes, Catherine Murphy, and Neal Blum flew in on the small, twin-propeller engine plane from the only airline with commercial service to the island. Once inside the old and dusty airport terminal which was about the size of a sandwich shop, Catherine approached the lone transportation desk, which offered the services of one taxi, a selection of three dilapidated used cars for rent, or a guided tour of the island. Catherine rented an old Citroen car to give them the freedom to move about any time of the day. She'd have to adjust to driving on the wrong side of the road.

They had a short drive to one of the few hotels in the area. The small hotel had that laid-back Caribbean feel. A gentle southerly wind was blowing and the few servants were rushing about the hotel in sandals, flowered shirts, and straw hats to service their infrequent guests. After checking into their rooms, the three met poolside for drinks overlooking the Caribbean Sea.

With a drink in hand, Steve spoke to Catherine, "Well, we're here where we think the money trail leads. The information on who is getting this Chinese money won't likely be revealed willingly. Let's review the plan once more."

Catherine said, "First, we'll setup surveillance on the bank and see if anyone suspicious goes in or out. At the same time, the FBI is working to get the data in their own way. Any record searches will support our cover story as a married couple, with Neal as your brother. We'll check with the American Consulate in Antigua for local information on the bank and its owners."

"Let's get started right away."

"We already have. Our hotel rooms overlook the Chambers and Son law office that handles all the Barbuda Caribbean Bank transactions for the Peoples First Bank of China accounts that we're tracking. We'll take turns cataloging who comes and goes."

Steve asked, "This doesn't look like a major financial center. What makes Barbuda such an attractive place for the Chinese money?"

Neal said, "To put it succinctly, its secrecy and lax financial laws make this place attractive for offshore bank accounts, especially the shady type."

"It must be a very good secret, because I didn't notice any banks on our drive from the airport and I didn't see any big financial district."

Catherine said, "Most of the bank transactions are handled electronically, and practically anyone can setup an offshore bank for themselves. Usually, you can be open for business here in Barbuda within twenty-four hours and for very little money."

"Where does the money go when it arrives in Barbuda?" Steve asked.

"The bank is setup by a Chambers and Son lawyer as a trust company and the money flows through the trust into an electronic account, or directly into the account in another bank. You have to have at least one Antigua Barbuda citizen in the trust. The Chambers and Son lawyer often fills that role for foreign companies."

Steve asked, "What's the significance of a trust account, Neal? Why not just put the money in a regular bank account?"

"The laws in many countries, including Antingua and Barbuda's, protect the names of the owners of trust accounts. It's just a way to further hide the source of the money."

Steve said, "I'd like to take a walk around over there this afternoon. Want to join me, Catherine?"

"Let's finish our drink and go over now. Neal can take the first watch. We'll switch every four hours during the business day."

Steve and Catherine strolled casually out of the hotel and around the small group of office buildings across the street. They didn't see any activity. No cars were moving on the road and no pedestrians were walking around. It wasn't quite noon yet, and much of the business and social activities in Barbuda's nightlife centered on the bars, which stayed open until 2:00 AM. Those people slept until noon in Barbuda.

There were two cars parked next to the Chambers and Son law office.

Steve knocked on the door, looking like a tourist in his sandals, shorts, and sunglasses.

A shout from inside said, "Come in."

"Good morning, we are lost and hoped you could help us," Steve said as he and Catherine stepped inside.

The attractive receptionist with a mixed British and mild Caribbean accent, said, "It's pretty hard to get lost around there. There's not much to see or to get lost in. What are you looking for?"

"We're staying at your hotel across the road and we wanted to find a farmer's market to buy some locally grown mangoes and pineapples."

As Steve was talking, a well-dressed man stepped in from the next room and spoke with a clear British accent. Introducing himself as Jonathan Chambers, he said, "I recommend you go to the Antigua Heritage Market. They sell fresh produce and are open every day. Do you have a car?"

"Yes, at the hotel."

"The market is located across from the West Street Bus Station in town. Take All Saints Road for about fifteen kilometers and then just follow the signs to the market. You can't miss it."

"Thank you. We'll visit it today."

"Can I ask who you are?"

"I'm Steve Jackson and this is my wife, Catherine. We're from the States, here for a little rest and relaxation from our crazy business."

"What business is that?"

"We run Willy's Delight, a chain of hamburger shops in the southeast U.S."

"If you're ever interested in putting your money away where no one will know you have it, I can help you."

"Uh, well. Hadn't thought about that before. What kind of business do you run here?"

"This is a bank, or more specifically an offshore bank. I set up trust accounts for the bank."

"Yes, I've heard of those. Are they that private? If Uncle Sam twists your arm, don't you have to give them information on your accounts and depositors?"

Frowning with an insulted look in his eyes, the lawyer said, "Your money deposited here would be absolutely private. We are not a territory of the United States. I'm proud to say that we're on their Financial Crimes Enforcement Network Watch List. They keep us on that list to intimidate us into giving them information. We never will!"

"Is there complete secrecy from your own country for these accounts or can countries get information on depositors and transactions directly from the Antigua Barbuda government?"

"Information about our accounts is very restricted. That's what makes them so attractive to businesses like yours or any individual who may not want your IRS to know about all your income sources. However, if there is substantial evidence that a crime in Antigua Barbuda has been violated, then information may be disclosed to our government. That still will not entitle your government to get those records."

"Does that happen very often?"

"Almost never. We have very business-friendly financial laws in this country; it is very unusual for account information to be divulged to our government in Antigua Barbuda, let alone a foreign government."

"Well, this is all nice to know. I might be interested in an account here. We'll be in Barbuda for a few days. Let me check with my accountant, and I'll come back to see you in a day or two."

Satisfied with the contact they made with Chambers, Steve and Catherine walked back to the hotel. Catherine immediately contacted the FBI when she got back to their room. After some discussion, the FBI put a smart-phone-like device on the plane to Barbuda. Steve and Catherine picked up the device late that evening after spending the afternoon at the market buying fruits and vegetables.

Other than the mailman, Steve and Catherine were the only visitors Neal saw go into the law office that day. The next morning, Steve and Catherine went back to the office. They sat down with the lawyer and opened an account. After the paperwork was completed, Steve and the lawyer walked to the receptionist's desk to get copies made while Catherine was supposed to call their accountant with the wiring instructions.

Watching the half-opened office door carefully, Catherine used the FBI electronic device to clone the information from Chambers' smartphone left on top of his desk. It was all done wirelessly and in seconds. The electronic device also planted a little malware on the lawyer's phone as Catherine suspected that it would be used to access bank accounts. Catherine pretended to look for a pen as she gave the wiring instructions on her phone and walked around the room to plant a small microphone under the lawyer's desk.

Later that day, they met Neal for lunch at the hotel. There had been one other visitor to the law office that morning, but their database didn't identify the local businessman as anyone suspicious. They discussed their day, then decided it should be Steve and Neal who met the American Consular Agent in Antigua for a local intelligence briefing that Catherine had arranged. The Consular Agent would provide more insight into the local banking and crime networks.

There was a knock at her door while Catherine was watching the law office from her hotel room. Expecting Steve and Neal, she simply opened the door. Two muscular goons pushed the door back and shoved Catherine back into the room.

The older man spoke English but with a heavy Caribbean accent. "Who dee fock ah you, lady?"

Shaken, but looking for items she could use as a weapon, Catherine asked, "Who are you? What is this all about?"

"Shut up, woemon! Bote you ah snoopin' roun' heeya. Whad you wan?"

With a fake nervousness, she replied, "I-I'm here on vacation with my husband. We visited the market yesterday and went to the beach here at the hotel."

"You lie woemon! Gimme dee purse."

The goon dug through her purse, taking out her passport, which

ID'd her as Catherine Jackson. Finding nothing unusual, they turned back to Catherine. "Yo mon at dee consolad! Whad he do?"

"His passport is about to expire. He's ordering a new one, to be picked up when we get back to America. I expect him back any second!"

The man picked her up and put his face against hers. "If you lie to me beetch, I kill ya. Tell ya mon is time ta go hom. Or else, I beat ya good." The goon threw Catherine down and they left her room.

Catherine immediately grabbed a floppy hat, sunglasses, and a shawl to cover her blouse. She peeked out the door to see the men enter the elevator, then ran down the stairs in time to see them walk through the lobby and out the door. She got a good cell phone picture of both. They got into a black SUV and drove to the Chambers and Son law office across the road.

Catherine called Steve to warn him of the danger while he was out of the hotel. She then went back to her hotel room to straighten up and continue surveillance. Just in case, she put a metal fire poker and steak knife within reach for protection.

When Steve and Neal returned that evening, they all concluded that Chambers suspected their cover story. They'd continue their surveillance, but would stay together for better security.

The FBI used the pictures of the goons to confirm they worked for the lawyer. Their arrest records for assault and larceny from INTERPOL showed them to be as they appeared, local muscle.

Steve had the morning watch the next day. It was quiet until a Chinese visitor entered the law office just after eight. Steve recognized the Chinese agent as the one they followed in Beijing. He called for Catherine and Neal. Steve watched him go in, and then two minutes later they heard him talking in Pidgin English with the lawyer through the microphone Catherine had planted.

"How our transactions going?" the agent asked.

"As usual, all monies deposited this week have been credited to the trust accounts."

"Is very important to my government to keep transactions secret."

"We pride ourselves on the utmost secrecy for our clients. Our banking regulations were drafted by an offshore banker, ensuring we took advantage of all Barbuda loopholes. There have been very few cases where Antigua Barbuda shared banking records with any other country."

"*Hão*. Make sure Chinese account don't become exception."

"The Chinese government is not identified as an owner or associate of any of the accounts we manage for you. Deposits come through legitimate businesses or shell companies. Money is deposited into trust accounts. I assure you that no one will know you're involved."

Apparently satisfied, the agent pressed on, "Anyone snoop around here asking questions about Chinese government?"

"No one has asked questions. I had one couple in here this week that also made a visit to the American Consulate in Antigua. We checked them out and everything is clean. They even opened a new account with us."

"What names?"

"Steve and Catherine Jackson from Florida."

"You have picture and address?"

"Yes. I'll have my secretary provide it to you on the way out."

"Keep eye on them. Make sure get message they being watched."

"We have already taken care of that. Anything else I can do for you?"

The team could hear a chair sliding back and paper rustling through the hidden microphone.

"I leave envelope with agreed fee for you. I trust this satisfactory to keep operation going?"

"Of course, I appreciate your business and I can assure you, you will remain anonymous."

"I go back to airport now. I take information on your visitor."

The Chinese agent left the office after Chambers provided him the pictures and addresses for the Jacksons. Steve followed him back to the airport, where he boarded a plane and departed Barbuda. Steve thought: *So, a quick trip in and out and a personal payment for services. This must be an important operation for the Chinese.* Regardless, the visit proved the link between the Chinese military and the accounts in Barbuda.

The next day, the American consular agent had a coded message delivered to Catherine. It was the information on the Barbuda Caribbean Bank accounts that the FBI had hacked into. The FBI used the malware planted on the lawyer's smartphone to exploit a weakness in the older version of the Unix operating system the bank used to manage its accounts electronically. As they suspected, the lawyer used his smartphone to access the bank records. With that direct connection and the passwords he saved, they were able to hack into the system and transmit the data from his phone to the consulate through local cellular networks. The bank accounts provided a lot more information than they expected for one account holder. Steve looked forward to discussing the information with Sherry back in DC.

The munitions case was solved. Loszer Vallalat was buying illegal ammunition from the Chinese manufacturer, Norinco, and they were being paid illegal kickbacks by the Chinese government. The corruption stopped at Loserz Vallalat. There was no evidence to suggest either First Persia or the Rock Island contracting officer had any knowledge of the illegal purchases or kickbacks.

With their business in Barbuda completed, Steve, Neal, and Catherine packed up the next morning and got in their car to drive to the airport. After Catherine's team had pulled out of the hotel parking lot, a black SUV cut them off, and the two goons who had attacked Catherine came out with guns drawn.

Steve told Neal to stay in the backseat as he and Catherine got out.

Confident of their ability to control the smaller Americans, the two goons, Island-dark, six foot tall, broad, hair in dreadlocks, strode directly up to each of them, guns in hand, shouting for them to stop and keep their hands in the open.

When the first goon reached Catherine, she blocked the gun he stuck in her face with her left arm and delivered a debilitating kick to his groin. The gun fired harmlessly into the car engine. Her next move was to kick the gun from his hand as he was dropping to his knees in excruciating pain.

Catherine kicked her attacker in the head. He rolled onto his back and she dropped her full weight with a knee to his abdomen and a straight jab to his throat. He was left writhing in pain and gasping for air.

Steve, moving when Catherine did, wasted no time subduing the other man. Using his off-balance weight against him as he strode in too close, Steve grabbed the goon's shirt, pulled his arm forward while firmly holding the gun hand, rolled the man over his hip into the ground and slammed the arm against Steve's knee to release the weapon. Twisting the arm around as Steve was crouched over the goon, Steve said, "Next time you lay your hands on a woman, try to be a little more kind, asshole." Then, Steve stood up and stomped on the man's head, incapacitating him.

Steve and Catherine tied the men up, dragged them over beside the SUV with Neal's help, left them for their friends to find and continued to the airport.

Washington, DC

Sherry picked up Steve at National Airport when he arrived back from his trip to Barbuda. They went to MacGregor's Irish Pub in Old Town Arlington to discuss Shankle's involvement with the Chinese.

After Steve got an Irish Coffee and Sherry got some iced tea, they talked about his trips.

"We hit the jackpot. We traced payments made by the Chinese military to Alex Shankle's bank account in Barbuda, and there were contributions from the Chinese PLA to a SuperPAC for the 'Election of President Shankle.'"

"Well, there it is. Shankle's dirty. How much did they give him?"

"Tons. The payments total hundreds of millions of dollars. No country throws around that much money without expecting something significant in return."

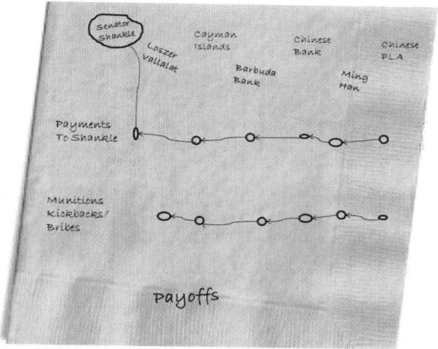

"How do you know for sure it's the Chinese?"

"I'll trace the money flow on this bar napkin for you. The money path is confusing, but the most important thing to know is that Army CID traced the money paid to an account in Shankle's name back to the Chinese People's Liberation Army. That's the same source that paid kickbacks to the Hungarian munitions supplier, Loszer Vallalat."

"Was there any relationship between Vallalat and Shankle?"

"Just their money source in China. We watched a known Chinese agent living in Beijing carry money from the Chinese PLA to a Chinese lawyer, Ming Han, who laundered payments to Vallalat. We followed this agent and he always carried cash to this law office. No electronic transfer and, presumably, no paper trail."

"What was in it for the PLA?"

"To slow down munitions and deliver poor quality rounds, I suppose. They also got a cut of the money our government paid Vallalat. We didn't see the munitions money go back to the PLA, but we're sure it did. Ming Han then made large cash deposits, which were broken up into dozens of accounts at the Peoples First Bank of China. Law enforcement calls that smurfing."

"The Chinese bank wouldn't just tell you all that."

"No. The CIA bribed a bank official to provide us information on these deposits. The official also provided records of the transfer of these funds to trust accounts at the Barbuda Caribbean Bank. Barbuda is on the U.S. watch list for the risk of money-laundering and other violations of international law. All the accounts were numbered, so there was no one to associate with them."

"This is why you spent a week on a tropical island?"

"It wasn't so I could work on my tan. The Barbuda bank transferred the money from these accounts to the Cayman Islands for Alex Shankle and the SuperPAC. We recorded the lawyer in Barbuda discussing the accounts with the Chinese agent from Beijing for added confirmation of the Chinese government's involvement."

"How did you know which accounts the Barbuda bank was

transferring?"

"Your friends at the FBI hacked into it to trace the trust accounts. With a little help from a bug Catherine planted in the lawyer's phone, they were able to exploit a weakness in their operating system to extract the account information."

"Did you hack into the Cayman Islands bank to get those records as well?"

"We didn't have to. The Cayman Islands have agreed to international standards and they cooperate in reporting funds coming from banks on the U.S. Treasury's watch list. That's how we determined that much of this money was going into Shankle's and the SuperPAC's accounts. There is no good, legal explanation for that money."

"Okay, Steve, we'll run with that information. I'll get with CID and the FBI personnel to get that account information tomorrow. We'll do further analysis to catch Shankle taking the money out of his bank."

"I look forward to watching the FBI take him down." Taking the last swallow of his coffee, Steve put the glass down and said, "On a happier subject, when can I see you again?"

"I'm in town all week. Check your schedule and let's go out."

"I'd like that. I'll text you with the day and restaurant."

22

Washington, DC

Sherry Adkison walked out of her office on a mild summer afternoon at FBI headquarters in Washington, got into her vintage 1960 Chevy Malibu, and left work, looking forward to her date with Steve Holmes. The sleek sedan with the eight-cylinder gas-guzzler engine, dark blue interior and black exterior, caught stares from drivers and pedestrians as she drove along the busy road. She had restored the car with her dad's help on weekends during college and had driven it ever since. Cruising in the Malibu around Washington made her trips in heavy traffic a little more tolerable.

Sherry turned off U.S. Hwy 1 in Arlington looking for a convenient on-street parking place as the end of the workday traffic departed. She had a few minutes to freshen up before her dinner with Steve. They both said they liked the authentic Chesapeake Bay crab cakes served at McConnell's Restaurant.

Sherry found herself missing Steve when they were apart, thinking about him most of the time. She was attracted by Steve's kindness, honesty, and big brown eyes. Seeing Steve often in the last few months, Sherry saw the same sense of fairness and empathy in dealing with people that she tried to have. It wasn't just what they had in common, including the FBI background, but the differences as well that she loved. Steve was trusting of people, maybe sometimes too trusting, she thought. Coming from a large family, Steve was more open, more apt to talk about problems he encountered or mistakes he made than Sherry was. Steve would talk about his alcoholic father openly, while Sherry discussed her family only with her closest friends and family. Whatever the chemistry was, it was strong and Sherry was happier than she could ever remember being.

Sherry requested a booth facing the front entrance and slid into her seat to wait for Steve. Her cell phone rang as she sat down. It was a *Washington Chronicle Observer* reporter Sherry occasionally used when the FBI wanted to spread some information.

"Agent Adkison, I wanted to get your comments on the story we ran today about the virus the Air Force discovered in their AWACS systems." Sherry had read the story that morning and was surprised how quickly after the Air Force found the bug that the *Chronicle Observer* knew about it.

"No comment."

"Not even a denial?"

"Why are you asking me? Why not call the Air Force?"

"The Air Force wouldn't comment. A friend told me that you are the lead FBI investigator for the convoy attacks involving failed communications from AWACS. After the suggestion at the recent Congressional hearings was made that the system may have been sabotaged, I thought this story might interest you."

"No comment."

"I expected that response. I'm willing to trade a little information with you."

"If I knew anything, what information could you have to trade?"

"I asked Shankle about the virus. You might want to know his response."

"I don't recall seeing any comments from the senator in your article. How did he respond?"

"Do we have a deal?"

"Let's hear what you have."

"The senator's reaction was kind of funny. I caught him alone in the Capitol as he came out of a committee meeting last evening. He acted very nervous and seemed to have a little difficulty speaking when I first told him about the virus. First, he accused me of lying about it. Then, when I showed him the article I was going to run, he emphatically denied any connection between this virus, which he claimed to know nothing about, and the Neka convoy communications failure."

"I appreciate the call. I promise that when FBI gets ready to comment, you'll be the first person I call."

Steve arrived fifteen minutes later. After parking his car at his apartment, Steve walked down the sidewalk to the restaurant in Arlington as pedestrians ran to make their connections home, whether by bus, metro, or automobile. Sherry had a pint of Guinness waiting for him. It was early, and the restaurant wasn't crowded. They could take their time and relax.

Steve sat down in the booth beside Sherry. "I hope this isn't too early to eat."

"Not at all, it's nice to get somewhere in DC before the traffic gets too heavy, and then stay there until it clears."

Steve reached across the table to hold Sherry's hand. "It's nice to have a chance to see you before I leave for London in a few days."

"China, Antigua Barbuda, and now London! You've been quite the world traveler the last few weeks."

"It comes with the job. The information we got on payoffs going to Shankle made it all worthwhile for me."

"Alleged payoffs. We're still working to confirm Shankle is receiving the money and that this is not some false identity or plan to frame him. That will be the first thing he'll claim in his defense."

"Good luck with that."

Sherry reached into her purse and pulled out the news article from the *Washington Chronicle Observer*. "You haven't read the newspaper today, have you?"

"No, I've been a little busy."

"This article reports that the Air Force discovered a virus in their AWACS communications systems. The article also indicates that it's a passive virus until it identifies its intended target. Then it's malicious."

Steve took a few minutes to read the article. "The FBI didn't know about this?"

"I didn't say we didn't know about it."

"I understand. It doesn't say what activates the virus or what the target was. There are thousands of viruses out there, most of them benign. What makes you think this is relevant to the Neka convoy?"

"Well, first, it's on the AWACS. And second, the Air Force is reacting very angrily to the release of this information. It would be embarrassing to have a cyber attack on the heart of their military communications systems. It would be unprecedented."

"Who do you think planted the virus? The Iranians?"

"Who knows? At this point, we're not ruling anyone out, friend or foe."

"Who has the capability to plant a virus like this?"

"Excluding our allies, the Russians, Chinese, North Koreans, and Iranians have been the most active countries for information warfare."

"What's your gut feel?"

"I can't see why the North Koreans would focus on AWACS right now. The Iranians would be the most likely culprits, but their infrastructure has been seriously disrupted since the start of the war. I don't see what advantage this would be right now for the Russians."

"That leaves the Chinese, who support Iran."

"Yes. We suspect the Chinese military's Third Department, Unit 61398, is funding hundreds of commercial companies to spread viruses that gather data and report information back. Some viruses have been disruptive; many have been to steal commercial secrets. We operate on the idea that there are only two types of companies in America: those that have been attacked by the Chinese and those that don't know they've been attacked. We confirmed an attack in twenty-thirteen on a U.S. company that provides software and systems to manage energy, especially power grids, and the flow of hydrocarbons around the world for many of the world's Fortune 100 companies. Another one happened in a UK company in twenty-seventeen. Our power plants, water supplies, and military equipment production facilities are among the highest priorities for any cyber enemy."

"Do you have any evidence that links this virus to the Neka convoy problems?"

"Not yet, but the *Chronicle Observer* reporter for this story just called me. He told me that Shankle rejected any relation between the virus and the Neka convoy failures."

Steve handed the article back to Sherry, with a raised eyebrow. "Really. How could he possibly know if it is or isn't the cause at this stage?"

"He can't. It doesn't fit his strategy to blame the President and contractors for the convoy failures. Perhaps he's just being political. Heck, if the FBI can't rule out the virus as the cause of the failures, he certainly has no basis for doing so. I know the reporter pretty well. He said Shankle acted like he didn't know about the virus and seemed bothered when the reporter first broke the news to him. I'll follow up and see where it goes."

Steve lifted his pint. "All the problems of the world can wait. Here's a toast to us."

With a clank of their glasses, Sherry said, "I'll toast with my tea. I guess you know our relationship isn't going unnoticed? We've been seen around Washington and people are talking about us."

"Yeah, when I told George Bird about us recently, he said he already knew. He ran into General Ron Lee in the airport on his last trip who told him. And I've gotten a couple of comments at work."

"I told my boss at FBI after our first date back in April, to see if they wanted me to step down from the case. He told me this week he's heard about it from his boss. Seems someone in Congress is worried about the appearance of conflict."

"I understand about the perception. I wouldn't want you to lose your job over this."

"No, it won't come to that. You were cleared as a suspect long ago. DC just has the fastest grapevine in the world. Everywhere we go, someone knows someone who knows us."

"Even my Facebook page says we're in a relationship. I'd like the whole world to know I love you."

Sherry reached up and gently stroked Steve's hair. "Let's enjoy our meal and then you can ride with me back to your apartment."

"I'll drink to that."

23

Pasadena, California

Ravi Cherukapally read the *Washington Chronicle Observer* article on the AWACS virus with alarm. As he sat in his office in Pasadena, California, working on yet another proposal for embedded systems development, he tried to think if anything unusual had happened when he worked on the AWACS upgrade back in 2017 to 2019. As the lead software design engineer and programmer for the upgrade, he would know if weird stuff had occurred. One incident came to mind.

He recalled one evening at the end of a long day for Ravi and his colleagues from ERP Digital Corporation when his vegetarian sub sandwich was delivered to the Hanscom AFB computer development laboratory. He'd had to gobble it down in a few bites with some mineral water, and then get back to work putting the final touches on the AWACS embedded software.

Major Abdullah Sharif stopped by as Ravi was finishing his meal. "How's it going, Ravi?"

While Ravi had supreme confidence in his own programming ability, it still intimidated him that the Air Force's program manager, who was in charge of the six hundred million dollars being spent on this program, would regularly visit him. "We'll make the deadline within our budget, Major."

"I don't care about the money, I just want it done on time. Are you sure you don't need more help?"

"No, we'll make it. I couldn't train anyone fast enough to help in the little time we have left anyway."

Seated in front of Ravi's desk, Major Sharif played with his key ring while Ravi and the remaining few programmers in the building worked. "How do you like the high-end speakers I got you?"

Ravi stopped typing and turned toward Sharif with a big smile. "The Klipsch P-39F tower speakers have incredible sound. I feel like I'm standing next to the rapper. But really, the gift was too generous."

"Not even. I give gifts to all my friends. I told you if you kept this program on schedule, I'd make sure you were taken care of. Is ERP treating you well?"

"I'll say. I got a bonus directly from the CEO last month after he got that letter of commendation from you. I think my boss is a little pissed 'cause I'm making more than he is, but he's too afraid I'd leave him to say anything."

"ERP is succeeding because they have you. This upgrade is bigger than the original design. You led the design of the architecture and modeled the software in our simulation laboratories for proof of concept. Your team coded all the communications interfaces for real-time signals. I'm talking hundreds of thousands of lines of software!"

"It's nice to be appreciated, Major. By the way, I thought I'd throw a little party at my apartment and invite some of the ERP staff and their dates. You could come by and checkout the sound of those speakers."

"Yeah, I'll do that. Do you have a date?"

"No, I'm not real good in that department."

"I know a couple girls. I'll bring your date."

When it appeared everyone else was gone, Sharif pulled a thumb drive off his key ring. "I want you to load this classified electronic warfare module into the AWACS code," he said bluntly.

"We should use the normal config and design procedures to log and test any new software."

"It has already been tested by Cyber Command. Some of the spooks developed it. They say it will operate at the machine code level and won't interfere with normal AWACS operations. It will protect the new, advanced jamming system from cyber-attack."

"As long as it's your head that rolls if anything goes wrong."

"No one else can know about the software. Trust me, nothing will go wrong."

24

London, England

Steve Holmes planned a series of Town Hall meetings with employees and performance reviews with the leaders of Kratos business in the UK, Middle East, and Australia. The trip this summer of 2020 would keep him on the road for two weeks, but it was important to keep his hand on the pulse of the organization. Steve started his trip in London to coincide with Jodie Arenas' visit; hoping a different setting away from the pressures of legislation and constituents in DC would make for a friendlier conversation. Jodie would be there to accompany the senator as he met with some of the U.S. coalition partners. Steve was anxious to find out how the senate investigation was going and what she thought about the communications virus.

Arriving in London at eight AM gave him one day to adjust to the time difference. After taking a black cab from Heathrow Airport, Steve checked into the Hilton near Tower Bridge. He liked to be close enough to walk to his meetings, and he enjoyed his jogs along the Thames River.

The afternoon drizzling rain was cold, hitting Steve's exposed skin as he started his jog along the river. He dodged the construction work, underway to widen the pedestrian walkway and improve traffic, as he ran along the smooth brick walkway under the Tower Bridge and out Lower Thames Street along its centuries-old cobblestone road. Turning around after logging a mile on his pedometer, he ran back by the Tower of London and the hotel, and down side streets until he reached London Bridge. He finished up his three and a half miles back at the hotel with a short cool-down walk in the now refreshing rain.

The next morning after a British breakfast of beans and sausages, Steve took his briefcase and walked out of the hotel and over the Tower Bridge to his meeting on Tooley Street. The pedestrian traffic was unusually busy. The nice, dry weather seemed to invite all of London to go for a walk. Once inside the section in the building temporarily reserved for the senator's business, the receptionist showed Steve into Jodie's office.

"Good morning, Ms. Arenas. Have you recovered from your flight across the pond?"

"Good morning, Steve. It's good to see you here in London. No, I haven't recovered yet, but thank you for asking. It usually takes me a night or two before I'm able to function effectively, and a week before I can sleep right. How was your trip?"

Steve was a little surprised by Jodie's unusually cordial attitude. "I was able to get a few hours sleep on the plane. Then I powered through the day without taking a nap. A jog along the Thames in the afternoon helped. Now, I'm ready to go, but I'm most effective in the morning. Sometimes when I've been here before, I've actually fallen asleep for just a fraction of a second while standing up. I'm not sure why I didn't just fall over on my face, but I never did."

"I would have paid good money to see you do that," Jodie said with a wicked smile.

"So, what's Senator Shankle doing here in London?"

There was no need for Jodie to hide the meetings. They'd be reported in the paper anyway. "There are many politicians among the coalition forces that don't like the way this war is going. The senator is meeting with some of them here in London to discuss how to make some changes or just end it altogether. If the British and Israeli people are as dissatisfied as many Americans are with how this war is being managed, we might be able to collectively bring about some positive change."

"You mean a change in policy or a new president?"

"We'll take a tactical policy change right now that will help end this war, but President Rubina will be very vulnerable in the elections later this year."

"I'm not sure about that. Rubina seems to be doing pretty good in the polls. He might not like the senator stirring up dissension."

"You may be right, Steve. Sometimes I can get polarized in my view of politics. I think like a Democrat. You, on the other hand, think like a Republican. Nonetheless, the senator is well within his duties to meet with coalition partners on matters of common concern."

Smiling a little that Jodie would agree with him so easily, Steve said, "Turning to another matter, I am interested in how your investigation into the Neka convoy is going since the hearings?"

Jodie relaxed and picked up the senator's itinerary. "Let me give you a rundown of our activities for the next few weeks. After the Congressional hearings, we've been building support for a bill that would rescind the law creating the Sponsored Reserves. The senator is calling-in many favors to get this signature piece of legislation repealed. It's going to take a lot of jawboning because the Sponsored Reserves were the president's pet initiative and he will not give it up easily."

"The broader use of contractors in combat roles and the draft have been successful in reducing the stresses on the military seen in Iraq and Afghanistan. And, the president has produced the cost savings he promised with the Sponsored Reserve Act. Why would the House approve billions of dollars in additional defense spending that would come with a repeal of the law?"

"I wouldn't expect a defense contractor to be in favor of this repeal. And don't pretend you give a damn about saving taxpayers' money."

"The cost savings are not even the most important outcome of the President's actions. Our soldiers, marines, airmen, and sailors aren't suffering the extreme levels of Post Traumatic Stress, suicides, and other mental and physical injuries that came with tour after tour in a combat zone. They knew back in World War Two that over two hundred cumulative hours of combat resulted in a high incidence rate of psychiatric illness. In Viet Nam, it was highly unusual, even viewed as extreme, for a military person to serve more than one tour in combat. In Iraq and Afghanistan, they routinely served three, four, five and more tours because we had such a small volunteer force."

"And, don't forget to mention that Kratos will make less money if we repeal the Act. Not that money is important to you," Jodie said with a condescending smile.

Ignoring the insult, Steve pressed on, "If you're successful in eliminating the Sponsored Reserves, how will you pay for the added cost of hiring and training soldiers to replace these reserves?"

"We're at war, Steve. We'll keep your ex-employees who are serving already. You just won't get contracts to employ them when they leave active duty. We'll go back to the way it was before the Sponsored Reserves when we maintained a core of expertise on active duty and standby reserves, and hired to fill in the rest when needed for war or other military contingencies."

They discussed the bill further, but did not change their opinions. Steve wanted to get on to Jodie's take on the *Chronicle Observer* story.

"Is the senator maintaining his position that the virus reported by the *Chronicle Observer* could not be the cause of the convoy communications failures?"

Jodie's eyes fixed on Steve with a penetrating stare. "That's a bunch of hogwash. Computer viruses popup all the time. There is not one shred of evidence that this virus in any way contributed to a communications blackout for the Neka convoy. Even if it were true, one person couldn't pull that off. Unless the FBI uncovers a massive conspiracy that would have to involve many people, including the senior ranks of government, I don't see how this virus could possibly be the culprit."

First with the senator's comments to the press and now here with Jodie, Steve felt they were too ready to dismiss the virus. "Why does cyber sabotage seem so unlikely? We know our enemies are engaging in the same techniques we are. We've caught them doing it."

"Yes, they've penetrated weak private company firewalls. And they've penetrated some superficial levels of government websites, but they've never demonstrated the sophistication and coordination for this kind of attack on hardened military systems."

"The reporter at the *Chronicle Observer* thinks the virus and convoy attacks are connected."

"Perhaps your girlfriend thinks it is suspicious, and she leaked the story? There is no proof, and until there is, the senator will continue to keep the focus on Kratos as the culprit."

Steve raised an eyebrow and paused for a moment, realizing Jodie was paying a lot of attention to who he saw and what he did. He said, "And how is that going?"

"You can expect more hearings, and you can bet your bottom dollar the Department of Justice will be looking at you."

The two discussed the investigation for another half-hour. As he got up to leave, Jodie said, "Let me call you a taxi. I notice that it has started to rain out there."

"I appreciate your offer, but that won't be necessary. I can walk down to the bus stop on the Thames and get to my hotel that way." After Steve had left the office, Jodie made a hurried call.

Upon leaving Jodie's London office on Tooley Street, Steve turned onto Horsleydown Lane for a stroll down to the Thames River to think about his meeting and catch a bus back to his hotel. *Why had Jodie's behavior changed toward him?* It was strange. And Jodie had seemed disturbed about the possibility there was a virus in the AWACS.

As Steve walked along the street, he got the feeling he was being followed. He stopped to tie his shoe and look behind him, but he didn't see anything that seemed unusual. He stepped to the curb at the corner bus stop to join the short queue. There was a young family, who were obviously tourists, waving their miniature Union Jacks. Business people and local tourists made-up most of the crowd waiting. Two women carrying briefcases, a Chinese man carrying an umbrella, and several other men reading either the *Sun* or *Times* gathered to wait for the bus.

Steve was standing on the curb, looking down the street for the next bus when he was pushed from behind and felt a small stab of pain in his hip. As he turned around, the Chinese man apologized to Steve as he chastised the man next to him, saying, "Mind your step, sir."

"Pushy British. I'd rather walk!" the Chinese man said as he picked up his paper. Appearing to wrap something with the paper in his hand, he quickly walked away from Steve toward the stairs up to Tower Bridge.

The Englishman responded indignantly to Steve's questioning

stare. "I did no such thing!"

Steve saw the Chinese man look back over his shoulder at him. Sensing something was wrong without knowing what, Steve decided to follow him to see what he did. The man looked worried as he started up the stairs and glanced back over his shoulder again. As Steve got closer, the man picked up his pace.

Steve picked up his pace as well.

Steve used his hand to examine his hip as he walked quickly. Feeling a small object under his skin at the point where he had felt the small stab of pain convinced Steve that the fleeing Chinese man had poked him with something, which brought a memory up from the depths: *Georgi Markov, a Bulgarian national working for a London newspaper. He was poisoned with ricin, delivered by the poke of an umbrella. A case study at FBI training.* Steve shook his head; it was a farfetched idea that someone would try to murder him, with poison or anything else.

The Chinese man started running. Steve started running, too, and caught the assailant on the Tower Bridge. Steve dove, grabbing his legs and tackling his assailant as they tumbled down the sidewalk. The Chinese man rolled over into a crouching position and produced a ring dagger. Steve jumped aside, just in time to sidestep the knife thrust. Pedestrians cleared the street as the assailant stood up, grasping the knife handle with the sharp edge turned out. He seemed confident he could end this fight, and Steve's life, here and now. He attempted several kicks, which Steve deflected. He tried to move to Steve's right to decrease Steve's punching leverage. Steve pivoted, but maintained his defensive stance, thinking: *A man in a hurry, with a knife, is bound to attack.*

That is just what he did. He attempted to thrust his fist and knife across Steve's mid-section. Steve grabbed the assailant's knife hand, pulling his arm out and forward, stepped in close, and slammed his hip into the Chinese man, using the assailant's thrust to pull him off balance. Steve rolled the assailant across his hip, twisting the knife arm up while throwing him to the ground. Steve had a death grip on the knife hand; he wasn't letting go. They struggled with the knife as Steve beat the assailant's arm into the bridge railing. The knife dropped, falling into the river.

Before Steve could capitalize on his advantage, the assailant swept Steve's legs out from under him, and ran to the other side of the bridge, which took him over the Thames.

Steve got up and gave chase. He leaped over the railing on the last flight of stairs, and landed just behind the assailant as he ran under the bridge toward the Tower of London on the sidewalk where merchants and sailors had come for centuries to deliver supplies. He picked up a jagged-edged pipe as he ran over the sidewalk construction area, and threw it into the assailant's legs, tumbling him to the ground. The man got back to his knees just as Steve lunged at him. He grabbed Steve's arms, rolled on his back, and flipped Steve over. Then he jumped on top of Steve and began choking him while pinning Steve's arms to the ground. Steve struggled to throw the man off him, but it was almost impossible. The struggle continued until Steve was beginning to get tunnel vision from lack of oxygen. By continually bucking his upper body, Steve got the man shifted far enough forward until he could throw his legs up from behind, catching the man's head in a scissors-hold, then pulled him backward.

Steve scrambled to his hands and knees and backed away to give himself some time to get oxygen and recover from the chokehold.

The Chinese man picked up the pipe Steve had thrown and charged Steve again. Steve rolled out of the way as the man swung the pipe at his head, striking the concrete just inches from Steve's head. Steve managed to roll under a chain guard and down to the second level sidewalk. This gave him a moment to get up for the pending attack. When the assailant swung the pipe at Steve's head, Steve again stepped in to avoid the blow, blocked the swing with his arm and used the man's thrust to throw him over his hip. When the man hit the ground, the pipe bounced out of his hand and rolled several feet away.

The Chinese man swept Steve's feet out from under him and retrieved the pipe. Charging the man to disarm him, Steve was stabbed in the shoulder with the jagged edge of the pipe. With a large crowd and several bobbies moving in, the assailant had to flee.

Steve was transferred to The Royal London Hospital. When he told them about the stab to his hip and that he suspected poisoning, they put him in a secure area designed for handling patients exposed to hazardous substances. Medical workers wore protective suits and all bodily material, including blood and urine, were treated like hazardous waste. The surgeon removed the pellet from Steve's hip, then he underwent blood tests and chromosome analysis to identify the type and extent of poisoning. The pellet was tested as well. They started blood transfusions immediately as a precautionary measure.

The doctor reported that Steve was correct; he had been poisoned, but it was polonium, not ricin. Fortunately for Steve, the poison pellet had only penetrated the outer skin layers and delivered a very low dose of poison. They determined the polonium was covered in a thin, flexible lead coating to protect the assailant from radiation poisoning. The coating did not breakdown rapidly in the body. Newly developed treatment was available now that hadn't been available in 2006 when the Soviet dissident, Alexander Litvinenko, was poisoned in London. Steve received prompt blood transfusions and medication for chelation therapy to attempt to remove the polonium from his system. It would take several weeks for Steve to make a full recovery. The superficial injection, quick medical attention, and slowly dissolving lead coating saved Steve's life.

By now, it was morning in Washington, DC and a decent hour to call Sherry before she left for work.

"Hello, honey, I'm glad I caught you before you left home."

Sherry wasn't surprised to hear from Steve at this hour, since it was midday in London, but something about his voice raised her concern. "Is something wrong?"

"Sorry honey, I should have called you sooner, but I had to think for a while. I am okay, but someone tried to kill me yesterday."

"My God! What happened? Why didn't you call me immediately? And you better talk fast!"

"First, I was medicated, undergoing tests and treatment. After that, I didn't want to bother you in the middle of your night. Plus, I needed some time to sort this out. I haven't come up with a good reason why someone would want to kill me. I figured you could help."

"I'm listening and I'm still mad at you."

"The assailant was Chinese and an expert in martial arts. There is nothing in my personal life that I can think of that would cause someone to want to kill me. So, it has to be something in my professional life with Kratos."

"Okay. So, who would want to kill you at work?"

"Well, I might've made Alex Shankle worry a little. If he's figured out I helped find his elicit Cayman Island accounts, he might be concerned enough to do something. But that information hasn't been released, and I don't see how anyone would know I was involved in that investigation."

"Are you doing anything as high profile as the Neka convoy matter?"

"No."

"I can think of a few reasons surrounding Neka why someone

might want to kill you. You're having a high-profile public argument with the Chairman of the Senate Armed Services Committee, you're pushing a theory of foreign saboteurs, and you're linked to President Rubina."

"I barely know the president. We shared a podium at Arlington National Cemetary, and that's it."

"You are a prominent executive among the military industrial sector and Rubina is closely tied to that sector through the war with Iran. That's enough for some nut to want to kill you."

"Yeah, more than enough."

"The common thread seems to be the war with Iran. You've been trying to find the root cause of the communications failures. You've pushed the Army, the FBI, and Congress to look into the matter. Perhaps someone feels that if they can shut you up, the pressure will go away. I'm scared for you, Steve."

"I can take care of myself. It's the unknown I worry about more than anything else. I don't know if they'll try again or what to expect. I feel a little vulnerable here in the hospital."

"Do you mean they don't have any security there for you?"

"No, and it didn't occur to me to ask for it until just now."

"That's where I can help. You sit tight, and I'll move heaven and earth to get someone there."

Sherry hung up the phone and immediately called her British contact at Scotland Yard. An armed police officer was outside Steve's door in thirty minutes. Steve was on a flight back to DC three days later.

25

Doha, Qatar

Unhappy with their progress on the Neka convoy investigation, CID decided to put Catherine Murphy in charge of the program. After a hand-off meeting with her predecessor on the case, Catherine jumped into reading all the background material, talking to other investigators on the case, and visiting critical sites. The E-3 AWACS was high on her list of sites to visit.

As Catherine stepped off the C-17 Globemaster onto the tarmac at Al Udied Air Base in Doha, Qatar, the sheer volume of activity was overwhelming. The noise from the KC-135 tankers, F-35 fighters, C-130 gunships, and E-3 AWACS aircraft taking off and landing was loud enough to make her regret leaving her headphones at home and losing her ear plugs, to boot.

Major Abdullah Sharif met Catherine as she walked into the military airport terminal. "Well, hello, Captain Murphy. I've been looking forward to your visit ever since I heard you were put in charge. Let me get your bags."

"Thank you, sir, but I can carry my own bags. And thank you for agreeing to be my sponsor. I have a lot of questions about AWACS."

"I volunteered for the assignment. I'm fascinated by police work. Kind of view myself as an amateur detective—but don't worry, I won't get in your way."

"Not at all. I intended to talk with you anyway," Catherine said as she tried to wrestle her bag away from him.

Before the last syllable left her lips, Sharif asked, "Do you have any leads on this convoy attack yet?"

"Nothing concrete, but I don't want to discuss too much about the case. I'm here to get a better understanding of your AWACS."

"Finest bird in the air. And with its upgrades, it protects everything on land and sea as well."

"When can we go up?"

"How 'bout this afternoon?"

"Great. I'll freshen up at the VOQ and do a little work."

"I'll pick you up at fourteen hundred and you can accompany me on my pre-flight communications systems check-out."

"Whew!" she said as Sharif drove away in the staff car and Catherine stepped into the Visiting Officers Quarters. *It's exhausting talking to him.*

Three hours later, Catherine was strapped into her seat on the E-3 as it took off for a mission over Iran. Watching the two dozen operators and crew go about their job was fascinating. Dozens of display screens provided situational awareness for tactical missions being run in the area.

As soon as the wheels left the runway, Major Sharif jumped up to show Catherine all the system capabilities. "AWACS has been around since the 'eighties. It managed over a thousand sorties in Bosnia in the 'nineties. In the first days of the war with Iran, we stayed operational in the air on this bird for two weeks without landing, doing aerial refueling every eight to ten hours."

Catherine walked through the communications center, spoke with operators, and got briefed on missions and capabilities with Sharif doing much of the talking. When they got a chance to view a ground convoy mission, Catherine asked, "How do you communicate with the convoy commanders?"

"He has an FM Falcon radio in his MRAP to talk to us and a laptop where we feed him real-time information on ground and airborne threats."

The operator called the convoy commander. When he responded, an icon popped up on the operator's monitor, showing not only where the commander was calling from, but who was calling as well.

The operator pointed to the area display. "He has the same aerial picture you see here, Captain. You'd see some flashing lights if any threats were identified around there."

Without pause, Sharif said, "Have you seen our computer upgrade that presents summary reports of social media comments on the real-time missions we're running?"

"Not interested. How often are your comms with the ground commander down?"

"Almost never. They depend on us," Sharif replied.

"You mean almost never, except for the Neka convoy?"

"Yeah. I forgot that."

Surprised, Catherine asked, "Has anyone been here to ask questions about the convoy?"

"Not that I know of."

"Weren't you the operator on the console monitoring the Neka convoy the day of the attack?"

"Yes."

"I'd think you'd know if anyone talked to you about this investigation."

"Well, no one has talked to me."

"Okay, so tell me about that day. What happened?"

Slowly, after a long pause, Sharif said, "I was sitting at the front console over there watching multiple operations, including the convoy. Everything seemed fine until they got near the town of Neka. Then we couldn't communicate with them anymore."

"Is that it?"

"What do you mean?"

Trying to remain calm, Catherine said slowly and mechanically, "Were any of your other comms down at the same time?"

"Well, we couldn't reach the Army Rangers in the area at the same time. Everything outside that area was fine. I checked the incoming signals from satellites and Mashad. They were all working fine."

Catherine waited impatiently for more information, when Sharif remained silent, she said, "So, why did it happen?"

"You mean the communications outage?"

"No, the damn fumble in the Giant's game that day. Are you giving me the runaround, Major?"

"Watch your tone, Captain."

"When you are forthcoming, I'll change my tone."

"I told you what happened."

"Okay, tell me why it happened. Do you have a theory as to why no one around Neka could communicate with your AWACS?"

"It would only be speculation on my part. May I call you Catherine?"

"No."

"I seem to have gotten on your bad side."

"Not at all. You flyboys blow my skirt up."

"That sounds seductive."

"*Not at all!* Now, what's your theory, Major?"

"It had to be sabotage by someone on the ground. Everything else was working fine up here."

"I've heard that theory. Do you have another one?"

"Perhaps someone was jamming the communications with some signal we couldn't detect?"

"Is that possible?"

"With a bug in their systems, it is. Everything is digital these days."

"A bug in their ground system. I haven't heard that theory. Thank you. I'll look into it. What about the bug the Air Force discovered in AWACS? Could that have blocked the communications?"

"That's impossible. I built this advanced system, including the security software. I was the Air Force Program Manager when we built this upgrade at Hanscom AFB. No virus could penetrate it. It's not connected to the Internet, and only pre-defined, classified feeds from trusted networks are permitted."

The clickety-clack of operators typing blended with the engine noise and voices to make it hard to concentrate. Looking around, Catherine was at a loss. She wanted to probe further. She felt there was something there, something else she should be asking. Then it occurred to her. "What about the operators?"

"The AWACS operators?"

"Yeah. They enter commands through the keyboard. Why couldn't they just turn something off?"

"They could, but it would show up on the electronic log. The computer maintains a record of every key stroke they make. I believe the Air Force reviewed all logs and found no such commands."

Catherine stood, looking down as she thought.

Sharif asked, "Do you want to continue?"

"What's that?"

"Do you want to continue the tour?"

"Yes, yes, let's continue."

26

Washington, DC

Steve Holmes awoke early on the Monday morning in DC after arriving back from London. Weak from the lingering effects of the poison to his system and carrying his arm in a sling to allow the wound in his shoulder to heal, Steve took a little more time to get ready and get to the light duty he had at work. By seven-thirty AM, he was driving the short distance from his apartment to the corporate headquarters in Arlington, thinking about his eight AM meeting with Bernie Tyler.

As he approached Tyler's office, he saw Janice looking his way, not smiling. "Bernie will see you immediately."

Bernie looked up to see Steve bandaged and moving slowly. "Come in, Steve, and sit down. You look terrible. I bet the other guy looks worse," Bernie said with a sarcastic chuckle.

"It will take a while to heal."

"You look like you're getting around okay. I need you back at work full-time."

"I'm engaged by phone and computer. What's the crisis?"

"You aren't sending work to our friends at Sadik Dost like I told you. Why not?"

Steve sat down slowly, lowering himself with his right arm. "I personally met with their president and provided a list of upcoming bids after you and I talked last time. I developed a plan to increase our oversight and involvement in their work to ensure they deliver and adhere to the law and contract on things like human trafficking. But, as I explained last time, Bernie, it has to go through a competitive government process. While Sadik has won some small projects utilizing cheap Turkish and Filipino labor, they just don't have the experience to deliver on the larger, more complex projects."

Bernie stood up angrily and began to pace. "I don't give a damn about the government process! If I am going to expand our business in the Middle East for our stockholders, I need to partner with companies in the region."

Steve knew when Bernie said, "I don't care about the process," he meant, "I won't tell you to break the rules. You'll never have a piece of paper that shows I told you to break the rules. And if anyone asks, I'll tell them we always follow the rules. What I'm saying is that you should break the rules if that's what it takes to get me what I want. Then, if and when you get caught, you'll be the guilty party who pays—I'll make sure of it."

Steve replied, "Well, you may not care about the regulations, Bernie, but I certainly do. I'm not going to jail for anybody. And while we're talking about doing what's right, you replaced my financial controller without even discussing it with me. Why?"

Bernie stopped pacing. He stood above Steve with his arms folded, and said, "I put who I want where I want when I want to. I need someone to watch over your activities and report back to me. I seriously question your ability to do your job. We have the Department of Justice, Congress, FBI, UK Serious Fraud Office, and the U.S. Army Suspension and Debarment Office after us, not to mention the many civil lawsuits that are arising out of your government work. What's a little more scrutiny for getting work to Sadik Dost going to hurt?"

"Investigations from those agencies come with the territory when you're a large defense contractor doing work in a combat zone, and you know it, Bernie. And the lawsuits often arise from those who can't sue the federal government. A soldier who's injured because cancer-causing chemicals were present in an area they assaulted can't sue the military for negligence if they subsequently get sick. However, they can sue the contractor.

"Contractors are left to defend ourselves and the cases hang on for years, even decades. We have the best lawyers in the world applying arguments like the government contractor defense, derivative immunity, and the political question doctrine to defend us from these lawsuits. But those lawsuits pale in comparison to the costs, fees, and damage to our reputation you've caused with your commercial construction operations in third-world countries. Kratos had to plead guilty to fraud and paid over one billion dollars in penalties for bribery in Syria, under the Foreign Corrupt Practices Act. Our commercial consultants made illegal payments to Syrian government officials to get construction contracts after President Assad was overthrown. The claims against Kratos on the commercial side of the business are triple what we are facing with our U.S. government services business, and you know that."

"It all sounds like excuses to me, Steve. You get Sadik business, or I'll get someone who will."

Steve stood up a bit too fast and grimaced. Standing two feet from Bernie and looking directly into his eyes, he said, "You should get that person now, Bernie. I stayed in this job for a year longer than I could stand it for the same reason I joined Kratos two years ago: to support our people who are doing important work for our military at war. However, I can't work for a man who is at a minimum unethical, who would pressure his people to do something that's flat out illegal. And from the moment you questioned my honesty over statements made by Sadik Dost, I knew I wouldn't work for you much longer."

Bernie gave a slight smile and after a momentary pause, in a calm, satisfied tone, said, "You know, Steve, sometimes a guy just has to do what he has to do. It's been my experience that a resignation can often be a win for everyone. Of course, you'll need to notify the Board officially." Bernie was smirking now like he'd called a bluff.

Steve removed a sealed envelope from his sports coat inside pocket. "I have a letter of resignation for you right here, Bernie. I put a duplicate copy of that resignation in a registered mail envelope Saturday addressed to our lead director. My contract Separation Agreement with the company says I will give thirty days notice before I leave, which will be one month from today."

Steve saw what he thought was a look of admiration that replaced the smirk on Bernie's face. "That's just how I would have done it, too, Steve."

"I'll work out my thirty-day notice period and support the transition as you see fit." It was pointless to make any parting comments to warn Bernie again that what he is trying to do was against the government rules. Steve suspected there was more to Bernie's motives than he knew.

"Yeah. I'll have HR contact you."

Steve slowly walked out of the room.

27

Two days later, Steve Holmes took a taxi to FBI headquarters in Washington DC to answer questions about the attempt on his life. Exiting the taxi as close to the front of the building as he could get, Steve moved slowly from sitting to stepping out of the vehicle to standing up. His nauseous stomach churned as he slowly made the short trek into the building and through security.

The FBI agent met Steve in the lobby. "Good morning, Mr. Holmes. I'm Alice O'Neal. I've been assigned to conduct the witness interview this morning."

"Good morning, Agent O'Neal. I apologize for moving like I'm a hundred years old."

Slowly making their way to the interview room, the bustle of activity with agents and visitors coming and going from offices, talking in cubicles, answering phones, and crowding into the elevator they rode to the fourth floor, gave the building a sense of importance Steve hadn't noticed on his first visit.

O'Neal showed Steve her badge when they arrived at the interview room. The room had a glass window, a small metal table, and three straight-back metal chairs.

"Can I get you a bottle of water or anything to make this more comfortable, Mr. Holmes?"

"Yes, water would be good." Steve couldn't help but scratch the rash on his arm as he opened the bottle and took a drink.

"This shouldn't take more than an hour, Mr. Holmes. I just have a few questions to add to the witness interview you gave to Scotland Yard."

"I understand the process, Agent O'Neal."

Switching on the video recorder, O'Neal asked, "Can you describe your attacker?"

"Short, muscular-looking Chinese, wearing a dark business suit, carrying an umbrella and newspaper. He was maybe five-foot eight-inches tall. No noticeable scars or tattoos. Brown eyes, black hair."

"I'll get a sketch artist in to see you. Any idea who might want to kill you, Mr. Holmes?"

"Not really. Maybe it has to do with my job in this war with Iran, I just don't know."

Alice asked about threats to him, other family and friends. They discussed his travel and people he encountered.

"Why were you in London?"

"To meet with the senator's staff to discuss the convoy investigation and to visit Kratos business operations. I met with Jodie Arenas just prior to the attack that morning."

"Was that all you discussed with Ms. Arenas?"

"Pretty much."

"What did you do when you left her office?"

"I walked down to the bus station. That's where I first saw the Chinese guy."

"Your hotel was just across the river from that office building. Do you usually take a bus for short trips like this?"

"No, but it started raining that day and I didn't bring my umbrella. Jodie offered to call me a taxi, but I told her I could walk." Steve squinted and pursed his lips slightly as he thought about leaving Jodie's office.

"Is something wrong, Mr. Holmes?"

"It's probably nothing, but it did seem unusual at the time that Jodie would offer to call me a taxi."

"I don't understand. It was raining, and she offered to call a taxi. What's unusual about that?"

"She was never courteous to me. In fact, she was unusually courteous during the whole meeting."

"Okay, I'll have a talk with Ms. Arenas."

Alice wrapped up the meeting by reviewing Steve's witness statement and confirming the contact information for his family and associates.

28

Feeling much better three weeks after the attack, Steve arrived by taxi at the Kratos corporate headquarters in DC a little before one PM, as requested. His invitation to the Kratos Board of Director's meeting had arrived at his home two days ago. As Steve approached the fortieth-floor boardroom, he wondered why they would ask an employee on his way out of the company to attend. As an employee, he'd only occasionally attended these meetings when invited by Chairman Tyler.

Steve knew the standard itinerary for the Board meetings. The Board subcommittee meetings, including Compensation, Security, and Audit, were held the day before the full Board met. They also held a social event somewhere in the city the evening before the full Board meeting.

As Steve sat waiting outside the boardroom shortly after one PM, the Board secretary stepped out to apologize for a delay caused by a last-minute, directors-only session that was going on. Steve couldn't make out what they were saying, sitting there waiting for the special session to end, but he recognized Bernie's voice and could tell he wasn't happy.

At two forty-five PM, the directors took a break and asked Steve to join them. As Steve entered the somber room, every director except Bernie walked over to shake his hand and thank him for coming. The room was deathly quiet when Bernie called the meeting to order and turned over the discussion to the Lead Director, Richard Allenby. As the former U.S. ambassador to Saudi Arabia, Richard had the diplomatic skills to lead matters where the Chairman might have a conflict of interest. Bernie presented a report on the current work Kratos was doing in Iran. He showed contract dollars, profit, numbers of people, locations, and several examples of current projects. Richard thanked Bernie, then turned to Steve.

"Welcome to the Board meeting, Mr. Holmes. We were shocked to read about the attempt on your life in London. I and the entire Board hope you have recovered from that heinous attack."

"I'm much better, and thank you for your concern."

"Turning to the Board's business at hand, we were sorry to receive your resignation from Kratos recently. Your passion for supporting our military was a point of pride for all the Board members. We were confident in your ability to lead that part of the company."

Steve glanced at Bernie to see his expression. He looked as uncomfortable as an unruly little boy being made to sit still.

"Thank you, Ambassador Allenby. I was proud to lead the support Kratos provides to our military."

"Those people truly do an outstanding job. When I was ambassador to Saudi Arabia, I traveled to the embassy in Kabul, Afghanistan that was supported by Kratos people. They were enthusiastic, dedicated people who did an outstanding job supporting us. One of the best meals I ever ate was in a Kratos-run dining hall." Allenby paused to pick up a page of notes. "I don't know if you are aware of it, Mr. Holmes, but the Financial Controller appointed by Bernie just prior to your departure has come under scrutiny by the Army CID. There is apparently a video floating around on the Internet that shows the controller taking a briefcase full of cash and smoking hashish with members of one of our prime vendors, Sadik Dost."

"No, I haven't seen the video. I have to say I feel a little uncomfortable here. I hope you can understand, Ambassador, that this seems highly unusual for me. You're calling an employee who has resigned from the company in to explain the behavior of an individual I didn't hire or appoint. Can you shed a little more light on what your purpose is?"

Bernie rocked back in his chair and put his feet on the table. "Yeah, Richard, what is your purpose here?"

Ambassador Allenby smiled at Bernie, then turned to Steve. "I'll be completely candid. That's a trait that didn't make me popular in diplomatic circles, but which proved effective in working for three presidents. It is the Board's fiduciary duty to protect the stockholder's interests. As these matters of the video and potential illegal activities have come to our attention, we wanted your perspective on what was occurring. We know that in addition to the Army CID, the Department of Justice is investigating and there are potential violations of U.S. law for bribing foreign officials and falsifying invoices, including the False Claims Act and the Foreign Corrupt Practices Act. Are you comfortable helping us understand the issues surrounding this financial controller, the video, and Kratos contractors better?"

"I appreciate your candor, Mr. Ambassador. Like you, I like to tell it like it is. I'll be glad to tell you what I know, but let me say first that I am unaware of any illegal activities by any Kratos' employees that haven't already been reported to the proper authorities."

Nodding his head, Ambassador Allenby said, "Neither your character nor involvement in any wrongdoing is being questioned, Steve. We heard informally that when you resigned from Kratos, it was specifically because this financial controller was being assigned to the program and that he would report directly to Bernie. Is that correct?"

"Not exactly, Ambassador. I resigned because I no longer respected Mr. Tyler, and I was concerned about the propriety of what he was asking me to do. Up until the day I resigned, I thought I had sufficient control of my workforce to prevent Bernie from doing something that would get us all in trouble. When it was clear I no longer had that control, I knew it was time to go."

Bernie snapped his feet to the floor, brought his chair upright and slammed his arms and papers in his hands on the table. "Now, stop right there, Holmes! You're a liar! There is not one shred of evidence that I ever asked you to break the law in any fashion. This bullshit story you're telling is only to cover your ass."

When Bernie paused, Steve ignored his rants and continued with his comments directed at the Board. "The day I resigned I had had enough and planned the resignation before I walked into Bernie's office. His appointment of his own private financial controller was just a final sign that I no longer controlled what went on in my operation."

"I wish you'd come to the Board with your concerns. It's our role to investigate any issues that would concern stockholders."

"That's hard to do when the problem is with the CEO, who is also Chairman of the Board. Nonetheless, I did raise my concerns about Bernie's general behavior to some individual Board members."

The ambassador made some notes and continued his questions. "What made you believe that Bernie would want you or others to do anything illegal?"

"Bernie was clever. I'd explain the rules and the fact that what he was asking me to do was against the law. He would just keep telling me he didn't care about the rules, 'just get Sadik Dost more work.' I already had a report from one of our employees in Dubai that Bernie had a meeting there with Sadik Dost that I knew nothing about. That he had direct contact in a somewhat clandestine way worried me even more."

Bernie glared at Steve, seething with anger. He wasn't used to being accused of anything.

Allenby said, "Do you have any documentation to support what you are saying, Steve?"

"I have my daily journal where I made notes on the conversations for each of Mr. Tyler's comments, and I noted the name of the person who informed me about his meeting with Sadik Dost. Otherwise, I have no documentation. Of course, if I had documentation of any actual wrongdoing I would have already reported it to the contracting officer or the FBI. I'm sure there are records that will document the meeting Bernie had in Dubai."

Bernie continued his rant. "Horseshit, Holmes. You're lying, and that's why there is no evidence of wrongdoing to support your claims. I'm the CEO of this company. I meet with subcontractors and customers and employees whenever and wherever I want. You're trying to make the meeting look improper to cover your own ass."

Ambassador Allenby said to Steve, "Will you give us the name of this person so we might question him further?"

"I will not, Mr. Ambassador. I know Bernie. He would take retribution on the employee. If and when the Army CID or the Department of Justice opens a formal investigation, I will give them the employee's name. In the meantime, if you conduct a detailed investigation of your own, I'm sure there are other people who can tell you about the meeting."

"As Lead Director, I'm going to ask Mr. Tyler to step out of the room for a few minutes. Without your presence, Bernie, we can ensure any investigator that we took every opportunity to dig into these allegations."

Bernie had sufficiently calmed down to recognize that this move was good for him as well, showing he tried to get at the truth. "Of course, I welcome the opportunity for Mr. Holmes to express himself freely."

After Bernie left the room, Ambassador Allenby asked, "Is there anything else you want to add, Mr. Holmes?"

"As I said, I resigned from Kratos because I believed Bernie would behave unethically, even illegally if given the opportunity. For me, the signals were strong enough that I started worrying about what I didn't know. What deals had he cut with Sadik Dost? What lengths would he go to in order to get work for them? What's in it for him?"

"We appreciate your candid feedback. I want to thank you again for coming. We will continue our investigation."

Before Steve departed the room, Richard pulled him aside. "I want you to think about coming back to Kratos. You're on our very shortlist of candidates to succeed Bernie."

"If and when Bernie departs the company, I would be interested in coming back. Not until then."

29

Tinker AFB, Oklahoma

Catherine Murphy was on her fourth cup of coffee and wasn't sure she could wait two more hours for relief as she sat in an unmarked vehicle at five AM, two houses down from Major Abdullah Sharif's home in the officer's housing section of Tinker AFB. Her best alternative was shaping up to be squatting beside the car, using her blanket as a tent. Then she saw movement at Sharif's home.

He walked to the street, dressed in a white jalabiya and sandals, got into his Corvette and pulled off. Catherine followed at first without headlights, turning them on only after Sharif made his first right turn.

She radioed for a backup to help her tail Sharif as he drove toward Oklahoma City. Catherine followed far behind Sharif in the sparse traffic. As they got closer to downtown, her backup tag-teamed with her to switch on and off as the tail car until they reached the mosque.

"Bingo!" Catherine yelled as she saw Sharif enter the mosque. Linking Sharif to the same mosque attended by the two Americans the FBI and CIA tracked to Muqtada Al Sadr in Iraq should be sufficient probable cause to search his quarters. After hitting the head at the first gas station she found, Catherine went back to her office to get the paperwork done.

Catherine made her case in the base commander's office later that morning with his JAG's representative observing.

The commander said, "What led you to Sharif in the first place?"

"I determined an AWACS insider had to be involved and Sharif acted like he had something to hide."

"Why an insider?"

"Signals came into AWACS, but they didn't go out."

"And you tracked him to a mosque."

"The same mosque that sent people to visit with Mahdi Special Forces and Muqtada Al Sadr in Iraq."

"Is that all you have?"

"Turns out Sharif headed up the software upgrade. Got a tip that he inserted some unknown software."

"Okay, Captain. You'll need JAG to get clearance for the Doha search. Keep me informed."

Four days later, Catherine was back in front of the base commander. She put a mail pouch on his desk as she walked in.

He picked it up. "What's this?"

"Coded set of prime numbers Sharif entered into AWACS to trigger the blackout. The code is for the date and location of the Neka convoy attack."

"Where'd you find it?"

"Took half a dozen investigators tearing his home apart, then there it was, under the floorboard in Qatar. Cyber Command broke the code in less than a day."

"It's postmarked DC."

"That's our big lead on who sent the virus."

"Pick him up. Good job, soldier."

***

Sherry Adkison got the phone call for an impromptu classified meeting with Army CID in Quantico just twenty-four hours before it was to happen. She pulled her vintage Malibu into the pre-rush hour traffic at five AM for the drive. Catherine Murphy greeted her when she cleared security and entered the meeting room. After introductions, Catherine laid the classified mail pouch on the table in front of Sherry.

"We're going to need your help to find out who sent the package from DC to Sharif in Qatar."

"Any prints?"

"Only Sharif's."

Sherry picked up the mail pouch sealed in a clear plastic bag, examined the labels, postmark, and addresses. "Who knew about the convoy in time to tell the Iranians?"

"We're on that now. Looking at his chain of command, intel channels, contractors, and legislators."

"What about those legislators? Any reason to suspect someone there?"

"That's where we need FBI. Congress requests this type of information as part of their oversight responsibility. Don't know yet if anyone requested the Neka schedule. Lots of staff handle that information, too."

Catherine gave Sherry an update on the case and Sharif's arrest.

"Okay, we're on it. The FBI is also looking at any communications the mujahideen received prior to the attack, and any potential or known spies who might have been involved. Haven't come up with much yet."

30

Washington, DC

The cell phone's old-fashioned telephone ring tone awoke Bernie Tyler from what had been a restless, tossing sleep. First the internet video showing his financial controller taking a bribe, followed by an FBI investigation, and now the Kratos' Board investigation felt like bricks dragging down his head and shoulders.

But it was all going to get better soon. Bernie had a plan.

Rolling over to see the time, 4:15 AM, and flipping on the light beside the bed, Bernie answered, "Give me some good news, Tom."

"Good morning, Bernie. You're up bright and early in D.C. today."

"You're funny. What work are you sending to Sadik Dost today?"

"Well, there's a large security project that we need to get moving on quickly. It's for construction of an outer ring of fencing and bomb-resistant roof structures. It's worth twenty million dollars and I've got the sole source subcontract ready for Sadik to sign."

Bernie smiled, relaxing, knowing he was getting what he wanted by making Tom Liddy his Middle East financial controller. "You've sent a bunch of work to Sadik already. Good job, Tom."

"It's not hard. I never understood why Steve Holmes couldn't do it. Just stupid, I guess."

"Am I going to see this project on an Internet video, too? That last mess of yours has caused me a lot of trouble." Bernie moved the phone away from his ear at the CLANG! of a metal trash can kicked across the room.

"That's not fair. I was set up! How was I to know they would tape the meeting and then someone would post it on line? Sadik Dost shot that video. They wanted to show the sheikh how good things were going. One of those idiots put the video on line and it went viral. But, since you bring it up, are you making sure I won't go to jail? You sent Andrew Sutter out here. Should I be worried about protecting my ass?"

With a reassuring tone, but sarcastic smile, Bernie said, "Don't worry, Tom. Andrew's an experienced clean-up guy and he'll protect you. When he's done, there won't be any paper trail to link you to any wrongdoing. And he's creating on-line evidence to show that video was faked."

"You better be taking care of me, 'cause if I go down, you go down."

Bernie's smile quickly became a frown, but he maintained his supportive tone. "Haven't I always taken care of you, Tom? Now, let's get to the business at hand."

"If I didn't have to produce all this documentation Andy is asking for, I could get a lot more subcontracts out. I put four people on our payrolls this week just to satisfy Andy's demands."

"Well then, hire more people. Get the documentation and get more work to Sadik. It's not that hard."

Bernie hung up the phone with Tom and immediately called Andrew Sutter.

"Hello, Bernie. What can I do for you?"

"How long will it take you to finish up your work there?"

"That depends on how much help I get from Tom. I'd say it will take at least another week. I'm warning all the key players not to speak to investigators. They are to refer any inquiries to our legal department. I'm also getting each of them to sign statements that they know of no wrongdoing by anyone in the company."

"Wrap it up fast. Tom's getting the hives about this whole thing. If this thing blows up, can it be traced back to me?"

"Don't *worry*, Bernie. Once I'm done here, the only person they'll be able to blame is Tom. Tom is the only link back to you. If he's arrested and squeals, then you'll have to defend yourself, but he won't have any documentation in the files to back that up with. It'll be his word against yours."

Taking a deep breath and releasing it slowly, Bernie relaxed a little more. "That's good. Get it done, Andy. I'll be out of the U.S. and hard to reach for a while."

Bernie stepped into his closet and removed the ticket folder from his sports coat pocket. He checked the departure time of his flight to Venezuela—plenty of time to get to the private airport near Stafford, Virginia. He set his suitcase on the bed, opened it, and reached under the layer of clothes he had packed to unzip the compartment below and removed a stack of hundred dollar bills from the one million dollars he carried. Preparation was key for Bernie. A little cash for the TSA official he'd used before. A little for the customs officer who used to work for him. And a little more for the pilot, would ensure his smooth transition to a country without extradition agreements with the U.S.

Bernie picked up his phone, and pulled up the financial app that showed his liquid assets page, including over five million dollars in the Cayman Islands and Switzerland. With a satisfied smile, he imagined how fast the assets would grow as Sadik and Sheikh Khaleed continued to receive contracts courtesy of him.

Bernie got dressed, ate breakfast, and picked up his two suitcases. His wife, Jane, said goodbye, expecting him back home in a week. Just after six AM, with the sun slowly rising in Washington, DC, Bernie loaded the luggage and climbed into his Bentley Supersport convertible. Revving the engine, he felt the rush of 700 horsepower of pure thrill he loved to race through Washington's streets with the top down.

As he backed out of his garage and onto the street in the private, gated community he lived in, suddenly two unmarked cars slid hard with brakes squealing to block Bernie's car in front and back. The WOOP! WOOP! WOOP! of sirens wailing drew neighbors' attention as uniformed officers stood up from behind cars and stepped out from the bushes by his driveway with guns drawn while marked squad cars pulled up with lights flashing.

Bernie's head whirled around to see all the people with guns pointed at him.

The officer standing behind the unmarked car directly behind Bernie said through a loudspeaker, "This is the FBI. Step out of your vehicle with your hands above your head."

Bernie slammed both hands on the steering wheel, looked for any way out, then gave up, trapped like a fish in a net without a chance for escape. He stepped out of the car with his hands up and his head down to avoid the accusing stares of his neighbors who'd been called to their windows and streets by all the noise.

The agent said, "Lay down on the ground and spread your arms and legs."

Jane heard the noise, walked out the front door, saw all the police around Bernie and gasped. She began to cry.

Neighbors now stood across the street and watched with both

sadness and a little vindictiveness. Wealthy, showy, and anti-social; that was the Bernie they all knew. To see him now, prostrate on the pavement, shattered that higher-class veneer Bernie tried to exude.

Bernie began to sob as the coarse, sharp street asphalt cut at his face. Two agents approached Bernie. While one agent knelt down to handcuff him, the other kept his gun aimed at Bernie. They then stood him up, leaned him against the car and began a thorough pat-down search. Finally, they read Bernie his rights, loud enough for everyone to hear.

"Bernie Tyler, you are being charged with grand larceny in connection with kickbacks you took for the Kratos contracts with the United States Army."

Still sobbing with his head lowered, Bernie was placed into a police car and driven to jail. The media had been alerted and were waiting to take the pictures that would be on the home page of today's Internet media sites and tomorrow's newspapers.

Simultaneously with the local news conference at the DC Metro police station at nine AM, United States Attorney General Elliot Park addressed the national media in the White House press room.

"Bernie Tyler, Chairman of the Board, Chief Executive Officer, and President of Kratos Energy and Logistics Corporation, was arrested today in Arlington, Virginia for bribery and violation of the False Claims Act." A video of Bernie Tyler's arrest was playing in the background as the AG spoke. "Let this be a warning from President Rubina and this Department of Justice to all those criminals who would illegally profit from our war with Iran that you cannot get away with it. Justice will be served. And, let it also remind the vast majority of honest and dedicated people working in the military-industrial community that by punishing those who would do wrong, we honor your service. Thank you."

31

Kratos Lead Director, Ambassador Richard Allenby, got the phone call from Linda Hines that morning just after nine AM. While continuing to read an article on his computer screen, Allenby heard, "Bernie has been arrested!"

Swiveling quickly from reading his on-line State Department magazine, he asked, "When and where?"

"The FBI arrested him at his home this morning. It's all over the news. The media were invited to film the whole thing."

"What is he charged with?"

"Stealing from taxpayers. Kickbacks he allegedly received and bribery of officials involving those Iran contracts. He evidently was a lot more involved than he let on."

Allenby jumped to his feet. "That lying, crooked bastard!"

"Yeah, and I'm pissed that we didn't do what we should've for Bernie's failure to ever take responsibility for problems, immoral behavior in Dubai, and his suggested involvement in payoffs. As a Board, we were chicken-shits. We should have stood up to Bernie and thrown him out when all those rumors and reports of questionable behavior from people like Steve Holmes first came up."

"There will be a time for chewing ourselves out. The Board has work to do right now. We have to terminate his employment today, Linda. I'll call the other Board members to get their vote, but now we do need to move fast. This will be devastating to Kratos' reputation and for our stockholders."

"I don't want Bernie to get one penny out of this!"

"Well, since we've been considering firing him, you know what's in his Severance and Termination Agreement: We have to continue to pay his legal expenses unless and until he's found guilty. If he's found innocent, we'll have to pay him that large severance and he may sue us, but we'll cross that bridge when we come to it."

Washington, DC

At Kratos corporate headquarters, two days later, Ambassador Allenby called the meeting to order. "I've called for this special session of the Board of Directors to consider the candidates for Chairman of the Board, Chief Executive Officer, and President of Kratos to replace Bernie Tyler. I asked Mr. Wayne Brown, the owner of the executive search firm Wayne and Associates, to present candidates for the position."

Wayne stood up and clicked his remote control for the first chart to popup. The Board members pulled up their copy of the charts on their electronic notebooks. "We're meeting under very unpleasant circumstances, but you should be proud as a Board that you are prepared with the three layers of succession plans you've been building the last few years."

Linda tapped her pen impatiently on the mahogany table as the succession plan for Bernie's position was discussed.

"You have the latest update for Bernie's succession plan in your hands. The first section is a list of current Kratos company employees that have been screened for consideration. The second section is a list of candidates from outside the company," Wayne said.

After a short discussion of the updates to the succession list, Director Ben Paul said, "The top candidates on this list haven't changed. I recommend we select the best two candidates, interview them, and move on as quickly as possible."

Linda couldn't keep quiet any longer. "Hold on just a minute. Let's not run out and grab the first Tom, Dick, or Bernie that tells a good story. That's how we got Bernie Tyler, remember? He was the first person we interviewed. He promised double-digit returns annually if we bought into his Mideast strategy. He had us spellbound, and he wanted it all; chairman, CEO, and president. You see where that got us. I suggest we split the chairman and CEO's roles first."

"I agree we should split the roles," Allenby said. "We can't avoid at least the perception that we didn't act to remove Bernie earlier, when allegations first started surfacing, because he was the Chairman of the Board. We have to take responsibility as the Board, and I as Lead Director, for letting Bernie continue on after that video came out, showing his hand-picked financial controller taking a bribe."

"We all share that blame. I have great confidence in your leadership, Richard. I nominate you for the chairman's job," Linda said.

The other Board members voiced their unanimous approval with applause.

"In good conscience, I can't take the job," Allenby said. "I want to be part of this Board to fix the problem I helped create, but as the Lead Director who failed to remove Bernie when indications of his criminal activities were strong, I will not accept the chairman's job."

Ben said, "We're facing big problems with this military work. Who would be better to get us through it than someone with your government experience and contacts?"

"Not to mention your diplomatic experience. It will take some skill to convince Congress and some of our customers that we're not the bad guys," Linda said.

"It's flattering, but as a stockholder myself, I wouldn't want the guy who was in a lead position when we got into this mess to get us out of it. I won't take the job, but I would proudly serve under Linda Hines as chair."

The nomination was met with surprise and initial silence. After some deliberation, Richard spoke up. "All in favor?"

Linda was unanimously approved as the new Chairman of the Board.

After a short recess, the Board continued to examine the candidates for the CEO/President's role.

"Don't forget the other internal candidates. I personally think our current CFO, John Carpenter, is a pretty strong candidate for CEO. He guides the company financially, he knows the business, and he has proven to be a straight-shooter and honest leader," Ben said.

"Before we decide who we want, let's agree on the most important criteria for the job," Linda suggested. "I don't want to fool ourselves by throwing names up and making this a beauty contest. We have a criteria; it's in the Succession Plan. Let's agree on what the two or three most critical characteristics of our new leader will be, then let's interview the top candidates and go."

"All those skill-based criteria seem to be among the least important I can think of for the right candidate for this job," Ambassador Allenby said, after looking at the criteria the Board had developed.

The comment surprised the Board members.

"We use these criteria all the time. What's wrong with it?" Ben Paul asked.

"It's all about their degrees, years of experience, past jobs they've held. What about their behavior? Isn't that important? After Bernie, behavior of a CEO jumps up as a much more important factor than skill. Are they honest? Will they do what they say they'll do? Are they good with people? And, I'd like to know their level of commitment to what we do here. Kratos plays a pretty important role in the world; shouldn't we expect to hire someone who is passionate about that role?"

Paul responded, skeptically, "How do you measure passion, ethics, people skills, and commitment?"

"We have behavioral tests that could give us some insight," Linda replied.

"The tests may help, but just because we can't measure it precisely, doesn't mean we shouldn't try to get someone with those characteristics," Allenby said. "If we focus on these behaviors, interview the candidates and observe them in our social interactions, we'll get a feel for them."

"I observed one example of Bernie's poor people skills," Linda said. "I was riding on a bus to a social event at the Kennedy Center for the Board members and the Executive team one evening. Ricky Anderson, who runs health and safety for Bernie, struck up a conversation with Bernie's wife, Jane. When they discovered they'd both gone to the same high school, Ricky started talking about people they knew, what they were both involved in, and other things they had in common. Bernie butted in, and said, 'Now stop that. We're not here to chit-chat about high school.' And out the window went any chance that Ricky was going to give a damn about Bernie or the company. Bernie ruined morale."

"Well, it's too late to wait until we hire them to discover their behavior is bad," Allenby said. "I want someone to do what's right. We can't just assume that everyone we hire will be ethical. But, we can look at their past behavior, listen to what they say is important to them, observe their behavior during our interviews and see if honest, do-what's-right behavior is high on their list of concerns."

"All Bernie ever talked about was openness. At the time, we thought that was pretty good. We thought he implied ethical behavior, but he obviously did not. And, as it turns out, while he wanted everyone else to be open with him, he certainly wasn't open himself." Linda shook her head, sad at what she'd missed about the man. "My bottom line is, if they don't talk about ethics then it's not very important to them."

After agreeing on ethics, people skills, and passion for the Kratos mission as the most important criteria, the discussion returned to the CEO/president candidates.

Allenby said, "I want to point out that in our last discussions with Steve Holmes we told him that he was our top candidate. We know his capability. Why dither? Let's interview him with one or two other of the best candidates on our list who meet our criteria and select the best one. Not only will we give ourselves a chance to challenge our preference for Steve against other top-quality candidates, but it will also demonstrate to the stockholders that we made a thorough search and selected the best."

"I'm not so sure about Steve. He quit, remember? I'd feel more comfortable with John Carpenter, our current CFO in the CEO/president's job," Linda said.

"Hasn't Steve's concern about Bernie's behavior vindicated his decision to leave?" Allenby asked.

"Well, yes, but he still quit. Who's to say he won't quit again? And he doesn't have the financial experience I'd want in a CEO."

"No CEO has every skill. That's why you surround them with other experts, like a good CFO."

The Board split into two camps. One favoring Steve Holmes and the other favoring John Carpenter. After some discussion, Linda proposed a compromise.

"I'd be comfortable with Steve as president, running the operation. We could put John in as the CEO, further splitting out those two roles. That way, we have a financial expert and current employee who stuck it out in the CEO's role to focus on stockholders and Kratos' financial health, while Steve focuses on running the operation."

After some arm-twisting by Linda, the Board agreed to split the roles and conduct interviews for the two positions, with Steve and John as their top candidates.

***

Ambassador Allenby called Steve Holmes later that day. "You probably know why I'm calling."

"I heard about Bernie's arrest and saw the Board's announcement that you'd fired Bernie. I hope you're calling me about the job."

"Yes. The Board confirmed that you're our top candidate for president. We are considering other candidates for CEO."

"It's an important role in a company that has an important mission. But, I have to admit, I'm a little disappointed the job does not include the CEO's role."

"After careful consideration, the Board decided to split the three positions out. We want to avoid the mistakes of the past where we gave near-total control to one person. It's best for our company and stockholders to have the best people in each role to lead Kratos. The announcement that we elected Linda Hines as chairman will go out tomorrow before the stock market opens. John Carpenter is our top candidate for CFO."

"Yeah, John's a good guy. He's someone I could work for."

"Does that mean you'll consider the President's job?"

"I've had a lot of time to think about coming back to Kratos since the last time we talked. And, yes, I'm very interested in the president's job and would like to be considered."

***

Steve went the following Monday to meet with the Board. The interview went extremely well. Among the many questions asked, was what Steve thought was the most important characteristic for the new President.

Steve said without even having to think about it, "A moral compass and commitment to the mission, in that order. If you aren't driven to do what's right, no amount of regulations or training sessions is going to change you. That lack of ethics will put the company in another legal bind at some point. Our mission is to exceed our customer's needs in commercial and military construction and services. We provide leadership in building the world's energy capacity. And Kratos' mission to support the military is important to not only the success of our company, but also for the successful operation of our military as well. I am committed to that mission, and I would consider it a privilege to lead the people who provide that service to our country."

"What is your most important consideration for whether or not you'd take this job?" Ambassador Allenby asked at the end of the interview.

"Working for an ethical company and having the trust of those I work for."

"Bernie left a stain on Kratos' reputation that won't soon be erased. And the Board lost sight of just how much good behavior reflects on our people, business, and reputation. I can assure you that traits like honesty and integrity were important criteria in our selection for this and all positions we fill in the future. And, as for trust, the Board knows you and we trust you to lead the operation in a manner that brings credit to Kratos."

"Thank you. I appreciate the Board's confidence. I have to evaluate these factors based on what I know about you and the company. I recognize that as president, I'd have a great deal of influence on the ethics of the company. The selection of your CEO and that person's ethics will be critical to my decision."

***

On Sunday night, after John Carpenter had been announced as the new CEO, Linda Hines called Steve Holmes at home. "After we voted-in John Carpenter as our CEO, and you interviewed with the Board, we are in unanimous agreement to offer you the job as President of Kratos."

"Kratos is a great company with passionate people who do an outstanding job. It would be an honor to serve as their President."

"Congratulations! You should contact John Carpenter on Monday morning and coordinate getting started."

32

Captain Catherine Murphy called Agent Sherry Adkison at 8:15 AM. "I have a classified report I need to discuss with you. Can I come over?"

"I'll have a cup of coffee waiting."

Catherine handed Sherry the sealed courier pouch containing the classified forensics report as she entered the FBI's secure conference room. "The AWACS virus came from the Chinese."

"China! How are they linked to Sharif?"

"Major Sharif received an email containing the virus from a Chinese agent, then put the file on a thumb drive and uploaded it to the AWACS software during its upgrade at Hanscom."

"He got an email from a known Chinese agent? In the open like that?"

"No, nothing that overt. He got an email that was innocent enough on the surface, but by examining the metadata we were able to determine it was suspicious."

"I thought metadata was just high-level identifier information like you might get on your phone bill to identify who and when calls were made."

"There's a lot of information contained in that metadata that the normal email recipient never reads. The email header told us the keyboard was Mandarin, the software font was a Chinese SimSun, and the country of origin. And the attacker used a fictitious Domain Name System, similar to what the NSA had seen before. By comparing those multiple DNSes, we triangulated, in a sense, back to pinpoint the attacker's location inside the Chinese military."

Sherry asked, "How did Cyber Command find the source for the virus so fast?"

"They've got lots of money and people. They believe the next nine-eleven will be a cyber attack."

"What proved the Chinese developed the virus?"

"We have a lot of descriptive information on past cyber crimes in our databases. We catalog and archive all the details about who, where, and how the viruses are generated. Each virus leaves telltale clues to its origin. We focused on source code patterns, language signatures, known behavior, malware design centers and similar events. The first thing we discovered in the underlying machine code was a reference to a malware file used in a previous attack."

"Used before?"

"The Chinese military's Unit 61398 used a similar virus, called Blaster, in the early two-thousands to creep into the Microsoft operating system. It's been copied, enhanced, and used many times since."

"What did this virus do?"

"It sent the command for AWACS to block transmissions in the Neka area when Sharif triggered it with that prime number sequence."

Sherry thumbed through the remainder of the report, then said, "This is a turning point in our investigation. The Chinese are also suspect in the attempted murder of Steve Holmes and bribes to Senator Shankle."

33

On a busy afternoon at work, Janice stepped into Steve's office to say, "George Bird is on the phone. Do you want to take it?"

"Yes, of course. Hello, George, you old jarhead, where are you this week?"

"I'm at home here in DC with Cathy and the family. I took a week off before I go to my new assignment in a joint-military operation with the navy."

"Let's get together and you can tell me all about it. I'd like you to meet Sherry, too."

"I'd like that. As a matter of fact, I was hoping you were up for a basketball game on Saturday."

"Sure. Just tell me when and where."

"Nine AM. I'll text you the directions."

Two days later, dressed in his sneakers, gym shorts, and Washington Wizard's jersey, Steve was driving in rural Virginia to meet George. As he pulled his old Cadillac CTS into the gym parking lot, he noticed the sign above the gym door that read "Arlington Youth Center." Steve saw there were more cars than he expected for pickup basketball.

George met him at the door and said, "I'm sorry for not telling you more about this, but I wanted it to be a surprise."

"Okay, but I'm not dressed to give a speech."

"No, it's nothing like that. All you'll want to do is watch. It's going to be pretty amazing."

As they entered the gym, Steve could hear the bouncing ball, referee's whistle, and squeaking of sneakers so distinctive in these Saturday youth games where several games ran on multiple courts at once. Excited parents cheering for their children on the court, yelled out instructions to "Get the ball!" or "Shoot, shoot!" while others cheered. What Steve first saw when he looked on the courts, wasn't players running up and down and the squeaking wasn't coming from sneakers. Steve saw children in wheelchairs rolling themselves up and down four courts, squeaking their wheels as they turned, catching, dribbling, passing, defending, and shooting.

They sat down next to Cathy and their other two sons. Steve said, "Where's Danny? Are you taking him out there?"

"Danny's already there."

"By himself?"

"Yes. He's there under the goal."

Steve looked up at the nearest court and picked out Danny wearing his dad's number 13 jersey and maneuvering his wheelchair, though not keeping up completely. "Amazing!" Taking a long pause, then, "I'm at a loss for words. When did he become capable of pushing himself around, much less playing without help?"

George said, "He's been working hard to be able to do this by himself. Cathy helps, but by working-out for hours every day, he has strengthened his arms and improved his dribbling and shooting. He called me six weeks ago in Iran and said, 'Dad, I want to compete.' 'Compete' was a word he'd never used before when I wheeled him around in basketball games or ran with him in races."

"It must have taken tremendous determination. I love Danny, but I didn't think he was even capable of this."

"Danny said he read a news report about a young teenage girl who was depressed about being paralyzed in a terrible accident. The girl didn't know how she could live. Danny said he wanted to show her and others who were paralyzed that they don't have to be helpless."

As Steve turned to watch the game, Danny missed the first pass thrown to him, but he kept playing. A few plays later he was under the goal and maneuvered to catch a rebound in his arms. Wheeling the chair with his left hand, he dribbled up the court as his teammates raced with him toward their goal. Nearing the basket, Danny heaved the ball a few feet ahead of him to his teammate who shot and scored the basket.

Steve jumped to his feet yelling, "Attaboy, Danny! Great pass." The crowd for both teams yelled and jumped up, encouraging all the players.

A few minutes later, Danny was thrown the ball from out of bounds. Avoiding a defender, Danny dribbled and rolled his wheelchair the length of the court. At midcourt, he glanced into the stands where he knew his parents were sitting, flashed a broad smile and dribbled on. Steve could feel the emotion welling up in his throat, watching George and Cathy grinning and bobbing their heads, high on pride.

After a few more dribbles, Danny lost the ball. His muscle coordination just wasn't good enough to keep it going. As the game went on, Danny got more chances to pass, dribble, rebound, defend, and shoot. His shots didn't go in or even hit the goal, but he kept trying.

Near the end of the game, while rolling hard and leaning over for a loose ball, Danny collided with another player and fell over, wheelchair and all. The crowd grew quiet as everyone looked to see if Danny was okay. George jumped up and ran over to help him. Just as he got there, Danny held his hand up to stop him and shook his head violently. He used both hands to pull himself across the floor to the tipped-over wheelchair. Balancing himself with one hand, he used the other to grab the large wheel and pull it over to set the chair upright. He adjusted the footrests out of the way, locked the wheels and pulled his back to the wheelchair. Reaching both hands up over his head, he pulled himself up and maneuvered into the chair.

Sitting in his wheelchair, looking at everyone who had gathered around him with a proud, big smile, Danny said through his computerized speech synthesizer, "I got this, Dad." The same words George used to comfort Danny in the past when they ran or played and competed together.

Steve and all of George's family ran onto the court to celebrate at the end of the game. Danny hugged them all and high-fived practically everyone else in the gym.

Steve leaned over to Danny. "I sure am proud of you, Danny."

Danny put his hand on Steve's shoulder, and with George and Cathy listening, he said, "I just did what mom or dad would do: I went for it. I'm going to be okay."

34

Steve Holmes was relaxing on his apartment couch one week later, feet propped up and sitting under the illumination of a small lamp, when the cell phone rang, interrupting his quiet evening. Laying his book on the end table, he stepped across the room and answered the phone sitting on the kitchen bar.

"Hey, Steve, Mark Darrow here. National news media are reporting that Iran's Mahdi Corps special forces, backed by Hizballah, attacked a radar site in Oman while mujahideen naval forces, backed by Basij local militia, simultaneously attacked ships in the Strait of Hormuz today," Kratos' General Counsel said.

"Where are our Kratos' employees in this fight?" Steve asked as he sat up, now fully alert.

"We've got over two thousand, some on daily ops support and some manning gunner positions on the ships. We've also got that contract to operate the radar site on the Musandam Peninsula in Oman. We can use both Americans and Turks on that one. I'm pulling together my risk managers and our media communications team to monitor the developments."

"Was there any warning of the attack?"

"Very little. I haven't heard any reports from our people or from the news people about the threat of an attack. The Pentagon said they thought their greatest naval threat was land-based from anti-ship missiles. They talked about suicide boats, like the one that attacked the *Cole*. The Free Iran Internet site is claiming that a swarm of hundreds of boats, ships, and submarines attacked the Fifth Fleet at four AM, Gulf Time, exploding thousands of mines to clog the Strait with sunken tankers and cargo ships. And they're reporting an amphibious assault against the radar complex on the Musandam Peninsula in Oman to take down the radar."

"Nobody thought Iran could pull off a big attack like this."

"Our military seems to have been surprised by the attack. You'd think we would have had some advance warning with our intelligence and electronics."

"This had to be a low-tech assault by the mujahideen using person-to-person cues and clock times to coordinate." Steve paused, then said, "Jesus Christ! I just realized two of our top people are over there in this mess. Bruce Williams is in charge of the security team defending the Musandam Peninsula radar site, and George Bird is onboard the *McCain* destroyer in the Strait of Hormuz."

"I guess they jumped right from the pan into the fire. Are you worried about them?"

Smiling, Steve replied, "It's the enemy that should worry. You couldn't ask for two better warriors. The Salty Sea Dog rides again!"

"How's that?"

"Just thinking about George as a Marine Corps gunner serving on a navy ship."

Mark continued with his report. "The Pentagon reported that the attack on the radar site occurred during a planned maintenance and repair operation."

"The only way the Iranians could know that was if someone told them. They knew about the convoy movements, and now they know our routine there on the Musandam Peninsula. This is no coincidence."

Strait of Hormuz, Persian Gulf

All was quiet on the USS *John S McCain* destroyer moving through the Strait of Hormuz earlier that evening as the night shift reported for duty. After a midnight meal in the officer's mess, Marine Corps Gunnery Officer Lieutenant James Gordon reported to the Executive Officer for his briefing of the day.

After a security briefing and general announcements, the XO said, "Gentlemen, Captain Taylor has directed that we run attack drills every two hours. Bunched together with only twenty miles between the Strait of Hormuz gap makes us and the oil tankers easy targets. Let's not be one. Gordon, that goes double for your weapons team."

"Aye, aye, sir. I'll drill 'em all night, alternating between a swarming and land-based missile attack."

***

Following their first attack drill, Lieutenant Gordon made his rounds, stopping at each of his gunnery positions. When he got to Sergeant-Major George Bird's station, he said, "How's your gun performing this morning, Marine?"

"Shipshape, sir. The Phalanx Gatling gun is battle ready; R2-D2 is the finest weapon in the navy. It will be ready for any threat." The canister-shaped weapon did look like something out of the *Star Wars* movie.

As they sailed into the Strait early that morning, there were hundreds of boats moving in every direction, or just floating with the currents. The Fleet task force ships were constantly warning boats off on the radio and with bullhorns in Arabic and English, using an occasional jet spray of water from the fire hoses.

"Sergeant-Major Bird, inspect all weapons in use and have someone double-check our inventory of back-up weapons, ammunition, and spare parts. We don't get into sustained small arms battles very often; I'm concerned we may run out of critical weaponry."

"Aye, aye, sir. You know I brought a piece of advanced technology commercial equipment on board, sir?"

"Yes. I saw some sailors setting it up below deck. I had a helluva time preventing the skipper from throwing it overboard. He stopped when I told him it manufactures spare parts."

"I hope we don't need it, but it's ready to go if we do."

"Can you make bolt and processing assemblies for the M60s?"

"Yes, sir, I can. I brought the engineering drawings for every part of our crew-served weapons, including the sixty."

"I hope they aren't rubber parts, Sergeant-Major."

"No, sir. The 3D printer uses nanofiber material to produce items lighter and stronger than steel. I would need three IT-trained sailors to assist me, though, if we had to use it, sir."

The lieutenant turned and looked out toward the sea. The wind was calm and the sky was clear. The water was as smooth as glass. The hundreds of small boats in and around the Fifth Fleet task force were visible for miles.

Lieutenant Gordon removed his helmet and scratched his head. "This would be one hell of a bad place for an attack: ferries, tugs, tankers, and fishing vessels all over the place. Identifying one of these boats as a threat before they got too close would be damned near impossible. It could sneak right up within a thousand feet before we identify them as a threat. They could ram us from there in less than a minute or fire missiles and torpedoes within such close range we couldn't react fast enough to stop them."

"You've got a very experienced crew here, Lieutenant. Many of them have spent their entire careers as gunners. They'd do well, sir."

"Oh, I don't have any questions about the men, Sergeant-Major. I just don't think the navy has done enough planning in shifting from large threats to small ones."

"The Salty Sea Dogs, with a little help from the navy, would protect the Fleet from any of these piss-ants getting past our destroyer to hit a carrier, sir. Or we'd die trying."

Chuckling, Gordon said, "I know you would, Sergeant-Major, I know you would." Lieutenant Gordon turned and walked out. George got up to stand at attention.

"At ease, Marine."

George immediately started his inspection of the weapons. Their best defense against a small boat attack would be the crew-served weapons and a modified Phalanx Gatling gun. The crew had small arms, including combat rifles, grenade launchers, and pistols. They also manned small M-60 machine guns, .28 mm chain-fed machine guns, and dual-barreled .50 caliber guns mounted on a swivel seat. The machine guns were spread fore and aft, starboard and port.

Bird examined critical components and asked for an assessment of each weapon from the sailors and Marines manning them. George then moved to the ship's Magazine Room to examine the inventory of spares and ammunition.

***

Another ship patrolling the Strait with the Fifth Fleet task force, the USS *Cole* destroyer, received a distress call from a small boat only two thousand yards from the ship. The ship's lookout on the bridge had identified the fire before the distress call and was preparing to launch a boat to inspect it. A patrol boat with an armed security team and firefighting equipment was dispatched to the fire. When they arrived, the boat was almost underwater and burned too badly to salvage.

Two women and one child were spotted nearby, floating in the water with their life preservers. The patrol boat rescued them, gave them blankets to keep warm and sat them in the cabin of the patrol boat.

The Arabic interpreter accompanying the rescue team questioned the female survivors. They were paying passengers on a ferry that was carrying them across the Strait. The patrol saw no other survivors.

As the Fleet task force patrolling the Persian Gulf was making its way through the Strait, two dozen high speed boats gathered in close proximity to the burning ferry and the USS *Cole*. The destroyers were positioned defensively around the carrier. When the aircraft carrier *Harry S. Truman* approached the area, the speedboats opened up their throttles and made a beeline for the carrier. As soon as the other mujahideen saw the speedboats make their move, other boats of all speeds and sizes sped toward the Fleet, all on different lines of attack.

Neither radar monitors nor outside spotters detected the mass assault headed the Fleet's way immediately. The movement wasn't along a single line or fast enough to stand out.

The patrol boat returned to the USS *Cole*, helped the two rescued women and child out of the boat and onto the ship, and planned to turn them over to a security officer. But, just as the women stepped onto the deck of the Cole, they yelled *"Allahu akbar!"* and triggered their explosive vests. The crater in the deck of the *Cole* was fifteen feet wide. Dozens of sailors standing nearby died instantly, along with the two Arab women and the child. The explosion ignited a fire below deck that spread quickly to other compartments.

Alarm bells rang and the call for battle stations sounded throughout the *McCain*. Captain Taylor raced to the bridge. While the Fleet task force initially focused on the burning destroyer, the attack boats, fast and slow, were closing on the carrier. As the first boats approached, they were individually hailed by the nearby destroyers and other ships positioned defensively around the carrier, and warned to stay back. As the boats approached the 1000-foot line, warnings began to go off about the coordinated encroachment.

George Bird was still conducting inspections in the Magazine Room when the alarm sounded. He ran out of the room, bounded up three flights of stairs, ran to his battle station, leaped over the half-wall of steel surrounding the Phalanx turret, and readied his guns. With his heads-up display mounted in the visor of his helmet and audio from the ship fed in through the speakers, he watched the monitor as the Aegis command and control system scanned the waters for targets the Phalanx Gatling guns could engage. His initial focus was the closest targets to the carriers and then to other ships. Each destroyer had its zone of fire and responsibility.

The sailors armed with M-60 machine guns and operating the .28 mm chain guns were already opening fire on threats within 1000 feet. These boats had ignored warnings and continued to approach the ships despite shots fired over their bows, which ended when dozens of boats began penetrating the close-in barrier at the same time, and serious shooting began.

The large and small slow boats were doing fifteen to twenty knots as they approached. George continued to scan the area without firing the R2-D2, letting the machine guns take care of the small boats while he searched for more threatening targets. Slower boats were sacrificing themselves to shield the faster boats as long as they could. The number of boats out there in the fight, moving among many boats not in the fight, was staggeringly difficult to sort out.

George spotted the first speedboat 3000 yards out doing about 40 knots and closing on the ship. George flipped the switch from Search to Fire and the automatic Gatling gun zeroed-in on the boat motors and opened up for a short six-second burst of 4500 rounds per minute. The fire was so rapid, it was a scorching sheet of metal that hit and obliterated the speedboat and its occupants.

The high-speed boats were each equipped with anti-ship missiles and torpedoes. They maneuvered around the other boats to get a clear shot at the carrier, which was clearly their focus. They wanted to score a tactical victory by sinking one. They weren't worried about surviving the battle.

The first Iranian missile was fired at the *McCain* a half-mile out. The Phalanx easily destroyed it before it made impact. As the boats moved closer, it got harder to target and destroy all the boats. It seemed the *McCain* was in the line for the main attack on the USS *Truman*.

Gordon was monitoring the battle from the electronic displays on the bridge. He could look out, see his gunners, and view electronic displays of the small-boat threats, and what he saw worried him. "Gun Team 1, this is Gun Team Leader, what's your status?"

"We have too many bogeys and our sixty is overheating, sir. Request more ammo."

"Roger, One. More ammo on the way." Gordon sent the message to the ship's magazine.

"Gun Team R2-D2, this is Gun Team Leader, what's your status?"

"Finding them and killing them as fast as I can, sir. Will have to switch to manual mode as bandits get closer."

By far the biggest threat to the ships was the torpedoes on the high-speed boats. The smaller, Chinese-built Iranian boats' anti-ship cruise missiles and torpedoes were deadly from short range. They could deploy advanced mines and highly effective anti-aircraft protection. Their submarines had fire-and-forget torpedoes that targeted a ship's signature in the water, maneuvering under and around other ships.

Captain Taylor wasn't dividing his defense commands. He had Lieutenant Gordon commanding both the anti-submarine warfare, and gunnery crews. Taylor turned to Gordon on the bridge. "How many torpedoes can your systems handle at once, Lieutenant?"

"We'd be strained with six torpedoes scattered and launched at short-range in the water at one time, sir. Our first effort is to divert incoming torpedoes with sonar decoys and maneuver. Our gunners and ASW teams can blast them, but that's only effective for near-surface skimmers."

"With this swarming attack so close to the Fleet, stopping six torpedoes may not be enough."

"No, sir. Our gunners are knocking out the bandits, but we seem to be catching the main brunt of the assault. We could be overwhelmed."

"Boats're attacking the Fleet three hundred-sixty degrees around our perimeter. We can't get another destroyer over here until we're sure there's not another assault wave coming. You'll have to hold them off."

"Aye, aye, sir."

With all the technology on the ship, it was incredible that the weakest link was becoming the reliability of the M-60 machine guns to blast the swarm of small boats. The bolt and operating rod assemblies were failing on the guns because of their light weight and heavy use. They had few replacements. Gordon remembered Bird's machine.

"R2-D2, this is Gunner Team Leader. Who can operate that manufacturing machine of yours?"

"This is R2. I'm the only one who knows how to work the 3D printer, Lieutenant."

"Roger that, R2. Prepare for replacement." Gordon handed command to the ASW Team Leader and sprinted to George's position. "Step out of that seat, Sergeant-Major Bird. Your commander is taking over."

"Aye, aye, sir."

"You're the last option I have, Bird. If you fail, we may lose the ship and maybe a carrier. I'll ask the skipper to send three sailors below deck to help you."

As he was unstrapping and moving out, George Bird said, "The commander may have forgotten I'm a can-do Marine first and always."

With a grin, Gordon said, "Get off my gun deck and go make those parts, Marine. Ooh-rah!"

George knew the technology would work; the problem was it took fifteen minutes to produce each bolt and rod assembly. He'd have to speed that up as much as possible. The 3D printing equipment was already setup, so he just needed to show the sailors how to operate it. "You've got to cut the cycle time down to make each item. The more you do, the faster you should get."

Fifteen minutes later, George personally took the first rod and processing assembly they'd made and put it in an M-60. He walked out on deck, looked at the horizon, and fired at one of the many boats now swarming around the ship. It worked just like it was designed. He returned to his R2 and relieved Lt. Gordon.

"Sir, they're cranking them out. We'll get one every ten minutes, if we're lucky."

"That should be enough to stay ahead of the failures. Get your ass back in this seat. I'm sick of doing your job poorly."

By now, the boats were swarming too close to the ship. They were within 500 feet. The Phalanx infrared sensor did not operate effectively that close to the ship or shooting downward within 100 feet of the ship.

George flipped the R2-D2 to manual control. He still had Doppler radar to highlight moving targets, but he had to choose them and fire manually. He looked like a tail gunner in the underbelly turret of an old B-25 bomber as he swiveled around for 360-degree search-and-track coverage to find and shoot targets. His precision was stunning: No sooner did he fire a 4500 rpm burst to destroy one target than the turret spun, and he fired on another.

Two speedboats eluded fire, got past the McCain, and were heading for the *Truman*. George saw the boats pass by the ship, but they were too close to fire on. They disappeared from his radar screen when they were passing by close to the ship. George waited for them to reappear.

"Where are you, towel heads? Come on. Come on."

It seemed like an eternity, but in reality it took less than a minute for the boats to reappear. Unfortunately, they had launched their missiles and torpedoes the moment they had line-of-sight on the carrier. Those rounds were now the carrier's responsibility to defeat.

The moment the boats appeared back on his screen, he locked on the first and delivered a quick burst of fire, then swung to the second and gave an extended burst of .20 mm cannon fire. The overkill gave him a little satisfaction.

George had no time to watch what happened to the carrier. He had to turn back to the attackers and continue to blast them out of the water. A few minutes later, during a lull, he swung his gun back around and saw that the USS *Truman* was still there, unharmed. A strange sense of pride and relief washed over him like a wave in the ocean. There was no time to relax; the battle continued.

George's pride wouldn't last. After eight hours of fighting in the Strait of Hormuz, the Iranian Navy and Basij fighters were defeated, but not before wreaking havoc on the shipping lanes. Sacrificing larger, slower boats to get the smaller, high-speed suicide boats through the defensive screen, the mujahideen successfully disabled the aircraft carrier *Harry S. Truman* and several of the larger, slower ships in the fleet task force.

35

Musandam Peninsula, Oman

Under a crystal clear Omani sky, lit by the August moon and brilliant starlight, standing on a sugar white sand dune, and looking out over a still blue Persian Gulf, Lieutenant Bruce Williams knew he was viewing the same picture Bedouins, traders, and pirates standing at this same point had seen for thousands of years. Admiring the sight in the early evening before his shift ended, he was inspired by the beauty of it all. This security assignment to guard the Musandam Peninsula radar site was a welcome respite for Bruce from the front-line service in Iran escorting convoys under daily attacks by mujahideen.

Security was surprisingly weak at the radar site, which was located on the highest point at the end of the peninsula, for an operation that controlled the Strait of Hormuz shipping, where thirty-five percent of the world's seaborne oil shipments passed every day. Upon his arrival, Bruce had instituted regular security patrols around the peninsula, setup coastal lookout stations, and posted perimeter security on the main road leading to the compound. He extended the security fencing out one mile from the site and manned permanent posts to guard the fence perimeter.

"I need regular naval patrols, continuous drones for aerial monitoring of the littoral region, and more Marines to guard the site," Bruce explained on the phone to his commander back in Qatar after his reconnaissance of the site on his first day of duty.

"I'll put a request into the navy for patrols and I'll find some drones. You won't get more personnel, though. We have every available Marine focused on winning the war in Iran."

Typical staff officer response: *Don't fight the system*, Bruce thought.

***

On the day of the attack, large ships disguised as cargo carriers dropped off hundreds of small boats and amphibious light tanks just beyond the horizon with over five hundred Hizballah soldiers supported by Mahdi Corps special forces. The boats were only able to transport troops and small Toyota pickup trucks.

The Mahdi Special Forces fighters swam ashore under cover of darkness a few hours earlier. Low-crawling through the surf and beach, they moved inland, then came up behind the shoreline spotters with deadly surprise. The remainder of the assault landed quietly at two sites on opposite shores in the early morning hours, on schedule to launch their assault simultaneously with the swarming naval attack on the Fifth Fleet in the Gulf at four AM.

As perimeter security leader for the night shift, Sergeant Marie Olivera varied her patrol pattern as she visited coastal spotters every two hours and perimeter fence security Marines every hour.

Just before four AM, Sergeant Olivera approached within five hundred yards of the perimeter sentry guarding the main entrance on the sole paved road into the site. The driver of her three-person Marine team flicked his headlights. When they received no immediate response from the sentry, her driver stopped the Humvee, turned the lights off for two seconds, then back on. Still no response.

"Jed, are you there?" She had waited almost thirty seconds before a radio reply came back.

"Yep."

Really, Olivera thought.

"Jesus, Jed, you scared the hell out of me. Is Jethro there with you?"

"Yep."

Switching from the perimeter sentry's frequency on her FM radio to the emergency channel, Sergeant Olivera said, "Scout One reporting an attack on perimeter security at the main gate. Repeat, we are under attack."

Alarms went off throughout the radar site and Sergeant Olivera's vehicle was immediately hit with small arms fire coming from the main gate. Lights off, with Olivera sitting in the fifty-caliber gunner's position with a third Marine manning the M-240 machine gun pointed out his gun port, Sergeant Olivera said, "Ram that damned gate!"

As the Humvee first spun its wheels on the pavement under the power of the five hundred horsepower engine, then surged forward toward the gate, Olivera was blasting fifty caliber rounds in the direction of fire from the gate shack. Their speed was slowed by the permanent cement gate barriers with reinforced steel, but with the Mahdi Special Forces unable to operate the electronic emergency pop-up barrier, Olivera's Humvee went through the sally port with ease as she continued to blast anything that flashed or moved.

The Humvees had been specially designed to operate in the desert terrain. They had oversized wheels, a larger diesel engine, reinforced suspension, and roll bars. When no one was looking, the Marines liked to go dune-jumping in their vehicles, which turned out to be good practice.

***

Bruce flew into action when he heard Olivera's attack announcement. Alarms were blaring and every Marine was scurrying to their battle station when he ran from his barracks to the armory. Site protection was their first priority.

***

Sergeant Olivera instructed her other two Humvee patrols to search the area between the shoreline and the perimeter fence for more mujahideen. With the main gate secured, she headed out the main road to help with the inspection. It didn't take long for the reports to come in.

"Command One, this is Scout One. We have hundreds of attackers landing on our east and west shores, with light armored trucks and amphibious tanks. The heavy attack is coming from our east, toward the main gate."

"I copy, Scout One. What is your status?"

"We're taking heavy fire. My patrols are okay. Request permission to consolidate firepower on the larger force attacking from the east."

Having secured the site operations personnel and positioned his interior defenses, Bruce was talking fast as he walked with his unusual gait; feet pointing out to each side, head bobbing and weaving like Joe Frazier, and arms swinging free. "Roger that Scout One. I'm sending out a mortar team to help, but that's all I can spare. Delay, disrupt, and fallback, but don't sacrifice the whole squad. We'll make our last stand here."

***

When news of the attack reached headquarters at Al Udied Air Base in Qatar, Bruce's commander called his satellite phone. "What's your situation, Lieutenant?"

"Spotters not responding, assumed dead. Site perimeter attacked, but Olivera kicked ass and the perimeter is secure, for now. Olivera is surveying the outer area. I'll have more details in ten minutes, sir. Request air support and reinforcements immediately."

With the Air Force heavily engaged in the Strait of Hormuz fight, air support was slow to arrive at Musandam. Bruce positioned himself, machine guns, and snipers on the top of the administrative building attached to the radar facility.

***

The desert sand terrain provided some cover and gave Sergeant Olivera a chance to surprise the enemy. She pulled her security squad back behind the sand dunes. She ordered mortars to fall back 300 yards to defend the guards as they conducted a tactical withdrawal with hit and fallback maneuvers.

"Scout One to Scouts Two and Three, do you read me?"

"Scout Two here."

"Scout Three reads you."

"Come to my location near Lookout One."

When the two patrols arrived, Sergeant Olivera was standing beside her vehicle stacking land mines.

"I want Scout Two to plant these mines in the road while I lay down suppressing fire with Scout Three. When I drop back, you blow the roads. Got that?"

"Yes, Sergeant."

"Let's slow 'em down and buy time for Lieutenant Williams to get ready."

Because of the craters in the only paved road into the radar site, the mujahideen light tanks and armored trucks were forced to travel in the sand, gaining valuable time for the Marines. When the Hizballah were about 1000 yards from the facility perimeter, they were surprised to see three Humvees from different directions flying over the sand dunes, converging on them with .50 caliber machine guns mounted on top, spraying steel in rapid five- to ten-round bursts.

Sergeant Olivera's vehicle went airborne as she crested the dune first. She was wearing goggles with her sand scarf pulled up to protect her face from the thick, blowing, gritty sand. The second she spotted the Hizballah, she fired .50 caliber bursts while still airborne. She could direct her fire down at the attacking Hizballah by extending her arms fully while holding and firing the gun and raising herself up out of her gun seat by bracing her feet against the turret. It took an athlete and training to keep the machine gun steady, brace herself for the landing, hold on in the turns, and fire the weapon accurately. Her Humvee hit the sand hard, bounced, fishtailed, and swerved perpendicularly to the Hizballah's line of travel. Olivera spun her gun turret around as they passed the Hizballah and kept firing until they were over the next sand dune.

The second Humvee crested the sand dune on the opposite side of Scout One and farther up the columns of attacking Hizballah an instant after Olivera. Their crossing pattern, with clear firing zones, caused the Hizballah fighters to scatter, some dropping their weapons in the hurry to get out of the way. When Scout Two's Humvee landed, firing perpendicular to the Hizballah's track, it almost crashed into the first light tank in their attacking force. The Humvee driver cut his wheels and spun through the oncoming Hizballah, with his gunner firing as he went.

The third Humvee crested the next sand dune in front of the Hizballah as Scouts One and Two were clearing the field of fire. The hot shell casings ejected from the belt-fed .50 caliber gun were bouncing off the Humvee. The Marine manning the M-240 machine gun wiped out a swath of Hizballah down the middle of the assault. The .50 caliber gun was focused on the vehicles, knocking out a truck, but having little effect on the amphibious tanks.

The three Humvees hit fast, and then disappeared over the next sand dune, only to return two minutes later from another direction. They were disrupting the Hizballah, making them turn and fight, but there were many more of them than Sergeant Olivera could handle.

"Scouts Two and Three, make one more pass, then fall back three hundred yards to provide cover for the mortar team to withdraw."

On Olivera's signal, the mortar team showered the Hizballah with fire to cover the squad's retreat. The mortar shells weren't very accurate, but they caused the oncoming Hizballah to slow down to avoid craters.

"Mortar One, destroy your mortars and fall back." They didn't have time to breakdown the mortars and transport them back to the radar site, but they didn't want the Hizballah to turn the mortars against them either.

Sergeant Olivera moved out ahead of the other two scout vehicles and took up a position on the backside of a sand dune.

Olivera leaped out of her vehicle and led the Marine in the backseat carrying the shoulder-launched Javelin up the dune. Stopping at a protected point just short of the top of the dune, she took the Javelin, knelt down, armed the weapon with help from the Marine, then stood up and fired, sending the armor-piercing projectile with the infrared seeker zeroed-in on the engine compartment of a Hizballah light tank. The tank erupted in a fiery explosion of destruction as Olivera and the Marine ran, fell, and rolled down the hill.

"Direct hit!" radioed Scout Two.

Sergeant Olivera quickly reloaded, ran twenty yards up another dune, stepped up and fired a second missile. "Missile two away."

"Hit!" radioed Scout Three.

Seeing the covering smoke left by Scouts Two and Three, Olivera said, "Time to go, Mortar One," Olivera said as she mounted the Humvee and withdrew.

"Read you loud and clear, Scout One."

"Commence fire, Scouts!"

As Olivera set up three hundred yards behind Scouts Two and Three, the fire, fallback, and fire withdrawal continued until they reached the perimeter fence. The Hizballah fighters by now recognized the inaccurate fire, and spread out their attack to make the Marine's suppressive fire less effective. And they were quickly closing the gap on the patrols.

"Scouts Two and Three, fall back to home base. Acknowledge."

"Scout Two falling back."

"Scout Three falling back."

As her team neared the radar site, she heard Williams' welcome voice on her radio, but he wasn't calling her.

"Radar Site Command, this is Hog Team Leader, do you read me?"

"Hog Team Leader, this is Lieutenant Williams, Command One. I read you loud and clear."

"We can see the bandits. Are your Marines clear?"

"Fire as soon as ready, Hog Team Leader. No time to delay."

The Hizballah fighters were closing fast.

"Roger, Hog Team coming in hot."

"Command One to all forces. Fall back to the Radar facility, now! Repeat, fall back."

Banking and rolling hard, the two A-10 Warthogs leveled out at 200 feet off the ground. They flew in low for strafing runs parallel to the radar site using their 30mm anti-tank canon. As they swooped in and fired, their cannons ripped through the light tanks and armored trucks with 4200 rounds-per-minute sheets of armor-piercing steel like they were made of plastic. The first A-10 took out two of Hizballah's light tanks. The second A-10 took out one more. They pulled up, banked hard, pulling three times the force of gravity, then swooped back down for a second run, first firing their machine guns and precision guided anti-personnel munitions focused on Hizballah fighters before their strafing run with the canons. The two A-10s destroyed or disabled all six amphibious light tanks and killed dozens of mujahideen, but many fighters and trucks surged on toward the radar buildings.

On the second pass, Scout Two was hit by an armor-piercing shell from the A-10. Sergeant Olivera slid her vehicle between the Hizballah fighters and the disabled Humvee. She and one Marine went to help the two survivors into her Humvee while the other Marine used the M-240 to hold the Hizballah back. Two of the Hizballah slipped in behind Scout One's Humvee and, armed only with knives, jumped the Marines as they were pulling out the wounded. One of the Marine rescuers was stabbed in his shoulder. Olivera was tackled, knocking her Beretta free.

Olivera pulled out her Kabar knife and got to her feet just in time to see and spin away from a lunging stab, then she fell on her attacker, ramming her knife through his throat. She immediately moved to the second attacker who had turned to face her. Stopping short, she stood ready to defend against a thrust. The attacker instead jumped feet first into her chest, knocking her down. She dropped her knife. She got to her knees in time to deflect the attacker's knife thrust into her Kevlar vest. Then she propelled her body up, right arm extended, with the palm of her hand open into the attacker's nose, driving him to the ground bleeding and disoriented. Sergeant Olivera grabbed her Kabar and drove it into the attacker's throat.

The Marines quickly loaded their wounded and sped toward the radar site.

The A-10s had to withdraw with the Hizballah approaching the radar building. "Hog Team Lead to Command One, we'll loiter in the area to wait for a good shot. Good luck, Marines."

"Thanks, Hog Team Leader. We'll take them from here."

The Hizballah were in hot pursuit of the retreating troops. Olivera's Marines reached the radar facility and secured the building from the inside. Bruce and his team on top of the building were trying to repel the attack, but they were quickly being overwhelmed.

When the Hizballah got close, they lobbed grenades on top of the building. Bruce saw the first one coming up and made a running intercept of it, batting the grenade back to the ground like a blocked shot in basketball. When a suicide bomber finally succeeded in blowing a hole in the outer wall of the building, Bruce ordered his rooftop force back into the radar site to repel the attack.

The radar site personnel were surrounded by Hizballah forces and had no relief coming soon. Eight-foot-thick concrete walls reinforced with sheets of steel, Kevlar, and bulletproof fiberglass windows protected the radar site personnel, so the Hizballah fighters couldn't easily get in, but they *could* get in.

Bruce directed the site's defense using the building and perimeter sensors and monitors located in the control room. He issued weapons to the radar operations staff and ordered non-combatants into the underground bunker beneath the site. Bruce was watching a losing battle. He could see enemy pouring into the outer room of the facility.

Suddenly, one of the sensors in the control room went off. A radiation sensor had suddenly gone from normal to off-the-scale. The video monitors showed the Hizballah were leaving in a hurry.

Lieutenant Williams surveyed the television monitors and sensors. He looked at the people in the control room for a long moment, then slowly turned toward his Marines. He knew what had happened. Furious, he said, "Sergeant Olivera."

"Yes, sir?"

"I see a bunch of towel heads about to sail away and they forgot to take a package with them. What do you see?"

Confused, Sergeant Olivera stared at the monitors for a long moment, then smiled. "Sir, I believe they forgot something."

"Sergeant, get me the radiation detector and two shooters. We'll go into the outer room and see what kind of present they left behind."

Sergeant Olivera got her two best shooters, one with the new M-40 semi-automatic sniper rifle, the other with an M-16. She carried a 9mm Beretta and the radioactive detector.

Bruce and the three Marines went into the main building without protective suits while he searched for the radioactive device. He ordered everyone else into the bunker.

The shooters covering Williams and Olivera came out first. With one sniper standing and the other kneeling on opposite sides of the door, they quickly eliminated the straggling Hizballah.

Williams and Olivera moved out immediately after the two guards. Using the radiation detector, they quickly located the source in a small briefcase with a timer on the outside.

Bruce could see there were less than three minutes remaining on the timer.

"Give me that damn thing. Get down in the bunker and warn the A-10 pilots."

Once back inside, Sergeant Olivera contacted the A-10 pilots. "Hog Team Leader, this Scout One. Do you read me?"

"Go, Scout One, read you loud and clear."

"We are in DEFCON 1, repeat DEFCON 1. Detonation is imminent. Two minutes to zero hour."

"Holy shit!" The pilot accidently keyed his radio, and everyone could hear his surprise. "Hog Team Leader returning to base. May God keep you safe."

Bruce scooped up the briefcase and ran out the same hole the Hizballah blew open to get in. He climbed into a nearby Humvee and took off down the road as fast as he could. In these few moments before he delivered death, he thought about his wife and family, thought about pain and suffering, and thought about death and punishment. Few people have a couple of minutes to consider their own death. *Is this suicide or self-defense? Will I go to hell?* Surely the nuke was going to kill them all anyway, wasn't it? *Doesn't the Bible say there is no greater love?* "Oh, my God, I confess all my sins for thy just punishment. Holy Mary, mother of God, pray for this sinner now in the hour of my death. Amen."

The Hizballah weren't expecting anyone to follow them, so Bruce surprised them as he started catching up with those running in the back of the pack. He ran over or shot anyone in his way as he went by, zigzagging to avoid the shooters. He managed to catch up to the main pack at the rear of retreating Hizballah with a few seconds to spare. In a crowd of scattering fighters, Bruce slammed on his brakes, jumped out through the gun turret onto the hood of the vehicle in front of the stunned Hizballah.

"You assholes forgot something before your ship sails. Courtesy of Uncle Sam. Bon voyage! *Safar khosh!*"

The explosion incinerated everyone within a half-mile of him. It leveled everything else on the peninsula. The mushroom cloud was visible for miles.

36

Washington, DC

You couldn't miss a mother's loving touch by just looking around the room. The floors in the apartment were clean and shiny. The clean play clothes the boys all wore could pass for new, but were mostly bought from a thrift store and handed down from one boy to the next. While there were plenty of toys from three boys scattered around, even that was limited to two rooms. Cathy's love was most evident in the kind behavior and care for others her boys showed.

"How will the children live, Mom?" Danny asked through his speech synthesizer as he sat in his living room watching the television news about the nuclear attack in Oman.

"It will be hard, honey. But, they have other family, just like you, who will love and take care of them."

"Will we be killed by a nuclear bomb?"

Cathy choked up for a moment, considering the death of her children. "It's not likely, Danny, but no one can rule out that possibility right now."

"My dad won't let that happen."

"Your dad is a brave man, but even he can't do everything. Pray that our President and military will protect us all."

***

President Rubina took the rostrum in the House of Representatives in front of a joint session of Congress with every member present. He looked out over all nine Supreme Court Justices seated up front, amid a gallery of standing-room-only visitors, with media prepared to televise, radio, and stream his words worldwide. Without applause and with near-quiet in the somber chamber, the President spoke.

"Yesterday, on a remote peninsula in Oman, near the busiest shipping channel in the world, the Iranian mujahideen carried out their long-threatened use of nuclear power when they detonated a suitcase-sized bomb. This heinous assault was combined with a simultaneous naval attack in the Strait of Hormuz, using conventional weapons. We can thank the heroic actions of our armed forces that the loss of American and allied lives, as tragic as they were, was relatively few.

"I have personally spoken with our allies and communicated with all nuclear-armed nations to ensure them there would be no unintended and misunderstood use of further nuclear weapons. The world understands the Iranians did this. Our enemy has no capability to launch land, sea, or air nuclear weapons to attack our homeland. Our safeguards will continue to prevent a nuclear weapon from coming in across our borders. It is only our fear that can defeat us. Only internal division can dilute our strength.

"I come here today to assure the American public and our allies of our defenses, to warn our enemies of our resolve to punish any and all countries that may have helped the Iranians in this attack, and to ask the Congress to approve emergency funding to annihilate this threat. I met with my cabinet, members of Congress, and our military leaders this morning and will convene a bipartisan set of advisors tomorrow to help guide us all to manage the threats, real and imagined, at home and abroad.

"At this moment, we have substantial forces in place, with more being deployed, to destroy Iran's last elements of command authority. There will be no place on earth they can hide!"

There was mild applause from Congress, with an occasional member standing with enthusiasm.

"Let us go forward, not with fear, but courage. Not with hatred, but resolve. Not alone, but together as one people, one nation under God resolved to rid the world of this evil."

Panic and fear of a nuclear attack spread rapidly across the U.S. Lone-wolf, suitcase-sized bombs were imagined at strategic power and water sites and in large cities. Alex Shankle fanned the flames on national television with accusations of contractor spies, sabotage, and the threat of an imminent nuclear attack on the homeland.

Taking the podium in the senate chamber of the Capitol building the morning after Rubina's address to the nation, Shankle pointed toward the White House across the Washington Mall, and said, "One leader's mismanagement as our commander-in-chief made us vulnerable. One President has been so indebted to his political contributors in the military-industrial complex that he outsourced this war that we may now lose. Our ships were not prepared to defend themselves from a swarming attack that our best military experts knew would occur. Their ammunition, weapons, and preparedness were not adequate to prevent critical losses to our fleet. Our forces guarding the Musandam radar site were understaffed, unprepared, and glaringly unprotected to even the most amateur military strategist. President Rubina's conduct, resultant failures, and bungled strategies have mired us down into this long war with Iran that experts predicted should have lasted only six months. He had all the resources to win this war. Instead, we now face an all-out nuclear war in the Middle East and possible nuclear attack at home, if President Rubina is allowed to continue as Commander-in-Chief. President Mark Rubina must go!"

The senate chamber erupted in applause from Democrats and sympathetic Republicans alike. Catcalls of "Impeach, impeach!" rang out.

"I move that this chamber pass today this S. 201, *Secure the Homeland* bill I hold in my hand, authorizing our military to spend whatever is necessary to shore up our defenses to protect our homeland from a nuclear attack."

Every senator in the chamber cheered, with calls of "Hear, hear!" around the room.

"I take the floor today to call for the Pentagon to stop payment for defense contractors who failed in their duties until we can root out the traitors from their ranks." Applause.

"And I ask that a special prosecutor be appointed to investigate President Rubina's criminal behavior with his relationship with contractors, and his decisions that brought about this nuclear threat." Partisan applause was heard.

"And, most importantly, I demand the House of Representatives draft and pass the Articles of Impeachment against President Mark Rubina, with an impeachment hearing to follow in the Senate chaired by the Chief Justice of the Supreme Court!"

Shankle stepped down from the podium to applause from all but President Rubina's most ardent supporters, and walked up the center aisle, shaking hands and hugging his fellow senators as he triumphantly left the senate chamber.

***

Alex Shankle walked into his senate office where Jodie Arenas was waiting. When he closed the door, she leaped into his arms for a long embrace, but Shankle couldn't remain still. His adrenaline was pumping as he paced back and forth in the room.

"This is winning! This is my victory! No one can stop me now!" Shankle said as he talked seemingly to the world with eyes wide open and pupils dilated big as saucers.

"You've got him, Alex! America is scared and you're showing them who to blame. This attack was a stroke of luck. It will sweep you into the Presidency."

Shankle stopped, his focus narrowed, looking sternly at Jodie, "Luck?"

With a bewildered look, Jodie said, "Well, no one could have predicted the Iranians would have the ability to coordinate such a successful attack after the devastation their military command and control has experienced."

"There was no luck involved. I gave our Chinese friend the maintenance schedule for the radar site. I gave them the schedule of our fleet movements. I made the moves like pieces in a chess game that led to this stunning defeat for Rubina. I did it! I made it happen! Now, I will rule the free world!"

Jodie sat in shocked silence for a few moments, then said, "This is more than a few contractors getting killed. Ships were sunk, hundreds of sailors were killed, and you may have started a nuclear war."

"I did what I had to do. The country needs me as its President and Commander-in-Chief. I was going to lose without this bomb! You should have known I would never let that happen."

***

U.S. coalition partners in the war weighed in on Shankle's claims. Sir Angus Pringle asked the British Parliament for a resolution to withdraw from the war with Iran unless President Rubina stepped down. The Archbishop of Canterbury made public appearances to condemn Rubina and the war. He participated in a large antiwar rally in Trafalgar Square calling for British military withdrawal from all territories outside the UK.

Israeli President Peres went on national television to ask for a referendum by the Knesset to negotiate peace. There was a firestorm of condemnation against Rubina and those who supported continued war.

Alex Shankle saw the tide of public opinion begin to shift more and more to support his views and his presidential bid. He was the preferred guest of the major Sunday morning talk shows. His Internet site was flooded with campaign contributions. Major newspapers and news blogs came out in support of Shankle for President.

Shankle's political team advocated a second-ballot nomination at the upcoming Democratic National Convention. They ran direct email, twitter, and Facebook campaigns to convince convention delegates to cast their votes for Shankle in a brokered convention.

37

Speaker of the House Lionel Johnson and Vice President Luke Walker sat at the breakfast table setup in the White House Rose Garden, waiting for President Rubina and scanning the morning papers and news clippings their staffs had prepared.

When the President arrived, Rubina said, "Alex certainly seems to have support for his wild ideas."

Walker said, "The impeachment talk is a stunt to stir up your critics. That won't go anywhere."

"I'm not worried about me. He'll cripple our ability to fight if the contractors are shutdown."

Johnson said, "At least he supports more money for the military."

"It's a small comfort. Stopping payment will be disastrous for small businesses. Small companies provide most of the materiel, supplies, and services the military uses."

"You're the Commander-in-Chief. Can't you stop it?"

"I can't change the law. He's pushing a bill right now in Congress to hold our Defense Department contracting officials criminally liable on these contracts."

"Yeah, he's got the votes to override any veto, too."

"Can you prevent it from coming up for a vote, Lionel?"

"Normally, yes. But they have the votes for a Discharge Petition which will force the bill to the floor for a vote. Maybe I can delay it for a few weeks until we get more votes on our side."

"What do you think, Luke? Can Shankle hurt contractors enough to impede the war effort?"

"It's never been done that I know of. During WW Two, conservative Republicans in the House accused the construction contractor Brown & Root of making illegal campaign contributions to LBJ for payback for getting construction contracts. They got the IRS after 'em. Ol' Roosevelt himself told the IRS to back off."

Johnson said, "Hell, it was worse after Dubya left office. Liberals were so determined to get Bush and Cheney that they marched contractors in front of Congress, filed lawsuits, threatened contracting officers with criminal action and slowed down payments. The auditors and contracting officers were so afraid for their jobs they started re-auditing repeatedly, delaying billions of dollars in payments to contractors damn near until Obama's first term was up. It took a batch of top level guys, including a retired admiral, to provide an independent opinion on these audits, before ACOs felt safe to render a final decision and release funds."

"It was brutal, but there were some real contractor problems, too. Don't forget the sexual assault charges," Walker said.

"More fiction than fact. Problem was, the Army and grand juries seldom found grounds to file charges," Johnson said.

Walker said, "That frenzy doesn't compare to what's happening today. The first ever nuclear attack against the U.S.! There's real fear out there. Shankle'll use it to push his crazy ideas, at least long enough to get elected."

Rubina said, "Damn the election. We've got to get out in front of

Shankle on this. We'll hammer out a strategy with my military affairs advisory team."

***

The impact of Shankle's actions against contractors on the battlefield and the war effort itself was swift and damaging. Senators and congressmen called the Defense Department's administrative contracting officials directly to challenge continued payments to battlefield contractors who were under suspicion for negligence or non-performance.

The House and Senate started hearings on the crimes of contractor's in Iran and the President's relationship with contractors. The hearings focused on the military's lack of readiness, the billions of dollars handed out for the Sponsored Reserves, and campaign contributions.

The Secretary of Defense, a former Democratic senator, supported the actions against contractors. His Defense Contract Management Agency, bowing to public and political pressure and sympathizing with the view of corrupt contractors, directed their contracting officers to scrutinize contracts to find cause to withhold funds. Contract closeouts for battlefield contractors were stopped, delaying hundreds of millions of dollars in final payments. Award and incentive fee payments were stopped either by direct withholding or by dropping performance scores to zero. The ACOs cited rules that ranged from contractor non-performance to unsubstantiated costs and inadequate business systems to justify withholdings. DOD withheld as much as twenty percent of invoices from thousands of battlefield contractors and their subcontractors. Billions of dollars of cost that contractors had expended in support of the war were going unpaid, which was driving the industry toward massive contractor default and bankruptcy.

Camp David, Maryland

The first strands of sunlight filtered through the blinds of the Laurel Lodge conference room at Camp David, giving the President's pre-dawn meeting of military, civil service, corporate leaders, and invited guests a visual reminder that time was moving on and there was much to do. The service's military chiefs and the Chairman of the Joint Chiefs of Staff were there. NSA, CIA, and members of the President's cabinet were in attendance. House and Senate Republican leaders were there. Defense industry leaders from Lockheed, Boeing, Raytheon, Kratos, and DynCorp were there as well.

Steve Holmes felt honored to be one of the guests. It was Richard Allenby's suggestion to President Rubina that got him and Mark Darrow a seat at the table.

"Good morning, ladies and gentlemen. I brought you here to get advice on how we can best counter the potentially disastrous effects of Alex Shankle's war on contractors. I can't summarize the external threat and our posture better than I did in my address to Congress and the American people. Since that address, the antiwar Democrats, led by Senator Shankle, have created a potentially significant internal threat to our war-fighting capability. The threatened legislation that would stop, or seriously decrease, funding for many battlefield contractors could cripple our war with Iran. I need your help to address these threats. After our session, I have teams here to brief you on the remaining Iranian threats, command-and-control structure, and size and complexity of their remaining forces as well as U.S. force strength.

"Let's start the discussion with you, Jerry. What impact will these financial withholds have on Lockheed Martin's business?"

Using the networked app connecting all attendees, Jerry projected his Government Services' Balance Sheet. "We've been expecting and preparing for these actions for the past week, since it seemed likely the Pentagon was going to do something. They'll go after three to five percent of our payments by claiming our financial systems are inadequate. We expect they'll withhold payments on the new Obama One laser-equipped killer satellite, claiming we are substantially behind in delivery. They'll delay closing out some of our services contracts where we're still owed a ten-to-fifteen percent final payment. All told, we think we could see ten percent of our overall contracts withheld."

"How long can you sustain that kind of shortfall?"

"We have the cash and credit on hand to manage for a year or longer. Our stock will take a beating. The reduction in cash will limit our ability to pay for computers, pay our shareholder's dividends, or acquire other companies."

"How about you, Steve. How will this impact Kratos?"

"The Pentagon could withhold as much as twenty percent of our payments, amounting to over a billion dollars this year by delaying award fees, having DCAA increase the amount of charges they question and subsequent funds they withhold, and generally delaying payments."

Rubina asked, "Do you have the cash to even go six months with eighty percent payment?"

"We'll have to get creative, but we can survive for awhile. We're in a strong cash position with about ten percent of our annual revenue, or about one point one billion on hand. Our revenue from the U.S. government business is about six hundred million per month, so we can't rely on cash alone for very long. About four percent of that revenue is pure profit, everything else goes to pay salaries, corporate operating expenses, building rent, taxes, subcontractors, supplies, and other direct costs. We will have to borrow more money to fill the gap, which increases the costs of interest we pay. And we'll have to get creative and slow down payments to subcontractors and vendors. Mark Darrow, sitting next to me, our General Counsel, can tell you what legal challenges that will bring us."

"How much will prime contractors slow down payments to small businesses?"

Mark responded, "It won't be immediate, and there are certain contractual and legal questions we'll have to address first. For example, we have a requirement with small business subcontractors to pay them when services are rendered. So, we can't just stop paying them. With larger subcontractors, we have 'pay when paid' agreements. We can withhold payments, but that will open up other legal problems for us."

"You mean lawsuits?" Rubina asked.

"That's one problem. They may also choose to stop work, claiming breach of contract or change of conditions," Mark said.

Steve added, "Small businesses will be in big trouble on their prime contracts. Many will close within a month or two due to the lack of cash. They'll find it very difficult to get credit."

"What about you, Larry, assuming you have similar problems at Raytheon, how do you think these actions will effect the industry?"

"Like Lockheed, we'll survive for a while. Billions of dollars of shareholder value will be lost. Contractors will begin to stop work and go out of business by the hundreds every day after the first month or so. Those contractors will have to reduce salaries or stop paying their employees altogether. In return, their employees will not be able to pay their bills. Houses will be foreclosed on, and vehicles repossessed. Employees don't have a lot in the bank for rainy days."

Rubina said, "It could be a hurricane! Okay, General Sherman, as Chairman of the Joint Chiefs, how bad do you think this will be for our military? The SecDef would be here to answer this question, but he's gotten on my bad side lately."

"The turmoil caused by the Pentagon withholding payment

actions will have a damaging effect on the military almost immediately. While the active duty military, including the contractors in the Sponsored Reserves, must continue to work whether or not they're paid, the support contractors don't. The military could literally start running out of fuel, bullets, blankets, food, and every other military necessity within six months."

President Rubina solicited discussion and opinion for another hour, then spent two hours brainstorming solutions before calling for a short break. The sun was now fully above the eastern horizon as the attendees made their way to the sandwiches the Camp David staff had prepared.

When the meeting reconvened, Vice President Luke Walker outlined the plan to counter the Congressional actions against contractors. "First, we are working with the Senate Minority Leader and Speaker to rally votes against S. 201, *Secure the Homeland* bill. Get your employees to contact their representatives to denounce it. Second, we're working with Senator McCastle to sponsor an amendment that would exempt small and disadvantaged businesses from the law. She's a Shankle protégé, but a strong business advocate. She'll help us ease the pain if S. 201 gets passed. Third, the President and members of his cabinet and Defense Department will go directly to the American public and media in a series of fireside chats, news conferences, interviews, and town hall meetings.

"All of you can help here by engaging public and local media support. Fourth, we are preparing an emergency appeal to the Supreme Court if the bill overrides the President's veto. Finally, in the unlikely event that this bill does pass and we start to see the damaging effects, we are drawing up contingency plans for nationalizing critical industries and workers necessary to support the war effort."

Steve said, "Our military customers on the ground will push the

Pentagon from their end. When that commander sees an impact to his war-fighting ability, he or she will raise hell."

Jerry added, "We'll act collectively with other defense contractors through industry groups, like the National Defense Industrial Association."

Steve added, "Lawsuits against the bill will be filed by large and small contractors."

Richard noted, "That could take months or years to sort out. Our best bet is to stop the bill from becoming law."

***

The next morning, Steve met with Harper McCastle in her Senate office at the Capitol at eight AM.

When Steve was shown in, the senator stood to greet him. "Good morning, Mr. Holmes. I appreciate you coming to see me. I am very concerned about the impact of the withhold-payment actions by Congress and the Pentagon."

"Thank you for seeing me, Senator McCastle. I was afraid I might not be welcome after those hearings on the convoy disaster a few months ago."

"Nonsense. You handled yourself well in that very difficult hearing. I have great respect for you and Kratos."

"I knew that with your background, Senator, you could help."

"As you know, I was CEO of Alchemy, before I was elected to the senate. I understand the financial burden this will cause and the cascading effect it will have on our economy and the war with Iran."

"I understand you're sponsoring a bill to help small businesses."

"Yes, I am prepared to take several actions if S. 201 passes. We'll earmark specific funding to go to product and service companies to buy the most critical items for the military."

"How can we help?"

"Politicians like to see proof of voter concern. Any independent evidence you can gather would help."

"Yeah, I can get some petitions going. What else can you do?"

"We have the Secretary of Defense and the Chairman of the Joint Chiefs of Staff appearing before the armed services committee this week. I'll get them to say just how bad this bill will be for our military."

"What can you do to ensure that critical equipment and services get delivered?"

"We'll have to nationalize some functions to get through this mess. I'm not sure our commanders and the military services have the know-how now to operate and manage these functions. But, we'll get through it."

"That'll be a goat rope."

McCastle said, "We did it in World War One, with railroads, telegraph lines, and even Smith & Wesson. We did more in WW Two, including nationalizing Montgomery Ward for a while. We can do it again."

"That may not be enough," Steve said.

"You have my commitment, Mr. Holmes, to do all I can to ensure we reverse or minimize the impact of the Pentagon's actions."

***

Senator Shankle kept up his attacks on contractors and the President through it all, and his popularity with the public grew—it viewed him as a champion of the little man who would stand up to the big corporation. In poll after poll, the public showed that they trusted him on military matters more than they did the President or other members of Congress. The wave of public opinion looked sure to sweep him into the Presidency.

38

Washington, DC

Jodie Arenas took the long walk around the Washington Mall to relax as she made her way to 935 Pennsylvania Avenue. Taking deep breaths and rehearsing her story as she slowly walked up Independence Avenue, she arrived late for her meeting with FBI agent Alice O'Neal.

She paced and shot continual glances at the clock as she waited a few minutes in the reception area for O'Neal to meet her. Jodie felt uncomfortably warm and her heart was beating fast.

"Hello, Ms. Arenas," Agent O'Neal said curtly.

Jodie could only manage a weak, "Hello," then followed O'Neal into the interrogation room. After introductions and background questions, O'Neal asked, "Did you know where Mr. Holmes was going when he departed your London office the day he was attacked?"

"He said he was going back to his hotel."

"Was he going to walk there?"

"He said he'd catch a bus."

"Was it unusual for Steve to take the bus?"

Looking O'Neal directly in the eyes for more than a moment for the first time in the interview, Jodie said, "I assure you, Agent O'Neal, I don't know what's usual or unusual for Steve Holmes. We've only met a few times and never before in London."

"Why didn't he take a cab or walk?"

"I don't know." Jodie once again glanced at her watch.

"Did you notice anything peculiar when Steve left your office?"

"No, I went back to my desk and continued working. We were very busy, know what I mean?"

"How do you know you went back to your desk and not to the bathroom or to the window to look out?"

"Because I had another appointment to get ready for. Hear what I'm sayin'? I recall hurrying to get my paperwork together for that meeting. Know what I mean?"

"Your London receptionist, Olivia, said she walked in your office after Steve left and saw you standing at the window talking on your cell phone."

"Well, she's mistaken!" Jodie said defiantly.

After another half hour of questioning which yielded little information, Agent O'Neal said, "Okay, thank you Ms. Arenas. That will be all for now. I trust you will be available if I have further questions."

The London police provided O'Neal with phone records that showed that Jodie made a phone call immediately after Steve left her office. The call was traced to a cell phone near her office that was found on the day of the attack near the Tower of London. Only one other call was made on that phone, and it was made from the same cell tower. The call was to a number with an '86' country code: China.

***

Alice met with Sherry Adkison the next day and updated her with the information.

"I've been looking at Chinese agents, but this number will allow me to narrow my search. We're digging through customs records, travel records, purchases, and lists of foreign agents to find a connection to the convoy sabotage," Sherry said.

"So what's your theory, Alice? What was Jodie Arenas' involvement in all this?"

"Not sure yet, but she's lying. She was more nervous this time. She used 'know what I mean,' and 'hear what I'm saying' over and over, like that would convince me she was truthful."

"So, you think she was involved in the murder attempt?"

"Maybe. All I know for sure is that Jodie called a disposable phone that was later used to call a Chinese number."

"That call is the best lead we have."

"By the way, I dialed that Chinese phone number and it's no longer in service."

"That figures. I'll check with Scotland Yard and NSA. They may have a recording or at least metadata for that call."

39

Washington, DC

Sitting on the two oversized couches with marshmallow-like seat cushions, the Attorney General, Secretary of State, Secretary of Defense, Chairman of the Joint Chiefs of Staff, and Secretary of Homeland Security didn't speak a word as they awaited the President.

Joe Brownly, the Homeland Security Director, could literally feel the weight of the nuclear crisis on his head and shoulders, weighing him down like an anchor in the ocean. Unlike the AG, Joe seldom met with the President in the Oval Office. Joe tried to relax while sitting across from the AG, with the plush carpet emblazoned with a brilliant eagle and emblem of the United States under his feet.

President Mark Rubina entered the room with a curt "Good morning," then pulled up a large, leather-backed armchair from his desk to sit facing them.

"I need answers, and I need them fast. Who made the bomb and did any other country help Iran? That's what I expect you to tell me, and I'm not going to wait months to find out. Joe, you can start by telling me what you've done so far."

Taking a deep breath as he pulled out a summary of the investigative progress report for the President, Joe said, "We have a team in Qatar to conduct the forensic investigation. The Army containment team has secured the site. We're collecting samples today."

"Who's running the investigation?"

"We are."

"What about Sultan Al Said?"

Secretary of State Paulette Ryan said, "I met with the sultan this week. They have jurisdiction for all incidents in Oman, but our Security and Assistance Agreement with them gives us the lead for the nuclear investigation."

"And we'll coordinate our activities with the International Atomic Energy Agency, as well. However, DHS will supervise the investigation," Joe said.

Rubina looked at FBI Director Stephens for a moment, then asked, "Can we get conclusive evidence to prove who did this, Elliott?"

"The FBI has an agent on the forensic team who will lead all evidence gathering. Between the trace samples gathered at the site and the satellite, cell phone, Internet, and human intelligence, we'll get 'em."

Musandam Peninsula, Oman

Alice O'Neal stepped out of the Army Humvee carrying her hazardous material gear. Joining up with the rest of the investigative team, they loaded all their protective clothing, test equipment, and gear onto the helicopter at Al Udied Air Base, and then flew to the Musandam radar site.

After suiting up in their HAZMAT suits prior to arrival, Alice's four-person forensic team exited the helicopter and boarded vehicles designed to operate in a radioactive environment. The vans had test equipment onboard and mechanical arms and sensors for gathering soil, air, and water samples remotely; the team did not have to leave the vehicle.

Two soldiers from the Nuclear Disablement Team out of Aberdeen Proving Ground physically collected samples and prepared all the hazardous samples for shipment back to the DOE laboratory for analysis. Alice and the FBI would ensure the proper chain of custody was maintained for all evidence gathered. The DOE's team member was a nuclear scientist, Dr. Phillip Mellon.

As she sat in the HAZMAT van waiting for the evidence to be collected, Alice asked Mellon, "How soon do you think we can know where the bomb was made?"

"A few days, if we're lucky. A few weeks or years, if we're not. I'll do some preliminary tests here. The most important analysis will be done at Lawrence Livermore back home and Siebersdorf, Austria."

"FBI Director Stephens wants to know immediately. He called me again last night."

"Based on the chemical makeup of the bomb, we can pinpoint the country where it was produced and which production facility made the bomb, but the process takes time."

"Can you determine if any other countries helped the manufacturer?"

"If they just aided and abetted without providing nuclear material, no, we won't know that."

"Well, with some shoe leather and electronic data-gathering, our FBI team should turn up those other countries. How do you get the data for verification from those nuclear factories?"

"The U.S. and international community have been building databases for decades."

"I doubt you get much through voluntary contributions."

"What we have is in our database. They aren't perfect."

"Who keeps this database?"

"That's a problem. There's not just one database and they aren't interlinked. A little help from our international friends sharing their data could help us find the culprits faster."

"Okay. That's another topic I'll bring up with the DHS director."

***

After the initial analyses had been conducted, a low-confidence, preliminary assessment suggested the weapon was made in Russia. Dr. Franz Leitz, the DHS Lead Investigator, met with the forensic team at Al Udied Air Base. "We're making progress. I'd say the investigation is moving along better and quicker than expected."

Alice replied, "The press is all over this story about Russia. It's causing irresponsible allegations by some politicians. Russia has their nuclear forces on high alert."

"We warned the President that the preliminary findings could be wrong."

"If it's wrong, why would the data appear to point toward Russia?"

Dr. Mellon said, "Bad samples, faulty testing, or any number of other factors could give a false positive reading. Could be that the material originated in Russia, but was manufactured elsewhere. Russia has had past agreements to provide Iran with nuclear fuel and assistance."

***

It took another week before all the data was analyzed and anyone could draw conclusions with a high degree of certainty.

Sherry Adkison phoned Alice after the final data collection.

"I was worried about you out there in Oman. How are you holding up?"

"It's not fun wearing those space suits in the desert. I'm looking forward to some privacy when I need to pee."

"It's the little comforts that mean the most. When will you be home?"

"We're just wrapping things up. I should be back in the states tomorrow."

"National media are reporting your team's final conclusions will point to Iran as the sole manufacturer of the nuclear weapon."

"I can't comment on the specifics of the investigation until Washington releases it. I can tell you that we're ninety-nine percent sure where the bomb was made and it wasn't in Russia."

"That will be news. Steve thinks we'll drop a bomb on somebody. I'm glad it won't be Russia."

"Let's wait until the news comes out."

"Okay. Hurry back. I've got an assignment for you."

"It's got to be better than this one."

40

Washington, DC

Rising early on an unusually cold, late August morning in DC, Shankle slid quietly out of Jodie Arenas' bed and into the bathroom. He slipped-on his Saucony running shoes, ultra-short gym shorts, long-sleeved pull-over shirt, skull cap, and runner's watch, then jogged through the streets of Arlington and Crystal City, hot breath condensing into a fog with every exhale.

***

Sherry Adkison peeled off her warm winter coat and the blanket covering her legs as she stepped out of the van forty-five seconds after Shankle jogged past. This time, the FBI was prepared. In addition to the RQ-170 Sentinel surveillance drone loitering high overhead, they had agents stationed along the way. Jogging about a tenth of a mile behind the senator, Sherry was close enough to observe him, but not so close to alarm him. Other agents, disguised as maintenance workers and joggers, walked, jogged, or strolled around the most likely locations for electronic communications.

It was clear someone in Washington DC was stealing convoy

movement plans and Alex Shankle was a prime suspect. The address found on the pouch in Major Sharif's apartment established the DC connection. The FBI had traced the postmark back to a post office, but the trail had died there.

The senator turned up Crystal Drive and jogged on the stone pathway, beside the nearly deserted highways, past office buildings, restaurants and businesses that hadn't yet opened for customers. At eight miles an hour, his pace was good for an older jogger. When he passed 18th Street, he glanced around several times as if searching for anyone who might look suspicious. Although it was light enough to see, the sun had not yet fully risen.

He turned into the Water Park, and stopped near a metal bench to tie his shoe. He adjusted the watch on his arm and stretched for several seconds, then continued his run. Sherry peeled off from trailing Shankle, and another agent continued the chase.

Continuing on 18th Street, Sherry stopped next to one of the maintenance trucks positioned nearby and began talking with Agent Hugh Walker.

"Did you see him pickup or drop anything off?"

"Over there." Hugh pointed. "He stopped at that bench. Nothing out of the ordinary, though." Hugh scanned the area for anything unusual-looking. "We've registered transmissions in this area before when we know the senator was on one of his morning jogs. I know he's transmitting or receiving something. I just know it."

Sherry heard the announcement from their command post, "Sentinel registered a transmission in the area of the Water Park."

Sherry paused to look around, then continued, "We have to find that transmitting device. Let's start with that park bench, then search a circular radius of two hundred feet out from where Shankle stopped; that'll be about the extent of a cheap Wi-Fi's range. If we don't find anything, then we'll broaden the search."

They waited until Shankle made his return trip and re-entered Arenas' apartment before searching for the device in the park. They brought out metal detectors to search the surrounding grounds. They searched the trees and poles nearby. They used ground-penetrating radar to scan the area as well, but didn't find anything. It took an hour of searching before Hugh finally found the electronic device hidden in the hollow metal leg of the park bench the senator had stood over.

Sherry walked over to the bench when she heard the radio call. "I can't tell what it is. Get it down to the FBI lab and let them examine it."

Philadelphia, Pennsylvania

Three nights later, a team of a dozen experts stood in The Patriot Restaurant's private dining room waiting for their leader to arrive. The drinks and relaxed conversation flowed like water down a mountain stream. Some were experts on spy gadgets. Others knew how to break codes. There were FBI agents, contractors, NSA analysts, and one Marine, all taking the time to get to know the others on their project. Fifteen minutes after the party started, Sherry Adkison entered the room to "Hear ye, hear ye! All rise for the honorable Judge Sherry Adkison."

Walking slowly in a regal fashion, with both hands on her gavel and wearing a gray wig tied in a bun, Sherry strolled through the room. Her head was tilted up as she looked down her nose through the granny glasses at the small crowd laughing and pointing. Her black robe billowed and flowed behind her as she made her way to the podium. Striking the gavel three times, she announced "Now hear this. By popular decree, and FBI authority, I welcome you to The Project. We are going to catch a criminal!"

A loud cheer rang out.

Sherry flipped on the overhead projector with a picture of a secretive-looking character in trench coat and fedora. "Who's spying? You be the judge."

She popped up the next picture showing a mouse running through a maze, "How'd they do it? You be the judge."

Sherry clicked for the next picture showing a jury pointing fingers at a criminal inside a courtroom, "Who's guilty? Let me hear you say it."

In awkward unison, the crowd said, "We'll be the judge."

The last picture showed exhausted hikers walking through the desert toward an oasis, skin scorched red, with tongues swollen and dry, "Are we done yet? Can we go home? Do we have enough proof? I'LL BE THE JUDGE!"

Everyone was laughing as Sherry turned off the machine and raised her glass of water. When they quieted down, she said, "That all starts tomorrow. Thanks for getting here on such short notice. Here's a toast to hard work and the satisfaction of getting our man, or woman."

"That's the Sherry I know," Agent Alice O'Neal said as she turned to General Ron Lee.

"Have you known her long?"

"We went to the FBI Academy together. She's fun, and determined."

"This case may lead to some unwanted publicity and accusations of political bias if a senator is implicated. She'll need that strong will."

"She's fearless. On one training exercise at the Academy, we were searching an old barn for a briefcase when a discarded cigarette ignited gasoline that had spilled on dry straw. The fire spread quickly and all the trainees, except Sherry, ran out of the barn. Sherry continued searching and in a few minutes she found the briefcase. By now, the fire blocked her exit from the room. Sherry wrapped herself in a blanket and ran through the door. The blanket caught fire, but she threw it off after getting out of the barn and, without pause, walked directly to the instructor and handed him the briefcase. Everybody cheered; it was fun."

***

The next day at the FBI's Philadelphia Regional Computer Forensics Lab, RCFL, the team gathered around the electronic device used in the high-tech dead-drop at the Water Park.

Sherry explained the project, then passed out assignments. "We've extracted the software from the hardware device. I'm dividing you into two teams to analyze what we have. I want regular reports from the Code and Hardware teams."

The Code Team had mathematicians, analysts, and computer engineers deciphering the software encryption and logic, supported by General Ron Lee as a technical consultant. Hardware analysts and engineers reverse-engineered the foreign equipment and systems.

***

Sherry and General Lee met in her office in the late afternoon of the first day.

"I'm glad to have you in on this investigation, General Lee."

"I lobbied the commandant to get this assignment. As an unreformed geek, I look forward to the challenge."

"Not your typical Marine, hey, Ron?"

"I still bench press two hundred-eighty pounds, so I don't get any flak about it. What happens if we find the convoy data we suspect is on this device?"

"I'm almost afraid to imagine. There is someone in Washington leaking classified convoy data. If we find it, then Shankle is a spy."

"No matter how much I may disagree with his political views, it's hard to imagine that someone at his level would be a traitor."

"Thanks for dropping by, General Lee. Now, get back to work," she said with a smile.

Dr. Juan Galvez, a Kratos quantum physicist on contract with the Philadelphia laboratory, led the hardware examination.

Sherry met with Dr. Galvez the following morning.

"What do you know about this device we found, Juan?"

"Pretty standard stuff, for the most part. The input and output channels were standard Universal Serial Bus designs. Data storage, power, and processing hardware were also standard commercial equipment. It was the transceiver that was state-of-the-art."

"Come on, spit it out, Doc, in terms simple enough I can understand."

"It's an optical laser used for transmitting and receiving information. Made by the Chinese. Very advanced."

"Have you seen the technology before?"

"It's been used by commercial companies for several years. The technique is quantum teleportation."

"So, I can beam your cat up to the starship *Enterprise* with this transceiver?" Sherry asked with a grin.

"You're not the first one to use that joke, Agent Adkison. It transmits electromagnetic energy, not biological creatures."

"Did Shankle need line of sight for that?"

"Yes, of course."

"What makes a laser such a big deal?"

"The really big deal is that the transmitted code theoretically can't be cracked."

"That's what they say about all new codes. It's kind of like the unsinkable *Titanic*, isn't it?"

"The problem here is that to read the transmitted message in free-space alters the photons, which changes the message and tells the receiver you've been eavesdropping. It's due to something called the Heisenberg Uncertainty Principle, which is probably more information than you wanted to know."

"Well, yes, but we didn't have to intercept the transmitted message in this case. We already have it encoded on the electronic device."

"That's right. We can look for fingerprints and other physical evidence, but the real challenge is for the software guys," Galvez said.

"You've still got a good fourteen hours left to get work done today, Doc. Get to it!"

Galvez laughed as he left the room.

***

General Lee and the coding team ran several sophisticated models to help break the encryption. They used supercomputers that tested the massive combinations and permutations of each potential code.

Sitting next to a young mathematician, Lee asked, "What have you done so far?"

"We're using previously decoded messages and our database of current and past technology to try to decipher the message," the young man said as he looked up from his computer screen. "We're looking for similarities and patterns in the message."

"In other words, you're working backward from the message to decode it."

"Yeah. That's how I was taught."

"Let that run and let's come at if from the other end as well."

"How's that?"

"Let's focus on their method of encoding the message. There has to be a key there. If we can find a loose thread, this whole code will unravel."

"Where do you want to start?"

"Just like picking your combination lock at the gym, we try combinations of Shankle's birth date, social security number, age, or dog's name. Personal stuff."

The supercomputer crunched the data for twenty minutes. They tried keys based on other time and date factors and statistical features gleaned from the code as well.

The mathematician said, "There does seem to be a pattern. I think they used some type of symmetric key encryption."

"You can read the message?"

"No, not yet."

"Remember, they have a civilian on one end who wouldn't be very technical. They wouldn't rely on anything too sophisticated. I suspect this algorithm uses a single key for both encoding and decoding."

"One key seems a little too simple for anyone."

"It's good enough to be approved by NSA for encrypting U.S. classified data."

"The computer isn't finding a key based on Shankle's personal information."

Lee said, "Let that program continue running. Maybe they used a pseudo-random number program to generate the key. It's been done before."

"Isn't that too complicated for your simplicity theory?"

"No. They give him the code generator, he types in the key word followed by his message and out pops the coded message."

"I'll check for it. We have a database of previous generators used."

"Both the sender and the receiver would have to have that generator. Kind of like the code generation device I was given for my Treasury Bonds ten years ago."

"The what?"

"That was before your time. With many of these algorithms, you get the same number out every time if you use the same input key. Not very random at all."

***

It took the FBI team a few more days, but they successfully broke the code on the encrypted electronic storage device. Sherry sat down with Dr. Galvez and General Lee to review their findings.

"You have the report summarizing the crypto-analysis with the decoded message attached. Giving troop movement plans and convoy travel schedule information to the Chinese is clearly an act of treason. The problem is, we can't yet prove it was Shankle who gave them the information."

Lee asked in a surprised tone, "It's not enough that you saw him stop at the bench where the device was planted, you recorded electronic emanations there, and verified Shankle had received this type of information routinely from the military?"

"It's enough for us to put him under twenty-four-hour watch. It's not enough to arrest a sitting senator from the President's opposition party who is Chairman of the Senate Armed Services Committee."

General Lee asked, "How do we get him?"

"We either have to get him to confess or find the watch he used with the data on it. The attorney general expects the evidence to be irrefutable."

Lee asked, "With what you have so far, including those payments from the Chinese military that CID linked to Shankle, can you get authorization for a wire-tap and search warrant?"

"I'm working on it with Director Stephens, who's talking with AG Park. The AG won't approve it unless the President agrees. That's still under discussion. Let's wrap this up and talk about the next steps of the investigation."

41

Washington, DC

Sherry met with FBI Director Elliott Stephens the next day at FBI headquarters in Washington.

"Thank you for the update," Stephens said when Sherry finished her briefing. "I also received a summary of the findings from the FBI regional lab. It's some pretty damning evidence against Shankle."

"I hear a 'but' coming."

"But . . . it's not enough to arrest the senator. I spoke to the AG and President this morning. Workup the search warrant and wiretap paperwork. I think we can get approval for it, first from the President and AG, then from a federal court judge."

Sherry worked with the FBI General Counsel to develop an application for a search warrant and wiretap and presented her case to Director Stephens. After listening to her pitch, Stephens said, "It's a compelling case. The surveillance tape of the senator in the park, the high-tech dead drop, the money from the Chinese, Jodie Arenas lying in her interview about the assassination attempt on Steve Holmes, and that prime number code Sharif used. Yeah, I like it."

"Okay, so what do we do next?"

"I'll need to speak with the attorney general again, and then the President. There are significant Constitutional and legal questions they need to address, not to mention the political ramifications, before they'll do anything on this."

The AG and the DOJ lawyers were brought up to date on the case. After a thorough review of the evidence and the legal precedents, the AG and FBI director again met with President Rubina in the Oval Office.

"The evidence is convincing. I'll agree to the wiretap and search warrant, but you'll have to give the senator the opportunity to review all evidence seized," President Rubina said.

AG Park said, "That gives him the opportunity to assert his Privilege under the Constitution's Speech or Debate Clause."

Director Stephens asked, "His privilege?"

Park replied, "He can assert that any information seized was in his possession for his duties as a United States senator. We should also include an independent observer to ensure the proper handling of all seized information for future separation-of-powers legal challenges."

Stephens got the search warrant and wiretap order signed by the federal judge of the U.S. District Court for the District of Columbia. The FBI executed simultaneous operations to search and seize evidence at the senator's homes in Washington and Dayton, Ohio, and his office at the Dirksen Senate Office Building.

***

Sherry Adkison led the raid on the senator's Washington home. When Audrey Shankle answered the knock at the door shortly after nine AM, Sherry handed the search warrant to her, and said, "Mrs. Shankle, I am agent Sherry Adkison from the Federal Bureau of Investigation. I have a search warrant for your home."

"For what?" Audrey asked as the agents walked through the door.

"We have probable cause to believe your husband is involved in espionage."

"That's outrageous!"

As the agents methodically went through each room, they first had to identify and separate senate-issued devices, like computers, blackberries, mobile phones, and storage devices. They started with the study and master bedroom.

After personally searching the study, Sherry went back in the kitchen where Audrey was talking on her cell phone with her husband.

"Just a minute Al, an FBI agent is standing here with your computer in her hand. What is it, Agent Adkison?"

"I apologize for the inconvenience, Mrs. Shankle, but I'll need to take that phone."

"What! This is my phone, not Al's." Sherry could hear Shankle yelling on the other end.

"It's evidence, ma'am."

They then did a complete search of the home and removed all other electronic devices and suspicious files. Unfortunately, none of the searches turned up the senator's watch. The wire-tap didn't provide any leads, either.

Without the watch, Sherry wasn't optimistic that the rest of the evidence would produce a smoking gun. Her focus shifted to the interviews. Principally, she wanted to interview the senator and Jodie Arenas.

***

Sherry opened the interview at FBI headquarters, "Ms. Arenas, I want to thank you for once again agreeing to answer our questions. Just to be clear, I'm interested in your knowledge about any connections the senator may have with the Chinese and the leak of this convoy travel schedule data, not the assassination attempt on Steve Holmes."

"Well, I don't trust you or the FBI. This is all politically motivated. You and the President are out to discredit Senator Shankle. He's an honorable man, a great senator and a proud American. You don't have one shred of real evidence. Otherwise someone would have been arrested."

"You've been advised of your rights."

"Yeah, you'd like me to take the Fifth so you can claim Senator Shankle is hiding something."

"Nothing could be further from the truth. We took extraordinary measures to avoid even the appearance of political bias in this investigation. The evidence was reviewed independently by both the FBI and Department of Justice and we included an independent observer when we executed the search warrants."

"Independent, my ass! You all answer to the same boss, and he just doesn't want to lose the election. Rubina is using blackmail to get the senator to drop the impeachment hearings."

Sherry spent a considerable amount of time going through the timeline of events for the transmission of the convoy data first to the Chinese, then to Major Sharif in Qatar. She asked about Jodie's knowledge of the events, the senator's Chinese contacts and travel. Jodie's belligerence continued until Sherry asked about the intelligence information.

"Has he ever asked you to get him information on the Army convoys in Iran?"

"You know the senate is investigating the convoy attacks. Of course I've gotten it."

"Have you provided convoy travel information like dates and times?"

"It's in the public record. Did you do your homework before you started this interview, Agent Adkison or am I here to educate you?"

Without pause, Sherry continued, "When was the last time you requested that data from the military?"

"I don't know, probably just before the senate hearings on the communications and intelligence failures."

"Who provided you the data?"

"All our requests go through the military liaison officer provided by the Department of Defense."

"You haven't conveyed that classified information to any unauthorized persons?"

"No. We ask the liaison officer and he gets the data."

"Are you sure, Ms. Arenas. I'm not talking about the senator's guilt or innocence here. I'm talking about what you did."

There was shocked silence. Jodie's eyes grew wider as she delayed before answering, "I . . . I did nothing wrong," she said weakly as she contemplated her own fate.

"And finally Ms. Arenas, are you aware that the punishment for espionage in the United States could include fines, prison, or even death?"

There was another pause, then Jodie said meekly, "I'm n-not guilty of es-espionage."

"Thank you, Ms. Arenas, I'll be in touch."

***

Sherry conducted the interview with Shankle at his office in the Capitol Building the following day. She thought it was a mistake, but Director Stephens wanted to honor Shankle's request.

"This is a beautiful and historic building, Senator Shankle. You must be proud to serve in this iconic place," Sherry said as she sat down across the desk from the senator.

"I deserve to be here. It is my destiny. When the histories of our times are written, this will be but one stop on my journey to serve my country. America needs men of virtue and intelligence like me to keep it strong."

"I believe you mean what you say, Senator. I am so in awe of the Senate. Just for inspiration this morning, I jogged by the Capitol and around the Washington Mall."

"That's good for your health, my dear. In my campaign to get America fit, I encourage that we all exercise every day. I'm a jogger myself, you know."

"Really?"

"There are lots of opportunities to do that in Washington with events like the Army Ten-Miler and Marine Corps Marathon."

"Competing in races like those would help my motivation to run. You must enjoy the great opportunities to run in spectacular surroundings."

"That's true, but I also like to just get out and run on the streets and trails around town."

"I need to get in great shape, like you. I just need to get a decent pedometer to track my steps."

"Don't waste your money. Get accuracy with a GPS watch."

Looking at the senator's arm, Sherry said, "Is that the watch you use for running?"

"No, I use the GPS Watch Phone QE103. It does everything. You can talk on it, and keep up with your steps, speed, distance, and heart rate."

"I'll check that out, but it sounds pretty expensive. Can I see your watch sometime?"

Betraying his suspicion with a raised eyebrow, Shankle said, "It's at the Congressional gym, but I'm sure you can find something similar on-line."

Sherry made a note and then changed the conversation, "Senator, I want to thank you for giving us your deposition. I'm sure these matters can be cleared up with a little help from you."

"You're not going to kill me with kindness, Agent Adkison, so stop the act. I agreed to this interview so the American people could see I have nothing to hide. Proceed with your persecution."

"I wanted to ask you about the leak of the convoy travel information in Iran that led to attacks that killed American soldiers and marines."

"What makes you think I had anything to do with leaking that information? And if I did, do you think I'm stupid enough to admit it?"

"Major Sharif had a package in his home with a postmark from Washington."

"That doesn't mean I leaked it."

"You were one of several people here in DC who received that information."

"You accuse me of leaking classified information! You ransacked my home, scared my family half to death, tarnished my reputation with these outrageous accusations, and now you call me a spy."

"I'm not calling you anything. Just asking you questions."

"I defy you or this government to prove one iota of that allegation."

"If you would just answer the question, Senator."

"I am falsely accused for political gain. President Rubina is behind this and the world will soon know it. You and your cronies will rue the day you accused this senator, I can assure you."

"Are you threatening to get me fired, Senator?"

"I'll do a lot more than get you fired, honey. You'd better decide where you can hide when I come after you and all those helping you smear my name. This conversation is over! Get out of my office."

Sherry walked out. She wasn't afraid. She wasn't intimidated. And she wasn't mad. In fact, she was smiling. The senator had unwittingly handed her a present. That QE103 watch has an infrared sensor capability. She noted his suspicion when he said it was at the gym, but that was after he told her what kind it was.

Shankle walked out of his office a few minutes later into the throng of reporters awaiting him. He stepped to the microphone his staff had setup on the steps of the Capitol, and said, "I will read a statement and take no questions.

"I met with the FBI today and have fully cooperated with their investigation. I continue to do everything I can to help find and fix the problems that led to the Neka convoy disaster. But, and I tell you this with great regret: My political opponents don't give a damn about our dead soldiers, marines, seamen, or airmen. They are driven by their egos, politics, and their desire to shutdown any opposition. And they want to destroy anyone who stands up for the average American. They are so corrupt, they are trying to destroy my reputation. They accuse me of treason, without any proof! That is tyranny in its most evil form. They asked their questions and I answered them. I will not answer any more of my government's questions on this unjustified claim. I will simply leave you with the words of Thomas Jefferson: 'When the people fear the government there is tyranny, when the government fears the people there is liberty.' Long live liberty in America!"

42

Washington, DC

President Mark Rubina picked up his morning news clippings report as he and Vice President Luke Walker had breakfast in the White House Rose Garden. CHINA DENOUNCES IRAN'S NUKES and U.S. PLANS FINAL ASSAULT were the first of many similar headlines this day.

Rubina shook his head. "I don't know what Iran expected to accomplish with a nuclear attack, but they've lost every friend in the world."

"I bet they didn't count on China abandoning them."

"Or U.S. public opinion. As much as the public is pissed at me, they're even more determined that we finish off the Iranians once and for all."

"The Persian Thunder plans are ready for your approval this morning to do just that, Mr. President."

Joint Base Mashad, Iran

Steve Holmes arrived at Mashad the next day to meet Major Albert

York, a Sponsored Reserve squadron leader for twenty-four F-35 Lightning II Joint Strike Fighters designated to support operation Persian Thunder, at the pilots' favorite hangout at Mashad, the Stealth Bar.

As they sat down at the bar, Steve asked, "What's good here? I'm starved."

"The Fighter Pilot sub is good, if you like hot roast beef and horseradish."

"That sounds good. What have you been up to, Major?" Steve asked as they ordered their meals.

"We've been running close-air-support for small Army and Marine missions the past few months and patrolling the no-fly zone. Pretty boring stuff."

"I guess there haven't been any dogfights lately to get you excited?"

"No, we knocked out the mujahideen Air Force in the first few days of the war."

"I didn't see much in the news about those fights."

"Not much to 'em. Their Chinese Vigorous Dragons and older U.S., Soviet, and French aircraft weren't much opposition."

"When do you expect to get the 'go' for this final assault?"

"They don't tell me when."

"Are you ready?"

"We have to be. We're conducting training missions around the Hindu Kush while we wait."

After searching for months, Special Operations had finally pinpointed the location of the remaining Iranian military command authority in the Elburz Mountains. The Iranians had started building a massive underground bunker over a decade earlier when sanctions and threats over their nuclear program drove them to make contingency plans for war. They initially focused on a command center underneath the city of Tehran. The system connected government, religious, and military centers throughout the city to a series of tunnel entrances hidden from sight. As consensus against a nuclear Iran grew among Western nations and economic sanctions increased, the government undertook a massive three-hundred-mile long, half-mile-wide underground combined highway and railway linking Tehran and the Caspian Sea to a command center in the Elburz Mountains; Persian Thunder's target.

"Kratos had the contract to build that training range in Afghanistan fifteen years ago. Is it still there?"

"Yeah, that's the one. We fly down there, run our missions, and get back fast. Pretty convenient."

"You get good weapons' practice that way?"

"We shoot at drones over unoccupied mountain ranges. And we practice dogfights. We can test close-air support on the ranges all right, but these bunker buster bombs are hard to test without blowing the sides off mountains."

"Will they do the job?"

"We've run a few tests, but I'm not sure we can get these bombs down deep enough to penetrate the bunkers."

"How deep will they go?"

"That's classified, Steve. Sorry."

"What other options do you have?"

"If we can find an entrance, we can drop the Hades thermobaric bomb to blast 'em, suffocate 'em and cook 'em deeper in the mountain."

"I can't imagine they have much of a remaining defense to stop you."

"Ancient SAMs and triple-As. That's about all."

"You make it sound so easy. I know you don't tell your team that you don't have any real threats."

"Hey, it only takes one well-placed missile to knock one of us out of the sky. The greatest threat will come if we have to run close-air support missions. Even old weapons are scary close in. Not much time to react. The Lightning's skin is pretty thin."

"We don't hear much about that limitation for the highly touted F-35!"

"The F-35 is a great fighter, but close-air ground support is its weakest mission. It's a hell of a lot easier to maneuver at thirty-thousand feet doing mach one than it is at two hundred feet at near stall speed."

"Why don't you send in the A-10s for close-air support? For Christ's sake, that's what they were designed for!"

"Washington canceled production of the A-10. There are very few left on active duty. With their limited payload and low-speed they can't handle the air-to-air threat that, although unlikely, still has to be considered."

"Thanks for the education. You were a barnstormer before the war, weren't you?"

"Yeah, I did some acrobatics in my spare time when I wasn't flying commercial cargo flights for Kratos."

"What was that like?"

"Oh, it was great! We'd fly around the country to air shows and do stunts with the Vietnam-era Grumman F-4 Wildcat."

"Just don't pull any stunts like that on this mission, okay?"

"Gotcha, Chief. You have my word on it."

"Is your team mentally ready?"

"Find hadjis and kill 'em. We're ready."

"Just watch your six."

"Roger that, Steve."

Elburz Mountains, Iran

The assault started with a four-hour naval bombardment from the Fifth Fleet in the Caspian Sea using newly installed electromagnetic rail guns and cruise missiles, followed by the air assault. Major York started his air campaign using high-speed assaults to knock out any anti-aircraft defense systems. They encountered just a few surface-to-air-missile, SAM, and antiaircraft artillery, AAA, sites that were still operational. Anytime one of the Iranian systems turned on a sensor to track the F-35, it was destroyed with an advanced anti-radiation missile. If the Iranians were using passive systems that didn't radiate, the Special Ops and Air Force forward observers, or secondary F-35s, illuminated the Iranian launch locations with a laser to guide bombs in on the target.

The next stage of the aerial assault was to attack the most vulnerable areas of the command center: the entrances and exits. Major York led the four aircraft attack flight to the target.

"Alamo Leader to all Alamo team, we'll go in two at a time. Follow me."

"Alamo Leader dropping to four thousand feet and four hundred knots."

"Roger Alamo Leader, Alamo Two on your wing."

"Alamo Leader set and over target in one mike, weapons hot. Release on my count."

"Roger that. Alamo Two weapons hot."

"Alamo One and Two release in 5, 4, 3, 2, 1. Bombs away; repeat, bombs away."

The first two fighter jets pulled up quickly and accelerated to mach one after launch to reduce their exposure to ground fire. Major York flared out ninety-degrees and pulled up while his wingman pulled almost straight up, leaving an exhaust vapor stream looking like two prongs on a fork. They joined back up at their cruise altitude, and then made a turn to await Special Ops' damage assessment.

"Darby One to Alamo Leader, I count splash, splash. Two hits on two targets each."

"Roger that, Darby One."

"Alamo Leader to Alamo Three, you're cleared to descend."

"Roger Alamo Leader, Alamo Three and Four dropping down to four thousand feet and four hundred knots."

"Alamo Three and Four, bombs release in 5, 4, 3, 2, 1. Bombs away, repeat bombs away." Again, the two aircraft split, and pulled-up, but as they started their ascent a warning light and alarm went off on their display.

"Incoming, five o'clock!" Alamo Three radioed.

The F-35 countermeasures systems immediately detected and reacted to the infrared signature of the Soviet-made Strela-2, shoulder-fired, heat-seeking missile. Flares shot out and the pilots banked hard, pulling five g's. When the missile missed them both, they pulled up and climbed to cruising altitude.

With Alamo Two illuminating the shooter with his laser, York fired his laser-guided bomb at the threat. Unfortunately, the mujahideen shooter had dropped his shoulder weapon and taken cover in time to survive.

After fifteen minutes, the Special Ops teams started reporting the damage. The aircraft hit their marks, but failed to completely penetrate the bunker entrance deep enough into the tunnel to reach the command center.

"Darby One reporting. No clear path. Repeat, no clear path."

Looking down at his fuel gauge, Major York could see they were running critically low.

I should get the team home safely, York thought. *Marines'll be exposed, digging out that entrance*, York worried. *We're almost out of fuel . . . survive to fight another day.* "Alamo Leader to Alamo Three and Four, your orders are to turn for home."

"Roger that, Alamo Leader. Returning to base. Will Alamo Leader be flying trail cover?"

"Negative."

York selected aim points from the fire control computer. "Alamo Leader to Alamo Two, set your aim points for targets one and two. I'll take three and four. We're putting another bunker buster bomb on each door, then we'll give 'em Hades."

"Roger."

"Approach at niner-zero to target line at thirty thousand feet. Descend to two hundred feet at mach one, then pull up and roll toward target. Release at one mile standoff. We'll do an over-the-shoulder shot, then rollout and come around for the second pass. Copy?"

Damned SAMs, York thought.

"Roger, Alamo Leader. Thought that practice shot at Nellis was just for fun."

The F-35s made a high-speed, steep descent to 200 feet. At one mile from the target, Major York pulled up into a 360-degree barrel roll. Holding the jet steady as the stick shook in his hand like he was holding a jackhammer, he climbed to the release point. Staying focused to keep on his aimpoint was hard pulling five times the force of gravity. He released just past vertical near the apex of his roll, launching his two bombs out toward the target on a ski-slope-shaped trajectory that threw the bomb up, then let it glide down, guided by its inertial navigation computer.

"Wow!" came the call from the forward observer.

Alamo Two followed one minute behind with the same maneuver.

"Splash 1, 2, 3, and 4. All targets hit. Great shooting, guys!"

Albert thought about his promise. Steve was sure going to be pissed off when he heard about this stunt.

After a second pass, with multiple entrances into the underground command center now opened, the Marines began the final assault to kill, capture, and clear all remaining mujahideen fighters. Sergeant Marie Olivera was on the Marine assault team awaiting the end of the allied bombardment. She dubbed her squad the "Bruce Brigade," named after the greatest leader she had ever known.

"Marine One, Squad Four in position to go," she radioed.

The Marines sent remote control drones to quickly scout the openings to the Command Center and test for chemical or biological matter. After receiving the call to 'go' from the Platoon Commander, Olivera gave the arm wave signal to move out and led her squad into the cave. Wearing night-vision gear, they quickly moved forward in a wedge formation to continuously cover, provide suppressive fire, then advance. Speed and firepower were the keys to their assault.

The Marines stepped over and around the remnants of an asphalt highway and metal rails from train tracks scattered in the dark shaft by the bunker bombs. Olivera thought it might have even been the path the mujahideen who attacked the Neka convoy had taken.

After two hundred feet they began to smell burned human flesh, then saw bodies of mujahideen who had been killed in the bombardment. When they encountered two armed, injured attackers still moving, Olivera swung her M-16 across each of them in a motion as smooth as sweeping a floor. She fired a double tap into each chest to neutralize the threat, and continued to move through the opening.

The squad encountered its first gunfire about five hundred feet inside the cave. Using shoulder-fired grenade launchers, rifles, and machine guns, the Marines surged forward, taking out the snipers. It was another three hundred yards before they reached the command center.

The Marines stepped out of the tunnel into a dimly lit, huge cavern that housed the command center and quickly moved to cover and focus on targets within their range.

The mujahideen were fighting a rear-guard maneuver. Each time the Marines pressed their rear guard, the enemy drew back behind a secondary line of fighters waiting to take up the battle. This successive fire and fallback maneuver delayed the Marine assault. A convoy of enemy troops and vehicles could be seen a half-mile away, moving out another exit.

Sergeant Olivera pointed to the private carrying the Javelin, and beckoned with her arm for him to join her.

Kneeling behind a rock pile for cover, she shouldered the Javelin and took aim. The convoy was moving away, but she knew the missile had the range.

Olivera gave the hand signal to commence suppressive fire.

When the fire commenced, Olivera stood up just enough for the launcher to have a clear path through the cave, exposing herself to mujahideen fire. In an instant, she angled the launcher in the general direction of the convoy and fired the heat-seeking missile. The missile's tandem warhead struck with devastating accuracy. The first explosion ripped away the outer layer of protection on the armored personnel carrier and the second explosion ripped through the base armor with explosive efficiency. The APC was lifted off the ground and engulfed in fire.

The next APC in the convoy pushed the wreck off the road and continued out of the cave.

"Reload that Javelin, Private. I want them to remember the Bruce Brigade as they run with their tails between their legs."

Olivera moved to another position, stood up quickly, aimed and fired. Another direct hit, but the convoy was getting away. The Marines were left to sweep the area, neutralize any threat and secure it for the intelligence teams.

Major York was halfway back to Mashad when the call came to turnaround. He was to join other fighters returning from Mashad to attack a massive exodus of people, vehicles, and equipment that were evacuating the Iranian bunker.

"Alamo Leader to Mashad Command, we'll need to refuel."

"Roger Alamo Leader, Tanker is in the area."

Major York switched his radio to the UHF frequency for refueling and contacted the KC-135 tanker.

"Alamo Leader to ARCO One, do you read me?"

"ARCO One to Alamo Leader, I read you loud and clear."

"Alamo Leader and Alamo Two request immediate rendezvous for refueling."

The tanker gave them a rendezvous position. After confirming proper separation, the fighters maneuvered their aircraft in for refueling while the tanker maintained a steady orbiting flight path. Once refueled, the two fighters joined other aircraft from Joint Base Mashad and destroyed the escaping mujahideen convoy.

Isolated in the world, defeated, and with the Iranian people in massive protest against the war, the highest ranking surviving Iranian leader, their Foreign Minister, joined by the mujahideen commanding general, surrendered in the town of Neka the following day. The United States, China, and representatives of Iran, from both the mujahideen and the exiled Green Party, entered into trilateral talks on how to secure the country and restore peace.

43

Washington, DC

Steve Holmes was on the job at Kratos early on Monday morning at corporate headquarters in DC when the trilateral negotiations began. Around nine AM he got a phone call.

His secretary said, "Steve, this caller says President Rubina wants to talk with you. I don't think it's a prank."

"Thanks, Janice. Put the call through and we'll see."

"Okay. You're on hold."

When Steve took the call, there was country music playing. It seemed a little strange for the White House, but Steve enjoyed it while he listened on the speakerphone and continued to work at his desk.

A female voice came on, and said, "Mr. Holmes?"

"Yes, this is Steve Holmes."

"Please hold for the President."

"Good morning, Steve."

"Mr. President! Good morning. I am a little shocked to get your call, but how can I help you?" Steve stood up at his desk instinctively.

"Steve, I've got a problem in Iran that I think you can help your country solve."

"I will do whatever I can, Mr. President."

"It's not something we can discuss on the phone. Look, I heard you were an NBA fan?"

"I follow the Rockets, but like the Wizards, too."

"Would you and your date join me and Judy for the Wizard's game against the Rockets tomorrow night at the Verizon Center?"

"Well, yes, sure, we'd love to. I'll check with Sherry to see what her schedule is, but I'm sure she'll cancel anything she has going."

"Okay, great. We'll see you there at seven-thirty. My aide will give your secretary the directions to the Presidential booth."

***

Steve and Sherry arrived at the game early, as always. After being searched, they were escorted by Secret Service through the private entrance up to the President's booth. The President and First Lady were already there.

"We're so glad you could both come. I'm a big Wizard's fan," the President said as they took their seats.

"We're both big fans. Sherry can spot a pass coming two moves ahead. We both still occasionally play."

"And, you like the Rockets."

"Yeah. Dwight Howard is fun to watch."

"He's getting a little too old to play now, isn't he?"

"After back-to-back championships in 'seventeen and 'eighteen, he's earned some rest. He doesn't get to play as much as he used to, but he's still one of the best centers in the league."

They spent some time getting to know one another and enjoyed the game. President Rubina and Steve moved at halftime to a private room that the Wizards' owners had had installed, and certified by the Secret Service, to ensure Washington's elected officials had a secure meeting place.

"How're you liking the new job as president of Kratos?"

"It's a great company. I'm enjoying leading the operations."

"Ambassador Allenby tells me you have a leadership initiative under way."

"Leadership isn't strong in the company today, or in American corporations in general. I aim to change that."

"Can you get them all into a room and explain what you want?"

"I can start with that and some training, but the biggest effort won't be teaching or preaching."

"What else?"

"We have to promote individual leadership person-to-person, like the military does it."

"Seems like Leadership One-Oh-One?"

"Not one-oh-one. It's one-on-one. How you treat others. Your concern for their well-being. How you value their opinions and concerns."

"I like it. Show 'em individually, don't tell 'em"

"Something like that."

"That's a good lead-in for my first order of business. I want to show you a picture."

It was a picture of Lieutenant Bruce Williams and his wife, Sharon, on their wedding day.

"Did you know this guy?"

Steve choked up a little. "I knew him well."

"I thought so. He worked for you before the war, didn't he?"

"He was a Sponsored Reservist. He was the best leader I ever personally met. He had a great sense of humor. I sometimes laughed so hard, my ribs would hurt. I miss him."

"I will present his wife with the Congressional Medal of Honor for his valor."

Steve nodded solemnly, not trusting himself to speak.

Rubina continued. "That will be a first. A Sponsored Reservist has never received the CMA. I'd like you to join me to make the presentation."

"It would be an honor."

Rubina put the picture away. "Now, have you been following the trilateral negotiations, Steve?"

Steve adjusted his position, straightened up just a little, and cleared his throat. "Yes. With a great deal of interest."

"It's so important for us to get this right to ensure a lasting peace."

"Are you making good progress on the fundamentals?"

"I think we are. We are close to an agreement for the future of an independent, non-militarized Iran."

"That can't be easy with China involved."

"They're being difficult. They want to maintain cheap energy and an ally against us. But with our two hundred-fifty thousand troops in the country, they won't get everything they want."

"How can I help with that, Mr. President?"

"I've found the right military-governor to lead the transition in Iran, but he'll need help to run the country, a kind of cabinet with assigned duties. That's where you come in."

"Me?"

"Getting their economy running again is a top priority. You have the understanding of the commercial business that my generals do not. You run a muti-national corporation today. And you know how the military works. No one is more suited for a cabinet role than you."

"They have a good foundation. An educated population with the know-how to mine, manufacture, and refine their raw materials, especially oil, to sell on the international market."

"So, you'll take the job?"

"I . . . I don't know. I have commitments to Kratos. I don't know what Sherry would think about it."

"We can work out those problems if you accept the challenge."

"I'm flattered that you'd consider me for this position, Mr. President. If I take the job, I'll need support from key parts of your administration."

"You'll have it. You'll be appointed to the Senior Executive Service for the duration of the job."

"Can I have a couple days to consider it? I have some matters to attend to before I could accept the position."

"Certainly, take the weekend and let me know one way or the other on Monday."

"I will, Mr. President. I may need your assistance. May I call you if I have questions before Monday?"

"I'll give you a direct number to call."

When Steve got back to Sherry, the game was almost over. Steve departed the coliseum in a bit of a haze. It was surreal. *Did that really happen?* He held the President's phone number in his hand as reassurance it had all been real.

Quantico, Virginia

On Sunday night, before he had to give President Rubina his decision, Steve asked Sherry to meet him at the Globe and Laurel Restaurant in Quantico, Virginia. After they sat down and ordered drinks, Sherry asked, "Well, so, spill. Have you decided if you're taking the job?"

"I don't know yet. There are still so many things to decide."

"You owe the President an answer tomorrow. Don't you think you better be making up your mind?"

"Tell me what you think about the position first."

"I think you'd be a damned fool if you don't take it. It's the opportunity of a lifetime."

"What about us?"

"If this is what you want, Steve, we can work it out. I'll visit as often as possible, and you'll need to come back to Washington from time to time to meet with business leaders and government officials."

"How was I so lucky to find someone like you? You know the long-distance relationship will be difficult, but you're more concerned about what's good for me than how difficult it will be to make this work. I love you."

"That's what people who love each other do: They work it out. Now, shut up and drink your wine. You're going to take that assignment."

There was a commotion in the back of the restaurant. Waiters and staff rushed around and men in suits appeared and took up positions inside the restaurant.

Sherry moved to the edge of her seat and prepared for action. When she looked at Steve, he was sipping his wine, smiling, and looking at her.

"Good evening, Miss Adkison, may I join you?" President Mark Rubina asked as he approached their table.

Sherry looked up, jumped to her feet, spilling her tea, to greet the President. "Yes. . . oh . . . please, sit down," Sherry said, uncommon nervousness exploding all over.

"Steve tells me he can't take the assignment in Iran."

"He did? Oh, well, we've talked it over, and I think he'd change his mind, Mr. President."

"Well, I meant to add, he said he couldn't take the job without you."

Tears of surprise moistened her eyes.

"Now, seeing as how I have a little pull around here, I thought I'd use it, and I talked to FBI Director Stephens. As it turns out, we really do have an assignment open for Chief of Station at our Embassy in Iran. It's a critical position and a promotion for you. Will you take it?"

When she turned to look at Steve, he stood up, pulled a box from his pocket, and knelt down on one knee. "Sherry Adkison, will you marry me?"

Sherry nodded and let the tears flow as she and Steve embraced.

"I think my work here is done. I expect both of you to report for duty in two weeks," Rubina said.

44

Washington, DC

Steve and Sherry met for lunch the next day at a corner bistro near his office. As they waited for their order, Sherry said, "We have so many things to do. Plan a wedding, prepare to move, finish up assignments. . . . It's overwhelming."

Without looking up from the newspaper he held, Steve said almost inaudibly, "Yeah."

"I love your interest."

"I guess."

"Okay. What is it?"

Steve turned the newspaper around to reveal Senator Alex Shankle's face with a headline that read, IS THIS THE FACE OF A TRAITOR?

Sherry reached across the table and gently squeezed Steve's hand, "We'll get him. You pushed this investigation forward. You've done your job; now let us do ours."

"I don't know why the FBI can't just arrest him now."

"We need conclusive physical evidence that directly links him to espionage."

"And you can't tell me what you have. I know. It just pisses me off that he walks free. He murdered my people at Neka, just as sure as if he'd pulled the trigger himself."

"We'll get him, honey. Just be patient."

***

Later that afternoon, Steve walked up to Shankle's receptionist in the Dirksen Senate Building and asked to speak with Jodie Arenas. "Do you have an appointment, Mr. Holmes?"

"No, I'm sorry, I don't. But Ms. Arenas knows me well."

"Are you a constituent from Ohio?"

"No, I'm not."

"Please have a seat in our waiting room. I'm sure Jodie will try to see you when she gets a moment."

Impeachment hearings, intelligence discussions, peace negotiations, and judicial appointments were on the senator's calendar. There would be key votes on legislative actions calling Shankle to the Senate floor throughout the day. Steve could hear the senator talking when his office door opened and closed when aides raced in and out. Walking toward the reading table, Steve bolted into Shankle's office when the door once again opened as an aide walked out.

"You killed my people, you bastard!" Steve yelled as he jabbed his finger in the air, pointing at Shankle.

The senator's aide pushed Steve back as other staffers ran in to help.

But Shankle said, "No, let him have his say."

Steve said, "I wanted to look into the eyes of a traitor. You'll pay for what you did. Your campaign, your political ambitions, your freedom will all soon be gone."

Shankle asked everyone else to leave the room, then said, "You're pitiful, you and that company of yours, Kraaatooos. Ooooh! I'm so terrified of the winged enforcers! So, spread your mighty wings and swoop down to do what you can. You can't touch me. Your people were only there for the money. They got what they deserved. Just what do you think is going to happen now?"

"You'll get the death penalty. I'll see to it."

Shankle stood up, walked around his desk, and said in an eerily calm, soft voice, "No . . . no. I won't be stopped. The whole world will call me 'Mr. President' one day. You'll see."

Steve laughed, and said, "You're crazy. Glory is not your fate," as he turned and walked out of the office.

***

Shankle watched Steve leave, convinced the FBI had found sufficient evidence to arrest him. It was time to pull out all stops.

***

In a clandestine meeting held in Washington, DC later that day, Alex Shankle met with the deputy to the Ambassador of the People's Republic of China to the United States of America, Mr. Zing Cheui. They met in the Chinese section of town in a small, but busy noodle restaurant.

The deputy ambassador spoke first. "It appears the investigators are closing in on you, Alex."

"I'm afraid so. They managed to sniff out the payments going to my Cayman Islands accounts. We had that money trail so tightly obscured, I can't believe anybody found it. Someone in *your* country must have ratted us out."

"No, Senator, none of our agents informed on you. Your FBI, CIA, NSA, and Army CID have been working together. They used considerable technology and detective work to trace the money from our military to you. They did manage to bribe one civilian banker in China to help them. That banker and his family never lived to regret it."

"The bungled assassination attempt on Steve Holmes was a stupid error by your agent. That got them on my trail."

"Yes, that was a mistake. But you wanted him dead. You thought he was asking too many questions and by eliminating him, the focus of the convoy sabotage would stay on Kratos. That was also a mistake."

"Holmes paid me a visit this morning. He thinks I'll be arrested. If they've linked me to the sabotage, Major Sharif, and the money, then they know your country was involved as well. What should we do?"

"*We* will do nothing. *You* are on your own, Alex. I think you have very little time to salvage this operation and achieve your goal."

"I am prepared to take drastic action."

"What will you do?"

"I have sympathetic supporters and radical groups who will assist me. We're going to stage an armed revolution in Washington."

"We will not help. We are washing our hands of you. However, if you are successful in seizing power, Alex, my government will immediately recognize you as the legitimate head of government for the United States."

"I understand, Mr. Cheui. We will not fail."

***

Steve picked Sherry up from work that afternoon for an early dinner and evening together. After Steve pulled back onto the highway, he said, "I hope I haven't jeopardized your investigation. I went to visit Shankle today."

"I knew you were mad at lunch. You're not in jail, so you must not have punched him."

"I wanted to."

"So, what did you do?"

"I looked him in the eye and told him I knew he was a murderer and traitor, and he was going to pay for it."

"What'd he say?"

"Well, he didn't deny it. He said the world would call him 'Mr. President' one day. I think he's nuts."

Sherry laughed. "Mr. President? He said that?"

"Yes. In a strange, hypnotic kind of tone."

"Sounds like he's delusional. He'll never be President."

"So, I haven't hurt your case?"

"Not at all. In fact, we plan to put a little more heat on him soon."

45

Facing exposure, Shankle met with Jodie Arenas in her Washington apartment that night. Sitting in her kitchen with both of them drinking a beer, Jodie asked, "What did you learn from the Chinese?"

"They're with us," he lied. "But they won't take an active role. We have to do this ourselves." Shankle took two loud gulps of his beer.

"It won't be easy, Alex, but we have supporters. The public will have to rally to our cause if we're gonna win."

"We'll provoke the military to fire on us in the streets of Washington. When the media shows civilians being murdered by their government, we'll have massive support," Shankle said confidently.

Jodie sipped her beer slowly, pausing for a moment. Then said, "I don't know how Americans will react to a coup, Alex."

"Look at what happened in Tunisia, Egypt, and the Ukraine. The citizens there overthrew democratically elected presidents and the world community rejoiced."

"Those were hardly model democracies, but I hope you're right. I'm ready to die to make it happen."

"We've exposed the incompetence and corruption in this government. When they murder civilians in the street, the world will see them as illegitimate. We will win!" Shankle finished his beer with two more long gulps, and then went to the refrigerator for another.

Jodie was skeptical, but Shankle was convinced.

Jodie said, "Okay. Let's go over what we've been working on since you lost the Illinois primary."

"We start with massive street protests. How many protesters can we expect?" Shankle asked.

"We have anarchist groups and some labor unions that will rally to our support and fill the streets with a day's notice. With a direct appeal from you to the general public, maybe three or four thousand."

"That'll be a good turnout. I'll make the Internet announcement today."

"The key protest leaders will rally the crowd to support the armed fighters when they arrive."

Shankle said, "You were there when I met with our supporters in the National Guard and the DC and Capitol police. They've promised hundreds of fighters and weapons. The police only have pistols, rifles, and shotguns, but the National Guard will bring the heavier armaments."

"Will their Kiowa helicopters and Humvees be able to withstand a military assault for long?"

"We have some awesome firepower on those platforms. High-powered machine guns, air-to-air and air-to-ground missiles, as well as rockets. I figure we'll have three to four hours before the government's military and police forces can stop us. That's why we have to have plenty of media coverage to show citizens being shot down in the streets."

"I'll alert some of the media just before the protest and assault. And, I'll be out there to give them good copy. They'll have cameras and cell phone videos on the air constantly, showing everything that's happening with the revolution when it's happening."

"DC crawls with media. The news will go worldwide as soon as all hell breaks loose."

"Yeah, and I'll have people posting on Twitter, Facebook, Snapchat, and YouTube. They'll get our message out."

"I still like the plan."

"What will you be doing in the Capitol?" Jodie asked.

"With the help of the Capitol Police, we'll grab a few senators for protection as we broadcast the word that we are taking over and Rubina must go."

"Then it's done. We start in two days. Long-live the revolution!"

"We say it's done, but we have to get to the hive now, to make it happen," Shankle said.

***

The high-tech situation room was a beehive of activity with multi-media displays running, and technology experts and campaign workers buzzing about when they arrived at their central campaign headquarters in the basement of the Washingtonian Hotel. The senator's growing popularity attracted some of the brightest technology and social-media experts in Silicon Valley.

"I want everyone out but the crisis team," Shankle said as he got ready to orchestrate his protest with the small crew committed to radical change.

Sitting at the head of the conference table in front of the bank of video screens with Jodie and Karl, his technology leader, Shankle said, "Show me the announcement." The text of the protest announcement filled the large center screen. To one side, CNN was running while, on the other side, a live video stream of the Capitol ran continuously above several active screens with blog-site activity.

After reading the message they had developed, Shankle said, "Just change the start time to read 'zero hour is nine AM,' then change the date to this Friday and send it out. The message will get all protesters there, and our 'zero hour' code words will alert our revolutionary forces."

With his red hair, long braids, mustache, and goatee, Karl didn't look like a technology expert, although his baggy jeans, sandals, and t-shirt reading "Citizenville, Government 2.0," would be right at home in Silicon Valley.

Karl typed in the changes. Shankle nodded approval, then Karl clicked the send button. "Done," he said with a chuckle.

"Tell me where you have the message going?" Jodie asked.

"Every major news agency, blog site, and social media outlet will receive it. It also goes directly to the Twitter, Facebook, email, and cell phone of every supporter we've targeted. We merged data from potential supporters into one large database, then selected those who fit our profile, including anyone who has contacted, blogged, messaged, called, or emailed our campaign. We run real-time analytics on Big Data to tap into on-line conversations, and the latest events and voter trends to ensure we're reaching the most active supporters. This is state-of-the-art stuff."

"Have you alerted our revolutionary leaders to standby for a call?" Shankle asked.

"Yes, here they are."

Karl brought up the individual video conference streams for the seven primary revolutionary leaders with just a few keystrokes: the Capitol Police, National Guard, DC Police, Colt Wayne, representing Communists Against the War, and the leaders of three anarchist groups.

After brief greetings, Shankle said, "Each of you and your armed forces, along with millions of others, should have just received my message."

Colt Wayne said, "My cell phone rang with the recorded message and pinged with a text message at the same time."

"There will be thousands of peaceful protesters in the streets. For those of you outside the Capitol building, mingle in close to the police barricades, then attack at zero hour," Shankle said as he stared at his trusted lieutenants.

After a short discussion, Shankle said to the fat guy on Screen 3, "I'm depending on you, Mike, to have our supporters from the Capitol Police in the Rotunda room a few minutes before nine. Wait for my signal before you start shooting."

After some discussion on the plans they had pre-arranged, Shankle concluded the call saying, "As Karl Marx said, 'Let the ruling classes tremble.' Our revolution starts in two days!"

***

By Friday morning, there were thousands of protesters on the Washington Mall and in front of the Capitol building. Police barricades were erected and crowd control forces were called out.

46

Washington, DC

Sherry called the *Washington Chronicle Observer* reporter on Thursday afternoon.

"This is Agent Adkison. I wanted you to be the first to know that we strongly suspect Senator Alex Shankle leaked classified convoy and troop movement information to the mujahideen."

"Can I quote you on that?"

"Not by name."

"Why don't you just arrest him?"

"We're missing a critical piece of physical evidence that ties him to it."

"What else can you tell me?"

"The circumstantial evidence is overwhelming. He passed secret information to Chinese agents in clandestine locations in Washington. Money exchanged hands. That should be enough for your story. You can fill in the rest."

"A nice juicy spy story. Why are you telling me?"

"I promised to call you after you told me about Shankle's reaction to the virus. If you prefer, I can give the story to another reporter."

"No, no, don't do that! This will be the best headline of my career."

Sherry immediately called FBI Director Elliott Stephens after the call. "Our story will run in tomorrow's paper."

"Good. We'll be watching which way the rats run."

"I have surveillance on Shankle, Arenas, and suspects in the Chinese Embassy."

"Call me immediately if any of them move."

***

The news of secret meetings and payoffs to the senator appeared that Friday morning in the *Washington Chronicle Observer*. Internet news sites splashed the story on their home pages. Blogs, Twitter, and Facebook were flooded with tales of spies and traitors. The *Los Angeles Times* delayed their publication to get the story out on page one. The news about Shankle and protests in Washington set off a firestorm of media coverage.

With help from several hundred volunteers, many of them corporate leaders, employees and their families, Steve and Sherry had the ten thousand voter signatures and over one thousand signatures of business leaders that Senator McCastle requested. Wading through the growing throng of protesters, police, blocked roads, and barricades, they arrived at the Capitol doorsteps at 8:00 AM Friday morning, before senate meetings started for the day.

As they moved through security, Sherry put her weapon on the conveyor belt and showed her FBI credentials. It was routine for the Secret Service and FBI to enter the building with their weapons. A Capitol Police officer stood just inside the security station, observing everyone coming and going. He was overweight, with a large beer belly, and wearing a wrinkled, ill-fitted uniform. He saw Sherry flash her badge and stepped forward.

"You cannot take that weapon into the Capitol."

"I brought it in before. Why would you take my gun now?"

"It's a matter of added security."

"I have authorization to carry a weapon here. I'm on your list. Get your boss out here and let's straighten this out. I'm not leaving my weapon."

The guard would not move. Sherry got louder and attracted the police sergeant's attention.

"What's going on?"

"This officer wants to keep my weapon. I've shown my credentials and I'm on your list as an agent authorized to carry my weapon in the Capitol building."

The Sergeant turned to the officer. "What's going on here, Mike? Not only is Agent Adkison on the Weapons Authorization List, but I personally recognize her. She was here last week."

"My mistake, sir. I didn't recognize her." Mike walked off and retrieved his cell phone to make a hurried call to Jodie Arenas.

Steve and Sherry met with Harper McCastle in her office on the third floor. As Chairwoman of the Intelligence Subcommittee, she would be most knowledgeable of the threat created by Shankle's actions. Some might dislike her political ideology, but her character was widely respected.

Steve handed over the signed petition and voter verifications. "We wanted to get this to you as soon as possible."

McCastle scanned the signatures. "Thank you. Solid evidence like this of voter and business leader support can help convince other senators to support my small business legislation."

"And thank you for *your* support," Steve said as he and Sherry took a seat.

Laying the papers down and picking up the *Washington Chronicle Observer* newspaper, McCastle said, "What do you know about the incredible news articles this morning that Senator Shankle could be involved in espionage, Agent Adkison?"

"We have a lot of incriminating evidence against the senator. The story in the major newspapers is mostly accurate."

"Why wasn't I informed?"

"Director Stephens told me your friendship was a conflict of interest. It is my understanding that select senators and representatives were briefed."

McCastle stood up and walked to the window. She could see protesters and police barricades in the streets. "It seems surreal. I've known Alex since I was a junior senator. But I couldn't have really known him at all. These charges. . . The protests. . ."

Suddenly, gunfire rang out in the north wing Senate chamber of the Capitol building. Alarms sounded. Secret Service agents scurried to get legislators to safety.

Steve and Sherry ran toward the sound of the gunfire.

***

Hundreds of news reporters later pulled together the first bits of the story: The violence commenced when Capitol Police sympathetic to Shankle's cause shot and killed other guards in the building. They blocked the doors, then put on camouflage shirts and caps to form Shankle's Revolutionary Guard. The Capitol subway and main highways into and out of the city were blocked and armed Revolutionary Guards stood watch to repel any attack from that direction. A shootout soon erupted inside the Capitol with Secret Service.

To secure their position, the revolutionaries grabbed a band of fifteen senators, bound them with flexcuffs, tied them all together, and held them captive in the Capitol Rotunda.

Sympathizers at the U.S. Army National Guard in DC stole Humvees and Kiowa helicopters to join the protesters outside the Capitol building. The armed assault on the Capitol had begun.

Explosions and gunfire could be heard from outside the Capitol. Rebels from the National Guard patrolled a perimeter defense a quarter mile out from the Capitol. The Kiowa's were particularly effective at keeping SWAT teams and initial military troop responders from the area. Rebel National Guard snipers were perched on top of museums and monuments.

Secret Service and FBI SWAT teams were among the first to arrive. They deployed for an assault on the Capitol building, but had to gather outside the rebel perimeter. Air force fighter jets and Marine helicopter gunships had been launched immediately, but they were reluctant to shoot into the crowd of unarmed protesters after they'd arrived. Combat forces, standing by on alert, were boarding aircraft to deploy in the city. Alerts to all citizens to clear the streets were broadcast through loudspeakers and the media. Communication, command, and control among the disparate forces were poor.

***

Steve and Sherry watched from the third-floor balcony and could see camouflaged men and women carrying AK-47s and holding the small band of senators captive down below. Senator Shankle was clearly visible, armed, and dressed in camouflage. He had five stars on his shoulders.

A speaker using a bullhorn with a cell phone video feed was repeating and broadcasting to international media: "The Democratic Liberation Front has declared martial law. Senator Shankle has been appointed interim president. President Rubina must resign."

Sherry was able to communicate her location and the situation to the FBI and the Secret Service outside the building before her radio was jammed. They told her to prepare for an assault. Sherry took charge as the senior agent onsite, and with half-a-dozen Secret Service personnel inside the building dead. They gathered with the remaining Secret Service agents and loyal Capitol Police in McCastle's office to make their plans.

The ranking Secret Service agent spoke first. "We have contingency plans to stand pat and negotiate, or assault. I'm told you're to make the call since we don't have communications with anyone outside. What will it be, ma'am?"

"Assault."

'Some of those politicians may die."

"We don't know what else is coming. You hear the gunfire outside? We're going to neutralize the threat."

"Yes, ma'am. We have snipers ready and an assault team standing by."

"How many agents and police in the building are assault-capable?"

"There are approximately a dozen Secret Service agents and another two dozen loyal Capitol police still in action who can handle the fight."

"Where is Shankle?"

"In the Capitol Rotunda with the hostages."

"Do you have the manpower to secure the exits and lead the assault?"

"We have to clear the building room by room and make the assault in the Rotunda. I can spare two police officers to secure the exits."

"Okay. Send them out clockwise. Secure the main second-floor exit on that side. Steve and I will go the other way and secure the other main exit. None of Shankle's team in or out."

"Here. Use this to start the assault," the lead agent said as he handed Sherry a smoke grenade.

"I'll give it to Steve; he'll know how to use it."

Sherry had to give verbal and visual commands. She positioned Secret Service snipers inside the building. Capitol police were sent to clear and secure rooms from the ground floor up. A firefight broke out with the Revolutionary Guard and Secret Service.

Outside the Capitol building, unarmed protesters intermingled with small, armed bands of rebels who broke through the barricades and ran toward the Capitol. The protest and conflict had escalated more quickly than the police could react.

As Steve and Sherry moved through the Capitol building and down to the second floor to get a better view of the rebels holding the hostages, they ran into three rebel guards exiting the Rotunda room. Both they and the rebels were surprised. There was not time to reach for a weapon.

Steve slammed his knee into one rebel and pushed him into a second. As they stumbled back, Steve attacked hard and fast. The second rebel was an awkward policeman, inexperienced in hand-to-hand combat. Steve punched him in the gut and then across his face, sending the rebel to the ground. Steve grabbed the fallen Kalashnikov and struck the first rebel across his head with the butt of the rifle.

At the same time, Sherry had kicked the third rebel in his gut and threw an elbow across his chin. He stumbled, then started throwing wild swings at her. She backed up twice to avoid his swings. After the second swing, Sherry stooped low, then thrust up with a punch to his solar plexus with the entire force of her body. The rebel doubled over in severe pain, unable to catch his breath. She took a short step laterally and back to jump and deliver a kick to the side of the rebel's knee, breaking it.

They quickly tied up the three rebels, and Steve grabbed a Kalashnikov and extra ammo clips as they continued moving through the Capitol.

Steve and Sherry secured the rear exit of the Senate chamber leading to the second-floor hall and Rotunda. They were already armed, but Steve wanted more weapons. As they ran by a fallen

Secret Service agent, Steve picked up his Glock and grabbed his ammo belt, with spare clips and a switchblade attached. He threw the belt over his shoulder and put the knife in his pocket.

Outside the Capitol building, the anti-aircraft artillery already in place on the top of buildings and Air Force jets quickly destroyed the Kiowa's and armed Humvees used by the rebels. Attack helicopters brought in from Quantico and snipers placed on buildings picked off large and small teams of armed rebels. The fight outside the Capitol was quickly being brought under control.

With all teams in position inside the Capitol, Steve rolled the smoke grenade into the Capitol Rotunda to start the assault. Smoke filled the room, coupled with concussion grenades and small arms fire.

***

Shankle got the reports on the losing battle his supporters were fighting outside the Capitol. Now he saw the strong assault being made inside the building. The media were reporting exclusively in support of the current government. Shankle was losing the armed battle and the battle for public support as well.

***

Just after Steve threw the smoke grenade in the rear exit, the doors from the Rotunda burst open, and Alex Shankle and two armed escorts came out firing.

Steve and Sherry instinctively dropped to crouch positions, sought cover, and returned fire. They aimed first for the legs, then the head, avoiding protective vests. They killed the armed escorts, but Senator Shankle's flash-bang grenade exploded directly in front of them, knocking them back; Steve's Kalashnikov and Sherry's pistol slid away as they fell to the floor. Sherry was groggy, but Steve, who had taken cover to protect his eyes and ears, was still functioning.

As Shankle ran past Sherry, Steve shoved a tipped-over brass stanchion into Shankle's path, knocking him to the ground. Steve drew his Glock, but before he could fire, Shankle fired a shot that shattered the narrow window in the stairwell door leading to the first floor, a few feet from where he was kneeling. Steve again dropped to the floor and started low-crawling to the stairwell door as fast as he could. Shankle fired another shot that hit the door. Steve rolled over and fired rapidly as he opened the door and fell down the stairs to the cement floor below. Dazed momentarily, Steve scrambled behind the water cooler to pull himself together.

Steve waited, but Shankle didn't come out. He listened for noise inside, but couldn't hear anything over the assault team's gunfire. *Did he leave? Was he going after Sherry?* He had to go back inside. He crawled back up the stairs and cracked the door open. He could see Sherry and she indicated she was okay, though dazed. He didn't see Shankle, but was sure he was still there just around the corner.

"Alex Shankle, this is Steve Holmes. There is no way out for you. Give up, and you'll get out alive."

Shankle laughed a little, then a little harder. "Get out alive? Is that what you think I want?"

"It's all you're going to get." Steve could only tell the voice was coming from the opposite side of the hall from Sherry. After Shankle didn't add anything else, Steve goaded him. "Okay, I give up. What do you want? Power, money, love of the people? All of the above?"

"I want the weak-minded inferior leaders running this country out."

"And you will take over, is that it?" Steve looked for any shadows or movement, but still couldn't pinpoint Shankle's location.

"Who else?"

"Why you? How are you better than everyone else?"

"I am simply the leader with the greatest right to lead the country!"

"You weren't elected to the job. What right do you have?"

"I have the natural right. My right is not inherited or elected; God endows it."

"So God selected you?"

"No, God didn't select me to lead the country. I'm not a religious zealot, Mr. Holmes, who believes God only talks to me. What I believe is that I have been naturally selected for my virtue and genius."

"You're the smartest and most decent guy around. Is that it?"

"Yes, in a manner of speaking. Anyone can get themselves elected, and sooner or later you get a truly inferior leader. The natural aristocracy has to rise up against these leaders and reset the democracy."

"But surely you know you can't win this fight. Americans are not going to accept takeover by force."

"What the people want is only now becoming clear to me. If I can get to the reporters outside and make my case, I can still win over the American public."

Realizing that Shankle wasn't going to be rational, and worrying about Sherry's vulnerability, Steve decided to make a move. He opened the door a little more. He didn't see Shankle, so he entered, staying low and moving carefully. Sherry was still lying injured and semi-conscious on the floor. As she started to get up, Steve yelled, "Stay down, stay down!"

Shankle raised his pistol and started firing from the far corner behind metal cabinets. A round skimmed Steve's hand; he dropped the gun and it slid out in the open floor. Steve got to Sherry and pulled her around the corner, out of the line of fire. As he pulled her in, he felt a sharp, burning sensation in his leg. He tumbled over Sherry and grabbed his last remaining weapon, his knife, just as Shankle shot him again. As he fell back, Steve felt the warm blood running down his chest.

Shankle stood up and, with his left arm bleeding and hanging free, he walked over, knelt down, and rolled Steve over. Kneeling over him with his gun six inches from Steve's head, he said, "I'm glad I could get you two together."

Steve felt his strength draining out of him. He knew he had failed. In an instant, he and Sherry would both be dead. God wasn't going to answer his prayers, and there would be no one to rescue them.

At that moment, Sherry yelled, "Mr. President!" and Shankle looked up and turned his head.

With every bit of energy he could muster, Steve plunged the knife into his neck. Blood spurted. Shankle grabbed his throat and fell back. In an instant, he was lying on the floor with the last drops of life draining down his shirt.

Steve pulled Sherry into his lap as he sat up and cradled her head.

She looked at his wounds, and shook her head, looked into his loving eyes, and said, "You shouldn't have come back."

Steve squeezed Sherry's hand. "I wasn't going on without you."

Steve heard Shankle gurgle and looked up to see him take his last breath. His open eyes and fixed stare seemed to be asking Steve, "Has fate dealt me this unkindly blow?"

Steve recalled the tale Aeschylus told of how Kratos kills the renegade God Prometheus. Kratos said, "Now take thine iron spike and drive it in, until it gnaw clean through the rebel's breast."

Mark Williams

spent over 30 years working with the uniformed military, government civilians, corporate executives and contractors throughout the military-industrial complex. He was an executive for two Fortune 500 companies running businesses that provided contractor support to the United States Department of Defense, the United Kingdom Ministry of Defence, and the Australian Defence Force. In the 1970s, he served as an Air Force security policeman in the U.S. and Turkey. He holds college degrees in engineering, mathematics and systems analysis.

Made in the USA
Charleston, SC
31 May 2015